CLASH

ELLEN WILKINSON

CLASH

ELLEN WILKINSON

Edited with an introduction
by Ian Haywood and Maroula Joannou

TRENT EDITIONS

Published by Trent Editions, 2004

Trent Editions
Department of English and Media Studies
The Nottingham Trent University
Clifton Lane
Nottingham NG11 8NS

Printed in Great Britain by Goaters Limited, Nottingham.

ISBN 1 84233 069 1

Cover illustration: The Car House Colliery,
Greasborough, Yorkshire, 1926.
By courtesy of the Central Library and Arts Centre, Rotherham.

Contents

Introduction

There has been as yet no great interpretative novel in English of working-class life
— Ellen Wilkinson, *Plebs*, December 1926, pp. 450-51.

After years of strenuous feminist propaganda, very many women still regard it
as the natural order of things that they remain in the home, cut off from the
world, entirely dependent on allowances from their husbands. The working-class
woman, of course, has to be a working partner, and that brings her more into
contact with the outside world.
— Ellen Wilkinson, 'Britain's Cave Women', *The Daily Mail*, 19 May 1931.

Red Ellen[1]

Ellen Cicely Wilkinson (1891-1947), known as 'Red Ellen' for the colour of
her burnished red hair as much as her politics, was born into a Methodist
working-class family in Ardwick, Manchester. Her mother and grandfather were
members of the Co-operative Society and her father was a mill-worker who later
became an insurance agent. She joined the Independent Labour Party at the age
of sixteen. The first person in her family to go to university, she won a scholarship
to Manchester University from which she graduated with honours in History in
1913. In the same year she began work as a full-time organiser for the largest of
the women's suffrage organisations, Millicent Garrett-Fawcett's National Union
of Women's Suffrage Societies. The NUWSS had abandoned its political
impartiality in 1912 and urged women to vote for the Labour Party, which had
declared its unequivocal support for women's suffrage. Wilkinson was appointed
National Women's Organiser for the Amalgamated Union of Co-operative
Employees in 1915 and during the 1914-18 war fought for equal pay for those
women doing jobs hitherto held by men. Inspired by the socialist-feminism of
Sylvia Pankhurst, Wilkinson retained throughout her life a passionate
commitment to improve the plight of low paid women.

By this stage in her career Wilkinson had contributed to and was a beneficiary
of two great social movements of her day: the rise in the status of women after
they gained the right to vote and to stand for parliament in 1918, and the increase

in the political power of the organised working class which was reflected in the election of the first Labour government in 1924. Many progressive women saw her as an example or role model – the novelist Winifred Holtby, for example, who had always liked and admired Wilkinson, used her as a model for the campaigning heroine of *South Riding* (1936), the petite, red-haired Sarah Burton.[2] Largely as a result of these campaigns to gain women the vote, better jobs, pay, working conditions and greater access to higher education, Wilkinson became one of 'hundreds of thousands of women between twenty and thirty, mothers, professional and working women', of whom Dora Russell wrote approvingly in *Hypatia* (1925): 'the principle of feminine equality is as natural as drawing breath - they are neither oppressed by tradition nor worn by rebellion'.[3]

Wilkinson's socialism was expansive. In the early 1920s she became a founder member the British Communist Party and visited the Soviet Union. She resigned from the Communist Party in 1924 when Communists were proscribed from membership of the Labour Party, although she retained a Marxist outlook for much of her life. After standing unsuccessfully as the Labour candidate for Ashton-under-Lyne she was returned as the Labour Party's only woman member of parliament in the first, short-lived Labour government of 1924, representing the Teesside constituency of Middlesbrough East (the Shireport of *Clash*) which she held until 1931. During the General Strike of 1926 she became an accredited representative of the Trades Union Congress (TUC) and was sent on speaking tours of the country. Her companion was a friend and fellow MP, the *Plebs* cartoonist Frank Horrabin (a model for the character of Gerry Blain in *Clash*). The regional information gathered on this tour was used for a Plebs-sponsored book, *A Workers' History of the Great Strike* (1927). During the miners' lock-out which followed the General Strike Wilkinson was a dedicated supporter of the miners' cause. She visited the United States to raise funds for miners' families and chaired the Women's Committee for the Relief of Miners' Wives and Children. Such was Wilkinson's commitment to the miners that she once embellished a speech in parliament by flourishing a miner's 'guss' — a harness used to haul coal tubs underground. According to her biographer Betty Vernon, these theatricals were ironically meant to evoke Edmund Burke's famous wielding of a dagger in one of his anti-Jacobite speeches of the 1790s. If the heroine of *Clash* had been an MP, no doubt this scene would have found its way into the novel.[4]

A long-standing member of the Labour Research Department, Wilkinson was involved with the Marxist journal *Plebs* for many years and lectured for the Labour College movement whenever she could. Possessing a natural flair for journalism she wrote for a wide variety of feminist, labour movement and popular publications, including the Labour supporting *Daily Herald*, Lord Beaverbrook's *Sunday Express* and Lady Rhondda's feminist *Time and Tide*. Though she had limited time in a busy life, Wilkinson was keen to write full-length fiction, and in addition to *Clash* (1929), which she composed in just two months, she wrote a second novel, *The Division Bell Mystery* (1932), a 'whodunnit' set in the House of Commons. Wilkinson travelled widely in her political work, visiting Hitler's Germany and reporting on the activities of the international volunteers during the Spanish Civil War. Her influential pamphlet, *Why Fascism* (1934), was written with a refugee, Edward Conze. It was decided by the Labour Party that Wilkinson needed a safer seat in the 1935 election and she was duly elected for the ship-building constituency of Jarrow in 1935. She is perhaps best remembered for leading the procession of hunger marchers from Jarrow to London in 1936 (an event which has become an icon of the 1930s), and for *The Town that was Murdered*, her impassioned indictment of the policies leading to Jarrow's neglect and destruction, published by the Left Book Club in 1939. In the wartime coalition government she was a parliamentary secretary in the Ministry of Pensions and the Ministry of Home Security, where she was given special responsibility for civil defence. Following the Labour landslide victory of 1945 she was made Minister of Education. In this post she was responsible for raising the school leaving age from 14 to 15, although she was only lukewarm in her support for comprehensive education. Her determination to carry out her public duties in the face of chronic asthma, bronchitis and a frail state of health almost certainly contributed to her death from exhaustion and bronchial pneumonia in 1947. A secondary school in south London has been named in her honour.

The General Strike

On 'Red Friday', 30 July 1925, the Conservative government led by Stanley Baldwin agreed to a nine-month subsidy for the struggling coal industry. It also set up a Royal Commission chaired by Sir Herbert Samuel to report on the future of the industry. The Samuel Commission published its findings in March 1926 and recommended that the Government subsidy should be withdrawn and the miners' wages reduced. The mine-owners gave notice that they would increase the working day from seven to eight hours, introduce local pay bargaining, and cut wages by between ten and twenty-five per cent. They announced that if the miners would not accept the new pay and conditions, a lock-out would come into effect from 1 May 1926. Not surprisingly, the Miners Federation of Great Britain (led by A. J. Cook) rejected the proposals. In order to bolster their campaign, the miners handed over the conduct of the dispute to the Trade Union

Congress (TUC). Talks to resolve the deadlock continued, but on 30 April a million miners were locked out of their pits. A conference of the TUC met on 1 May and declared that a General Strike in defence of miners' wages and working hours would commence two days later. A TUC delegation led by Jimmie Thomas of the National Union of Railwaymen continued to talk to the government but the talks were broken off by the Prime Minister when printers at the *Daily Mail* refused to print an anti-TUC editorial. The General Strike began at midnight on 3 May and lasted for nine days. It was called off unconditionally by the TUC at midnight on 12 May 1926.

The TUC strategy in the first instance, was to call out on strike over three-and-a-half million 'front-line' workers: railwaymen, transport workers, dockers, printers, builders, iron and steel workers. In the absence of daily newspapers, propaganda was supplied by the TUC's *British Worker* and for the government by Winston Churchill's *British Gazette*. On 7 May Sir Herbert Samuel had secretly approached the TUC offering his services to help to end the strike. Without informing the Miners' Federation, the TUC negotiating committee met Samuel and worked out a set of proposals which included a minimum wage, a temporary continuation of the government subsidy while negotiations took place, and the establishment of a national wage council. These proposals were accepted by the TUC negotiating committee despite the fact that Samuel had cautioned that a reduction in wages was likely to be rejected by the executive of the Miners' Federation. On 11 May 1926 the TUC accepted Samuel's terms although, as predicted, the miners refused to do so, the TUC called off the strike the next day. In July the mine-owners announced new terms of employment for miners based on the longer working day. The miners remained on strike but by November 1926 most had drifted back to work. Some joined the company-friendly Spencer Unions, while large numbers were victimised and all miners had to accept longer hours, lower wages and local bargaining. In 1927 the Government passed the Trade Disputes Act which made 'sympathy' strikes illegal, required union members to 'contract in' to the political levy, prohibited the Civil Service unions from affiliating to the TUC, and declared mass picketing illegal.

The General Strike was a major defeat for the labour movement but for many on the political left it nevertheless demonstrated, however briefly, the revolutionary potential of the working-class to exercise some control over history. In deliberating upon the meaning and significance of those nine momentous days in May 1926 it is necessary to extract this emancipatory narrative from beneath the indisputable reality of humiliation and defeat and to consider the way in which the General Strike has been constructed and contextualized both in historiography and literary narrative. Considering its iconic status, and its well-authenticated existence as 'the most dramatic single event in British domestic politics between the two world wars'[5] the General Strike has been markedly under-represented in the cultural record. Understandably, there was a flurry of interest in the strike in the immediate aftermath. Most early accounts were written by labour movement activists anxious to come to terms with the defeat and learn the lessons of history.[6] Wilkinson herself published *A Workers' History of the Great Strike* with R.W. Postgate and J. F Horrabin in 1927 and also wrote the introduction to Scott Nearing's *The British General Strike: An Economic Interpretation of its Background and its Significance* (1927).[7] Several academic studies appeared on or around the fiftieth anniversary of the strike, including important new work by G. A. Phillips, Margaret Morris and Jeffrey Skelley, but this intensity of interest has not been sustained.[8]

This relative neglect of the General Strike could be a consequence of the way in which, as Margaret Morris has pointed out, the memory and significance of 1926 has tended to become subsumed into the familiar iconography of the 1930s: poverty, unemployment, the slump, and the rise of Fascism.[9] This slippage, in which the General Strike becomes associated with the troubles generated by a near-global economic recession, does not adequately reflect the resurgence of trade union power in the aftermath of the First World War and the circulation of radical ideas within social, political and cultural movements in the 1920s. As John Lucas has argued persuasively in his book, *The Radical Twenties* (1977), the 1920s was in many respects more radical than the following decade.[10]

Yet even working-class and socialist writers showed only a mild interest in the General Strike, probably because an overwhelming sense of defeat was carried away from those nine days. Close to the event, the strike does figure in stories by ex-miners, but only in the background, as in Harold Heslop's *The Gate of a Strange Field* (1929), Lewis Jones's *We Live* (1939) and Sid Chaplin's short story 'Easter 1927' (published in his collection *The Leaping Lad* in 1946). The General Strike also appears indirectly in some forgotten dystopian narratives of the period, in which the dominant tone is one of disenchantment and fear.[11] It is particularly noteworthy, therefore, that the two key inter-war novels which deal directly and substantively with the strike are both by women: Wilkinson's *Clash* (1929) and Storm Jameson's *None Turn Back* (1936). Moreover, *Clash* differs from other interwar novels concerned with the impact of the political ferment of 1926 æ John Galsworthy's *Modern Comedy* (1929), Heslop's *The Gate of a Strange Field*, Leslie Paul's *Men in May* (1936) — by following the events from the perspective of a politicised woman.[12]

Appropriately, both *Clash* and *None Turn Back* were re-printed in the 1980s by the feminist publishing house, Virago. *None Turn Back* appeared in 1984 during the Miners' Strike of 1984-5, while *Clash* appeared in 1989, when much of the British coal industry had been closed.

Women and the Miners' Strike

As Griselda Carr points out in *Pit Women*, 'every reference to miners' wives in regional writings on coal communities, from Leifchild's *Our Coal and Our Coal Pits* (1853) to Dennis, Henriques and Slaughter's *Coal Is Our Life* (1956), comments on the hard labour of the women in the coal mining areas'.[13] To the long daily labour, begun in the very early morning and ending after other members of the family had gone to bed – preparing meals, boiling water for baths, doing the laundry, cleaning the house, sewing, mending and baking (all without labour-saving devices) – was added the loss of household income and the demoralisation, stress and insecurity that attended strikes and lock-outs. As a feminist and socialist, Wilkinson was particularly drawn to the experiences of these women.

The best account we have of women's experience of the 1926 miners' lockout is Marion Phillips's *Lock-out: The Story of the Women's Committee for the Relief of Miner's Wives and Children*.[14] Phillips was the formidable chief Women's Officer of the Labour Party. She appears fleetingly in Clash as the character Mary Peters while the character of Beryl Gaye is recognisably modelled on the Secretary of the Labour Women's Committee, the redoubtable Barbara Ayrton Gould. Phillips provides a comprehensive account of the massive humanitarian effort expended in raising the £313,000 which women distributed in clothes, food, milk, shoes and medicines to the families in the coal fields. The efforts of this 'industrial red cross' literally stood between the miners and destitution. The miners' leader Arthur Cooke wrote in appreciation:

> The miner's wives and children will never forget how the Women's Committee worked night and day to collect funds, to arrange for our choirs and bands, and to dispatch money, clothes and boots. How many a mother dried her eyes when a visit from the local Women's Committee brought clothes or food. The Labour Women cared for Humanity when the Government led by Baldwin tried to starve our people.[15]

But while the miners were appreciative of Labour women's support and Arthur Horner readily admitted that 'the women had saved the British Labour movement from disgrace. Had it not been for what the women had done, except for one or two unions, nothing would have been done', the relationship between the trade unions and organised feminists was sometimes strained.[16] The miners were the last of the major unions to support women's suffrage. At the Labour Party

Conference in 1926 Dora Russell argued that it was four times as dangerous for a woman to bear a child as a man to go down a mine. She told male trade union delegates that birth control was a matter of women's occupational safety and compared the demand for birth control with their demand for a seven-hour day: 'Surely you will not turn the women down on this question because it was the women who stood four square with you in the dispute?'[17] As we shall see, some of these tensions between feminist and labour movement agendas are explored, if not wholly resolved, in *Clash*.

Wilkinson's Attitude to the Strike

Wilkinson's credentials for writing a novel based on the General Strike were impeccable. To begin with, she had extensive first-hand experience. She travelled about 2000 miles as an official propagandist for the General Council of the TUC and addressed 47 meetings in provincial cities and towns, including Oxford, Banbury, Woodford, Coventry, Crewe, Hereford, Darlington, Stockton, Middlesbrough and Hartlepool. Moreover, although the events of 1926 represented an enormous defeat for the British labour movement, and effectively signalled the end of the syndicalist project that had underwritten so much of its thinking and action since the first decade of the century, Wilkinson's attitude to the General Strike remained essentially optimistic. She threw herself wholeheartedly into it, brought back enthusiastic reports of solidarity wherever she had spoken, and reacted with amazement and disbelief when it was called off. Like many radicals, her anger was reserved for the 'abject surrender of the General Council' and the timidity of the trade union leadership who were 'not accustomed to face class issues' and who thus 'broke under the strain'.

Wilkinson had come to know many trade union leaders personally and concluded that 'the tragedy of this strike consists in just this fact, that it was led by men who did not believe in it, who could not want it to succeed.'[18] Her introduction to a book on the General Strike written for sympathetic readers in the United States underlined her belief in the revolutionary potential and significance of what had taken place and her faith in 'the marvellous powers of organization latent in our working class'. She wrote: 'The General Strike may not be Britain's 1905 (a reference to the events leading to the Russian revolution), but it undoubtedly has been a rehearsal for something bigger. Who knows how soon the performance will be staged?'[19] If the predominant feeling on the political left was that the miners had been abandoned, Wilkinson made sure that in her career, and in her fiction, the miners were supported and symbolically remained at the centre of the class struggle.

Clash and Genre

Clash is Wilkinson's attempt to politicise literary romance, a mode of writing widely considered at this time as inappropriate for the transmission of serious political ideas.[20] The inter-war period had, however, witnessed an upsurge of interest in popular romantic writing. The love stories which featured regularly in magazines like *Peg's Paper* (founded 1919) were avidly read by working women and girls. Although many socialists were highly critical of popular romantic fiction for its supposedly deleterious effects upon working class readers, Wilkinson deplored such distinctions between 'high' and 'low' art as a major impediment to the creation of a popular socialist culture.

Indeed, this debate finds its way into *Clash*, in the episode where Gerald Blain wants to launch a new popular political magazine to be called the *Wednesday Weekly*. He invites the heroine Joan Craig (obviously modelled in part on Wilkinson herself) to contribute a regular series of 'Simple Stories from a Woman's Heart'. This incident is a wryly self-conscious reference to the fact that Wilkinson's narrative method in the novel is to use a romantic plot within a class-conscious and feminist framework of ideas. The novel tries to find a balance between the individual woman's desire for emotional fulfilment within a heterosexual relationship and a political commitment to the working class which ultimately qualifies and limits such individualistic longings. *Clash* makes a case for the education of desire.

The emphasis in the novel is on Joan Craig's sexuality: she is at once desirable and desiring. Joan and the married Tony Dacre are 'modern' lovers. However, Joan also has a relationship with Captain Gerald Blain who wishes to marry her. Joan is a typical romantic heroine in that she knows that she loves Dacre passionately but the familiar questions of popular romantic fiction – who does the heroine really love, and does the man who is the object of her desire reciprocate her feelings? – provide a critical focus in *Clash,* despite the fact that the reader knows the answers from a very early stage. The very language and form in which these questions may be posed is altered by the fact that Joan is both a socialist and a feminist. Dacre satisfies the romantic heroine's need for a relationship premised on intimacy and tenderness but he possesses none of her class consciousness and the novel illuminates the patriarchal as well as the pleasurable aspect of their relationship. The issue to be resolved is whether or not Joan should comply with Dacre's wishes and give up her work in the labour movement, or whether she should opt for marriage to Blain, a marriage of equals to be based on the understanding that her work must come first. The unravelling of the romantic triangle, therefore, is inseparable from and partially determined by the wider context of class politics.

As Wilkinson noted in a *Plebs* article in 1929, 'There has been as yet no great interpretative novel in English of working-class life'.[21] In an interview given to *The News Chronicle* in 1935, Wilkinson stated that her ambition in the novel was to 'get across' to working class people, those that are 'as naturally the centre of th[is] book as middle-class people are of other sorts of novels'.[22] The episodes in *Clash* in which Joan goes to the Yorkshire coalfields to help with the relief work are good examples of the social realism which she admired in middlebrow writers like A. J. Cronin. She depicts the day-to-day reality of the miners lock-out in telling and studied detail, picking out vivid images for her reader as part of her mission to convey the desperation of lives lived on the edge of the abyss. Notable examples are the mother with no hot water or clothes for her new baby and the women and children who look 'like maggots on the refuse heaps trying to find precious bits of coal to sell for bread' (p. 146). But Wilkinson's chosen genre made it more difficult to show how circumstances such as poverty were the result of particular economic systems or of socially structured patterns of inequality. Her focus on the individual, implicit in the conventions of both realist and romantic fiction, made her reliant on reportage and inter-personal dialogues for much of the novel rather than on analysis of underlying determining forces and causal relations. Despite these limitations, Wilkinson was able to explore the important new social, emotional and literary territory of gendered class struggle through the actions and consciousness of her heroine, Joan Craig.

If politicised men feature only too rarely as the subjects of fiction, politicised women feature even less frequently. Beatrix Campbell argues that literary representations of industrial strikes often indulge in the stereotype of the complaining and obstructive wife.[23] Though she perhaps simplifies things somewhat, the fact remains that women have rarely been represented as industrial or political activists. It is this focus in *Clash* which makes it of unusual interest.

The semi-autobiographical heroine, Joan Craig, is a 26-year-old northern organizer for the National Industrial Union of Labour. The standard picture of men as the bearers of authority and prestige in public is immediately inverted in the novel. There is no male character to compete with Joan or to distract our attention. The men who congregate around Joan, including her immediate superior in the union, William Royd, come and go spasmodically. It is Joan who makes key decisions, knows her own mind, and is determined to exercise it. It is no coincidence that it is Joan's attaché case, symbolising the power and status of the public sphere, which is the first accoutrement associated with this successful, down-to-earth and politicised heroine.[24]

Although Wilkinson needed a protagonist sufficiently mobile to cross between conflicting social and sexual worlds, the character she creates in Joan might seem, at first glance, lacking in plausibility, were it not for our knowledge that Wilkinson moved between these worlds herself. Joan is a trade union organiser but she also inhabits the fashionable world of bohemian Bloomsbury. She is patronised by the wealthy socialite and veteran suffragist, Mary Maud Meadowes, who is based on Wilkinson's friend, Margaret Lady Rhondda, editor of the feminist journal *Time and Tide*. The cultural geography of this division in Joan's life is both socially and sexually symbolic: the north is a place of grim industrial reality, unrelieved patriarchy and duty to 'the cause'; the seductive south is a place of enlightened attitudes to gender, pleasure and high culture. There is an anticipation in all this of the symbolic national landscape mapped out by the Angry Young Men of the 1950s, and a reworking of the depictions of 'two nations' found in the 'Condition of England' novels of the 1840s. We presume that Joan will reconcile these two worlds by subordinating the south to the north, pleasure to duty. Her duty is her pleasure: 'Personal contacts wearied her. Family or friends were carelessly shed if something exciting in the way of a strike or a good organizing row called her to any distant town' (p.5). The reader suspects, rightly, that 'personal contacts' will test her mettle in the course of the novel as the romance plot asserts itself. Additionally, erotic temptations are thrown up precisely by a 'good' strike and an 'organizing row'. The crucial difference is that this 'row' takes place not in a 'distant town' but in London, the very site of the pleasure principle of which she is supposedly in control. As history is being made in the Memorial Hall in Farringdon, where the TUC took the decision to call the strike, Joan becomes enmeshed in the contradictory pleasures and politics of her Bloomsbury 'set'. The early chapters of the novel oscillate between the two locations: the spartan Methodist hall and the luxurious West End of London.

Some of these rapid transitions seem to beg the reader's disapproval. At one point Joan is whisked from the hall in which 'the middle class was completely absent' (p.27) to a lunch of omelettes and sherry in a Soho cafe.[25] This bifurcation of her social identity cannot be satisfactorily explained as a romantic choice between two upper-class suitors (Dacre the suave writer and Blain the idealistic First World War veteran), though her affair with Dacre provides the narrative opening for Joan's confrontation with the realities of being an emancipated woman in the 1920s. Wilkinson shows that the meanings of the strike reverberate far beyond the walls of Memorial Hall, not just in 'any distant town', but also in a revaluation of the idea of the independent woman. Class conflict is infused with gender conflict and *vice-versa*.

The strike has the paradoxical effect of initially lowering social and sexual barriers for those involved in the dispute whilst also sharpening the antagonistic, determining forces of property whenever the narrative comes up against the looming threat of revolutionary change. Likewise, the novel's pursuit of women's emancipation, which starts with a confident assertion of Joan's autonomy, begins to falter. Having been permitted access to the highbrow world, Joan is faced with a painful theorization of her 'lived' ideal of independence. When Joan hears that Dacre's wife, Helen, is prepared to help strike-breakers in order to raise funds for her latest modernist theatre production, Joan ask Dacre to intervene, but he is scathing about this appeal to his patriarchal authority:

> 'How can I? We're not in the Stone Age, and I'm not a cave-man. My wife earns her own income and lives her own life. I have no more influence over her than the next one.' (p.25)

Although Dacre may be rationalising his weak will, his critique opens up the question of the remaking of gender roles in a situation of equalised property, a conundrum which shadows the wider class struggle symbolised by the General Strike. Mary Maude's formulation of the dilemma of the modern woman also has a resonance for the meanings of the strike:

> 'Whether we can stretch the old Victorian codes to fit, or whether we should throw codes over altogether, or whether the modern woman can evolve a new code.' (p.59)

In some respects Mary Maude, whom we are told went to prison as a suffragette, is a compromised figure. She derives a private income from the coal mines and has only a superficial attachment to the working class. She wants Joan to live up to her name (Joan of Arc, who was the patron saint of the suffragettes) but at the cost of any romantic fulfilment. Mary Maude believes that acquiring a husband will divert Joan's energies away from her mission to become a leader of women and to further the next stage of feminist progress, entry into the professions and parliament. Thus feminist ideals about widening women's participation in the public sphere are represented as having middle-class origins and stewardship.[26] The narrative insists that feminist advance must be reconciled to the ongoing struggle of the working class. As we shall see, the attempt to resolve this problem is by establishing a set-piece dramatic plot climax, which allows Joan to recommit herself in public to the working class and simultaneously to make an acceptable choice of romantic partner.

So the question of precisely how the 'codes' of feminine identity should be reinvented in the modern world parallels the dilemma of legitimacy posed by the 'public' history of the General Strike. The central contradiction of the strike is articulated by numerous characters, including Joan: without recourse to revolutionary action there is little prospect of victory but insurrection will meet with a bloody response from the State (a scene of slaughtered workers mown down by machine guns is envisioned more than once in the novel). When Ernest Bevin tells the TUC delegates 'you have placed your all upon the altar for this great Movement' (p.36) the rhetoric captures the apocalyptic significance of this confrontation between labour and capital. But it is also clear that the labour movement cannot abandon constitutional machinery. Wilkinson's political ally, J. F. Horrabin captured the irony of this situation in a cartoon used on the front covers of *Plebs*: a huge elephant named 'Labour' refuses to tread on a tiny pea called 'The Constitution'.

The image of the State in *Clash* is also ambiguous. The government is depicted as a 'broker' between the mine-owners (capital) and the unions (labour), but there are obvious and sinister contradictions in this role. The EPA (Emergency Powers Act) and OMS (Order for the Maintenance of Supplies) were in place before the strike began, and Joan notes sharply that the OMS 'had all the powers of the state without any of its inconvenient constitutional checks' (p.36). In reality, the Conservative government led by Baldwin did not need to mobilize all its volunteers or troops since the strike collapsed after only nine days (though 3000 arrests for 'seditious' activities did take place). All the government had to do was call the TUC's bluff. When Joan ponders why all the 'fine stuff' of the working class is being wasted, the only word that emerges is 'muddle' (p.30).

The same sentiment does not apply uniformly to Joan's experiences with the women of the coalfields. The novel shows that the strike has both mobilized and intellectually emancipated many 'simple working women' (p.148). One conspicuous example is a *Plebs*-educated wife who initiates a discussion of birth control (a cause Wilkinson supported) and denounces patriarchal working-class culture: 'Do 'em good. The men are too uppish anyway. Let 'em see what we have to put up with for a change' (p.162). Inspired by such women, Joan recommits herself to the labour movement which is her true home (Joan's family is conspicuously absent from the narrative, as if 'sacrificed' to her cause). This allows her, in the closing scene, to emphatically renounce bourgeois culture despite its attractions (personified by Dacre and Mary Maud). Blain sums up the romanticised appeal of this class renunciation: 'the only thing for the men and women who can lead the workers is to stick with them, live their life, eat their bread, and resolutely refuse to go one step beyond the standard of living of the people they are leading' (p.168). Granted, Joan's choice of Blain as a marital partner is a concession to the conventions of romantic love (in which the heroine must marry above herself and is never allowed to stay single).[27] Joan has also become a fledgling writer, but it is clear that her literary talents, and her marriage, will enhance rather than impede her work.

Hence *Clash* explores the tensions between Wilkinson's commitment to feminism and her awareness of the marginalisation of feminism within the labour movement.[28] In common with Ethel Mannin, Ethel Carnie Holdsworth, Mary Agnes Hamilton, Leonora Eyles, Storm Jameson, Naomi Mitchison, Sylvia Townsend Warner, Lettice Cooper and many other left-wing women writers in the inter-war period, Wilkinson attempted to write her signature as a woman into the labour movement, throwing herself wholeheartedly into its campaigns and sensitively dramatising its preoccupations, while at the same time maintaining a critical distance from its more chauvinistic and insular proclivities. Long before the women's movement of the 1970s had pinpointed and publicised the connection, *Clash* insists that the personal is political. The dilemma of the central character, Joan Craig, is still recognisably the dilemma of many women: how to realise some degree of personal, professional, sexual and emotional fulfilment in a world where relationships premised on equality are more of an ideal rather than reality. In twenty-first-century 'post-industrial' Britain, it is tempting to conclude that only the feminist themes of *Clash* remain active and relevant. While this aspect of the book may well be the most immediately appealing to the modern reader, the challenge and achievement of *Clash* is its conspicuous refusal to separate issues of class and gender, the individual and the collective, the personal and the political.

The reception of *Clash*[29]

When *Clash* was published on 19 April 1929 it was extensively reviewed and on the whole favourably received. Wilkinson's public reputation and the novel's uniqueness (the first novel by a woman MP) probably contributed to this media attention. The degree of coverage was impressive. There were dozens of reviews in both mainstream and radical English newspapers and journals, but the novel was also favourably reviewed in Scotland, Ireland, the United States (where Wilkinson was a popular figure) and as far away as Australia.

The novel was published by Harrap at 7s 6d, a price which put it well beyond the working-class readership which Wilkinson claimed she wanted to reach and influence. A desire to redress this limitation may have been one of the factors behind her agreeing to have the novel serialised in *The Daily Express* between May and June 1929 and some of the paper's readers expressed their gratitude at being able to read the novel in this form. Although the novel was not reprinted, it was popular enough to warrant an edition in braille.[30]

Most of the reviews recognised that the novel's title was a play on words which signified two parallel conflicts: the heroine's attempt to reconcile romantic and career aspirations, and the class struggle of the General Strike. In an article in *The Daily Express* (15 April 1929) which appeared a few days before publication and was undoubtedly designed to 'soften' (or feminise) the novel's appeal, Wilkinson played up the former theme at the expense of the latter, claiming her primary goal was to write a 'modern' love story against the background of the strike. Different reviewers expressed a preference for one or other of these two themes, although many expressed doubts about their successful integration, and usually attributed this failure to Wilkinson's inexperience as a novelist. *The Times* (19 April) noted some 'crudity' but praised the novel's 'passion and feeling', a view echoed by the *Daily Mail* (23 April) which found the book 'vigorous' if callow. *The Telegraph* (19 April) was impressed by the sections describing the coalfields; similarly, the *Daily Chronicle* (19 April) praised the novel's historical accuracy and authenticity. *The Reynolds's News* (21 April) praised the book's socialist and feminist sympathies and its frankness about issues such as birth control (the latter was also singled out by Vera Brittain in *Time and Tide* (3 May) as 'good propaganda'). Similarly, the *Manchester Guardian* (19 April) highlighted the novel's 'expositions of attitudes and aspirations' although it regretted (in an acute observation) that the dominant point of view was that of the 'sympathetic middle class'. Perhaps the most sophisticated assessment of the novel's realism came in Nicholas Newcroft's review in *The News Chronicle* (25 April). Anticipating Georg Lukács, Newcroft claims that the best realism 'is a transcript of the social situation as this finds expression in the lives of individuals' and praises *Clash* for its 'epic' evenhandedness in not demonising the class enemy (Newcroft's comment that Wilkinson thus 'triumphs over her theory' also recalls Engels's 'triumph of realism'). *The Manchester Dispatch* (19 April) on the other hand, felt that the love story expressed Wilkinson's humanity far more effectively than the 'minor affair' of the political struggle. The conservative *Yorkshire Post* (23 April) found the 'Socialist' bias offensive but praised Wilkinson's engaging wit.

The June issue of *Plebs*, on the other hand, hoped that further novels about the labour movement would flow from Wilkinson's successful debut: 'it must appear as frequently in the novel as it does on the political platform'. The literary history of the twentieth century does not bear out this aspiration, a fact which reaffirms the continuing importance of *Clash*.

Mary Joannou and Ian Haywood

Footnotes

1. We are indebted to Betty D. Vernon, *Ellen Wilkinson 1891-1947* (London: Croom Helm, 1982) for biographical information.
2. See Vera Brittain, *Testament of Friendship: The Story of Winifred Holtby* (London: Macmillan, 1940), p. 420.
3. Dora Russell, *Hypatia: or Women and Knowledge* (London: Kegan Paul, Trench and Trubner, 1925), p. 7.
4. Vernon, *Ellen Wilkinson*, p. 90.
5. Patrick Renshaw, *The General Strike* (London: Eyre Methuen, 1975), p. 19.
6. See: Robin Page Arnot, *The General Strike, May 1926: Its Origin and History* (London: Labour Research Department, 1926); Emile Burns, *The General Strike, May 1926: Trades Councils in Action* (London: Labour Research Department, 1926); A. J. Cook, *The Nine Days* (London: Co-operative Printing Society, n.d.); R. Palme Dutt, *The Meaning of the General Strike* (London Communist Party of Great Britain, 1926); Henry Hamilton Fyfe, *Behind the Scenes of the Great Strike* (London: Labour Publishing Company, 1926).
7. Frank Horrabin, Raymond Postgate, and Ellen Wilkinson, *A Worker's History of the General Strike* (London: Plebs League, 1927); Scott Nearing, *The British General Strike: An Economic Interpretation of its Background and its Significance* (New York: Vanguard Press, 1927).
8. See: G. A. Phillips, *The General Strike: The Politics of Industrial Conflict* (London: Weidenfeld and Nicholson, 1976); Margaret Morris, *The General Strike* (London: Penguin, 1976); Jeffrey Skelley, ed., *The General Strike* (London: Lawrence and Wishart, 1976). The only major book-length study published after 1976 is Keith Laybourn, *The General Strike of 1926* (Manchester: Manchester University Press, 1993).
9. See Morris, *The General Strike*, chapter 14. See also Raymond Williams's brief but moving essay, 'The Social Significance of 1926' (1977), reprinted in *Resources of Hope: Culture, Democracy, Socialism* (London: Verso, 1989), pp. 105-110.
10. John Lucas, *The Radical Twenties: Writing, Politics, Culture* (Nottingham: Five Leaves Publications, 1997). Lucas argues that the General Strike was 'the definitive moment for the 1920s' (p. 4), an event which sharpened class antagonisms and therefore had a major influence on the ideological climate of reform which led to the election of a Labour government in 1945. He adds that 'the General Strike was inevitable. The only surprise was that it took so long to arrive' (p. 149.) See also John Stevenson, *British Society 1914-45* (London: Penguin, 1986), pp. 196-9.
11. See Lucas, *The Radical Twenties*, chapters 5 and 7.
12. Mention can also be made here of Menna Gallie's *Strike for a Kingdom* (1959). Although Gallie's novel has a male protagonist it pays sympathetic attention to women's perspectives and, as Stephen Knight has argued, makes a spirited

attempt to feminise the strike. See Stephen Knight, 'The Uncertainties and Hesitations that were the 'Truth': Welsh Industrial Fictions by Women', in H. Gustav Klaus and Stephen Knight, eds., *British Industrial Fictions* (Cardiff: University of Wales Press, 2000), pp. 163-180, pp. 167-170.

13. Griselda Carr, *Pit Women* (London: Merlin, 2001), p. 34.

14. Marion Phillips, *Lock-out: The Story of the Women's Committee for the Relief of Miner's Wives and Children* (London: Labour Publishing Company, 1927).

15. Quoted in Phillips, *Women and the Miners' Lock Out*, p. 25.

16. Quoted in Pamela Graves, *Labour Women: Women in British Working-Class Politics, 1918-1939* (Cambridge: Cambridge University Press, 1994, p.95).

17. Quoted in Graves, *Labour Women*, p. 96.

18. Ellen Wilkinson, *Plebs*, 18.6 (June 1926): 209-12 (211).

19. Ellen Wilkinson, Introduction to Nearing, *The British General Strike*, p. xxi.

20. For a substantial treatment of Wilkinson's reworking of romance motifs and romance ideology, see: Pamela Fox, *Class Fictions: Shame and Resistance in the British Working-Class Novel, 1890-1945* (Durham and London, Duke University Press, 1994), pp. 85-89, 169-76; Mary Joannou, 'Reclaiming the Romance: Ellen Wilkinson's *Clash* and the Cultural Legacy of Socialist-Feminism', in David Margolies and Maroula Joannou, eds., *Heart of the Heartless World: Essays in Cultural Resistance in Memory of Margot Heinemann* (London: Pluto Press, 1995), pp. 148-61.

21. *Plebs* (November 1929): 247.

22. See J. L. Hodson, '"Before I Die": Ellen Wilkinson's Ambition to get Working People "Over" in a Novel', *The News Chronicle* (13 December 1935): p.3.

23. Beatrix Campbell, 'Orwell — *Paterfamilias* or Big Brother?', in Christopher Norris, ed., *Inside the Myth: Orwell, Views from the Left* (London: Lawrence and Wishart, 1984), p.131.

24. This detail is also autobiographical: it was noted by the press that Wilkinson carried an attaché case to the House of Commons when she was first elected in 1924.

25. On this topic, see Jonathan Rose, *The Intellectual Life of the British Classes* (New Haven and London: Yale University Press, 2001), chapter 13. Rose points out that 'In the 1920's, London's Bohemia offered plenty of inexpensive diversions for the working girl' (441) and provides several real-life examples to parallel Joan Craig (though he does not refer to Wilkinson).

26. See the discussion of this issue in Janet Batsleer, Tony Davies, Rebecca O'Rourke, Chris Weedon, 'Fiction as politics: working-class writing in the inter-war years', in their book, *Rewriting English: The Cultural Politics of Gender and Class* (London: Methuen,1985), pp. 52-54.

27. According to Pamela Fox, this alliance is at the expense of sexual fulfilment: 'Joan in effect accomplishes her martyrdom' (Fox, *Class Fictions*, p. 175).

28. On this topic more generally, see Graves, *Labour Women,* chapter 4. According to Graves (pp. 152-3), by the mid 1920s the 'older generation of labour women who had absorbed feminist ideas as part of the suffrage campaign' had accepted 'a secondary status' in the labour movement and had 'lost ground to the much more numerous postwar generation.' Moreover, middle-class feminists outside the labour movement sometimes criticised the movement in public. 'Thus "feminism" became associated with an anti-labour position'.

29. Wilkinson pasted all the reviews of *Clash* into her scrapbook (Labour Party Archive, W1/6).

30. Letter from George Harrap and Co. to Wilkinson, 30 July 1929 (Labour Party Archive W1/6).

Suggested Further Reading

Archives

We have consulted scrapbooks of Ellen Wilkinson papers and press cuttings in the following archives of the British Labour Party: Bodleian Library Oxford: X. Films 83/19 — 32, X. Cat. Ref 51d (this collection is a microfilmed copy of papers held in the National Museum of Labour History, Manchester: LP/W1/1-8); Modern Records Centre, University of Warwick: MSS. 209. We are grateful to the staff of both libraries for their assistance.

Contemporary and Early Sources

Arnot, Robin Page (1926). *The General Strike, May 1926: Its Origin and History.* London: Labour Research Department, 1926.

Arnot, Robin Page (1949). *The Miners: a History of the Miners' Federation of Great Britain 1889. Volume 1.* London: Allen and Unwin.

Burns, Emile (1926). *The General Strike, May 1926: Trades Councils in Action.* London: Labour Research Department.

Cook, A. J.. (n.d.). *The Nine Days.* London: Co-operative Printing Society.

Crook, Wilfred Harris (1931). *The General Strike: a History of Labour's Tragic Weapon in Theory and Practice.* Chapel Hill: University of North Carolina Press.

Dutt, R. Palme (1926). *The Meaning of the General Strike.* London: Communist Party of Great Britain.

Fyfe, Henry Hamilton (1926). *Behind the Scenes of the Great Strike.* London: Labour Publishing Company, 1926.

Horrabin, Frank, Raymond Postgate, and Ellen Wilkinson (1927). *A Worker's History of the General Strike.* London : Plebs League.

Mannin, Ethel (1930). *Confessions and Impressions*. London: Jarrolds. This contains Mannin's impressions of Wilkinson (pp. 167-70).

Nearing, Scott (1927). *The British General Strike: An Economic Interpretation of its Background and its Significance*. New York: Vanguard Press, 1927. The Introduction to this book is by Ellen Wilkinson.

Oxford, Margot, ed., (1938). *Myself When Young by Famous Women of To-day*. London: Muller. This contains an autobiographical fragment by Ellen Wilkinson.

Phillips, Marion (1927). *Women and the Miners' Lock Out*. London: Labour Publishing Company.

Secondary Sources

Ayers, David (1999). *English Literature of the 1920s*. Edinburgh: the Edinburgh University Press.

Batsleer, Janet, Tony Davies, Rebecca O'Rourke, Chris Weedon (1985). 'Fiction as politics: working-class writing in the inter-war years', in *Rewriting English: The Cultural Politics of Gender and Class*. London: Methuen.

Branson, Noreen. *Britain in the Nineteen Twenties* (1975). London: Weidenfeld and Nicholson.

Branson, Noreen, and Bill Moore (1990-91). *Labour and Communist Relations 1920-1951*. London: Communist Party History Group.

Gaffin, Jean, and David Thomas (1983). *Caring and Sharing: The Centenary History of the Women's Co-operatve Guild*. Manchester: Co-operative Union.

Fox, Pamela (1994). *Class Fictions: Shame and Resistance in the British Working-Class Novel, 1890-1945*. Durham and London: Duke University Press.

Graves, Pamela M. (1994). *Labour Women: Women in British Working-Class Politics 1918-1939*. Cambridge: Cambridge University Press.

Haywood, Ian (1997). *Working- Class Fiction: From Chartism to 'Trainspotting'*. Plymouth: Northcote House.

Haywood, Ian (1999) '"Never Again"? Ellen Wilkinson's *Clash* and the Feminization of the General Strike', *Literature and History*, 8.2: 34-43.

Hinton, James (1983). *Labour and Socialism: A History of the British Labour Movement, 1867-1972*. Brighton: Wheatsheaf Books.

Joannou, Maroula (1995). 'Reclaiming the Romance: Ellen Wilkinson's Clash and the Cultural Legacy of Socialist Feminism', in David Margolies and Maroula Joannou, eds., *Heart of the Heartless World: Essays in Memory of Margot Heinemann*. London: Pluto Press.

Laybourn, Keith (1993). *The General Strike of 1926*. Manchester: Manchester University Press.

Mason, Anthony (1970). *The General Strike in the North-East*. Hull: University of Hull Press.

Lucas, John (1997). *The Radical Twenties*. Nottingham: Five Leaves Press.

Morris, Margaret (1976). *The General Strike*. Harmondsworth: Penguin.

Phillips, G. A. (1976). *The General Strike: The Politics of Industrial Conflict*. London: Weidenfeld and Nicholson.

Renshaw, Patrick (1975). *The General Strike*. London: Eyre Methuen.

Skelley, Jeffrey, ed. (1976). *The General Strike*. London: Lawrence and Wishart.

Symons, Julian (1957). *The General Strike*. London: The Cresset Press.

Thompson, Willie (1992). *The Good Old Cause: British Communism, 1920-1991*. London: Pluto Press.

Vernon, Betty (1982). *Ellen Wilkinson 1891-1947*. London: Croom Helm.

Williams, Raymond (1977). 'The Social Significance of 1926', rpt. in *Resources of Hope: Culture, Democracy, Socialism*. London: Verso, 1989.

Wrigley, Chris (1982). *The General Strike in Local History*. Loughborough: Loughborough University Press.

CLASH

CHAPTER I

Joan Craig stamped into her small office. She dropped her attaché case on the floor, tossed her hat on one chair, and her coat and gloves on another.

"I'm through," she said to herself viciously, "absolutely through." She turned and slipped the bolt on the door. "If I see another human face this afternoon, I shall hit it." She sat down by her desk and let her head fall on her arms. "I'm tired. I can't go on doing this work every day. You can't go on handing out bits of yourself to people who don't want to be bothered. Anyway, I can't ... I just can't." Joan was having one of her 'crises.' She was tired, with that kind of tiredness known only to those who set out to organize their fellow-men. At moments the world seems to them just a mound of other people's worries pressing on their shoulders. Joan had spent eight years organizing women, first as a munition worker, and since the War as a trade union official. At the age of twenty-six she had begun to think of her fellows simply as pink faces before a platform, or as lines of dark figures into whose hands she thrust meeting bills.

Sitting in the little room which she shared with another woman organizer at the Yorkshire offices of the National Industrial Union of Labour, she felt that she had come to the end of a chapter. She was bored as well as tired. For an hour at least she wanted to be free of people, relieved from contact with other personalities.

There were taps at the door ... someone made Morse signals with the fingernails. Joan knew who it would be and dragged herself wearily to draw the bolt.

"I'm not fit to speak to, and I shall either weep at you or quarrel," she said, managing a grin. William Royd was her refuge as well as her chief in the male staff she had to work with. He was a tall, strongly built Lancashire man with a reserve of power that was kept hidden under a vague air of general geniality. Every one called him William, but no one had tried to presume on that familiarity. Royd was from the work-shop and of it, more at home any time with his tools than with his pen. Success in leading a long and difficult strike in the works where he was employed had brought him on to the official staff of the union, and since then his rise had been rapid. He was now an executive member as well as an official, the youngest among a body of cautious and ageing men. He had the power among them that comes from at least giving the appearance of being able to get things done — and in his case somehow the things did get done.

As he came into the room, Joan went dejectedly to her seat by the fire.

"What's up?"

"I'm fed, William, just fed. I'll sweep streets before I'll address another works gate meeting, or give out one more beastly handbill. If the women won't organize they can jolly well stew. I'm through."

"'S'pity."

"Why? Spare me any appeals to 'build Jerusalem in England's green and pleasant land.'¹ I've done. I've made too many fervid appeals. I've protested against too many injustices. I know how the wheels go round. Is there a Trappist monastery² for women? I'll get a single ticket there."

"Oh, a cheap week-end would be better. You won't feel like that on Monday." He thrust some tobacco into his pipe. There were strict rules against smoking in these offices, but rules seldom worried Royd.

"It would be a pity to run away just when things were getting exciting," he said.

"Exciting!" Joan groaned in mock despair. "I've had to make the same speech twice a day for the last fortnight, and you call that exciting!"

"Well, a general strike would be exciting enough, even for you, wouldn't it?"

"A general strike! William, you've been reading the *Morning Post*,³ and at your age too! … Tut, tut!"

"Oh, there's going to be a general strike all right," said Royd, applying yet another match to his pipe.

"There'll be a lot of bluffing about one," retorted Joan, "as there was last July,⁴ but can you see our crowd fighting on that scale, or the Government letting them if they wanted to? Things don't happen like that in England. It's not as though the Communists had any influence now, and the best of them are in jail, anyway."⁵

"Joan, my child, it's you that's been reading the *Morning Post* if you imagine that a revolution in England will be produced by your earnest young Communist friends. British revolutions are made by British church-wardens. That's why they have been successful."

"Will the churchwardens run a general strike?"

"Their trade union equivalent will. If the stolid fathers of families who make up this blessed union of ours decide to get a move on to help the miners things will move, my girl."

"Yes, but I can't see them deciding."

"Oh, the Trades Union Congress General Council will probably do the deciding — but I'm pretty sure from what I've seen lately that there's a general feeling abroad that if the miners go down in this fight the wages of every other section will be attacked."

"Your tea, Miss Joan. Oh, I didn't see you, Mr Royd. Yours is on your desk, sir."

"Never mind, Emily. Mr Royd can drink out of my saucer or the sugar-bowl or something."

"I just won't be a minute, miss, just two little seconds. I'll …"

Joan jumped up and threw her arms round Emily's waist.

"Now that's all right. Your rheumaticky knees aren't going up and down stairs for any six-footer's tea-cup, bless you."

Emily was one of Joan's 'finds'. She had been victimized after a recent strike for telling the employer exactly what she thought of him. Joan, having heard Emily's choicest bits, felt a private sympathy with the poor man, but with Emily dressed in tidy black, all quiet, demure, and patient, Joan had no difficulty in convincing her Executive that here was a victim of injustice, sentenced to starvation for her self-sacrificing defence of her fellow-strikers. So Emily was installed to provide tea, to wash up pots, dust office desks, and adore Miss Joan, though the last was not specified in her list of duties.

"You shall have the honour of the cup, William, as a bribe," said Joan, pouring her own tea into the little china sugar-bowl.

She sat on the arm of the chair like a bird poised for flight. Much too thin, with wiry black hair that stood away from her face, and quick black eyes, Joan Craig always gave an impression of excessive energy. Her horse-power was too big for her body, her gear ratio too high. People trying to describe her features found they couldn't. Her face was thin and pale. She left the impression of a breeze rather than a woman. The men she had worked with during the crowded years since 1918 had often tried to reach the woman, but Joan eluded them. Personal contacts wearied her. Family or friends were carelessly shed if something exciting in the way of a strike or a good organizing row called her to any distant town.

Royd was surprised that she didn't go up into the air at once at the mention of such a thrill as a general strike. She sat very still until Emily's heavy foot had bumped down the last stair. Then she got down from her perch and sat on the chair seat, and looked at Royd.

"Do you know more than there has been in the papers? Is there any further news? Do you *really* think there will be a general strike, or was that a bomb just thrown to wake me up?"

Royd put down his cup. "Well, a bit of both. Something's bound to happen, and apparently it's going to happen soon. I've just received a summons that has been sent out, calling all the Executives of the unions to meet the General

Council[6] in London, so that looks as though they were meaning business."

"But it might mean all sorts of things — negotiating and all that."

"The General Council have got the power to do anything of that kind, and the tone of this summons suggests something more."

"It looks like a deadlock, you mean?"

Royd shrugged a shoulder. "Well, the subsidy which the Government gave to the coal-owners[7] has tided them comfortably over the winter, when it would have been awkward for them to have a strike. Stocks are big and the summer's coming, so they're all right. Why shouldn't they let the notices run out on May the 1st? And as for the miners, do you think they *will* give in?"

"And I suppose the Samuel Report[8] is in the W.P.B.?"[9]

"Looks like it."

"Then the Government will have to do something. Governments always give in when things are really uncomfortable," said Joan with an air of finality.

"I've a pretty shrewd idea that this time they are not going to," replied Royd. "I think they will just see if the unions are bluffing with all this talk about a general strike."

"Well, aren't they?"

"I'm not so sure. The question is, can the other unions afford to let the miners go down? If they do, it's all up with any hopes they've got of improving things for a good bit."

Joan rose to put some more coal on the fire. She looked thoughtfully at the piece she held between the tongs. "Queer stuff, isn't it?" she said. "All the hidden possibilities, the light and power and heat and scent and healing, all being squabbled over like a mangy bone some prehistoric cur has buried."

"And wasted, as though the sole use of it was to grub it out of the ground as quick as possible and chuck it at any price to anyone who'll have the stuff," added Royd.

Joan stood with the tongs still in one hand, while the other arm lay along the mantelpiece, her forehead resting on it as she looked thoughtfully at the fire. Royd was outwardly placid, but his jaw was locked on his pipe stem. The grace of her thin body, her tousled black hair above her white neck, went to his head. He was too physically strong for the life he was leading. The transition from heavy manual work to a sedentary life had been too abrupt. Though his own marriage was a perfectly happy and peaceful one, the wild strain in Joan appealed to deep fires in Royd's nature. He ached to stand behind her now, grip her wrists, and force that alive body against his. But he would rather have died than embarrass a woman who had to work under him. He controlled himself sufficiently to say evenly:

"Don't you agree to my summing up?"

Joan roused herself. She was too intently sensitive not to feel the impact of Royd's sudden strong desire. She felt bewildered ... she didn't quite know why ... the room had grown too small.

"It all seems to depend on whether the Government want a fight, and I don't see why they should," she said slowly.

Royd blew out a cloud of smoke. "Baldwin[10] won't want a fight. I don't think he ever wants anything very positively, except that things should be kept going somehow, which I suppose is all a Tory Prime Minister ought to want, though he's lucky if he gets it these days. But what about Churchill?"[11]

"It *is* Churchill I'm thinking of," said Joan. "He has got imagination. I shouldn't think he would want a country with a broken back, which is what downing the miners would mean."

Royd leant forward to knock out the ashes of his pipe against the bars. "You didn't see him as I did in the House of Commons last July, when the Prime Minister announced the coal subsidy in order to avoid having a general strike then. Baldwin was quite dignified about it, but Winston just snarled at the Labour benches. 'You wait,' he said."

"He would. And he would hate the trade union leaders as he hated the Boer commandos,[12] but there is a stray strain in Churchill of what I should call Imaginative Democracy. He'd make a lovely revolutionary leader. He's wasted in a morning coat." She laughed.

"It's odd to find a tenderness for Winston in you. I shouldn't call him a woman's hero."

"Well, he isn't exactly a sheik, I admit, but — oh, well, there is a touch of something daredevil in him ... I mean, he is a bit different — most men are so much alike."

"The unsuspected romantic attachment of a woman Red," laughed Royd. It was good to laugh. It released the emotional tension of his body.

"Not much of a romantic attachment," said Joan. "I will sentence him to execution, if I am at the head of any tribunal that happens to be around during the revolution, with the greatest satisfaction. When are you going to London?"

"To-night."

"Let me come."

"What about work?"

"I've none on at the moment. That was why I was so deep in the dumps when you found me. I've finished off those negotiations at Rochdale. You know we got a five-shilling advance for the girls and the lower-paid men? And, anyway," she continued, as Royd nodded, "if there is going to be a rumpus, ordinary trade union work will be impossible, and your li'l' woman organizer may be a useful thing to have about."

"Joan doing the pathetic as a li'l' woman," he smiled.

"I'm not," and she went very red. Joan always declared that she hated women who used sex appeal in business relations, being magnificently unconscious that she could no more help her sex appealing to men like Royd than she could help breathing.

"But what about that Trappist monastery you were asking the address of?" he said teasingly.

"Come off it, William. Is this to be a private little fight of the Executives, or are the staffs being allowed in on it?"

"If it really comes off, every one will be in up to their necks, but I was rather thinking" — and to the excited girl he seemed to be speaking maddeningly slowly — "I was rather thinking that you could help me if you came along to these preliminary stages. An ordinary secretary would be more bother than she's worth."

"Oh, William, bless you. I'll carry your bag and write your secret letters, or fight a policeman, or any other little job you want doing."

Royd laughed. "Something very humdrum like drafting handbills and circulars is likely to be more useful."

"When are you going?"

"To-night. Can you be ready?"

"Listen to the man! I could get ready to go to Pekin with a couple of hours' notice."

"Good. The train is at twelve-fifteen. I'll meet you at the station."

CHAPTER II

When they arrived in London in the early morning, Royd went off to an hotel in Southampton Row, while Joan took a taxi to Gordon Square.[13] She had a key to a house there belonging to Mary Maud Meadowes. Mary Maud was a wealthy bachelor woman, an intimate of an exclusive Bloomsbury circle[14] who bestowed fame on themselves by writing reviews of each other's books. As each slender work appeared it was greeted as a new Tchehov, a more sensitive Dostoievsky, a respringing of the fountain of Shelley's genius.[15] Most people read the reviews and not the books, and as all they wanted was to be told which was the book of the hour the circle was accepted as the last word in literary genius. The advertisement was none the less effective because the reviewers were far too highbrow to stoop to personal publicity. The tightly shut door on the paragraphist from the daily Press was as subtle a method of creating an impression as if it had been most carefully thought out.

Mary Maud didn't write novels or reviews or paint modernist pictures. She bought. She was amiably willing to pay for her rooms to be redecorated whenever another bright young person was taken up by the circle. She financed publications, one-man shows, eccentric theatrical productions, all with a rather detached enthusiasm. But she had a genius for friendships. Utterly without a sense of class or wealth, she loved to bring people together who could help each other. She was so willing to go to endless trouble herself to help people that her important acquaintances were shamed into helping too. She was fat and rather tall. In a room of fashionable skeletons people gravitated to her, she looked so comfortable and happy. At fifty her handsome face had hardly a line.

Joan and she had met at Leeds, where Mary Maud had gone to attend a try-out production of a more than usually eccentric prodigy, and went in to a Playgoers' Club afterwards to explain what it was about. The Leeds highbrows were suitably impressed and murmured the correct mumbles of "Marvellous," "So modern," "That inner Truth."

Joan had startled the club and attracted Mary Maud by putting a firm foot through all this. Her speech in the discussion was characteristic. The play, she said, was rotten. The author had nothing to say and tied himself in knots trying to say it. He had no first-hand contacts with life. New stage-devices, however startling, could not fill the blank left by an entire absence of original thought.

Mary Maud thought, "This girl is good stuff. She is the only civilized being in this wilderness of factories," and insisted on taking Joan off to supper at her hotel, where the provincial girl's porcupine quills were smoothed in Mary Maud's generous atmosphere. The friendship started that night had become very precious to both of them. The older woman, who was always reaching out for contacts with hard life, felt the need of Joan's uncompromising realism. Even Joan hardly realized how immense was the compliment when Mary Maud gave her the key to the house in Gordon Square. Miss Meadowes, in a world of careless callers, had fought with determination to preserve the privacy of her lair. Even the very latest in eccentric novelists had to telephone before he could get past Mary Maud's French dragon Suzanne. But Joan she encouraged to come in at any hour, because she fitted in. The girl would have been surprised to know how deeply Mary Maud loved her.

Joan let herself into the hall and cautiously tiptoed upstairs. Very quietly she opened the door of the balconied room on the first floor. The big standard lamp was still alight, and Mary Maud, huddled in a green and gold velvet wrapper, lay on the divan, a cigarette-holder still in her fingers, though the cigarette had burnt to ash.

She started up in surprise. "Who is it? What's the matter?"

"It's only Joan, dear. I'm awfully sorry I startled you. I've come up on the midnight. I thought I'd just dump myself on a couch until some one woke up."

"My dear, I'm glad you've come. What on earth is the time? I ..."

"Just past six."

"Heavens! Why didn't I go to bed? I was so tired that I just dropped in my tracks. Had a party at Michael's and didn't get away till nearly four."

"You won't help your schoolgirl complexion at that rate."

"My massage bill, my dear — really, it's awful. But look here, what about you? No, I'm quite wide awake," as Joan made a gesture of protest. "Let's have some light and be cosy. The dawn is too grim to look at us yet."

Mary Maud went hastily round snapping on lights and the electric fire until the room glowed like a jewel box.

"Oh, Mary Maud, how lovely. You have had it all redone since I was here."

"It *is* rather nice. It's by a woman decorator. You must meet her. I got so tired of Gornuikh's cubes and angles — bleak, sharp things to live with. This is Helen Dacre's. She loves comfort as I do. Don't these velvet purples and greens and reds seem cosy?"

"It is lovely. I hated the Gornuikh."

"Oh, I've left the bathroom as he did it. Sharp corners seem fitting there.

Which reminds me, you are not to stand talking another minute. You go and get a bath and I'll waken Suzanne."

"Oh, poor Suzanne!"

"Not at all. She likes getting up early, but usually I can't bear her pottering about. I'll lend you a dressing-gown, and we'll have a comfy breakfast by the fire."

Mary Maud put her arm round Joan and went to turn on the geyser. "Enough bath salts to dye you like a rainbow," she laughed, as she lit the gas.

"What dinky jars! But what on earth do you want this lot for?"

"It's Princess Karaylov, Gornuikh's mistress — at least, she was a week ago. I don't know if they've changed. She is trying to make a fortune selling coloured scented soda at a fabulous price. Each colour is supposed to fit in with a different mood."

"My mood in a hot bath is one of gurgling content," laughed Joan, "so which do I choose?"

"Take my advice and leave them looking pretty. Here's some plain pine stuff that comes from the Black Forest. Not much to look at, but makes you feel real good. There, that's hot enough. I'll hang a wrap outside the door."

When Joan, all pink and pine-scented, wrapped in a warm crimson dressing-gown whose soft lightness seemed to kiss her body, returned to the sitting-room she found that Suzanne had laid breakfast on a low table near the cheery electric fire. There was a lovely smell of bacon and toast and coffee.

Joan slipped into a low chair, and revelled in the luxury of it all.

"Oh, Mary Maud, it's so easy to be philosophical about the world and its troubles if you have a bolt-hole like this."

"I know, my dear. It's easy to wallow, but it's harder to live — well, life as *you* understand it, anyway. Two lumps? None! You should, you know, you are too thin. Now, what's it all about? *Had* you to rush down on a midnight train, or were you just breaking out?"

"I've come up because there's going to be a general strike." Joan enjoyed throwing the bombshell into the centre of all this comfort.

"A what?"

"A general strike — everybody — no trains, no buses, no bread probably."

"But there can't be. I mean, surely it's all a newspaper scare? I thought those millions we gave to the coal-owners had settled all that."[16]

"Well, it hasn't. The money is spent. Trade is no better for it. The owners say they must have a reduction in costs, and the colliers aren't having any."

"But that won't stop the buses — I mean, the summer is coming on, and it will take a long time for a coal strike to have much effect, won't it?"

"Precisely," said Joan. "It's just because the miners can't starve until the comfortable people can be made to feel it that the other workers are coming out too."

"In England — in this stodgy place! Dear heart, I'm beginning to wish it were true, but I don't see it happening."

"Well, between ourselves, neither do I, but William Royd seems positive. I came down with him. I say, this honey is good."

"It ought to be. It takes a lot of trouble to get it. But who is this Mr Royd? Is his word law?"

"William Royd? Oh, he is my boss, you know. The organizing secretary of my union."

"A Bolshevik?"[17]

"Good Lord, no. He has twin daughters."

"Don't Bolsheviks have twin daughters?"

"I don't know, but William Royd isn't one. He says he's the typical conservative English working man. And he always says that it's his sort that makes revolutions. When people like him get fed up, things have got to move."

Mary Maud looked interested. "There's something in that, I should think. But when is this revolution of yours coming off, if ever it does?"

"May Day — first of May."

Mary Maud sat up. "But it can't, it simply can't happen then. You must put it off or something."

"Ajax defying the earthquake for a change![18] But what's wrong?"

"My dear, that is the week of all weeks. We are all working on Helen Dacre's production of *Resurrection*.[19] It is going to be marvellous. It's her great masterpiece. If there's going to be no buses, no trams or taxis, the thing will be ruined."

"Can't you postpone it? The strike may never come off, but really the threat is serious enough. I would put it off somehow if you can."

"My dear child, do you know what it is like to get a theatre these days? We've been negotiating for the Princess' for months, and can only get it for three weeks as it is. Oh, why must you have this beastly strike just now?" she wailed.

Joan put down her cup and looked her friend straight in the eyes. "Mary Maud, you ought to be ashamed of yourself. Damn your Resurrection. These miners will be starved back into their holes unless something is done to help them now. It really isn't like you to talk like a Bloomsbury highbrow."

Mary Maud rubbed her hands through her curly, unshingled hair and was silent for a moment. Then she looked up at Joan with that sweet smile of hers that made Joan feel how gracious a person she was. Characteristically she didn't gush.

"Forgive me, Joan. It does sound beastly, I know. But we are beasts in

Bloomsbury. We are absorbed in our little arty schemes and get all hot and bothered if we hear one growl from the world outside that is keeping us in comfort. We know less about Monmouth than we do about Mars. But I'll be all in with you ... if it comes off you must let me help. Tell me what to do. I've got a bit of conscience left" — shyly — "I get half my money from coal, did you know?"

"You! Oh, Mary Maud, and I've been denouncing coal-owners as too bad to burn!"

"We're a mixed lot, like most others, I suppose. But I've never been able to find who is the villain of the piece. The managers blame the shareholders for being greedy, and we blame them for not managing better. But where does the trouble lie? My dividends have been extra good this year."

"Where are your mines?"

"South Yorkshire, I believe."

"Yes, they're all right. New seams and new plant. They'd be glad not to have to lock the men out, but, of course, they'll have to stand in with the rest."

"Couldn't I do anything? I'm a pretty big shareholder."

"No. Individuals are helpless at a time like this. It's mass that counts — both sides."

"But, Joan, the individuals make up the mass. There are brutes among the coal-owners, as, for that matter, I suppose there are among the miners, but I don't believe they want to starve the men. You've met the Kindersleys and the Vansittarts here — are they baby-starvers?"

"You can't do anything as individuals, anyway," persisted Joan. "You might get a move on if you organized, but I don't know where you could begin. The most difficult thing to find in modern industry is the place where the power is. Every one blames every one else. The man you are talking to vows that he is all right if it wasn't for somebody else ... whom no one seems able to meet.

The telephone bell rang. Mary Maud answered it.

"For you, Joan. Mr Royd."

Joan clutched the instrument. "Yes, yes, all right. I'll be there ... " Those maddening monosyllables of a telephone conversation to the other person in the room.

"Mr Royd thinks there might be a possibility of getting me into the Memorial Hall Conference.[20] He's been 'phoning the secretary. I'm to meet him there at ten o'clock."

"And what is the Memorial Hall Conference?"

"That is *the* centre of attraction. All the Executives of all the trade unions affiliated to Congress, the General Council of the Trades Union Congress, the

Labour Party Executive, and any other bigwigs happening around are to meet and decide what's to be done to help the miners. Oh, I simply shall die if I don't get in to it." Joan was a girl again after her seriousness.

"Anyway, it's not much after seven now. You are going to lie down, Miss Quicksilver, and get two hours of a nap. I'll send you along to your conference in the car."

Tucked up on the big couch, Joan was asleep almost immediately. Mary Maud looked down on her thin, almost childish face. An odd mixture of child and woman, a girl yet with big possibilities of leadership. The older woman found herself breathing a prayer that in the clash of hatreds into which the girl was so light-heartedly throwing herself, some power would shield that thin, sensitive body from the worst of the storm.

Not the loss of dividends nor the threat to her own comfort seemed so important to Miss Meadowes at that moment as somehow dragging Joan unscathed through it all.

CHAPTER III

The scene at the Memorial Hall reminded Joan of a beehive. Men were pouring in, while others were pushing themselves out. Communists, single-taxers, credit-reformers, were trying to push their papers on the delegates. Unemployed sandwich-men paraded in front of the hall. Press photographers tried to lure the big-wigs to pose. The inevitable mild middle-class lady gave out leaflets on birth-control. A little apart from the hubbub a typical group of London workers looked on with their usual air of cheerful detachment. A taxi-man, wearing his union button, surveyed the scene with immense benevolence. "Good old Ben," he called to a well-known transport leader[21] pushing his way up the steps.

As Joan walked into the stone and granite entrance-hall, she could not help feeling it a grim joke that this chilly temple of Nonconformist respectability[22] should be chosen as the place in which a great social upheaval might be launched.

William Royd met her with a long face. "Sorry, there isn't a dog's chance of your getting into the Conference. I've seen Weston, but they have had to bar out every one who isn't a delegate."

"But I'm only a little one, can't you tell him?" pleaded Joan.

"Absolutely no use, but I'll take you into the Press waiting-room. You will be at hand if I need you, and you will hear anything there as soon as we know it. I'll give you a faithful report at lunch. Will that do?"

Joan squeezed his arm. "I'm being an awful nuisance. Would you rather I just went back to Gordon Square and waited for you there?"

"No, I'd like you to stay. I've promised Weston to lend you to him for the duration if the strike comes off, and you might be wanted right away."

"Oh, William, have you really? I'll work my head off. Now park me somewhere and forget all about me till you come to collect the parcel."

Royd smiled and took her along to a side room where a group of Pressmen were chatting to various officials and Labour big-wigs.

"Let me see, who do I know who can look after you?"

"Now, please, don't you worry. Just leave me to float around till I find my bearings. I don't want to be attached to an unwilling male who'll feel he has got to be polite in jerks. I'll be all right."

The ringing of the chairman's bell in the adjoining hall reminded Royd of his duty.

"I must get back. Will see you at lunch, and if you get bored here I'll meet you in the Lyons[23] round the corner."

When Royd had left her, Joan perched herself on a wide, low window-sill and looked round with interest. She was glad she hadn't to make conversation with some busy, preoccupied Pressman. It was more fun to watch the crowd. She hadn't seen the London Press at work before — their elaborate air of detachment, and the carefully casual way in which anyone who appeared to have one item of news about him was surrounded and cut off from all means of escape but an actual bolt.

"Will it bore you if I introduce myself? Mr Royd asked me to look after you." Joan turned hastily to see a tall, fair man at her side. "My name is Dacre, Anthony Dacre," he said apologetically. "William Royd is a friend of mine."

"But how nice of you! Dacre — are you the man who writes short stories? I've read heaps of them."

"That is nice of *you*. You are Joan Craig. I have seen you before."

"Oh, but I can't have forgotten!"

"We didn't meet. It was soon after the War. You came up to London to speak to a big women's conference about women and trade unions. Don't you remember? In the Essex Hall. I was awfully impressed by your speech."

"Now that is unblushing flattery."

"No, really. It wasn't what you said, it was your awful familiarity with initials. You talked about the A.S.L.E.F. and the A.U.B.T.W. and the A.S.E.[24] and — oh, scores I can't remember. And you seemed to know what all of them meant."

Joan laughed. "It's awful, I know. Sort of besetting sin of the Labour Movement. We think in initials. Now I've collected celebrity Number One, tell me who your fellow-lions are. I've never seen so many interesting people."

"Celebrity Number One bows," said Dacre solemnly.

"Let me see, who's here?"

While he was looking round the room Joan was able to take stock of him. It was an interesting face — square and brown and strong. The hair above it was very thick and stood up like a brush. "Looks as though his face had been carved out of wood by one of these modern Germans," thought Joan. "Not smooth anywhere, and I like strong, thick hair like that, but how awfully tired his eyes look!"

"Hello, there's Parma de Pratz. You ought to put her on your list of 'finds'."

"What a name! Who is she? That fashionably dressed beauty? What is she doing here?"

"She's London's most celebrated sob-sister," whispered Dacre hurriedly, as Miss de Pratz moved forward to greet him.

She was dressed in a perfectly fitting suit of dark purple cloth, with a tiny toque of her namesake violets and a cubist scarf that Joan envied intensely.

"Off your usual beat, surely," said Dacre. "Let me introduce Miss Craig to you."

Miss de Pratz gave Joan the fleeting attention that she might have bestowed on a grain of dust on her sleeve, and turned to Dacre.

"This is going to be the scoop of the century. I couldn't possibly miss it. I'm covering it for the American Press. There will be a great story in it."

Parma drifted on casually.

"Really smart woman, that," commented Dacre.

"She will have a heartrending story of how Jimmie Thomas[25] thought of his dear mother as he declared the strike on or off, and though the poor man may never have seen her he won't be able to deny it."

"She's a beast and a snob," choked Joan.

Dacre looked down at her in surprise. "Snob — not Parma — oh, she didn't just glow at you, I know, but meet Parma when you're news, when you are the centre of the heart throbs, she'll make you *love* her."

"I'll hate her for evermore," said Joan, managing to smile, "She made me feel as though I had 'provincial' written all over me. Never mind, tell me about the others."

"Well, let me see, you ought to know Bennett, a good chap, he's your own *Daily Herald*[26] man."

"I don't know the *Herald* crowd at all. He'll be well in the front row in a show like this?"

"He ought to be. His paper is too poor to have a news service like the others. Their only hope is in exclusive Labour Scoops. Some of the Labour men are sports and reserve their titbits for him, but for most, well — I suppose you can't blame them if they are tempted by the big circulations for anything they want to put across. And for official news — well, that has to be given out to all the papers equally."

"M-m," said Joan. "Who's the large squashy man?"

Dacre shuddered comically. "God, he *is* a swine. He's the star man of the *Daily Wire*. He'll get news from the keyhole if he can't get it anyway else. He's got an uncanny nose for the coming headline. Never makes the mistake Parma does. Now if you become news over something you do in this strike you'll be a bit chilly if Parma de Pratz comes round for a story."

"Chilly! My manner will be guaranteed to make ice in five minutes from pure drinking-water straight from your own kitchen tap, as the advertisements say."

"Exactly. Now if Elphinstone had seen you brought in by Royd he'd have figured it out that the friend of the organizing secretary of the Industrial Labour

Union was a potential source of news and he'd have been all over you."

"I'm glad you arrived first," said Joan, with emphasis.

By the end of the first hour Joan felt completely at ease with Anthony Dacre and he with her. They might have been pals for life. From his manner of greeting various people who obviously knew and liked him, and addressed him as "Tony," Joan guessed that Dacre was not an effusive person. His social manner was rather stilted. But to her he was a delightful companion. Joan's appearance of loneliness amid the crowd, her thin, elfin face in its cloud of black hair, had gone straight through Anthony Dacre's barriers. Intending to be kind to Royd's 'lonely little friend' he found himself talking to a woman whose inside knowledge of the Labour Movement, and whose grasp of industrial conditions and the reasons behind the strike, far surpassed that of the journalists among whom he lived. This girl was alive, intelligent, and completely unself-conscious. Dacre had not met her kind before.

It was after one o'clock when Royd came to seek Joan. He looked very worried. "I'm glad you found each other," he said.

The journalists crowded round him, but he waved them away. "Only official news to-day, boys" — and got Joan and Dacre into a corner.

"The position is very serious," he said hurriedly. "The General Council's Negotiating Committee are with the Prime Minister and are expected back early this afternoon with a final answer. If he turns down our offer, there will be nothing for it but an ultimatum. I have got to go to lunch with the E.C.[27] to talk things over. If you two get some sort of a meal, there ought to be news by four o'clock … That's all right for you, Dacre?"

"Of course," said Anthony warmly.

"Oh, but —" stammered Joan.

But Royd, with a smile, had gone, pushing his huge bulk through the importunate Pressmen.

"This is really too bad on you, Mr Dacre. You must have people you want to see, and I've been dumped on to you."

"Is this a polite intimation that you would prefer to be alone?"

"Heavens, no, but I don't want to be a nuisance."

"Then stop being polite. If you'll put up with me I'll be all sheer gratitude. You don't know what a godsend you are. Making odd scraps of conversation as people drift by in a crowd worries me intensely. There are so few people to whom one can really talk. Now about lunch — no need to pack into the local Lyons, thank heaven! If we have till four, that gives us time to get right away. Where shall we go?"

"Is it polite to say 'anywhere' — or may I really choose?"

"Do, please. I hate making decisions. If you say 'anywhere' I shall weep."

"Then let's go to the Español Restaurant in Soho and have omelettes and sherry."

Dacre was surprised at her excellent choice. He had expected some mauve and grey tea room.

"A1. I've never been there, but I believe it's the goods. How do *you* know of it?"

"I do come to London once in a way, you know," said Joan very demurely. "The provincials are known to travel occasionally."

Dacre laughed. "That's right. Sit on my head if I get uppish. Londoners are apt to forget that it is the hub of the wheel that moves slowest. Oh, Lord, here comes Parma. Let's make a bolt before she can seize me."

At the Español Restaurant Joan was evidently much at home. Old Roderigo knew her, and Dacre very thankfully left to her the ordering of the lunch. He was always grateful to be relieved of the small decisions of life, and Joan was the first young woman he had met who could quietly take command without making any fuss one way or the other. The type of female who, while quite obviously competent to command an army corps, found it necessary to be coy, or else to deliver him a lecture on women's rights while she insisted on paying her share of the bill, tired Dacre. He had to meet so many women like that.

Joan frankly gloated over the quaint menu. "*Tortillas* — why didn't we take that word instead of the French *omelette*? Haven't you really ever had a Spanish *tortilla* before?"

"I'm duly apologetic, but Londoners haven't time to experiment with London. I usually drop into the nearest Slater's if I have to have a meal out. I prefer bread and cheese at home anyway."

Joan wondered if he were hard up. His clothes were well worn, but obviously from a good tailor. His shirt was *crêpe-de-Chine*[28] and looked new. No, he couldn't be poor and buy shirts like that.

It was a merry lunch. Joan had an impish quality of making a picnic out of any meal. Her daily work organizing factory girls in grim industrial towns was so gruelling that she lived to the brim the moments of escape to London. Besides, she had never met a man who fitted in so perfectly as Tony Dacre. By unspoken agreement they let the strike alone and talked London, theatres, politics, finding themselves thoroughly in tune.

When the waiter had set down their coffee-tray, Dacre lit the cigarettes.

"Tell me something about yourself. We've talked about everything else."

"There is nothing to tell — the most ordinary, uneventful life. I was born in a slum and nearly in a factory, for Mother worked at her looms till the last minute. I went to an elementary school, worked for three months as a dressmaker's apprentice (my goodness, that was awful), then in a shop — not so bad. Got sacked for trying to get the girls to join a union. Then I went into a munition factory. Led a strike, got arrested, and they would have sent me to prison except that the girls threatened not to work while I was inside and the magistrate discovered that I was only eighteen. That settled that. Royd came down to negotiate a settlement, and offered me a job as trade union organizer, and I've been with the Industrial Union of Labour ever since."

"And you call that an uneventful life? It seems like a circus of thrills to me. Mine seems pretty slow compared to it."

"Tell me and let me judge. That's only fair." Joan helped herself to some more coffee. Dacre. Where had she heard the name recently? Mary Maud that morning had talked of a Helen Dacre. She looked up with sudden interest.

"Is Helen Dacre, the theatrical producer, any relation to you?"

"You know Helen?" said Tony in surprise. She is my wife," and he turned to catch the waiter's eye. "You know Helen?" he repeated, as he settled the bill.

"No, not personally. Mary Maud Meadowes is my friend. I always stay with her when I am in London. She was telling me about *Resurrection*. She was worried out the effect of the strike on the production."

"M-m, yes. I hadn't thought of that."

"Mrs Dacre must be worried."

"I don't think it would ever occur to her that anything could stop what she had decided to do. And the whole crisis is so sudden to us Londoners, you must remember. You've seen the storm brewing up there, but we are so used to scare headlines that they don't make much impression. And so you know Mary Maud? Great person, isn't she?"

"Is your wife like her? They are fast friends, aren't they?"

"Helen like Mary Maud? You couldn't find a greater contrast anywhere. But you must meet my wife, Joan. I'm sure you'll like each other."

Joan was silent as the taxi ploughed its way through the Strand back to the Memorial Hall, and Tony respected that as a sudden return to the grim realities they would meet there, after the merry lunch amid the gay tiles of Spain.

CHAPTER IV

When they got back to the conference they found that the delegates had overflowed on to the steps, smoking and laughing in groups, rather enjoying the curious glances of the spectators who kept forming in a half-circle a respectful distance away and being continually shuffled about by the police. Royd was nowhere to be seen.

From a member of her Executive Joan found that the Negotiating Committee had been back to report about three o'clock. They had nothing much to say except that the Government were very stiff, but that they were hopeful that progress was being made. Three expert advisers, of whom Royd was one, had been added to the Committee, and he was now at 10 Downing Street. They were not expected back for some time yet, and some busy officials within a telephone call had left for an hour or two at their offices. From inside the hall came strains of *Swanee River, Annie Laurie*, and *The Red Flag*.[29] Every delegate seemed to be bubbling with excitement. Executive members of the unions, who had been called from the bench and the loom and the mine, felt themselves in the midst of great events. It was a wonderful break in the deadly monotony of the lives of these men. They had rebelled in their souls so long, and here was a chance to hit back openly and with a grand gesture.

Dacre, who had left Joan to get what information he could from his Press colleagues, returned to her side.

"There will be nothing doing here for hours, that is evident," he said. "Pity we missed Royd at three, but he couldn't have told us anything more. The general Press opinion is that the Government will fight and that the strike will be called to-night. If that is so, I think I'd like to go home and warn my wife."

"Please don't let me keep you. I feel I've taken up such a lot of your time already."

"Now don't say that, and don't let's start being polite. You and I are going to be pals — at least I am if you'll let me. We can cut through formalities when there's a war on. I was going to suggest you came with me. I'd like you to meet Helen and I'd like you to talk to her about this business. You know more than I do, and I'd like her to understand."

"*You and I are going to be pals.*" A great wave of soothing seemed to wash over

Joan. What did it matter if Tony had a hundred wives? — he and she were going to be pals. She wasn't to lose this interesting new friendship when Royd came to take her back from the conference.

"I'd just love to," she said, but Dacre had already hailed a taxi, and was giving the address to the driver.

"Russell Square is only a cockstride. Do you live in taxis?" laughed Joan, to whom an occasional cab was a wild extravagance.

"I'm sorry. Yes, always. Once I have made up my mind to go anywhere I hate to be bothered. I want to get there as quickly as possible."

The ground-floor of the house just off Russell Square at which the taxi stopped was used for offices. The Dacres had the first floor and upper part. Tony ushered his new friend into the front room and went off to find Helen. After the glowing comfort of Mary Maud's flat Joan was surprised at the starkness of Helen's own. The room was a study in silver and red. The walls and ceiling were covered in dull silver. The woodwork was quite straight, no mouldings, no curves anywhere, and painted a bright red. The chairs were of ebony and upholstered in silver-grey, and the table had a top of hammered silver. Dulled white glass with geometrical black and red lines drawn on it made curious lampshades. Against this background a vivid primitive[30] with a gold sky shone like a jewel in a case.

"It is only that picture over the fireplace that prevents the room from looking like a super-celestial bar," thought Joan, but she had to admit to herself that the chair in which she sat was very comfortable and that the electric fire looked delightful in its basket of polished steel. The books which were on shelves carefully fitted into an alcove by the fire all seemed to be about the theatre or interior decoration.

"It doesn't seem much like *him*," muttered Joan.

Dacre returned at this moment. "My wife will be down in a minute. She's been at the theatre all the morning and is having a bath. How do you like this room?"

"It's lovely and unusual, but I don't think I should like to live in it," confessed Joan. "Your wife's treatment of Mary Maud's flat was so much more cosy."

"Well, strictly speaking, we don't live in it. This is Helen's showroom to tempt her millionaires. It's changed quite often. The whole place is rather the same. You must see my wife's bedroom. It would give me a nightmare. But Helen's very good. She leaves my den and bedroom alone, and I don't care what she does with the rest. In fact, it's interesting and it pays her very well."

"So they don't share a room," thought Joan, to whom marriage, a vaguely conceived idea at best, meant a Victorian bedroom with a suite of furniture and a large brass bedstead. The Dacre *ménage*[31] seemed queer, but Joan found herself intensely conscious of Anthony. His head was poised so beautifully on his square shoulders. She found herself noticing the back of his ear, and making up her mind to dislike Helen.

But when Mrs Dacre came in a few minutes later she found it difficult to dislike some one who was so business-like and so neutral. Helen was as tall as Tony. Her hair was a dark brown and shingled to look like a silken cap. Her high cheek-bones and complexion of dull fawn gave her a queer foreign look. Her clothes were perfect. Joan summed up in a flash the expensiveness of the simple jumper suit in two shades of fawn, with a cubist design woven as a strip down the front, a red swastika at the waist emphasizing the note of a wonderful ruby ring on her long brown capable hand.

"My husband tells me that you have arrived from Leeds to call everybody out on strike just at the moment that my play is to be produced," said Mrs Dacre, offering her hand with a smile.

"I wish it rested with me to save you the inconvenience," replied Joan politely. "Miss Meadowes has already threatened to cut my head off if the thing happens."

"Tony was telling me you know my beloved Mary Maud. Well, for her sake, you shall be forgiven and have some tea in token of truce. And I really want you to tell me all about it."

A maid in a red dress without cap and apron served tea in red cups, seemingly made of lacquer, and a cubist silver tea-set.

Joan found that telling Helen Dacre "all about it" was like facing a cross-examination in the Courts. She had never met anyone with such deadly concentration. She felt that every secret thought was at the mercy of this quietly determined brown woman. How could Tony stand the strain of living with her? After half an hour's questioning Joan felt exhausted, and Helen leaned back apparently satisfied.

"*Resurrection* can't go on, that's clear. No one will want to go to a theatre next week, and if the buses stop the thing's impossible. Anyway, we couldn't get the right atmosphere for our advertising."

"You will have the theatre on your hands. You are paying five hundred pounds a week, aren't you?" asked Tony, who had sat smoking in an armchair while Joan pitted her wits against his inexorable wife.

"All the more reason for not throwing another couple of thousand away on expenses," said Helen. "We must do something dramatic with it. Something that will give us a great advertisement and make Arkwright Farmiloe ashamed not to give us an option on the following month. I know that he hasn't actually let the theatre for that time, but he hopes to get *Lady, Love Me!*"

"Question is, what can you use a theatre for during a general strike?"

"Bright boy, that is the problem I am facing. Can't you be more helpful? Let me see," looking through Joan thoughtfully, "the Government will be asking for volunteers to run the buses and taxis, won't they?"

"Of course they will," replied Joan hotly. "They've got all that ready. It will be the War atmosphere back again. Young men in plus-fours looking important, and silly society girls patting their heads and sitting up all night to give them cocoa."

"Excellent. The War atmosphere.[32] The very thing."

Even the cold Helen flushed with excitement. "Thanks very much for the advance information. We will run a late concert each night for the volunteers, or for those who are waiting to go on night duty. People will love to help, and we will run all the bars as a free canteen. I will make Hooke Lattimore pay for that. He has made enough money out of coal-mines, goodness knows."

Joan was wild with indignation. "Do you actually mean you are going to help the blacklegs?"

"And what are blacklegs, pray?" inquired Helen, lifting her left eyebrow.

"These beasts who are going to do our men's jobs, when they are well off themselves. Oh, you couldn't! Mr Dacre, tell her she can't."

This appeal to her husband from a girl she had only just met made Helen lift both her eyebrows. Dacre said nothing. He knocked out his pipe on an elaborate steel arrangement by the fireplace.

Joan turned again to Helen. "You must see what you are doing. These miners are starving. They can't live on their wages now, never mind taking a heavy reduction. If the other men come out to help them they must win quickly or they can't hold out. If you want to feed people, feed the pickets. God knows they'll need it. The plus-four men will have plenty, anyway."

Mrs Dacre remained calm. "Of course I should like to help the strikers. I don't want anyone to starve, least of all myself and my husband. But I am dependent for my orders on people with money, and if I fed the strikers at my theatre — even if Farmiloe allowed it, which he certainly wouldn't — that would be the end of all my work. And I happen to think that my art is important. But I am sorry to have worried you with my concerns. I can see your point of view, of course. If there is any special case of hardship you find, you must let me know and I will send money and food. I think that is better than helping these big funds. One never knows where the money goes. Will you be in to dinner, Tony? Can you stay, Miss Craig?"

Joan could not have trusted herself to speak at that moment. The cold detachment of this well-to-do, cultivated woman cut like a lash across her face. This was Tony's wife. This was the woman who had the right to love him. Joan wanted to creep into a hole and just cry. She felt queerly homeless and alone.

"No, sorry we can't," Tony was saying in a completely matter-of-fact voice.

"I want to be back at the Conference when the news comes through. Miss Craig must get back too. She may be wanted."

"Oh, of course," said his wife indifferently. It was obvious that her mind was fixed on her new plans and that she wanted to get busy. But she held out her hand to Joan with a smile that, furious though the girl was, made her understand something of the secret of Helen Dacre's charm. The set fawn face came to life for a moment.

"Good-bye. I hope your miners will win — and that they won't be too long about it. Don't have a revolution if you can help it."

In the taxi back to the hall Joan, still under the influence of that strange smile, turned impulsively to Anthony.

"She can't realize what she's going to do. Don't let her help the blacklegs. You simply must stop her."

"How can I? We're not in the Stone Age, and I'm not a cave-man. My wife earns her own income and lives her own life. I have no more influence over her than the next one. Once her mind is made up no one can shake her, though, to do her justice, she doesn't use my name for her own affairs. Professionally she uses her maiden name, Helen Hanray."

"Well, it isn't *my* ideal of married life," and Joan stuck out her determined little chin.

"It isn't my *ideal*," Dacre replied quietly. "But I wanted Helen and had to accept her terms. You have preached equality and organized for it. Why should you grumble at the results when they don't turn out quite as you like?"

Joan did not reply, and for the rest of the journey they were both silent, each busy with their own thoughts.

CHAPTER V

The Negotiating Committee had not returned from Downing Street when Dacre and Joan reached the Hall. Joan could stand exclusion from the centre of interest no longer. The temperature was rising. When the Committee returned with the Premier's answer it might be the most dramatic moment that would ever happen in her lifetime. She would not be kept out.

"I am going to get into that hall somehow," she said to Tony.

"Couldn't I come too?"

"Rather. Let me think. It may be hours before they come, and if we find a hiding-place we shall have to stick it. Let's go and buy some tuck and then we can dig ourselves in."

"Great mind," said Tony. "Let me go."

"No, you'll buy up the shop and we shall need a sack to carry it. I'll be housewife."

They bought oranges, nuts, and dates in little packets, and some chocolate from a Fleet Street fruit-stall, and then crept in like conspirators. The watch on the hall doors was as strict as ever, but Joan found a narrow, twisting staircase in the back regions which led to a sort of emergency exit from a narrow balcony. Tony put a cautious head inside.

"There's no one on the balcony," he whispered. "If we creep in and lie doggo we should be all right. Damn ... there's some one coming."

"'s only me."

"Blain! What the hell ...?"

"Don't spurn the little orphint boy. He wants a peep too."

Joan looked with interest at the young man. He had thick black hair and bright black eyes. But one-half of his face was slightly paralysed, the result of a terrible crash when he was an Ace of the R.A.F. during the War. It remained set, while the other half was lively and expressive.

"'I'll be good. But I guessed you were up to something. I've been trying to find a way into this damned hole, but those dragons of stewards are allover the shop. So I just followed your trail. Don't hate me," he grinned, looking impishly at Joan.

Joan could just have hugged him. There was something so gay and care-free about him, while his poor pathetic paralysed face touched her emotions, which were already keyed up in the hectic atmosphere.

"We'll share our last nut with you, and our three skeletons shall be found together," she whispered.

"Excellent. I'm all for it," Blain whispered back.

"We must keep pretty quiet or there'll be the devil of a row," warned Dacre.

Leaving the two men sheltering behind a back pew, Joan wormed her way cautiously to the front. The men soon followed her. The hall was by this time suffocatingly hot and they looked down through a haze of tobacco smoke. It was more a rank-and-file conference than many Labour gatherings, because it was composed of the Executives of the trade unions, most of which had a rule that membership of the governing body was confined to men actually working at their trade. The middle class was completely absent. Joan felt her heart beat in sympathy with these men. They were her own. She knew their lives. They had so much to lose. The strike-call, if given, would mean that some of them would lose jobs that they had held for a lifetime, others in railways or municipal jobs would jeopardize pensions on which the comfort of their old age depended, the men in power-stations would be rendered liable to heavy damages, perhaps prison. All would risk the livelihood of their wives and children. It was easy for her and the young bloods of the Socialist Party[33] to hope for a strike, but these men down here would have to face the music. There were very few women present. They were quiet and rather prim.

At the moment, with the cheerful refusal to cross rivers till they got to them which had carried their class through the horrors of the trenches, these grown-up men were as gay as schoolboys. The chairman of the gathering being at Downing Street, the chair was being occupied by a large transport worker who had evidently had considerable practice in chairing at 'smokers'. He called out men from the audience to "oblige". Some of these impromptu turns were really excellent, but good or bad they were rewarded with hearty applause, and the unanimous singing of the chorus:

> Oh, my, what a rotten song,
> What a rotten singer too![34]

It was nearly midnight before the Committee returned from Downing Street. Joan's little party was thankful for her oranges and nuts. The whisper went round, "They're here," and delegates poured back into the hall from the corridors and the street.

The Committee filed on to the platform behind the chairman, a thin, bald man with a scholarly expression and gold eyeglasses. Joan noticed the burly figure of Herbert Smith, the miners' leader,[35] and the decorative, curly grey head of the handsome leader of the Labour Party.[36]

In a voice none the less impressive for being completely unemotional, the chairman quietly reported that all their efforts to find a basis of peace which would prevent the driving of the miners to lower depths of poverty had failed. When the railwaymen's leader[37] rose there was a murmur of expectancy. His moderate views were well known. If he agreed to the strike-call, then indeed there was nothing else for it. Into an atmosphere so still that every word sank like a pebble, the man who once had driven trains and now guided a great trade union said solemnly:

"In all my experience — and I have conducted many negotiations — I never begged and pleaded like I begged and pleaded all day to-day ... But we failed."

The speaker paused dramatically, the audience held its breath.

"We have striven for peace. We have begged for peace, because we want peace. The nation wants peace."

A chorus of murmured agreement interrupted him. This leader was also a great orator, but he was himself too moved to think of oratorical flourishes at that moment. He looked round the hall.

"Those who want war must take the responsibility."

That sentence shattered the self-control of the audience. This meant war. Cheer after cheer was given. "If they want it they shall have it," was yelled from every part of the hall.

The chairman duly called the gathering to order. Speaking as unemotionally as the director of a company meeting, he reminded the delegates that there was much work to be done.

Proposals for co-ordinated action ("God, what a name for a strike," murmured the irrepressible Blain) would be laid before the unions. The Conference would disperse now and reassemble next morning.

"Wouldn't have missed it for worlds. We are in for it now. It's worth having come through that war for. I've often wondered lately why I did. We'll show the beggars ... fighting their war, and then our men getting treated like dogs!" The young ex-Air Officer was nearly delirious with excitement. He gripped Joan's arm. "They must let me help. I know I'm a crock, but I can drive anything — land, sea, or air. I don't need sleep or eats for days when I'm on the job. I don't know one blessed soul among the leaders, and they may suspect me. You'll answer for me, you'll get me a job, won't you?"

Joan might have replied that her sole knowledge of his trustworthiness consisted in being jammed tight against him for four hours in the dust of an unused balcony, but there are times when friendship ripens rapidly. At that supreme moment she would have gone to the stake with or for Blain and Dacre with equal certitude.

"Of course we'll use you." Joan felt herself the representative of the whole trade union movement before these two men. "The first thing now is to get hold of Royd. We mustn't miss him. Let's get down quick."

As they raced to the narrow staircase up which they had crept four hours before, their feet seemed to have grown wings. Blain hobbled down painfully. "You go on. I'll collect some of the lads and wait for you outside. We'll have a spot of supper together and see what we can do."

Royd was still in committee with the men who were considering plans. To Joan's urgent note he sent a scribbled reply. "I can't meet you now. Sorry. Go back to Miss Meadowes' and get some sleep. I'll 'phone you in the morning. Of course we'll use your friends. We shall want every kind of help."

This was the magic talisman for Joan into the favour of the group of young men whom Blain had got round him. The trade union leaders were remote as gods. Here was an approachable liaison officer. Joan found herself a queen.

"Now for Lyons' Corner House. We'll pack into taxis and talk there."

Joan found herself jammed with six hilarious young men, two Pressmen, and Anthony Dacre, into a Ford that some one produced from somewhere. At the Strand Corner House she was surprised to find that Parma de Pratz was included in the party. She remembered Tony's words: "If you are news she'll make you like her." This flushed and excited girl certainly was a different Parma from the exclusive haughty lady of the morning. Joan learnt, to her amazement, that she was a member of the Hampstead Labour Party.[38]

But it was Parma, not the men, who secured from an obsequious manager a comparatively quiet table in the crowded restaurant. It was Parma who ordered supper without bothering people who didn't care what they ate which of a hundred and fifty items on a menu they preferred. Joan respected efficiency and began to forgive the fancied slight of the morning.

The paper boys were already crying "Special" on the streets. The news had got round the tables and there was general excitement. A group of noisy young men in leather overcoats, wearing some kind of badge, took the next table to them. They had a large placard which they were displaying among themselves with great joy.

"I wonder if that is the O.M.S.[39] thing that Thomas spoke of at the conference?" said Joan.

"You leave it to me, captain. As a spy I rather fancy myself." And Blain, no longer the rebel but apparently the conventional ex-officer, strolled over to the men at the other table. They evidently took him for a man and a brother, and he stood chatting with them for a few moments.

"I say, that's queer," he told them when he returned to his friends. "It's an official placard issued by this Government O.M.S. stunt, and it's *dated yesterday*. That looks as though they had meant the negotiations not to succeed."

"Not necessarily," said Dacre. "Some over-zealous idiot stepping over the traces. Anyway, why shouldn't they prepare? I guess our people have been getting ready."

"I wonder," said Joan, and let the talk flow round her. She was desperately tired, too tired even to make the effort to get back to Gordon Square. The thrills of the day, following a night in the train, had left her utterly exhausted. There came to her at that moment the queer clearness of vision that sometimes happens when the body falls asleep of itself. Through the chatter of the crowded restaurant she seemed to see England — the great steel towns of the north, the mining villages she knew so well, the little homes in which she had stayed during her organizing tours. Decent men and women working far too hard, crowded together in uncomfortable homes. Lack of obvious things like baths and hot water, lack of comforts, and, for at least five years, lack of food and warm clothes. What fine stuff they were, what excellent material out of which to build a fine race. And instead ... muddle. Those men and women of the employing class meant well, no doubt, some of them, but oh, their *hauteur*, their assumption that people, because they were manual workers, were of an inferior race! The unblushing lying to preserve a competitive system that the really intelligent among them knew was breaking down, the refusal to organize or to allow resources to be organized except on a basis that would yield excess profits to some one! They wanted inequality. They could not conceive a society without some one to bow before and others to cringe to them. The Socialist ideal of a commonwealth of equals "simple in their private lives and splendid in their public ways" made no appeal to the class that governed England in 1926. The bolder of them wanted a world in which they could gamble. The timid wanted security — Government bonds and six per cent.

And now this strike. What good would it do anyone to drive the miners down farther? It was stupid to say that some mines were not paying. Some would never pay again, except in another war. Yet no attempt was being made to reorganize on a national basis, to cut through the tangle of ancient rights and wayleaves and royalties, to stop cut-throat competition, to work the mines as a great national asset. If the British miners' wages were lowered, the German miners would have to take less, and the old competition in semi-starvation would start again. The twenty-four million subsidy of the Government might, under wise direction, have been used to start a reorganization scheme. Instead, it had been thrown into the bottomless pit of unlimited competition.

What good could a general strike do unless it ended in a revolution and the workers really took control? Joan found herself smiling at the bare thought.

Weston and Arkwright and Hepplestone — were these trade union leaders likely to lead a revolution? Still, things might get out of hand. Joan shuddered to think what that could mean in the mining areas if some of these ex-officers were given a free hand. The miners would be fighting machine-guns with only their bare hands and the faith that was in them. She suddenly felt very cold and hopeless.

Dacre noticed her shivering. "What beasts we are. You must be dead tired, you poor little thing. I am going to take you back to Mary Maud at once. And you fellows too," he said, interrupting the hot argument that was going on as to whether Thomas or Baldwin really meant to fight. "It's no use being dead tired when you're wanted. Let's get to bed now and meet at the Hall at noon tomorrow. I'm taking Miss Craig off at once. We've nearly killed her!"

In the taxi Dacre put his arm round Joan. "Just lean on me and rest till we get there." It was a decent brotherly gesture that Joan, who hated being touched, did not resent. She felt the need of a friendly arm.

"Tell me about Blain," she said. "Who is he?"

Dacre smiled. "Well, he is Captain Gerald Blain, D.S.O., D.F.C.,[40] among other things. And he is the best pal and the biggest nuisance that ever plagued his long-suffering friends."

"What is he doing in the Labour Movement? Is he just taking an academic interest in us, from the height of his D.S.O. and Distinguished Flying Cross?"

"Does he seem like it?"

"No, that's why I was interested."

"At the moment his friends are trying to keep him out of the Communist Party, and I'm a bit worried as to where he will land if this strike business goes on."

"But how did he get among this crowd — the Socialists, I mean, not Bloomsbury?"

"I accept the distinction," smiled Dacre. "Am I Socialist 'us' or Bloomsbury 'them'?"

"I don't know. You haven't told me."

"Is that so? But really I feel as though I'd known you all my life and told you everything I'd ever heard."

Joan realized that Dacre wasn't paying an empty compliment. He just seemed to take her for granted. She was proud of that. It seemed a fine thing to have won a friend like Tony Dacre.

"I suppose we live quicker when things are happening on this scale," she said slowly. "But you were telling me about Blain."

"Where was I? Well, as you can guess, he is always known as the Chilblain to his friends."

"What a shame."

"What could you expect with a name like that? He was in the Army at sixteen and got his flying certificate at seventeen — usual lies about his age, I suppose. How he lived through the last year of the War, God knows. Finally he was shot down after bringing down five German 'planes. He landed in the sea, and was mercifully near one of our hospital ships. His inside is in bits — all silver tubes — and he is strapped together outside."

"Poor lad! What happened then?"

"They patched him up marvellously — on Armistice Night[41] his father got him out of the convalescent hospital for a party at the Savritz.[42] The old man made millions out of Army supplies, and it was some party, for he was as proud of his son as if Gerry had won the War off his own bat. Every one got frightfully drunk, of course, but Gerry didn't have much — at first I suppose because of the state of his inner tubes, but as the night wore on he just blazed with anger. He felt the drunken gaiety as an insult to his dead comrades, and treated the guests to some of the profanity they deserved. That night seemed to make a man of the Chilblain. He soon quarrelled with his father about the war profits, and won't take a farthing. Says he'll burn the lot in a furnace if the old man leaves it to him. Now he is living on his pension and what he can make by journalism. He has rather a *flair* for writing things men like. Does quite well when he wants to, but he gives quite a lot of time to organizing pacifist meetings."

"Blain a pacifist! But I thought you said he wanted to go Communist."

"It's capitalist wars that Gerry objects to. He says he would man barricades in a revolution with joy. Frankly, that is why I'm a bit afraid of what he will do if he is let loose now. Hello! Here's Gordon Square. I'll come in and tell Mary Maud you've been in good hands."

Dacre paid the taxi-man, but before Joan could open the door he said very seriously:

"It's a shame to worry you now, but just one thing more about Gerry Blain. He finished the War with some horrible complexes about women. He didn't seem to meet a decent one from the time he put on khaki to that night at the Savritz, when the women were pretty ghastly. There is some other story as well, but he won't talk about it. He never speaks to a woman now if he can help it. I was surprised to see him talking so easily to you. It may be that you can help him. You will if you can, won't you?"

"But what can I do? I hardly know him."

"I know, but you will. You'll probably see a lot of him during this strike. Blain ought to have some women friends who don't want anything of him, neither his love nor his father's money."

"Well, most don't."

"The crowd he used to meet did. And he keeps strictly to the men's side of the Labour Movement. But don't think I mean anything more. It was just that you are one of those women who isn't always remembering she is a woman, and I'm fond of the old Chilblain."

• • • • •

"At last!" was Mary Maud's greeting. "You've nearly killed the child. Where have you been?"

"Don't let her talk to-night. She's had her supper, it's bed she wants now," answered Dacre.

"I should think she does. And it's too much talk she's been. having — and you too! Have a drop of whisky before you go?"

"No, thanks, I must be getting along." And with a smile Dacre was gone. Joan vaguely realized that Mary Maud and Suzanne were undressing her and sponging her very grimy face. With a gurgle of the content that the feel of the sheets brought, she nestled into her pillow and was fast asleep.

CHAPTER VI

It was nearly eleven o'clock when Mary Maud took Joan her morning tea.
"Rested?"

"My dear, I've slept like a pig. This tea is lovely. I won't bother with breakfast."

"Oh yes, you will. It's all ready for you. You are going to be looked after properly while you're with me — no living on tea and aspirin."

"Are you coming to the conference?" Joan asked later on, when in spite of Mary Maud's injunction she was gulping down her food in haste.

"I would love to, but I'd be in the way. I'll call for you later."

Mary Maud's tone was wistful. She hoped Joan would contradict her, for she had all the rich woman's instinct to collect the craze of the moment, whether crises or china.

But Joan was too occupied to give much thought to her friend.

"Good. We shall be through by four. If not, I'll 'phone," she said, gathering her things together hastily, and giving Mary Maud a hug as she passed her.

When she reached the Memorial Hall she had hard work to force herself through the crowd. By this time the Press was full of the threatened crisis and the conference was in the spotlight. She did not see Dacre, but Gerald Blain, arguing fiercely with a group of Pressmen, gave a cheery shout: "Let's collect for lunch if we can." Joan nodded, and went on to inquire in the Press room if there was any message for her. She was given a letter from Royd which enclosed a precious admission ticket. The note said: "Robinson has had to go home ill and has left me his ticket for you, but keep quiet, as you really ought not to have it. Will see you at lunch. Hope you slept well. W. R."

It was thrilling to hand her ticket to the steward and to be passed so nonchalantly into the well-guarded hall after the difficulties of the previous day. She found a form at the side where, sitting perched on the back instead of the seat, she could get a good view of the conference.

Excitement was rising. These men, Joan thought to herself, were in the centre of a crisis in which actually they, working men, were being consulted and had to give the final decision. In all the history of their class, wars had been decided for them. Their job was to fight and die. At the most they could but grumble under their breath. But now Cabinet Ministers were waiting to see what *they* would do, and whether *their* decision was war or peace.

Joan's gaze travelled to the platform, where a group of well-known Labour leaders, members of the General Council of the Trade Union Congress, and others were chatting together, waiting for the chairman to start the meeting. She had met many of these men both as a Socialist propagandist and as a trade union organizer.

She smiled to think how different from the reality would be the bogies that the Press would present to a frightened public next week. They were decent, kindly men, whose last thought was any real desire to upset the present system unless some anaesthetic could be applied all round during the process. The trade unions which they led had become as much part of the capitalist system as the employers' associations. They were closely linked up with their trades. Their older leaders, locally and nationally, hoped somehow for an ideal set of employers who would be content with a fair profit, pay a fair wage, and give fair treatment to their workers. In their hands the trade unions were as constitutional as borough councils. Yet the revolutionary germ was there. Among the younger set were men and women who had a wider vision than their own trades, who felt the grinding of the wheels of a giant Capitalism, under which the individual employer was almost as helpless as the individual worker. But the leadership of this mass strike would be in the hands of the older men. Among them, too, was a Marxian group led by Preston and Sankey, but they were officials of minor unions. The men who controlled the big unions, men like Thomas, excellent organizers themselves, were furious with the coal-owners for the incompetent mess they were making of things. They looked complacently at their own better-ordered industries, with proper agreements unquestioningly enforced by both sides. The breakdown and chaos in the basic industries was affecting their men. They wanted to help the miners, but they were as anxious as the Government could possibly be to get the whole thing over with as little trouble as possible.

The word Government set Joan's thoughts on a new track. Were the Government anxious for peace? They had been bluffed by the General Council and had given the coal subsidy nine months ago. Would they allow this to be a constitutional wage-struggle and, if not, what would the Trade Union Council do? Were they ready to face the Government if it threw away the pretence of impartiality and came down with all the force of the State on the side of the coal-owners?

It was this question of 'preparedness' to which Joan's thoughts came back continually as if to a sore tooth. She had heard from friends on the local town councils of the Home Office preparations through some sort of organization called the O.M.S. — the Organization for the Maintenance of Supplies. Apparently this body had all the powers of the State without any of its inconvenient constitutional checks. Joan shook herself. Of course there must have been preparation on the trade union side. Responsible men like these leaders did not start a fight such as this struggle without knowing where they were going and what was to be done. They had had nine months to get ready. But naturally they were keeping their secrets. They had more sense than to talk too loudly about their plans. Joan had reached this comforting conclusion when the chairman's bell brought back her thoughts to earth.

Somehow the very coldness of the chairman, his composure and efficiency, seemed to give confidence. As he called the Conference to order, the wild hubbub of conversation, greetings, and laughter died to utter silence. The crisis was at hand.

One stroke of the dramatic the chairman permitted. A roll was read of all the unions, and the general secretary of each had to say whether his union was voting for or against a general strike to aid the miners. The first called said "Against." It was some little unimportant craft union. After that the "Fors" piled up until the tenseness became unbearable. Three and a half million votes for the strike, barely fifty thousand against.[43] Joan found herself gripping the arm of a big collier near her, saying: "It's fine, it's fine, oh, isn't it fine!" The man steadied her from falling backwards from her precarious perch. "It is fine, miss, it means a lot to us miners. This time it looks as though we shan't be left to fight alone."

"You won't, you won't," half chanted Joan. "We're all in it. It's just great!"

Now for action. What had to be done next? The Conference having taken its decision was ready for anything. The man who announced the plan for the Executive was a great, rough-hewn figure — a transport workers' leader who had started life by selling ginger-beer from a cart, and was now one of the ablest of the younger leaders.[44] He demanded discipline. At that moment he seemed a Napoleon. Joan's obstinate critical faculties were silenced by the powerful voice. The industries to cease work immediately were transport of every kind, printing, and the Press. (The Press ... a master-stroke. "That'll larn the *Daily Mail*,"[45] whispered the miner.) Iron, steel, and heavy chemicals, all building except houses and hospitals. Electricity and gas. ("Gee, the lights will go out in London. Hit 'em where it hurts," muttered the miner.) The different unions would call their own men out. "Oh, damn," the collier took out his pipe. "There might be a muddle there." "No, no, it will be all right. See how willing they are," urged Joan.

The transport leader paused until the silence in the hall almost hurt Joan's ears. Then in quiet tones he concluded: "We look upon your 'Yes' as meaning that you have placed your all upon the altar for this great Movement, and, having placed it there, even if every penny goes, if every asset goes, history will ultimately write that it was a magnificent generation that was prepared to do it, rather than see the miners driven down like slaves."

Joan could have knelt to receive the speaker's benediction. Sacrifice her all on the altar! Her whole being contracted to one passionate, intense wish that she might be worthy. She looked at the matter-of-fact miner, smoking stolidly at her side, with a feeling of shy worship. The man from Durham would have been astonished if he had realized that the eager girl beside him was regarding him as a representative of a crucified class. He had managed to prevent her falling over backwards, and he thought she looked a nice little thing.

"Do you speak at meetings yourself, little lady?" he asked.

"Yes, I'm a trade union official," was her proud reply.

"Then if this goes on, you come and talk to us in Ashlington. We like a fresh face and we don't get many women speakers."

"Rather, and if the railways don't run I'll bike there."

"Well, here's my address. You just drop a line. A couple of hours' notice is enough to get thousands when there's a dispute on."

Joan glanced at the address which was on the envelope of an opened letter. Her new friend was a County Councillor and a J.P.[46]

"It will be useful being a J.P. just now."

"Ay, but the Government won't let us do much for the lads, don't you fear. Hello, Ramsay's speaking."

Joan didn't wait for the final words of blessing. She wanted to find Royd. She saw him standing in the hall with Dacre and waved to them. Dacre drew a quick breath at the picture she made as she stood there poised at the top of the wide stairs, like a slender bird alighted on a rock. Just a second she stood with one hand waving, and then ran down the steps, her eyes shining like stars, her whole being lit from within.

"The fight is on," she said.

Dacre released his breath. He had an odd feeling at that moment that if this girl had flown to them and gushed "Isn't it *too* marvellous?" in the fashionable flapper jargon of the day, he would have turned and left the hall. But there was no shallow gush about Joan. He felt the power, the reserves of strength and spirit, in her thin body. Queerly he felt afraid for her — this girl who seemed to know no fear, who was so used to being alone. Anthony Dacre, the suffragist, the egalitarian, understood at that moment why harems were invented.

Joan and Royd were deep in trade union technicalities. Blain blew up to them.

"It's nearly three, and my turn is all for a spot of lunch, if Joan of Arc doesn't think it too awful for a fellow to mention his deep desires at such a moment. See, I'm sitting up and begging."

"Rather. Let's." Joan jammed on her red cap. "I'm pining for a poached egg."

"Listen to the woman. A poached egg. Do armies fight on poached eggs? Can commanders lead. ...?"

Dacre gripped him by the throat. "We stand no dissertation on poached eggs from you, old flick. Come on, or else every blessed place will be full. The conference seems to be over."

"Well, so there you are!" Mary Maud's ample figure barred their way.

"Oh, Mary Maud, the strike is on and we're going out to lunch," chanted Blain.

"Lunch! Do you mean that that girl has had nothing since breakfast? I'm ashamed of you."

"Please, none of us have."

"Well, get in my car and Suzanne will produce something." Miss Meadowes looked inquiringly at Royd.

"Oh, you haven't met. Mary Maud, this is my boss. I tremble at his nod. William — Miss Meadowes."

"You can see her trembling," Royd grinned, and Mary Maud liked his genial face and kindly eyes. He was much younger than she had gathered from Joan's description.

"We really are rather a lot to plant on you," murmured Dacre. "Wouldn't it be less trouble if you drove us out of this area to Soho?"[47]

"Well, it might be quicker," said Miss Meadowes. "How many are there? Mr Royd, you, Joan, me, Tony, Gerry Blain — couldn't we take some one else? The car can take eight easily."

"I think Mr Royd is very tired — it means long arguments over lunch if we take a conference crowd. Just let's slip away and rest him all we can," whispered Joan.

Mary Maud nodded. "You must get me some miners, though, to a party — can you ask them for to-night?"

"I'll collect some — they are sure to be at the Southampton Hotel. They always stay there. Oh, Lord, now William is captured."

"Leave it to me." With an air of apology and command Gerald Blain extricated Royd from a group of excited trade unionists, piloted his flock to Mary Maud's car, and told the chauffeur to drive to the Bella Vista.

Joan found herself comparing Tony and Blain. During all this performance Dacre had been quite still, smoking a pipe. He had allowed himself to be managed by Blain as much as the two women. She stole a quick glance at his mask-like face. He allowed anyone to take command. He faded into the background of any group, and remained silently sucking his pipe unless he was actually being addressed. Yet he was not in the least shy or self-conscious. He just didn't 'grip' a person or a situation unless there was no one else to take hold. Joan felt there was strength there, but wondered at the complete inexpressiveness of a man whose brilliant short stories had become classics already.

Blain's restless energy seemed fussy by contrast. Beside these London men — obviously dissatisfied with life — without roots, Royd was like a man who had put his feet upon a rock that was under the shifting sands of modern life.

"I feel flat," said Joan wearily.

"What you all want is stimulating food. Tell him the Hindu, not the Bella Vista, Gerald. It's quiet, with soft lights — and curry is what you need."

They laughed and called her "the stoker," but they were grateful for the shaded silence of the Indian restaurant.

Blain felt one little squeal had to be made. "Much too expensive, this. Labour leaders guzzle while urging others to starve. The strike is on, you know."

"Mr Royd tells me it doesn't start till Monday night. After that you'll all be living on ham sandwiches, anyway. Now, can anything be done to-night for the strike, or shall we declare ourselves by having some miners to a party, or taking them to a theatre, or what? If Helen's going to feed blacklegs, I'm due to entertain the fighters," and Mary Maud turned to Dacre. His face remained as immobile as ever. "Quite," was all he said, but somehow Mary Maud regretted that remark. What *was* he thinking about Helen? Why didn't he do something? — but then, with a shrug, that was what people were always saying about Anthony Dacre.

"My work starts again at six." Royd helped himself to curried chicken. "I expect we shall be at Downing Street to-night again."

"But I thought the Conference had told the Cabinet to go to hell." They all laughed at the dismay in Blain's voice.

"We aren't having a strike for the fun of it, young man. This morning was a good counter-bluff to the Government's O.M.S. placards about recruiting appeals. Now we've got to see which bluff will call which."

"Bluff … that conference … bluff! I'll never believe in my fellow-man again if that speech of Bevin's was bluff." Joan sounded desperate.

"Not bluff in the sense of being insincere. When the unions handed in their cheque to-day they meant it to be cashed — if necessary. But is it necessary? That's the whole question. Who wants to plunge into a general strike if it can be avoided? Not the union leaders or the men either, I can assure you of that. We want to help the miners. If we can convince the Government that we mean business, they will then have to decide whether we or the coal-owners can make things more unpleasant for them and make up their minds accordingly. That's why we shall meet them to-night — probably all night and all to-morrow."

Dacre helped himself to more rice. "I suppose you've discussed every alternative pretty thoroughly. It occurred to me — of course I know nothing about it — but it seemed as though an embargo on the import of foreign coal, the movement of any coal in this country, except for hospitals, might be a bit slower, but it would be dead sure."

"We did think of that — but it isn't practicable. The first railwayman who refused to move coal would be instantly sacked. That means a railway strike to support him. That means widespread unemployment, anyway, and the draining of the union funds. Our hope, if this thing has to come off, and I tell you frankly I'm praying to heaven it can be avoided, is in shock tactics. If the Government are really put up against it, they may feel it is easier to coerce a few coal-owners than several millions of workers. There'll be some intricate manoeuvrings for position this week-end."

"You'll forgive my saying it," and Blain's gay voice was very quiet," but that doesn't sound to me like the spirit in which one can win a great crusade."

"But in those crusades that were worth anything the leaders counted the cost beforehand," Joan broke in impulsively.

"True," replied Blain, "but they didn't bargain with Saladin[48] at the very moment they were giving the call."

Royd laughed. "Now do come down to earth, you two, and look at the problem we're all faced with. The coal-owners can't make the mines pay, antiquated methods, world conditions, the gold standard, cut-throat competition — whatever the reason. They want to reduce wages. We say, 'The miners' wages are low enough, you must try some other way. The miners want nationalization to be tried. An expert Commission has recommended that by a majority.'[49] Are we striking for nationalization of the mines? Could we? At least it would be a definite issue, but the Government make the obvious reply that they were elected as an anti-Socialist Government, and if we want a Socialist measure we have to get a Labour majority first. What's left? Ordinary trade union action. We say to the bosses: 'You are not going to lower the miners' wages. We will ruin every other industry before we'll let you. You won't let us offer suggestions now to meet the situation. Then it's up to you to find the remedy.' The coal-owners sit tight, as last July, and the issue is thrown back on to the Government. Obviously, then, if we can come to some agreement with them, it's no use going into hysterics and smashing the parlour ornaments."

"It's a silly business, anyhow. Why couldn't they use some of that subsidy for reorganization?" asked Dacre.

"The word reorganization smacks of Socialism. Every man who owns a bit of property says, 'This is mine. My will on it is law.' Well, you can't run a complicated civilization like ours as a mosaic of exclusive bits of private property — though we are trying to do so — and a strike can't smash up that mosaic unless it becomes a revolution. That's what's worrying me about the whole thing. We are in the position where we can't avoid it, and yet I can't see what good it's going to do."

Blain was chilled, but Dacre was interested in this well-balanced, clear-sighted man.

"Suppose the Government are ready?" he asked. "Suppose their bluff calls yours? Might it not become a revolution?"

"Only if they are such fools as to arrest my colleagues. There'll be no fear of a revolution while they are in control."

Blain put his hands together in mock prayer. "Please, eternal spirits, where'er ye be, make Churchill arrest the General Council and let him hurry up about it."

"Now, now, Gerry, you really mustn't say things like that," reproved Mary Maud. "Mr Royd, I'm a shareholder in coal and I'm ashamed of my class. But a revolution won't do any good. I'm glad there are sane men like you at the head of affairs."

Royd gave her a queer look. His eyes were hard.

"*I* shouldn't save you from a revolution, Miss Meadowes. I've been through the mining districts lately. I would lead a revolution to-morrow if I thought there was the faintest chance of getting one. Our people are far too patient, unfortunately."

"You make me shiver. I'm glad our people aren't like those excitable Russians. Now, what's every one going to do?"

"That reminds me," said Royd. "What are you doing to-morrow, Joan? I've got that big meeting at Shireport. It's impossible for me to go, and I don't want to leave them without a speaker. Could any of your friends motor you there? You don't want to be held up in case of difficulties with trains."

"Our first job. Something definite at last," said Blain. "'Scuse my butting in, Joan. Let me drive you. I want to see how folks are taking this. My old bus will stagger there somehow. Or could I borrow yours in the great cause, Mary Maud?"

"Of course, but can't I come too — and Tony? Let's all go," said Miss Meadowes. She wanted to be in all this excitement.

"Does Miss Craig want us?" Tony's voice was almost prim.

Joan looked up in surprise. "Heavens, since when have I become Miss Craig? Question is, can either of you two talk, in case there's an overflow?"

"Joan, dear child, the springs of oratory surge in me," said Blain, striking an attitude. "At least, it's either that or the curry, but I feel equal to addressing the universe. Mary Maud, yours is the commissariat department. I will drive and Joan will orate."

"And my job?" asked Dacre.

"Tony will look after Joan," murmured Blain. And the eyes of the two men met.

Dacre took Joan and Mary Maud back to Gordon Square. He sat quietly by the fire while Joan was telling her adventures. The telephone bell rang. "For you, Tony." Mary Maud had answered it. "It's Helen."

From his curt monosyllables she could gather nothing of what Helen was saying. "All right. I'll come round now. I'm at Gordon Square." Tony put the 'phone down and looked at Mary Maud. She patted his hand.

"Difficult?"

"Very."

"You'll do no good with Helen till you stand up to her and win."

"There are some victories that may not be worth the winning."

"Tony, it's no use. Your whole life is at stake. Your work is showing it. It's getting bitter, cynical, and not like you."

Mary Maud, it seemed to Joan, was continuing some discussion between her and Dacre.

"Fifteenth edition of *Marred Souls!*"

"I don't care if it's the fifteenth million. That book isn't you. It's Helen's power over you."

"My dear friend." And Tony leaned over her and kissed her hair.

"Shall you come back?"

"I will come back to you both." He left the room.

"What is the matter between them?" Joan was comfortably settled in a chair, and felt rather inclined for a gossip.

"You've seen Helen. What do you think of her?"

"I thought she was so cold. Beautiful in a queer way, or anyhow — unusual. I suppose she is very clever?"

"Devilishly clever. Yes, devilish is the right word. She can be almost uncannily cruel — and she knows Tony to the last flicker. What a change there has been in him since he married her."

"How?"

"He was so gay — not like Gerald, all over the place, but sunny and as unselfish as St. Francis.[50] She has played on all that. Used him for her own purposes to the last shred. When he rebels she knows just where to hurt most. Somehow, in the early days, it was like a child being tortured."

"But why did he stand it?"

"He was passionately in love when they were married. I think sometimes he hates her now. But no one knows what Tony really thinks these days. He has grown a shell to hide in. My poor Tony!"

"Can't he leave her?"

"Does any man leave his wife except with another woman? There's been no other woman in Tony's life. Helen has seen to that. It gives a woman a great advantage when her man works under her eye. Besides, he has had to keep his nose pretty well on the grindstone to pay her bills."

"I thought she worked too."

"She does. Earns a lot, and spends more. Tony's house is her workroom and her showroom. Tony works in the attic."

"He was grateful to her for not decorating his room," said Joan.

"He might be more grateful to her if she would leave him alone," Mary Maud replied hotly. "He can be dragged off any work at any time for Helen's purpose. That is her ultimate mistake, for Tony has the makings of a great writer really, and he knows his work isn't what it ought to be. It sells because he is writing from the depths of his own bitterness, but that fashionable stuff isn't what he wants to do."

"What's the way out?"

"Goodness knows. Another woman, I think, but heaven help her when Helen gets her claws in. She feels Tony is as safe as her sideboard, and treats him like a piece of furniture. If her property rights are threatened there'll be sparks."

"Could Tony face that?" Joan's voice was very detached.

Mary Maud shrugged her shoulders. "I don't know."

"I think I'll write some letters," said Joan. "I'm glad we are doing that meeting to-morrow. This waiting is terrible. I feel that we ought to be planning things. I suppose some one is doing that, but I wish I could be in it."

"Royd means you to be in it, so rest while you can," replied her friend lovingly.

There was a comfortable silence in the glow from the fire, as Joan's pen scratched at her letters, and Mary Maud held a book in her hands and worried about Tony.

• • • • •

Suzanne had just brought in the tea-tray when Dacre reappeared, carrying a small suitcase. He put this down the door and stood looking at Mary Maud.

"What's the bag for?" she asked.

"I've left home for duration."

"You've left home … what on earth! What does Helen say?"

"Nothing. I've told her I won't live under her roof while she feeds blacklegs. She intends to go through with her scheme, so I've left her to it. I'll 'phone the Russell for a bed."

"There's a spare one here. I expect I'll have Gerald and the whole lot of you sleeping on the floor like sardines before this strike's over."

Mary Maud Meadowes was a wise woman. She refrained from comment, asked no questions. Soon afterwards she excused herself till dinner, saying that women of her figure needed to put it away quietly times. Tony and Joan settled by the fire for a good long talk.

CHAPTER VII

Dacre had not accepted Mary Maud's offer of the spare bed, but had spent the night at the Russell Hotel. He telephoned Blain, and they went together to Gordon Square in the morning to find Miss Meadowes very excited about her dash to Yorkshire.

"This mink coat is so cosy; you don't think it looks too extravagant — mocking the starving miners and all that?"

"The miners aren't starving yet, and being polite people they will comment far less on your coat than your friends would if they saw miners wearing watchchains," said Joan severely. "They will accept what you are wearing and won't make rude comments as your class do."

"Dear me. Now that's quite pointed. Our Joan is going all class-conscious." Mary Maud remained cheerfully unperturbed.

"Well, really one might think they were Hottentots,[51] the way your crowd talk about the miners, instead of decent, ordinary, respectable people."

"I apologize — I grovel — not one word will be wrung from me against these marvellous miners. Tony, protect me. The Chilblain's getting fierce too. Dare we let him drive? Will it be his duty to some one else's class-consciousness to drop us two *bourgeois* into the nearest ditch?"

"Have you got the lunch, Mary Maud? My bourgeois instincts are all for looking after the innards." Tony felt a little tact was indicated.

"These certainly aren't proletarian eats," replied the hostess; "Suzanne has been determined we shall not starve in the wilds. There's chicken, foie gras,[52] a marvellous pie, cake and wine and things."

"Oh, come, Mary Maud. I mean, we ought just to have collected bread and cheese. We're on the job now," protested Joan.

"You children can eat bread and cheese if you like" — Mary Maud comfortably gathered her coat round her — "but Tony and I are middle-aged. We've learnt by this time that no job is done worse for a bite of good food."

"Tell that to your coal-owners. This the basket? Good Lord, it would feed a regiment. Suzanne, we'll love you later," and Blain blew the smiling Frenchwoman a kiss as he hoisted the basket. "All aboard for the Revolution," he called, leading the way downstairs.

In the car Mary Maud put Joan next to Gerry and tucked herself into the back seat of the comfortable saloon with Tony. She noticed that he made no effort to alter this. Joan and Gerry were soon deep in a close discussion of strike possibilities, from which a sentence floated backwards now and again.

Mary Maud was glad they seemed to be getting on so well. For conscience was troubling her. She had loved Tony with a deep, maternal love since his marriage. She had known Helen Hanray years before, and they had been good friends. But Anthony stole her heart. Her large fortune, anything she could do for him, was his. She had watched the sunny, golden-haired lad become the cold, self-centred man. She had watched him suffer, and watched Helen use his passion subtly, cruelly, to gratify her every wish, her lust for domination. How often had Mary Maud almost prayed that there would be another woman, but Tony remained faithful.

In spite of her modern smartness, Miss Meadowes was a really old-fashioned woman at heart. She loved to plan marriages for her friends, and to imagine romances for them and, where possible, give a helping little push. She had not engineered Tony's acquaintance with Joan Craig though she knew them both so well. The strike that had crashed into all their lives had thrown these two together. In a couple of days they were on more friendly terms than they might have been in months. Mary Maud admitted, as the smooth-running car zoomed along, that she had greeted Tony's interest in Joan with joy. But was she being fair to the girl? Suppose she and Tony really fell in love, what future could there be with Tony married — and to such a wife? Joan had character and the courage of her youth, but Mary Maud shuddered as she thought how little these would count when fighting a Helen roused in defence of her property and comfort.

No, it mustn't happen. Joan mustn't be wrecked on a hopeless intrigue. Tony was so much her senior. Gerald was so suitable. He had been at ease with Joan at once — so different from his usual glowering gaucherie when girls were about. For the thousandth time Mary Maud found herself wondering what was that war story that had turned Gerry Blain, of all men, so much against women. Why had he never confided in her? Most people did. Gerry was always amiable, but never confidential. Yes, Gerry would be a good husband for Joan. His father was so rich — and that little matter of war profiteering could be got over. With a wife, Gerry might think differently. Yes, of course it would be suitable — but her mind went back to Helen Dacre, and she sighed deeply. She wanted some one to fight Helen for Tony's soul.

"Well, have you solved it?" said Tony, offering a cigarette.

"Solved what?" Mary Maud was startled and leaned to his hand for a light.

"When you are thinking your face is like a cinema film. One can almost read your thoughts."

"Read them, then."

"Joan and Gerry."

"Partly. I wonder about Joan. She told me last night she had never been in love."

"Plenty of time."

"She's twenty-six. I wonder if the modern girl isn't losing a lot — romance, I mean. Aren't the best of them getting too keen on work to have time to fall in love?"

"I never generalize about women. Joan's not like that, anyway. She is so virile. I believe she would go over the top like an avalanche if she really loved."

"Why do you think that?"

"You forget I'm a novelist by trade."

"That means you romanticize."

"No, but I observe."

"Joan and Gerry — pooh, children."

Tony leaned forward to flick his ash into the tray. He didn't answer.

Joan turned round. "This lad says he can drive through without a stop, but I'm thinking of chicken. Is anyone else? Gerry will hate me, but I think he ought to have a stop."

"Squash Gerry. We're wanting a stretch." Mary Maud didn't want a diversion just then, but evidently Tony did. They had a gay lunch by the road side. Joan and Gerry were in high spirits, and a load seemed to have fallen from Tony's shoulders. Only Mary Maud felt depressed. Somehow this lunch had a last-time flavour. The storm clouds were gathering. The excitement of the crisis was rushing them along into an intimacy that would not have ripened so quickly for months under ordinary circumstances. What would happen? The good-natured woman felt responsible, but she didn't quite know what for.

After lunch Blain drove like one possessed. They were in Shireport by half-past six, Mary Maud having contrived cups of tea from a thermos[53] without another stop. They drove as directed to the house of the Shireport Trades Council secretary. As she stepped out of the car Mary Maud felt that she was really putting her feet into the strike. The secretary's wife welcomed them to a great Yorkshire tea — ham and bread, heaps of homemade cakes, shining crockery on a clean cloth. The secretary took Joan into the kitchen to discuss technicalities. Gerry had frozen again, but Dacre lured the wife into talking of the strike. The woman was calm, but obviously worried.

"A strike gets one behind so," she confided, liking Dacre and the obviously friendly Mary Maud. "Tom gets three pounds regular wage, and there's a lot of overtime now and then."

"That's very little, isn't it?" asked Mary Maud, thinking of her own expenses.

"A man who gets three pounds is well off in Shireport — most of them are on the dole. We are the lucky ones; but if the strike lasts long I get behind so — clubs, rent, you know."

"Do you belong to many clubs?" Mary Maud was surprised, the only 'clubs' she knew were the expensive social affairs to which she belonged.

"Clothing clubs — yes, three. It's the only way to get our boots and clothes and things. You can't buy everything right out. But if one can keep up a shilling or two shillings every week then it helps. I hate running into debt, but four children, you know ..." And the lady of the house smiled at Mary Maud as at one who would, of course, understand. Miss Meadowes felt humble.

The Joan who came into the sitting-room was a different person from the laughing girl of the drive down. Her manner was decisive. She had the facts of the situation in hand. "They are a bit afraid of trouble here. The docks and engineers are all right and so are the miners," she explained. "It's a heavy chemical place that works on a bonus system that may lead to difficulties. The men may not want to risk their six months' bonus. You had better talk class solidarity, Gerry. It ought to be your line. 'You stuck together in the trenches, lads, the same spirit wins here.' You know the sort of appeal."

"Aye, aye, cap'n," Blain saluted.

"Is the other gentleman going to speak?" asked the secretary.

"Are you, Tony?"

"Me! *Me!* I never made a speech in my life."

"Well, you may have to try. If there's only one overflow meeting Gerry and I can change over, but if there's two you'll have to do your best."

"But — really, Joan — I'll go to the stake, but ..."

"The stake's not needed. What these fellows want is news. They are thirsting for first-hand stuff. Don't think you are making a speech. Tell them what you've seen."

"Tony lit a pipe. "All right — God help me — but don't inflict me on these poor blighters unless there's a real need."

The men's main task when they arrived at the hall was to get Joan inside. The drill-hall was packed to suffocation. Anywhere where a human being could perch some one was hanging on. Blain was taken off to the overflow meeting. Tony thought Joan would be squashed to death, but in her own way she managed to worm her way through. A policeman tackled the job for Mary Maud.

The party's appearance was the signal for a great burst of cheering. These were the folk who had come from London with the great news. Mary Maud, minus the mink coat which she had left at the secretary's house, found herself, to her amazed amusement, regarded as a Labour leader. All her life she had hated crowds, but she revelled in the sheer friendliness of this one. "The dears, they *are* dears," she found herself saying over and over again.

The chairman read out the typed instructions from London; the men who were ordered to cease work cheered. The engineers called out, "Why not us, too? Let's have a right scrap and finish it." "Why don't they call out the lot," men shouted from all parts of the hall. The chairman remained stolidly calm. He was a trade unionist of the old school. "These are your instructions, worthy brothers, and you have got to stick to them. No fight is possible without discipline. We have a worthy sister sent here from London and she will tell you what they mean."

Cheer after cheer rose as Joan stepped to the front. She had taken off her heavy coat and was dressed in a bright red frock. Her face was flushed with the heat. Her thick, wiry black hair made a setting for her small thin face. Against the packed mass of men of the platform behind her, she stood like a living red flag, the spirit of revolution.

Joan had not a great voice. With so slight a frame that would not have been possible, but she knew how to use what she had. Her enunciation was clear. Every word finished with a click. The musical timbre of her voice made her clearly audible through the hall. The men and women hung on her words. Briefly, impressively, she told the well-known story of the muddle of the mines — the profits in war-time, the sudden decontrol in 1921,[54] the disastrous lock-out and long struggle, the loss of Continental markets, muddle and waste at home — the 1925 Budget[55] which made further reductions inevitable — the subsidy to carry the mines over the winter — the lock-out in the less prosperous mines for May 1st. It was familiar enough in its details to her audience, but, told as she told it, the case was terrible.

"There *must* be another side," thought Miss Meadowes uneasily. Joan's bitterness frightened her. She dreaded the girl's effect on these people.

Joan's voice by now had a passionate quality. She told of the trade union desire for peace and the negotiations with the Cabinet that week-end for some agreement that might help the miners. She told them of the railway leader's[56] words: "I have pleaded for peace, I have grovelled for peace." "If the Government mean war," she said, "they shall have it." The roar that greeted this shook the building. Mary Maud looked at Tony. His gaze was grimly set on that red figure.

Altering her voice, Joan spoke of the conditions in the mining areas, the poverty in the iron and steel towns, the want in Lancashire. The pitiful facts were lived by her hearers in their own daily lives. Joan touched the grim details with the flame of her own revolt. "It is the miners first. If they go down we are slaves." Again the cheers reached the roof. Women wept at her pity and men cheered her passion. There was silence again. Joan had spoken for over an hour, her strength was failing. In a voice that shook, but kept bravely on, she flung a last message of defiance to the owners:

"Wherever a mine's blown skyward,
We are buried alive for you;
There's never a wreck drifts shoreward,
But we are its ghastly crew.

Go search for our dead by the forges red,
And the factories where we spin;
If blood be the price of all your wealth,
Good God, we have paid it in."

She sank back to her seat exhausted. There could be no question of any other speaker. The audience surged towards her. Tony struggled to reach her, but was helpless in the press. But Joan was safe. The crowd pressed back and let her through. Somehow Mary Maud and Tony got to her and the secretary jumped beside the driver. They drove slowly through the packed throng. No queen could have had such a reception in Shireport.

Mary Maud was half hysterical — a mixture of admiration and fear. Joan sat quietly back — very silent. The virtue had gone out of her. When they got back to the secretary's house, the sensible wife bore the girl away, and came back to announce that she had put her to bed. By this time the little house was full. Blain went off with some of the men to a neighbouring pub and Tony took Mary Maud to the hotel where rooms had been booked. He was so obviously disinclined to talk that the kindly soul could only press his arm. She felt the waters were flowing too deeply for any aid of hers.

When he left Miss Meadowes, ostensibly to go and find Gerry, Tony walked rapidly along the mean, slummy main street out of the town. Men were discussing the meeting at street corners and Tony heard scraps of praise of Joan as he passed. "Yon were a gradely lass," came to his ears in a deep Yorkshire voice. Dacre wanted to be alone to think, to understand where he was drifting. He recalled Royd's hurried words — "Look after that little friend of mine, Joan Craig — girl in the red hat" — that had brought this girl again into his life. Her easy friendliness had been such a new thing after the strain of his sophisticated circle. Joan was young, fresh, in touch with real things. It was like opening the window of a heated Bloomsbury drawing-room into the freshness of the square to talk to Joan of her work.

But to-night had shown him another Joan — a woman of flame and passion. He gripped the gate on which he was leaning. He meant to think things out, but he could only want. His body seemed to become just one ache for this girl. He couldn't think of Helen — his life had dissolved into mist. There was nothing in it but a girl in a red dress. It couldn't be. It was mad, of course. Joan was not like his wife's friends who would accept a night with an attractive man as easily as an invitation to tennis — or, for that matter, suggest it themselves. But her unapproachableness only added to the fire. Tony, for the first time in his life, at the age of forty was really in love. His passion for Helen had been a strong, physical thing. She had killed it by using it so cleverly.

"This is ridiculous," he said, shaking himself impatiently, as though he could shake off the obsession that was gripping him. "I've only known her two days" — and then he knew it was not so, that, seven years before, this girl, seen only once at the meeting at which she had spoken, had had a great effect on him. For days then he had not been able to forget her, and wondered how he could meet her. The feeling had worn off in the routine of everyday life, but it had come over him again like a wave when he had seen her in that Press room. But whether he had known her seven years or seven hours, what did it matter? He *knew* he loved her, there was no point in arguing with himself about that.

"I couldn't have felt like this when I was twenty," he muttered. "A man must have lived, have really grown up, to know what love is." He stared at the moon and tried to think — to renounce. His mind seemed a whirring chaos.

"They told me you had gone out to look for me." Blain's voice behind him brought him back to reality with a start. "If you would rather be alone. .." The look in Tony's set face embarrassed the young man.

"No," said Tony, "I'm coming back."

Gerry stood very near to him. He didn't take his arm, but just rested his body against Dacre. He had been through deep waters himself and knew the comfort of the feel of a friend.

The two men walked silently back towards the town. The tall dark chimneys of the chemical works stood black against the red glow of the iron works across the river. These giant industries thrilled Blain. The struggle to control them seemed the biggest thing in life to him. If only this strike could take them out of the hands of men like his father, the men to whom they represented only percentages and dividends — figures in a ledger — and put the workers in control, the researchers, the men who could build a great world. To Blain the working class, the men crowded into his meeting that night, had become the Hidden God. Tony interrupted his thoughts — speaking hesitantly." Joan made a fine speech to-night."

"So I heard. The men were full of it. I'd like to hear her in full blast."

"She's not a works' siren, man."

"I know — sorry — at top form, I meant."

"Gerry" — Dacre hesitated so long that Blain realized he was trying to confide in him — "Gerry, are you keen on Joan Craig?"

"I like her very much — she's a ripping kid, isn't she? Got brains and go and all that."

"You seemed to be getting on with her very well to-day."

"Well, she's the sort of girl a chap can get on with — level-pegging. I just can't stand girls who set out to be attractive — aren't they awful? Joan doesn't care a damn what you are thinking about her, she's interested in life and what's going on."

"Forgive my asking, Gerry — I'm not prying, you know that — but, well, I mean ... are you thinking of wanting to marry her?"

"Good Lord, no! Why, I've only known her since Friday. Bit rapid, wouldn't it be, even for these days?"

"Oh, I don't know; anyway, I didn't mean that you were likely to ask her next week — I only wondered if, well, if it was likely to be in the wind."

"Not for me," said Gerry emphatically, "or with anyone else either. I can't marry, old man, now how can I? I mean, just look at me."

"Your face? You are not sensitive about that, are you? Every one loves you for it. Besides, no one knows what their partner's face looks like six months after they've married 'em."

"It's not only my face, but I'm a complete crock. The doctors have done pretty well with their spare parts inside me — but it wouldn't be fair to any girl, would it now?"

Dacre kicked a stone in the road. "When I think of my cushy job in the War," he said, "and what kids like you went through in France ... oh, Lord ... I ..."

"Silly ass. We all got the packet we were due for. But, anyway, I shan't marry. I've got things to do in life that marriage wouldn't fit into. Anything that's left of me goes into the Labour Movement." Blain offered, and Tony took, a cigarette. They paused in the shelter of a tree to light them, and then walked on in silence for a time. Gerry at last said rather shyly, as though he had brought up the remark with difficulty from his boots:

"But I say, Tony, have *you* fallen for Joan Craig?"

The older man laughed — a short, bitter laugh. "Yes, I suppose I have, God help me." And then as Blain was silent he said: "Idiotic, isn't it?"

"I don't know — one can't help these things. But Tony — I don't suppose Joan's had time to fall in love with you yet, but I think she's pretty keen — and I guess she will — that is, if she ever stops still long enough to realize what is happening to her."

Tony would have given his hope of heaven to say: "How do you know? Has she said anything?" but obviously he couldn't, and Blain said nothing more.

"I love her, Gerry. I came out to face it, but there's no way out. I can't waste a woman like Joan. And Helen wouldn't divorce me."

"If Joan will have you, tell Helen Hanray to go to hell."

The viciousness of Gerry's tone surprised Tony.

"A man can't do that to his wife very easily, Gerry."

"I'm not generalizing. I say tell Helen to go to hell. She's badly needed some man to tell her that these last ten years, and that's straight, Tony."

They had reached the hotel, and a sleepy nightporter told them it was two o'clock.

"Lord alive! We must start not later than ten tomorrow. Joan will be wanting to get back to London. So long, old chap. Shaving water eight prompt, Boots."

Tony didn't undress. He threw himself on the bed and laid his head on his arms. Blain came in. "Yes, I thought you'd do a damn-fool trick like this. Go to bed, you silly idjut.[57] Daddy'll tuck him in." Blain literally tore off Tony's clothes, got him into his pyjamas anyhow, and pushed him into bed. "Look here, Tony. I came in to say one thing. If you feel about Joan like you looked when I dug you up in the lane, you've got to tell her. No — wait till I've finished," as Tony moved in protest. "I know you're married. I know Helen. I know Joan's standards aren't Bloomsbury. You can't say anything till this strike's over. Joan will have more on her mind than love affairs, but when it's over you've got to tell her if you feel like that."

"This from you, Gerry!"

"I know. Woman-hater and all that. I'm not, Tony. I know a damned sight too much about women not to appreciate a decent one like Joan when I see her. I am talking about what I know."

"Can't you tell me, Gerry? Come under the bedclothes, you're shivering." Tony was so much in love that he wanted to talk about love affairs like a schoolgirl.

"No, I'm not coming into bed, and I'm not going to keep you awake all night talking like any Ethel and Poppy. I'll tell you some day. It looks as though I'll have to, the way things are shaping. But you take it from me — you tell Joan when this business is over. She's got to decide, not you. There now, Uncle's bedtime lecture is over. Here Tony Boy goes to sleep. Bye-bye," and Gerry was gone, but Tony had seen that his eyes were wet.

CHAPTER VIII

When they got back to Gordon Square they found Royd stretched on the couch, being given tea by Suzanne. "You said I might come along," he said, as he rose to greet Mary Maud.

"Of course! This is open house while the trouble's on — eat, bathe, sleep, anything you like." Mary Maud's only regret seemed to be that she couldn't feed the entire coalfields.

"Had a good time?" Joan looked so glowingly happy that Royd couldn't help a pang of jealousy of young Blain. The idea that Tony might be concerned did not cross his mind.

"Oh yes" — impatiently — "but never mind about us. We want the news. What has happened? I know I'm a grubby sight" — Joan flung a hat on one chair, a coat on another, and sat at Royd's feet — "but I'm not moving till I've heard all about it."

"Is the strike still on?" Gerry looked suspiciously at the Labour leader.

"More or less."

"What's the less? Let's hear the worst. Has that man …?"

"Oh, let the poor man tell the story his own way," pleaded Mary Maud. "Please begin at the very beginning, Mr Royd. Two lumps, Gerry? — and we will all be quiet."

Gerry chuckled. "I *like* that from Mary Maud. But I'll be good."

"Let me see, where was I?"

"Did you go to Downing Street when you left us?"

"Not quite. We went for a snack, having telephoned to see when we could see the Prime Minister. He fixed nine and we left him at two-thirty this morning."

"You poor things." Mary Maud was all sympathy.

"Whom did you see?" Joan had naturally assumed the cross-questioning. "Was Cook with you?"

"No, that was the devil. And to make things more difficult, the Miner' Executive had all taken the first trains home after the conference."

"What on earth for? Are they as trustful as all that?" said Gerry suddenly, sitting bolt upright from his usual position of being flat on his back on the floor.

"The miners are always homing pigeons," Royd explained. "They won't stay in London one second after a meeting is over."

"But why wasn't Cook[58] there? " asked Joan.

"I don't quite know," admitted Royd. "Probably the Council thought that the matter was entirely in their hands. Anyway, he wasn't along.

"And what happened? Whom did you see?"

"Well, Baldwin was amiable all round for a few minutes and then we appointed a committee of three to meet him, Birkenhead,[59] and that solemn Minister of Labour — I never can remember the man's name. He always looks like a Plymouth Brother,[60] and talks as though he had just found you out."

"Sir Arthur Steel-Maitland."[61] Joan supplied the name with a promptitude that made every one laugh.

"That's him," said Royd, "and it is obvious that he wouldn't count with Birkenhead around. I've been on several deputations to him. His main asset is an impressive manner."

"Isn't that a bit hard?" asked Dacre. "He's got sense, I've always heard, and a fair knowledge of industrial conditions."

"Maybe, but since Charles Booth took him to see Darkest London[62] he's got a sort of feeling that some of the workers have a rather uncomfortable time," Royd replied.

"And that's a fatal complex in a Tory Minister," added Joan.

"Joan, I won't have you say such bitter things." Mary Maud stroked the girl's hair rather helplessly. Listening to this conversation she felt that if only people would remember that most people were all right at a dinner party, all this bitterness wouldn't be necessary.

"Let's get on. What happened?" Blain said impatiently.

"Well, of course, I wasn't in for these negotiations," replied Royd, "but about two o'clock Weston came in with a formula."

"Blessed word," Gerry murmured.

"This was a model of blessedness. It simply said that the Prime Minister had been satisfied by the trade union men that if notices were withdrawn and negotiations continued, the trade union representatives were confident that a settlement could be reached in a fortnight."

"Good Lord," said Gerry.

Tony leaned forward and knocked the ashes from his pipe. "But what does it *mean?*"

"Bullying the miners for a fortnight to make them take reductions of wages," Joan answered decisively.

"M-m. Not necessarily permanently," Royd replied. "The Prime Minister said it meant acceptance of the Samuel Report and readjustments of wages and hours till we saw how things worked out."

"Heads we win, tails you lose. The wily Mr Baldwin. But are the miners going to accept that, Royd?" Blain again pulled himself to a sitting position.

"The difficulty was to get hold of them," said Royd impatiently. "Why, in God's name, didn't they stay in London? They were telephoned for to the ends of the country. Cook protested against our meeting the Premier without them. But they could have gone with us if they had been there."

Joan rose to the defence of the miners. "They didn't know — how could they?"

"Then they ought to have guessed. Anyway, we have hung around all day. But we can't let things drift without another meeting, so we are seeing the Premier again at nine."

"To-night!"

"Yes, of course. The notices operate to-morrow."

"Without the miners?" Joan was horrified.

"The miners will come with us if they get back to London in time. Really, Joan, we are not anxious to sell the miners, as you seem to think. But there is no point in letting the strike happen if it can be prevented, and the miners helped at the same time."

"God help the miners," murmured Gerry.

Joan got up from her cushion beside Royd's knee and walked up and down the room. Then she sat by the fire and looked her chief straight between the eyes.

"That's all right as a newspaper report. What do you think about it? What is going to happen?"

"It would be easier to answer that, Joan, if I knew who exactly was in this business. You know that the General Council don't want to fight. Trade union funds are low and they are not prepared. As far as I can gather they haven't let Weston make any plans. Frankly I don't think Baldwin wants a fight either. It's against his instincts. He isn't a fighting man and doesn't want to be."

"Who, then — Birkenhead?" asked Tony.

"We haven't met him at first-hand in this, but the Negotiating Committee have got on well with him. That formula is his."

"I should have thought he had fighting quality."

"Yes, but he's a curious mixture — careerist with a lawyer's brain."

"Ulster?"[63]

"He's lived in quieter circles since then. And he isn't an Irishman, remember. Carson[64] wants to join in anyone's fight, but I have the feeling that Birkenhead wouldn't half mind being the man who saved the country. And, unlike Baldwin, he has not one atom of concern about the coal-owners as such."

"Or about anyone else but F. E. Smith,[65] I should imagine," murmured Dacre.

"Then, if neither Baldwin nor Birkenhead want to fight," said Blain, "and Thomas certainly doesn't, we can regard the fight as off, and some one will come round with brush and shovel to sweep up the bits of the Miners' Federation. Give me a cigarette, Joan — and your match."

"It is not as simple as that." Royd accepted a cigarette at the same time. "There are people behind the scenes who do want to fight. I'm told that at least Seven Cabinet Ministers have threatened resignation."

"Led by Churchill," asked Tony.

"No, Neville Chamberlain,[66] I understand — but, of course, that is Press rumour."

"I'm Neville the Devil,
The one with a will,"

chanted Gerry. "So you are going back almost immediately?"

Royd looked at his watch. "By Jove, yes. Can some one get me a taxi? I've cut it rather fine."

Joan took him down to the street door. She leaned on his arm. I wish I believed in something to pray to, for you," she said wistfully. "And I feel so helpless, so useless."

"You help *me* more than you know, Joan."

"Bless you, my big man. All the very best. We'll wait here till you telephone or come — come any time. We shan't go to bed till we've seen you."

It was a dreary wait. Gerry did not move from the floor, where he was stretched out as if crucified. Though he wouldn't admit it, he had badly overstrained himself with the two long drives and the big meeting. Only by keeping flat could his wretched body get any ease. His mind was pounding miserably round. Was he going to have a breakdown again, just now of all times? Would it mean another three months in hospital? Curse that war. Joan was restless and Tony on edge. They fratched his nerves.

"Why don't you two go for a walk? Go and walk it off. Royd won't be back for hours."

Mary Maud made a movement as though to protest, but Joan jumped up.

"Shall us, Tony? I'm all bubbly and worked up."

A light might have been lit inside Dacre. "Come along, we'll leave them to it," he said, following Joan from the room.

"It's no use looking at me like that, Mary Maud. I'm not after Joan."

"Well, I'm afraid Tony is."

"Of course, but what of it?"

"Tony is married." Mary Maud looked so severe that Gerry howled.

"That from you — and in Bloomsbury!" he said.

"Why, you can never remember who's living with who as it is."

"Joan isn't our sort, and I feel responsible for her. She will take love deadly seriously."

"Maybe, but she is too sensible to worry whether a marriage service is read over her."

"I don't want Joan to be wasted, Gerry."

"With Tony Dacre? He is a man in a million. He's the silentest bloke that ever happened, but the girl he loves can count herself lucky, wedding or no wedding."

"It's not that. I'm not thinking of them as man and woman."

"What on earth else is there to worry about then?"

Mary Maud was silent.

"Let's have it out, my Mary. Joan and Tony will probably be in a hectic crisis by the time this strike business is over, and we may have to help. What is worrying you? Is it Helen?"

"Partly, but it's like this, Gerry. You know I was a keen suffragist — went to prison and all that. No, let me finish. Well, the Women's Movement has been the only thing I ever really cared about. I've had too much money of my own, too many love affairs to get any work done myself, but always I've dreamed that some day there would arise a woman leader who would carry on the tradition."

"Show the men where they get off," commented Gerry .

"No, I wasn't meaning that. I meant an heiress of the work those women did. Some one who could really be a rallying point for women."

"There are plenty of A1 women about, or do you see Joan as the directly inspired one?"

"Don't sound so cynical, Gerry. I'm desperately in earnest. There are lots of women leaders but they are all snowed under. As soon as a woman emerges from the crowd, she gets married."

"She can still go on leading, can't she?"

"She can, but it isn't the same. Marriage takes so much more out of a woman, demands so much more time than it does for a man. And a love affair is worse."

Gerry dragged himself into a sitting position. "What sort of a creature do you imagine your marvellous woman leader is going to be if there are to be no men in her life? Some gaunt spinster who thinks of nothing but 'leading'? Whom in heaven's name do you think she is going to lead — not women, I'm sure?"

"You don't understand, Gerry. I know the women I dream of must come before we can get the status we want. Women to whom men will not be in the first place in their lives, put it that way if you like. Some women who will devote themselves to their job as men do, and make their private lives fit in."

"Oh, well, if you bring your ideal on to that sensible plane, I agree. Maybe

Joan is that type. But it's casting her for the *rôle* of some celibate female Pericles I objected to. And Pericles wouldn't have been the man he was without Aspasia.[67] But I don't see Anthony Dacre as a male Aspasia. He is terribly in love with Joan, and if Joan goes over the top too, you can whistle for your she-Pericles."

"But, Gerry, don't you see that that is just what I'm dreading. Joan is the most unusual girl I've met. You didn't hear her at Shireport, but a girl who can hold an audience like that can climb to any height. She might even be in Parliament. But she's only twenty-six. If she goes off with Tony she's finished. Helen will see to that. And she can't be happy with all that vitality concentrated on one man, and denied any social or public outlet. She would kill Tony by sheer pressure of personality."

"Would that be any better if they married?"

"She wouldn't be denied an outlet then. She could work off her superfluous energy outside. But I'd rather she didn't marry yet. I want Joan to grow to all she might be by herself. Some women will have to do it, Gerry, in our generation. Social codes may alter but it's now I'm thinking of."

Gerry lit another cigarette. "Don't go all mystic about Joan, Mary Maud. It's your Irish blood, you know. You'll romanticize about her till you've fitted her up with a Celtic twilight all her own. And she won't fit in. This 'flame' business is all very well, but she seems to me to be a pretty hard-headed Yorkshire woman underneath. The way she tackled the Shireport business showed that."

"It's because she is all that, that her sacrifice of her personal happiness would be the more worth while," said Mary Maud.

"After all the blurb about sacrifice during the War, I want to give that word a rest for a bit," replied Gerry quietly. "Apart from emergencies like a shipwreck or an explosion, most self-sacrifice is the line of least resistance, passively suffering something, instead of using one's brains to alter things so that sacrifice is unnecessary. If the men who sacrificed themselves in the War had put in a spot of work previously as ordinary citizens to get peace, that beastly horror need not have happened. Sacrifice is a mania with some women. That was all right when it was their strong suit, but isn't it time to drop all that blurb and get things altered?"

"What things?"

"Well, this very thing you are up against with Joan, for example. You women with brains and money or a career of your own, most of you a damned sight more independent than any man is ever allowed to be after he's twenty-five, you all go round pretending that you are living according to the narrowest conventions of the Victorian female. Every one knows that you are not. Most folks don't want you to, anyhow. But you are all shamming hard, and if anyone of you shows signs of putting her foot through the sham, people like you bleat about her sacrificing herself. And if some one says 'Sacrifice for what?' then you go all mystic and talk about the Higher Good."

Mary Maud sighed. "It's so difficult to explain, Gerry, and I know it sounds all woolly to you as I put it, but what I mean is that now so much has been won, the vote, open professions, and all that, there must be some women in this generation who will put their job first and who will tackle some of these problems that are left lying around — this very question you mention of whether we can stretch the old Victorian codes to fit, or whether we should throw codes over altogether, or whether the modern woman can evolve a new code and a new etiquette to suit her new status."

"Etiquette?"

"Oh, I don't mean leaving cards or stuffy things like that, but if a life is to be lived graciously there must be some code, some traditions, the courtesies that take so much for granted. Freedom doesn't mean just slopping around anyhow as so many young women nowadays seem to think."

"But I can't see why Joan — " he interrupted.

"I know, Gerry. I feel I can't get it across to you, this idea of mine that big things for humanity are only won by some one's sacrifice. Your generation has been asked to sacrifice too much already."

Looking up, Gerry saw that Mary Maud was weeping quietly. He patted her hand. "It'll all come out in the wash, I expect," he said sympathetically. He dragged himself to his feet, got out her patience cards, and put them on the table in front of her. "There now."

"Giving baby something to play with," she smiled through her tears. Gerry laughed too and then stretched himself out flat on the rug. Mary Maud felt his need of silence. She made a pretence of playing with her cards and soon began to nod.

• • • • •

It was nearly two hours later that Gerry wakened her by saying: "Hello, here they are."

"Settled the strike, you two?" called Dacre.

"Any news from Olympus?"[68] their cheery voices echoed from the hall.

"Joan, you are wet through. Wherever have you been?"

"Been!" Tony staggered to a chair and mopped his face. "I'll never take Joan out again without a pair of reins. She doesn't walk, she flies. I panted after her along the Embankment. We then took a taxi to Putney for what she called a stroll over the Common. Stroll! My father's gods!"

Mary Maud felt thankful. At that rate they could not have had a sentimental promenade. Joan came in, having changed her dress and shoes, rubbing her head vigorously with a towel. Her wiry hair soaking wet was a mass of little curls.

"Golliwog Joan," teased Gerry.

"Beast. I always think my hair quite fetching when it's wet, it's like wire when it dries."

"Well, you both look fit and open-aired. I've been having a terribly long lecture from Gerry. Now I know where I'm to get off, as he says."

"No word yet? What time is it?"

"Gone eleven. Goodness, wouldn't anyone like any supper? Suzanne has had a rest this evening, so let's have it by the fire. You set the table, Tony, and Gerry can make the toast."

"I'm going to ring up the *Daily Herald*." Joan sounded worried. "Why don't you have a wireless,[69] Mary Maud?"

"I'll get one put in to-morrow."

"All the electricians will be on strike to-morrow."

"Dear me, what a world! What about it, Gerry? You are some sort of an engineer."

"Buy a portable and we can take it round with us in the car."

Joan put down the telephone. "No news. They are all at Downing Street. The miners got there about eleven. So there's nothing to do but wait."

Supper over, Joan threw herself on the divan and was soon asleep. Gerry stretched himself again on the floor. Mary Maud returned to her patience. Tony sat deep in the armchair smoking, content with the sheer joy of looking at the sleeping Joan. In his heart was the peace that comes when a human soul knows it has found its mate. Dacre was not at that moment thinking of the breakers ahead.

The ringing of the telephone-bell roused them. Joan shot up, cleared the stretched form of Gerry at a bound, and seized the 'phone. "Yes, yes, this is Museum 0909. (Bother these call-offices.) That you, William? What's happened? Not really! I say. Oh, come along here … yes, we are all here."

The others were in a bunch behind her. "What's up? Is it off — have they settled?"

"Not they. My hearties, the strike is ON and it is the Government who have declared war."

Gerry bounded to the piano and began to hammer out *The Red Flag*, which he and Joan proceeded to sing at the top of their voices.

"What a tune," murmured Mary Maud. "It almost makes me like the National Anthem. Now, if Mr Royd is coming here, he must have some supper."

"Bless the woman!" Joan, who was bounding about like a young colt, gave her a big hug. "When Jix[70] has condemned us all to be shot, Mary Maud will come in with a basket and tell the firing party they must first join us in having a bit of supper."

"And welcome she'd be at such a moment," said Dacre. "Far be it from me to discourage her. In our house we regard it as a find if the cupboard produces one decomposed sardine in an emergency .Here's the lad," as the bell rang.

They hurled themselves on Royd, who looked very white and weary.

Mary Maud tore them off. "Now, do be sensible. Not one word does that man say till he's had a bite."

Conscience-stricken, they all became embarrassingly helpful. Gerry took his hat. Dacre helped him off with his coat, while Joan, not to be outdone, insisted on sitting him in an armchair and taking off his boots; Mary Maud wheeled forward the supper wagon.

"This is really good of you all," said Royd, gratefully.

"We are not worrying you to death? If you'd like just to talk to Joan ..." Mary Maud was determined to be unselfish.

"Now, none of your sacrificing," said Gerry. "Kick us out afterwards, but I'll die unless I hear what's happened."

"Of course. And the tale wants an audience." Royd smiled benevolently on the young man, while taking large bites of sandwich. "Just two more bites and I'll begin."

"Were the miners there?" asked Joan eagerly.

"They came at eleven ... I ..."

"Now, look here, Joan," Gerry said firmly. "We must have a chairman or you'll get out the bits you want and we shall lose the thread."

"Right. I'll be quiet. Begin at the beginning."

Royd accepted another cup of coffee. "We went back to Downing Street, as you know, about nine and smoked in a sitting-room, while our Big Three went at it with theirs for two solid hours. Then our lot came back with another formula."

"Put not your faith in formulas," murmured Gerry.

"They are useful things sometimes, Blain. This one was also Birkenhead's. It was in his handwriting, in fact. It accepted the Samuel Report as a basis of settlement, and negotiations were to go on with the understanding that it might involve some reduction in wages."

"Thank you for nothing, Lord Birkenhead," said Joan.

"Well, of course, it wasn't particularly satisfactory. It left everything just where it was."

"But you could have done all that before the notices expired, surely?" Dacre asked.

"Quite. But you know what Baldwin is, or the whole crowd, us included, for that matter. Every one was manoeuvring for position till the storm was actually on us."

"Did the miners accept that?"

"They didn't get the chance. We 'phoned for them and they came about eleven o'clock. Thomas was determined that the miners should accept, and we were hard at it with them when a servant came in to say the Prime Minister wanted to see Mr. Thomas and the Negotiating Committee. Thomas said, 'Let's finish this point.' Then a secretary came up. Thomas was very impatient and said, 'We're coming. Let us finish this point first.' The secretary came back and said to Thomas, 'The Prime Minister wants to see you at once.' Of course we thought that some small point wanted clearing up and we started in to pacify the miners while Thomas was away."

"Cook was blazing, I suppose," said Blain.

"No, it was the actual miners from the districts who wanted to bite. Then Thomas came back. He was thoroughly angry. Apparently when he dashed down to see the Prime Minister, Baldwin handed him a letter, and said that 'something had happened at the Daily Mail and that negotiations were therefore at an end.'"[71]

"What was in it?" asked Joan breathlessly.

"Well, of course Thomas couldn't know then what was in the letter, but it appears that the machine men of the Daily Mail had refused to print a leading article which described as revolutionaries all those who sympathized with the miners."

"Good for them, but what had that to do with Thomas?"

"Nothing, of course. We didn't know anything about it. He read us the Prime Minister's letter which said something about 'overt acts have already taken place, including gross interference with the freedom of the Press.'"

"Good Lord, is the *Daily Mail* part of the British Constitution that we must fight for its right to say what Lord Rothermere[72] likes?" Dacre suddenly felt himself an outraged citizen.

"Apparently. Anyway, the letter asked for a repudiation of this, so of course we repudiated it. The printers' action was quite unauthorized."

"Sporting thing for them to do," said Blain. "I wish they would kick oftener."

"Possibly. But you wouldn't have liked to have private soldiers' battles on your hands before the zero-hour when you were in the trenches," replied Royd quietly.

Gerry kicked a pouffe. "What did the Prime Minister say when you went down to repudiate the printers?"

"He wasn't there to say anything. The room was in darkness and a servant told us that every one had gone to bed and we could see nobody."

"What cheek! Well, of all the ..." Blain and Joan chorused.

"Do you really mean that Baldwin had gone to bed and left Thomas and you people in his own house without a word? " This from Dacre, who was staring at Royd in amazement.

"That was just exactly what happened."

"What did you do then?"

"What could we do? The servant intimated that our presence was no longer desired, so we came away. Thomas was naturally in a blazing temper, because his work had been at the point of success. He told the Pressmen on the steps of Number Ten that the Government had declared war. Then he turned to Cook and said, 'Now, Cook, we must fight for our lives.'

Joan drew a deep breath and remained very still. Blain was jubilant. "Lucky for Cook and the miners. Now we are in for it. It is more than one could have wished for."

Dacre looked at Royd. "This means," he said quietly, "that the Die-Hards[73] in the Cabinet have used this *Daily Mail* affair to force Baldwin's hand."

"That's about it. Baldwin and Thomas were both fighting on two fronts," replied the trade unionist.

"Then, in effect," said Dacre, "this means that the direction of the strike passes out of Baldwin's hands — I mean as far as the Government is concerned."

"I imagine that a good deal of that has been done already. He declared he didn't know about the O.M.S. appeal for recruits on Friday when we challenged him about it. Well, Joan. And what do you think now?" Royd smiled down at the girl sitting silently on the floor beside his chair .

"It comes to this," she replied in a low voice. "Our side, the Trades Congress, I mean, not the miners, have been forced into a fight that they don't want and that they haven't prepared for."

"That doesn't make their moral position any less strong, Joan."

"Ten years hence, no, but who's caring about moral positions now? The Government will have all the moral position that is going. Can't you see all the respectable people, the people who don't want to be bothered, and who only want the miners to be quiet and if they've got to starve just put up with it, can't you see them all doing mock heroics and saying, 'We must stand behind the Government. Law and order must be maintained'? They'll never stop to think that this Government is as much on one side as Cook and the miners are on the other. All the Press will be shrieking that Thomas is a revolutionary."[74]

"That will have its humours, Joan," Dacre reminded

"You forget, there won't be any papers," said Royd.

"Of course. Well, that's one good thing, anyhow."

"What are the orders, captain?" Blain was on his feet.

"I'm going to strike headquarters at nine to-morrow and we shall want all the help we can get."

"We'll be there," said Gerry.

"Then let's all go to bed now," Mary Maud said firmly.

CHAPTER IX

Mary Maud handed over her Lanchester[75] to Gerry "for the duration."

"My sacrifice," she said, looking at him with a significant smile.

"All sacrifices are justified in emergency, as I said," he replied with mock gravity.

When she had seen them safely away to collect Tony and Royd, she set off on foot to visit Helen Dacre. Nothing had been heard of her since Tony left home.

She found Helen fully dressed for out-of-doors, in smart tweeds, having a sketchy breakfast in the kitchenette. Tony's joke about his food at home was not without foundation. Helen cared nothing about food. Her smart maid did not live in, and the daily char couldn't be expected to cook. Consequently, what meals the Dacres had at home were hastily collected when required from the nearest *delicatessen* shop. Helen seemed to have no notion of stores or even of quick cooking.

"Well, your friends have made a pretty mess of things," was Helen 's cool but not unfriendly greeting, as she looked up from a pile of morning papers.

Mary Maud had come determined to be pacific under any provocation. She did not want to lose touch with Helen during the trouble. "Pretty mess all round," she replied comfortably.

"Is Tony still enjoying your excellent cuisine, or has he eloped with this *protégée* of yours?"

Mary Maud looked at her keenly, but Helen's voice sounded quite detached. Evidently the idea of Tony eloping did not strike her as a likely event. "He's not staying with me. I think he is at the Russell," Mary Maud replied.

"You *think* he is at the Russell?"

Mary Maud coloured.

"I'm sorry. He is at the Russell.[76] He has been at Gordon Square a lot, of course."

"Well, what does he think of this business? Are you bearing an olive-branch?"

"Is one necessary? Tony is just as keen on helping the miners as he was, and has gone to their headquarters, I believe."

"But this isn't a question of the miners now. As all the papers say — it's a challenge to the Constitution. The Government simply must win. Anything else would be unthinkable. I mean, life wouldn't be worth living."

"The other unions think their life wouldn't be worth living if the miners lose."

"Then people like you and me, Mary Maud, have got to decide. We've got to stand in with the Government until this threat is withdrawn. I never saw anything so clearly as I see that. Tony and you simply must see it. Oh, who's that?" — as the bell pealed loudly — "Sorry, I must answer it. Alice doesn't come till ten."

Helen returned with two men. Commander Knowsley was an ex-naval officer whom Mary Maud knew well and liked. He was tall and spare, with the keen blue eyes that seem peculiar to navy men, and he was a really marvellous bridge-player. The other man, whom Helen introduced as Captain Bowyer-Blundell, a colleague in the O.M.S., was rather small, very stiff, and obviously suffering from an acute attack of national crisis. His hair was so well groomed that it looked as though it had been painted on.

"You've given up the concert idea, then?" said Mary Maud. "Of course," Helen retorted. "This is too serious for that plan. I have volunteered for the O.M.S., and Commander Knowsley is in charge of a district and we are under him. We've to report at ten o'clock."

Helen an officer in the O.M.S.! This would about finish things with Tony.

"You are coming to help us, Miss Meadowes?" asked Knowsley.

"No, Mary Maud is a Bolshevik — lending her car to help the rebels."

Mary Maud went very red, but held her ground. "I feel a responsibility, Commander. I do not want the miners to starve."

"But of course not. Who does? I have a great deal of sympathy with the miners, fine fellows, but we can't have this challenge to the Constitution. Where should we be? Any union with a grievance could go to this Trade Union Council and demand a general strike. If they do it for the miners, why not the plumbers or the roadsweepers?"

"Isn't it just because the miners' case is so desperate that there is any question of such action?" pleaded Mary Maud.

"There is a lot of exaggeration about the miners, Miss Meadowes," put in Captain Bowyer-Blundell, adjusting his monocle. "I know plenty who are earning fifteen pounds a week.."

"Oh, surely not."

"But it's true. My people are coal-owners. I know what we pay. Of course some get much less than that, but even if they only get three pounds a week, when you have five or six sons working in the mines with their fathers, it means a family income of eighteen to twenty pounds a week. There are plenty of workers who would be glad to change places with the miners." The captain held himself very stiffly.

Mary Maud longed for Joan's help. There must be some reply to Captain Bowyer-Blundell. She couldn't call him a liar. If only Joan were here! "I'm sure there must be lots earning less than that," she persisted.

"Possibly — but then there are over a million unemployed earning nothing at all. No one suggests a national strike about them." With an air of having ended the argument Bowyer-Blundell accepted a cigarette from Helen.

"And, besides," said Knowsley, his pleasant voice a contrast to the captain's parade-ground manner, "there is discipline to be considered, Miss Meadowes."

"Yes, discipline of their class by ours." Mary Maud felt quite proud of that reply, remembered from Joan's address at Shireport.

"Good Lord! Hyde Park!" Bowyer-Blundell took out his monocle and put it in again, as though some adjustment was necessary before he could see this extraordinary person properly.

"Come now, is that quite fair, Miss Meadowes?" said Knowsley. "Every class has to accept the discipline of the common good. The man owning the three-thousand-pounds Rolls-Royce who could race everything on the road has to obey the policeman as much as the man with the donkey-cart. After all, it is the workers themselves who will suffer most from this sort of thing. Suppose they get a Socialist Government next time …"

"God forbid," said Bowyer-Blundell.

"But suppose they do, they will rightly expect us to obey their laws, however much we may dislike them."

"It is a different thing when you are starving," protested Mary Maud weakly.

"Starving! Nonsense!" said Bowyer-Blundell. "No one need starve in this country. Too many doles and pensions. The fact is the men are just spoiled. They put up with far worse in the trenches without a murmur. They knew it couldn't be helped. Well, they'll have to be told that the coal trade can't help it. A firm hand and a straight talking to, and less of this starvation sobstuff." Bowyer-Blundell refixed his monocle. He was impatient to be at work, exercising that 'firm hand.'

"Well, I'm going to stick by the miners," said Mary Maud.

"And we must be getting along to stick by the nation," Helen replied. "When we've saved the situation for her, Mary Maud's dividends will come in again quite nicely, and then I shall work hard to please her with some new decorations. Blessed are the very rich, for they alone can afford revolutions."

Mary Maud faced the blow squarely. "I know that's justified, Helen. I have accepted my money without caring where it came from or how it was earned. I've got to reconsider a lot I've taken for granted. But it is true that most of these miners are working for terribly low wages. I don't know about Captain Bowyer-Blundell's fifteen pounds a week. There may be stray cases, but even the Press admits that wages are low. Our comfort, yours and mine, rests on the underpaid work of these men. Is it right to turn round fiercely and say 'Back to your kennels' if they find life intolerable when we are so comfortable?"

"But really, Miss Meadowes" — and Commander Knowsley's voice had that patient, gentle tone which kindly men assume when things have to be simplified for the intelligence of a woman — "really, you know, as I said, it is the challenge to the Constitution that we must keep in mind. We cannot allow one set of people to challenge the whole nation."

"Challenge our comfort, you mean," fired Mary Maud, jumping up and facing him.

The Commander would not quarrel with a woman. He stooped to pick up Mary Maud's mink coat, which had fallen to the floor, and helped her into it.

"What a lovely coat, Miss Meadowes," he said. "You have the most perfect taste in clothes."

Mary Maud's eyes filled with tears. His polite remark hurt far more than Helen's sneer at "rich revolutionaries." She knew she had been idle and luxurious, easily generous with money easily come by, but with a generosity limited to a circle of pleasant acquaintances. Her patronage of every new movement of art and drama and music mocked her with its triviality at this moment. She could only *feel* she was right about the miners. She ought to have *known* how to put their case.

With an effort Helen forced down her own rising anger. Life would have to be lived when this crisis was over, and she had no intention of permanently estranging so profitable and influential a customer and so generous a friend. Damn that girl Craig! For the first time the dangerous thought entered Helen's mind: If it had not been for her, Tony would have been content to stay at home, giving a sentimental lip-service to this Socialism, as he had always done, and Mary Maud's money might have been behind Helen's schemes. There was no time to think of that now. Helen's mind concentrated on keeping Mary Maud. She held her arm affectionately, and said: "Don't let's quarrel, you and I. We aren't fighting the miners really, you know that. But this bigger issue has to be settled. The Government must win, of course, and then you and I will do something for the miners' children."

At one time Mary Maud would have succumbed to the stronger woman, but at that moment she resented the way in which they all treated her as a child, or as some slightly mentally defective person who had to be humoured. Joan took her into partnership and explained things. But for Tony's sake she also didn't want a quarrel. She let Helen dry her tears, and forced a smile in return. "Well,

I mustn't keep you," she said. "Let me know how you get on. Good-bye." The men shook hands politely, but Mary Maud felt their hostility. She had betrayed her class, she had gone back on her side. To their public-school code it was the last crime. Mary Maud felt pathetically out of things as she went back to her empty house. Like all rich people who join a proletarian movement on mere emotion, she did not care to question her colleagues for fear they might think her lukewarm in the Cause, and so, when faced with the old arguments on which she had been nourished from childhood, she had nothing but feelings and emotional platitudes to offer. But it was not in Miss Meadowes' comfortable nature to remain worried long. She settled herself before the fire and allowed herself to be petted by Suzanne with a lovely cup of hot chocolate. She wanted to help the miners, but it was pleasanter to dream about Joan.

• • • • •

At the strike headquarters everything was in a wild confusion of preparations. Tony and Gerry were soon placed. The trains were to stop at midnight, so that messengers or speakers sent long distances had to go by motor or they would be stranded. Gerry was sent to take some important transport officials and papers to Liverpool, and to bring them back as soon as their job of silencing the docks was done.

"Hadn't I better go as a relief driver?" asked Tony doubtfully. "Mr Blain isn't too strong, and I'm not very used to driving. My wife always drives our car."

"Can't afford relief drivers," said the decided woman in charge of the Transport Department. "We are so short that if you can drive at all you will be needed. Can you lend us your car?"

Joan saw Tony go rather white. He could not say that he had not been strong enough to prevent his wife commandeering his car for the O.M.S. Instead he said quietly: "I am sorry , it isn't available; but I will gladly pay for the hire of any car you can get and drive it for you."

"I am afraid hirers won't lend for a risk like this."

"Go and buy a second-hand one," said Joan promptly. "You can sell it afterwards if anything of it's left."

"Brains!" said Tony, overjoyed. "I'll go at once. A man I know is in the trade. Coming?"

"No," said the decided young woman. "Miss Craig is needed. Off you go and buy the biggest you can afford. An old five-seater will be more use than a new two."

Joan was soon put to work by this lady, who introduced herself as Beryl Gaye.

Joan recognized the name at once as that of the wife of a famous poet and the daughter of a still more famous woman doctor. Beryl Gaye had been a notorious suffragette and was now a Labour candidate for Parliament.

From the first the two women liked each other and worked well together. Like most women who spend much of their time pleading for women's rights, Joan had had very little to do with her own sex. The working women of her meetings adored her, but Joan's contact with them was purely professional. Her trade union office was staffed by men, she worked almost wholly with men, liked them, and understood them. With women other than Mary Maud she was rather shy. Beryl Gaye was a joy to work with. Good-looking, competent, with an orderly mind trained by a scientific mother, she remained a woman, and had not become a martinet. She knew how to humanize a machine, keep overtired workers up to the mark by some odd little kindness or a joke at her own expense. Beryl appreciated Joan's quick mind and air of self-confidence, but her great value to the hastily improvised transport section was her knowledge of the industrial North. There was hardly a town of any size in which Joan hadn't spoken or whose Labour *personnel* she had not met. So Mrs Gaye simply handed over to her the task of getting speakers and instructions conveyed north of the Humber.

If Joan had stopped to think about it she would have been appalled at the task she had been given. In fourteen hours every motor-bus, every transport wagon not conveying food, would stop. There would be no letters, the telegraph wires would be jammed even though the post-office men were not called out. No newspapers.

"Thank heaven for that, anyway," thought Joan. "They wouldn't print our instructions, and that stops theirs." But in that brief time they had to improvise a service of news, despatch-riders, conveyance of speakers and instructions, almost an alternative Government, and that in a country which was used to having the latest news served piping hot in the streets three times a day.

For that emergency no preparation had been made by the General Council. The Transport Department were sending out then to buy maps and extra supplies of stencils and stationery .

At her first free moment, during which she and Mrs Gaye stood together swallowing a cup of coffee and eating a sandwich, which was all the lunch they had time for, Joan asked her why nothing of this had been foreseen and why, since the Council had known for nine months that a crisis was almost certain to arise when the Government subsidy to the coal-owners ended, no preparations had been made to deal with it. "The Government has not only been preparing, it has bragged about its preparations."

Mrs Gaye shrugged her shoulders. "What do *you* think?" she inquired of a tall, thin official, the head of the Research Department, a man who, in spite of greying hair, maintained an air of neat youth. "He is the Movement's official apologist," she explained, introducing him to Joan.

George Blackburn grinned. "Some job that. But it's no use getting bitter. Our folk have a difficult problem to face. If they had started making preparations to meet the Government's activities, they would have been steam-rollered by the Press. Can't you see the headlines in the *Daily Mail* or the *Morning Post*? 'General Council prepares foul blow at the Nation.' They would have been glad enough to have had a stunt like that to take people's minds off the miners. Weston did press the Council to do something, but they passed a resolution that no preparations were to be made. Sounds idiotic, but in the circumstances there was something to be said for it as a piece of strategy."

"I quite see that now," said Joan thoughtfully. "But why didn't they make that a public declaration and get on with their preparations in secret?"

"Perfidious woman!" laughed Blackburn.

"Innocent woman," amended Mrs Gaye. "My dear, don't you know yet that if you go into your bedroom, lock the door, wrap your head in a blanket, and murmur a secret about the Labour Movement, it will be in the Daily Express next morning? A secret that thirty-two men with thirty-two wives and families knew! Simpler to write a leader for the *Herald* about it. It would attract less notice."

The little group laughed and returned to work. Tony arrived shortly afterwards in high spirits. He had bought a roomy Austin twelve from his friend in the motor trade, rather old but in excellent order. Joan stopped her work for a moment to admire it.

"I've christened her Red Joan," he whispered. She smiled at him happily and in the middle of the storm there was a little oasis of peace. They stood in silence for a few seconds, just enjoying each other's nearness. Then, "Where are you going to send us to?" asked Tony, and Joan's mind swept back to her work.

"Could you get as far as York to-day. meet the strike committee to-night and give them their instructions, and then to-morrow make a tour of the big towns between York and Newcastle — you know — Hartlepools, Darlington, and the Durham colliery area?"

"You don't want me to speak at meetings? I should be terrified."

"I'm terrified at what *I've* got to do and I'd love to speak at meetings," replied Joan. But your job is to carry news, hearten the local people, and bring us back news as to what is happening. If there's any trouble, send back anyone who has got a motor-bike. If you can get a relief driver, drive back through Thursday night and report here Friday morning.

"You think it will go on as long as that? I had thought twenty-four hours would have been enough."

"If the Government means to make a fight of it, it should last a week, they say. But come along and I'll give you your papers and credentials and have your car registered."

Just for one second did Joan's official mask slip. She stood on the steps of the office and looked back at Red Joan. "I wish I were going with you. I'd like to see the boys on the job," she said wistfully.

"Do come," he urged. "You'd hearten them for the fight as you did at Shireport. There must be heaps of people here who can organize, but who can't hold crowds like you."

"They don't know the North, though. Haslingden or Nelson are spots on a map to them. This London crowd know no more of Lancashire than an intelligent Hottentot," which shows that Joan was more exasperated than fair at that moment.

When he was duly registered and instructed Joan had four men ready to go with him, to be dropped at places on the route. "Keep us in touch at each point that you can get a wire through," she said, but though Tony looked back as he started his engine, Joan did not come out to see him off.

"I'm glad I'm on the job with her. She makes one feel keen, and it's a man's job," he muttered to himself. He was glad at that moment that Helen had bullied him into some acquaintance with gears and clutches, but his wife seemed a vague blur in a peaceful but incredible past.

CHAPTER X

The days, of that fateful and crowded week went by like a blur. Looking back later to try to remember them, Joan found she could not. Punctual to the minute at Monday midnight trains and transport stopped. No newspapers appeared on Tuesday morning. The pulse of Britain was stilled. The only news that came through was on the wireless, which had been taken over by the Government. The bulletins were so obviously what the Government wanted people to think, that they defeated their main object of assuring the public that this alarming general strike was a storm in the nation's tea-cup which the Cabinet had well in hand.

Some newspapers came out in stencilled typescript. Winston, ever ready for adventure, left Whitehall and installed himself in the editor's chair of a leading London newspaper. He produced the *British Gazette*, which in its first issue tactfully gave full particulars of "Latest Wills." The General Council answered with the *British Worker*,[77] which added to the pressure at the strike headquarters. Ordinary distribution was, of course, hopeless, so stereos had to be got through to Glasgow and Newcastle for local printing, while impatient motor-cyclists, sent from towns within a radius of a hundred and fifty miles, clamoured for supplies. The crowd of volunteers got in each other's way, but in the press Beryl Gaye, George Blackburn, and the permanent officials of the Labour Movement kept their heads, encouraging, planning, smoothing difficulties, and dealing with the Olympians in the Council rooms. Most of these Olympians were in a state of utter bewilderment, but Mrs Gaye and Joan had occasion to thank their stars for a few of them — men like the burly transport leader, whose temper became steadily worse, but who was able to think on a big enough scale, and was ready to listen to plans conceived on a bigger scale than the limits of a trade union office. There were two officials of minor unions that Joan would have liked to have seen with more power, men equal to vigorous action and decisive thought, but, for the most part, the Council was concerned to avoid 'provocation.' It put a seal on the lips of the Parliamentary Labour Party and tried to sit on as much extraneous activity as possible. Sub-committees dealing with transport and communications, strike instructions, information, food supply, and other essential parts of the organization were set up.

Mrs Gaye was almost in tears after two hours' wrestling with her sub-committee. "Some of them seem mainly anxious only to do things that the Press will approve of when they let it come out again," and she managed a smile. "There's six of these men who are the salt of the earth, but why can't the others go home and sleep through it?"

"Six just men is a high proportion on any committee," Blackburn reminded her. "We only see our own troubles, but imagine the joyous time Baldwin must be having with his little lot! I hear Winston is going to parade tanks with troops in gas masks through the East End to-morrow."

Joan worked all through Wednesday night and was sent home for some rest on Thursday afternoon. She wondered what was happening to Tony. His telegrams didn't come through to her, but went to the Reports Department, and she had not liked to ask about him. She had no right to show the slightest interest. Tony had said he would wire to Gordon Square, and she hoped there would be some message. To her surprise she found Helen Dacre sitting with Mary Maud. Helen really looked charming. The excitement and unaccustomed energy had quickened her blood. Her face was flushed and her eyes bright and eager. She was perfectly dressed in a suit of brown and red. She knew how to wear clothes. "Not worrying her much," thought Joan contemptuously, in which the overtired girl was hardly fair. Mrs Dacre was as eager to overwork herself as ever Joan could be, but in place of a host of ill-equipped volunteers the O.M.S. had highly paid, perfectly trained Civil Servants at their command, and fleets of cars. Apart from the men who had volunteered to fill the striker' places, there was little need for help, and Helen was indeed lucky to be placed, through Commander Knowsley's influence, in charge of a central canteen depot. Helen glanced at Joan with amusement. Really, it was almost a pity that Tony was in the North. If this girl had ever interested him at all it would be good for him to see her now. Joan had not even washed her hands in the last twenty-four hours. She had slept leaning on her desk with her head on her arms for a couple of hours. Her woollen dress was crumpled and soiled. One stocking was laddered. Her face was lined with fatigue and grime. At Helen's appraising glance she looked down at her dress and hands. Her complete lack of self-consciousness made her equal to Helen's *chic* appearance.

"Heavens, what an untidy pig I am! Please forgive my meeting you like this, Mrs Dacre, but we've been up all night. If you'll forgive me I'll dash off and get a bath."

"Please," protested Helen pleasantly. "Of course I understand. It must be very exciting for you. But I was just going. Good-bye, my dear," she said, turning to Mary Maud. "I thought you'd like to know that Tony was all right. At any rate, he will not be able to say he can't drive when this is over. Good-bye, Miss Craig.

Don't overdo things, you know."

When Mary Maud returned to the sitting-room after taking her guest to the door she found Joan sitting by the fire as though some one had drawn out her backbone. "Tony had wired Helen when he wired to me yesterday from Newcastle. I thought you would have a report at the office, so I didn't send it over."

"Oh, yes, of course," Joan replied. Of course Tony would wire his wife; of course he would do the correct thing and wire Mary Maud at Gordon Square, assuming she would see it. Tony was Mary Maud's friend, after all. She was just an acquaintance thrown across his path by the strike. She suddenly realized how tired she was.

"You are tired to bits, mavourneen,"[78] said Mary Maud. "Have this chicken Suzanne's cooking for you before you bother to bath."

"No, I'm filthy. I must have a bath. Oh, Lord" — as the bell rang — "some other visitors for you, Mary Maud. I must get to the bathroom before they see me."

The door opened. "Tony!"

" 's me. Please, it's me. How are you?"

"Tony, where have you come from? What on earth have you been doing to yourself?" The questions were Mary Maud's. Joan hung back from sheer happiness.

"I'm a striker, I am. Don't I look it?" Tony looked even more disreputable than Joan. He hadn't shaved. His eyes were ringed with grime and his mackintosh was stained with oil and mud.

"I don't know which of you would take a prize for being the dirtiest," laughed Mary Maud. "Who's going to get into the bath first? I think Joan has it — come along, Joan, and don't start talking till you are both ready for your meal." Mary Maud bustled out. Tony caught Joan's hand.

"You are fagged to bits, you poor mite," he said. "Is all going well down here?"

"So, so, I'll tell you. What about up north?"

"Splendid. Oh, my dear, it hurts to see you look so tired." Then utter fatigue lowered their barriers for a second. Tony caught her in his arms. She thrilled to feel the pressure of his unshaven face.

"Forgive me," he muttered, as he let her go.

But Joan darted to the bathroom on wings. Her tiredness had dropped from her like a cloak.

> "Then, comrades, come rally,
>   The last fight let us face," [79]

came gaily through to Mary Maud, as she mixed a whisky-and-soda. She looked inquiringly at him, but Tony drank it down with great innocence.

"Bathroom's clear," called Joan a few minutes later.

Tony avoided Mary Maud's look. "I'll be through in a jiffy," and he darted from the room. He couldn't exactly tell Mary Maud that it was thrilling to use the bath immediately after Joan.

When they were sitting by the dining-room fire eating Suzanne's perfectly cooked meal, Tony said eagerly, "Now, your news."

Joan told him in a few pungent sentences. Tony laughed. "What a shame! God, if leaders were only worthy of the men they lead. I've never seen anything like the strike in the North. If only you had been there, Joan."

"Don't rub it in. Begin at the beginning. I've got to be at the House of Commons to meet Arkwright at six."

"Without a rest?" said Tony.

"Never mind, I'm really fit and I am to go to bed to-night. But tell me all you've been doing."

"Well, we got to York first. I met the strike committee that night. Of course they didn't need any help. The railway men were running the show, and as they were used to running a complicated business like York station, running a one-eyed town like York was child's play. All the towns along that route were marvellous. Every one out, and the others wanting to come out. Why on earth couldn't they stop the lot?"

"Strike pay," said Joan. "No use paying non-effectives."

"Then they ought to have tried to stop electricity. Hit the middle classes quicker."

"Don't forget you are one of them yourself," murmured Mary Maud.

"Well," continued Tony, with a smile at his hostess, "when we found the big towns and colliery districts going strong we thought we'd take a look at the smaller towns coming down."

"Who's 'we'?" asked Joan.

"Oh, didn't I tell you? I've collected two great lads, both Communists. One is a transport driver from Newcastle. I took him on as a relief driver, and he brought along Tom Openshaw."

"Not Openshaw, the Communist leader?" said Mary Maud with a shudder .

"The very same. And a great lad he is too. He's the only man I've met so far who has got the strike into proper perspective. He doesn't see it as a bolt from the blue. After he had put the case, one saw the whole thing as an inevitable part of a new phase of capitalism. He knows you, Joan."

"Yes," said Joan. "I know him very well."

Something in Joan's tone made Tony glance at her quickly. "Don't you like him?"

"Oh, he's all right. Has he made a Communist of you, Tony? He is regarded as a dangerous persuader."

"Well, I don't know enough of the Labour Movement to wander along by-paths of my own finding, Joan. I'm sticking to you and Gerry and Royd, but at least he had worked out the ideas for a fight and knew what the fight was for. He didn't go meandering round declaring that this was not a challenge to the Constitution. He said, 'Yes, of course it is a challenge, and the Constitution that expects miners to work underground for two pounds a week and be quiet about it ought to be challenged.'"

"It's easy enough to be logical if you don't worry how far ahead of your followers you go, or even whether you have any followers," said Joan.

"Well, I'll take your word for it, but, anyhow, he was a good companion, and I learnt how not to seem too out of it. We visited all those funny towns south of York that no one hears of — Worksop, Retford, Newark. They had got a real live lord at Newark trying to run a train, punch tickets, and do everything else. The men leaned over the gate and gave him tips on how to do it. He was quite game, I believe, and stood the pickets drinks round when his shift was over."

"Are the smaller towns solid?"

"To a man. It's absolutely unbelievable. Quiet country towns that had always been dominated by the big houses. And, Joan, it was such a queer feeling for me — don't think this sounds snobbish — but really it was a thrill to be with railwaymen and porters and waiters and people you'd tipped, and realize them as human beings without their uniform. They know such a lot about life, Joan, that chaps like me never learn. I'd always thought of them as a respectable background. It was good to get their viewpoint on us. It made me realize how helpless Helen and I and folks like Mary Maud are when democracy stops touching its hat and refuses to answer the bell."

The telephone-bell rang.

"It's Royd," said Joan, when she had answered it. "I promised to go with him to the House at six and he's calling for me. Would you like to come, Tony, or are you too tired?"

"I'd love to. I want to see all sides in this business. I shall be so much more use giving news to my chaps when I get on the road again."

Royd's friend, a miner M.P., met them at the House of Commons. Royd was wanted at once for a special conference, but as Joan wouldn't be needed for another hour he managed to get tickets for the Members' Gallery for her and Tony.

"It's like looking at fishes in the tank at an aquarium," whispered Joan, as they took their seats and looked down at the crowded floor.

"I suppose it's this top lighting," agreed Tony.

The House was packed. Joan looked with interest on the heads of the Labour women members.

"Do you know them?" whispered Tony.

"No. Poor dears, they have to spend so much of their day knowing everybody that they haven't time to know anyone in particular. Oh, there's Lady Astor."[80] Lady Astor, in the course of the preliminary business, was trying to convey to the Labour members that she thought them perfect horrors for causing all this trouble, and to her own side that she considered them a collection of idiots for allowing it to happen.

"Hardly any need for her to make a speech," Tony murmured admiringly. "She talks with her whole body."

An eminent lawyer rose to make an important pronouncement telling the workers that the strike was illegal.

"He looks like a lily," said Joan wrathfully.

"Queerly removed from the world," agreed Tony. He had much to do to keep Joan quiet during the speech and he took her out to find Royd immediately it was over.

"It is just wicked," said Joan when they got into the outer lobby. "He used his position to put the side of his own class and give it the prestige of law."

"He probably believes that, you know," said Tony. Joan's utter incapacity to give credit for any sincerity to those with whom she disagreed made him smile.

Royd smiled too. "Let them have all their legal opinions. If our people remain solid — well, they can't put three million people in jail."

"But they could arrest the General Council."

"Would that be an unmixed evil? And if they sequestrate the funds — well, we haven't enough strike pay, anyway, so it won't matter."

"All the same, it's wicked" choked Joan.

Royd put one hand on her shoulder. "Keep that indignation, my dear. Use it when you get into Parliament. You'll need it." Tony felt his heart miss a beat.

"Is *Joan* thinking of Parliament?" he asked.

"Didn't you know the great news?" Royd looked surprised.

"Oh, I am sorry," said Joan rather shyly. "I forgot to tell you in the rush. Shireport Labour Party are asking me to stand at the next election."

"But they have got a Labour member, haven't they?"

"Yes, but he's very old. He won't stand at the General Election and he may resign before then."

"Five thousand majority last time," put in Royd.

"Congratulations, heaps of them."

Tony managed a smile and a hearty handclasp, but he was glad when Royd took Joan off to her committee, and he could walk along the Embankment alone.

The river was empty of boats. No trams or taxis speeded along the roadway. Occasionally a private car passed. Tony was glad of the quiet. The possibility, now the certainty, of Joan entering Parliament had hardly occurred to him. Though he lived in a circle where the women were as keen on their work as the men, that work had never seemed to stop them doing anything they wanted. But here was a woman with a career that had to be considered.

Even now Tony would have been indignant if he had been accused of wanting Joan to be his mistress. He wanted Joan, ached for her. Away from her he was moody and restless. She was a perfect companion. He had been almost afraid to let his thoughts wander to anything else. Manlike, his mind had realized to the full the difficulties of his own situation — his marriage, Helen's temperament — but at the same time he resented barriers round the woman he loved.

With long strides he walked from Westminster Bridge to Blackfriars and back trying to face the situation. He thought of Joan's glowing welcome earlier in the day. Her kiss. A girl like Joan wouldn't have let him kiss her if she was indifferent to him. But would Joan want to marry if she was keen on becoming an M.P.? Could she love him more than her work? Would Helen be willing to divorce him quietly? Could Joan marry him even then? He knew that the obvious thing to do was to see Joan and have it out with her, but somehow he felt he couldn't. Joan was now an officer of the strike. Against the background of this great struggle he felt ashamed of intruding his own concerns. Round and round his mind worked in an agony of indecision.

Reaching Westminster again he stood and looked up at the clock. Big Ben seemed a prison tower in which they had put Joan, and he couldn't reach her.

"Stop being a fool," he said to himself savagely, and walked rapidly to Eccleston Square. He offered to go on immediate duty and was given urgent dispatches and copies of the *British Worker* to take to Durham. He drove out of London without seeing Joan and he left no message.

CHAPTER XI

Though she was hurt that Tony had left no message of any kind for her before he left London, Joan was much too busy to worry about it. In two small and inconvenient houses in Eccleston Square[81] an organization was being improvised that would have bathed the whole resources of Whitehall in peacetime. From every part of the country every hour of the day messengers, deputations, dispatch-riders, swarmed into the narrow passages of the strike headquarters. Were the power men to come out or not? Why were the engineers left in? Could they be allowed to come out on strike if they wanted? What were the arrangements about strike pay, about permits? Could a cargo of rabbit-skins be allowed to go as 'food' if the rabbits they had been on were left to feed the strikers' families? Sub-committees had been formed to deal with these thousands of questions and questioners, but they became bottlenecks, choked with the work. George Blackburn and Beryl Gaye conspired to give the soft answer which turns away pickets whenever possible, and Joan was taken off her transport organization to help.

"Why can't they just call every one out and have done with it?" she would say impatiently to Blackburn — and that perfect official would adjust his eyeglasses and say with a grin, "Why can't they have a revolution and have done with it? It would be much less trouble to organize than this tight-rope cake-walk."

When Gerry breezed in the next Monday Joan could have hugged him. He looked fagged out with his almost continuous driving, but he was as cheery as ever.

"Bless you, Boadicea,"[82] was his greeting, and how goes the fight at G.H.Q.?"[83]

"It's more like a bargain basement than a battle," said Joan ruefully, glaring round the disordered room with its mass of miscellaneous strike gear, and the crowd of people at the door struggling to get in or out. "Oh, Gerry, at least in a real war people do sometimes get killed."

"But never the ones you want, my dear. Our li'l' ditty was 'Big brass-hats never die, they only fade away-ee.'"

"Fade! If only any of this crowd would fade away for a bit I'd be thankful."

"When did you have your last meal?" asked the ever-practical Gerry .

"Oh, a ham sandwich about eleven."

"And it's now five o'clock. Tummies, my child, are the source of all defeatism. Can't keep a schoolgirl complexion on an occasional ham-sandwich. That is," he looked at her teasingly, "if you still have one."

"I know I'm a dirty pig." Joan rubbed her face vigorously with her grubby handkerchief and looked with dismay at the dirt that came off.

"You are coming out for a meal. No, don't you worry about asking. Who's your brass hat? Mrs Gaye? Righto, I'll tackle the gorgon."[84]

"The gorgon is here to be tackled."

Gerry turned to face Mrs Gaye. Joan noted with amazement how he froze into the 'perfect gentleman' when he had to talk to any woman outside the little group of those he liked. "Miss Craig is very tired. Would it inconvenience you if I took her out for a meal, Mrs Gaye?" he said with cold courtesy.

Mrs Gaye, not knowing his little idiosyncrasy, felt snubbed by his distant manner. She briefly gave the required permission and turned away rather hurt.

"Gerry, you're a beast to every woman you meet. Why do you act the iceberg even to jolly decent sorts like her?" said Joan impatiently, as she climbed into his car.

"I'm not an iceberg to you, am I?" he said, occupying himself with brakes and self-starter.

"Well, I can't go round explaining that," Joan objected. "I can't say. 'This little dog is quite harmless but he barks at petticoats.'"

"Never mind, women soon won't be wearing them." Gerry was evidently anxious to avoid discussion of the point. "Where shall we go?"

"Somewhere where I can wash first."

Freshened by soap and water, Joan gratefully sank into a soft chair in the corner of the Sylvan Restaurant, which Gerry had chosen.

"You eat that sole before you say one word."

"Then you do the talking. Where have you been and what are things like in the front trenches?"

"Well, not to begin at the beginning, things are just marvellous."

"That's illuminating. At least *you*, of all people, can't follow up with the bromide that 'the women are wonderful.'"

"Some are," he answered to Joan's laugh. "One place I went to, the police and strikers had a football match. I kicked off and the Chief Constable's wife entertained us to tea. Great woman. She didn't know what all the trouble was about, but she had spent the entire War handing out cups of tea to British Tommies, and these were British lads, and of course they must have tea. She organised a cocoa canteen which served pickets and O.M.S. with an equal cheeriness throughout the night. It's a weird country."

"But the strike …?"

"She's not interested in my bright gossip 'pars,'" said Gerry pathetically to the ceiling.

"Because one amiable woman … you seemed to get on all right with her, by the way!"

"Rather. Under six and over sixty I get on with 'em beautifully. My old lady was a great female. Seemed to think that if only she could show my paralysed face to Mr Churchill, he would fall on my neck and give the miners everything they wanted as a small token, *et cetera, et cetera.*"

"Still, there is a strike on and I want to hear about it."

"Bless the girl, she shall. Now prepare." Gerry cleared his throat, gripped his lapels, and began with an oratorical flourish.

"This strike is in no sense a challenge to the Constitution. We solemnly declare that she shall not sheathe the picket badge …"

Joan fingered a chocolate éclair menacingly.

"Forgive me. Well, it's like this. In most places the strike committees are really great. It just shows what a lot of organising ability is running to waste among the workers in this one-eyed country, when a man is called a 'hand' and allowed to think. Crewe and Coventry, and a score of the towns I've visited, are being run by sheer soviets. The permit business is marvellous. Just to see the big employers of the town coming cap in hand to ask for permits to move cargo does one's heart good. Joan, I'd die happy if I could have seen the Pater[85] having to do that. Except that, poor lad, he'd probably have died of apoplexy."

"It's all right while the strike's on, but …"

"I know." Gerry sobered down. "That's what Harry Browne, the Kelsall lad, said. God help us unless we win. Some of us will get no work for miles round if we don't. That lad Browne — just a young engineer, but he's got that town organized to the last flicker. The employers know just what they can or can't do, and because it can be enforced they are putting up with it and doing what they are told. Browne's only trouble is the contradictory orders from London. Some of the transport men have had to march in and out as though they were Morris-dancing."

"God help us if we don't win," Joan quoted, quietly, her eyes looking beyond the rose-shaded lights.

"But we are going to!"

"Gerry, are we, can we? Can the unions stand the strain? If the men would stand out without their strike pay … but they've got to eat, and their reserves are so small. And then the miners aren't in these negotiations. Will they accept the terms?"

"Negotiations? Is there anything in this Samuel talk? I see he says he has come back from Italy[86] just to see if Nelson's Column[87] is still there, or something like that. Is there anything in the wind? Personally, I thought the Archbishop was a game old sport, but I see he has been kyboshed and told to mind his own business." [88]

"There are rumours. I believe something is being offered, but, Gerry, I'm afraid."

"Of course you are. All you G.H.Q. crowd have got the breeze up because you haven't seen what's going on. You can't see the wood because your noses are stuck in the Forestry reports. I wish you could see the lads."

"Yes, I wish they all could. I must be getting back. It has been good to see you, Gerry."

"Where's Tony?"

Joan's lip quivered. "I don't know. He just went off north."

"Poor Tony."

"Not poor me?"

"I don't know about you, Joan. But when a man loves a woman as Tony loves you, he has either got to clear out ... or ..."

Gerry left his sentence unfinished, but the sun shone out again for Joan. It wasn't a bad old world after all. She could even feel charitable towards the O.M.S. She wanted to tell all the women in the world that if they could only find Tonys to love and Gerrys to play with, everything would be all right.

Reporting back to Beryl Gaye, Joan found Royd and Blackburn with her, looking very serious.

"Joan," said Royd, without any preliminary greeting, "I want you to go off to the Kelsall area to do a series of meetings for me. I can't leave London. There will be meetings of engineers. Tell them to stay in at the moment and prepare them for coming out on Wednesday. There's no one to send with you. You must do your best. Can Blain drive her down?" Royd turned to Mrs Gaye.

"Yes, certainly, he has just signed off his other work."

Joan was now indeed in the sunshine. Calling at Gordon Square to leave word for Mary Maud and pick up a bag, she was soon speeding in the Lanchester along the road to the Midlands. No level-crossing hold-ups, very little traffic, no speed limit — Gerry's speedometer rose to sixty and stayed there. Having wired Harry Browne to meet them, they drove straight to his headquarters in the great engineering town of Kelsall.

"Better come and meet our secretary," Harry grinned, as he met them on the door-step. Browne was a small, spare, pale-complexioned young man, nothing about him that would cause anyone to give him a second glance under ordinary conditions; but in these few short days of power he had assumed quite unconsciously the habit of command, something of that air of knowing what he wanted and expecting to get it that is supposed to be the result of the careful training of a governing class.

The contrast with the nominal head, the secretary of the Trades Council who had held that position for years, was amusing. Joan found him, rather fat and rather bald, with a copy of the club rules in front of him, under certain lines of which he was ruling with red ink. He greeted the newcomers rather grudgingly, and insisted on finishing his work before he would discuss what was to be done. The correct ruling of the red lines seemed really more important than the meeting of eight thousand engineers who had to be coaxed into obeying orders they disliked.

"The whole thing is a mistake, I tell you, and no good will come of it. There's young Harry there, issuing orders to men like Mr Ponsford, one of the biggest manufacturers in this town. It's against nature, I tell you. Put a beggar on horseback and he'll ride to the devil, and that's where the whole trade union movement is riding. Masters will be masters. You can't alter nature. And let me tell you, young woman, I don't approve of females racing round the country with young men, and telling men old enough to be their fathers to strike against lawful authority. It's against nature, I tell you."

And that was all they could get out of the stolid Midander. They left him to his red-ink underlining. Browne then took them along to the Town Clerk, a typical old-fashioned solicitor, compelled, much against his instincts, to obey the orders of a Labour Town Council. Here Joan realized how effective was the stopping of the Press.

"No newspapers, no *Times* — really, Miss Craig, without *The Times* in the morning one doesn't know what to think," said the worried Town Clerk.

"Couldn't you try thinking for yourself, just for once?" asked Joan, very demurely.

At the meeting itself Joan found the air full of the wildest rumours. Some were declaring that victory was to be announced next day, others that the miners would be let down, others that Churchill had had a tank corps out and destroyed the East End of London. Joan's announcement that the orders were for the engineers to come out on the Wednesday morning was received with cheers. Here was something definite. Evidently headquarters meant business at last, and the men who had fretted on the leash and the men who had chafed to see them at work were united again.

An old man approached Joan as she was leaving the meeting with Browne and Gerald Blain. "Pardon me, miss, could I have a word with you?" he said respectfully.

"Of course!" Joan stepped aside to speak with him privately.

"It's this, miss. Don't think I'm intruding my own concerns, but could you tell me if it is really necessary that the engineers should come out?"

"I'm afraid it is. Don't you want to?"

"I'm anxious to do my bit, and I want to help the miners, but, you see, it's like this. I've worked for this firm for fifty years and I get a pound a week pension from December for fifty years' uninterrupted service. Ours is a hard firm, miss; fair enough employers, but hard. If I come out, I'll lose that pension, miss. It's in the contract."

Joan's eyes filled with tears. "Perhaps you had better stay in, then. One man can't make much difference."

"No, miss, I stand by my mates. I'll never be a blackleg, come what may. I only just wanted to know if it was really necessary like. Thank you very much, miss. It was a fine speech of yours to-day, very inspiring to us chaps. We haven't had much news."

He touched his cap and walked away, leaving Joan with an awful doubt her heart. Was it necessary? There must be hundreds like this man. Had they come out at the beginning, they might have helped. Was it too late now?

CHAPTER XII

Joan stayed two nights with Harry Browne's mother, and the wise old lady flatly refused to call her too early. It was very late on Wednesday morning when, conscience-stricken, Joan ran up the steps of the Trades Hall. There were excited groups in the big room. "The Trades Union Congress is at Downing Street," they told her. "It's come through on the wireless."

"Don't you believe all you hear on that fib-machine," she warned them laughingly. As she turned the handle of the secretary's door she heard Tony's deep voice. Her heart almost stood still for a moment. Pulling herself together, she walked in.

"Tony!"

"Joan!"

"What are *you* doing here?"

The older men smiled at the glowing welcome in her eyes, but Gerry turned to the window.

"I had to come through to Birmingham. I heard you were here from one of the dispatch-men, and so came along to tell you the news."

"What news? What is this about the T.U. men being at Downing Street?"

"I believe we've won, Joan."

"Well, I don't," Gerry said gruffly to the window-panes.

"Do tell us what you know. We left London Monday afternoon. Have the miners accepted the Samuel Memorandum?"

"I hear they have. I was on the 'phone to a man I know well, a great friend of that crowd. Told me positively the strike would end to-day."

"Oh, wouldn't that be fine!" Joan clasped her hands together.

"Would it?" Gerry turned on her with a fierceness that surprised every one. "What is there in these terms? Have the Government said they would accept them? I believe the miners are being let down."

No one would listen. Joan and the others fussed round Tony as though he were responsible for victory. When later on that fateful Wednesday the news came through that the strike was called off, and the local paper struggled out with a bill, "Terms of Peace," Kelsall was beside itself. In some towns the men hung back, distrustful of the wireless, fearing they were being got to work under a pretext, but because Tony had come in that morning from the outside world his version was accepted. At a great meeting in the market-place he was induced to make a 'victory' speech.

Gerry sat glum at the driving-wheel. He drove Joan and Tony through the cheering crowds without a word.

"Now, let's get back to London, shall we?" asked Tony, as they steered out of the crowd at last, and got some food in a *café*.

"I'm not leaving here till I know what's really happened," said Gerry sternly.

"But don't you think we've won, Gerry?" Joan was worried.

"No, I don't. There was nothing in London on Monday to indicate anything of the kind. I don't know what's happened, and I'm not leaving Harry Browne and his lads to face the music till I know. You go with Tony, Joan. He can drive you, and I'll come when can."

"Of course not. If you feel like that, Gerry, I'll stay too."

Tony was frankly impatient. The strike was over and he wanted to get back to London. He had never been absorbed in the Labour Movement as were Joan and Gerry. It was only a casual offer of help in publicity to Weston, the Trades Congress secretary, whom he liked, that had caused his presence in the Press room in which he had first met Joan. He had been caught up in the strike whirl because of Joan, and had worked hard. But now the immediate interest of the fight was over, his own problem loomed large. Above all, he wanted Joan to himself in London. He thought longingly of evenings by the fire at Gordon Square, with Mary Maud tactfully absent. Tony didn't mind living hard when he had to, but he wanted his own comfortable surroundings now that the need was over.

"There really isn't anything you can do now, Joan," he pleaded. "Let Gerry stay and I'll drive you back."

But Joan was immovable. The long drive back together, Tony realized, wasn't even being considered against the possibility of helping the strikers.

"Of course, if you prefer to stay with Gerry," he said acidly, and then saw his mistake. Joan looked straight into his eyes, and her own filled. "I'm sorry, my dear," he said in a low voice. "Forgive me, I'm a brute, but I haven't seen you as much this trip as I had hoped, and I had thought we should be working together."

Gerry had got up from the table and was looking at the crowd, his hands deep in his pockets. "There's Browne," he said suddenly; "I'm off."

But he met the young engineer on the stairs and came back with him. Browne's face was white. He sat down heavily at the table. "Gerry was right. Unconditional surrender."

"But the Samuel Memorandum?" asked Tony.

"Miners wouldn't look at it. Said there was no guarantee that the Government would accept it, and it meant reductions, anyway."

"But how do you know?"

"I've been at the *Courier* office — my brother is a reporter there. They've been on the 'phone."

"But the news they got may be doctored."

"No. They let me use the 'phone. I was lucky. I got through to Blackburn at Eccleston Square. He confirmed it. Unconditional surrender. Oh, my God, what will happen to our lads?" and his head dropped on to his hands.

"Damn," said Tony.

Joan left her place and pulled a chair beside Browne. "Listen, Harry," she said. "We must act quickly. Let's call the men together and get them to pledge only to go back as one body. No victimization. All or none."

Joan's quick brain had remembered her old engineer. He must be saved.

Browne looked doubtful. I doubt if we could organize it. I've thought of it." But Joan's optimism was infectious. "All right, then," he said. "Come on. I'll get the boys out to bell a meeting."

There was no need. By evening the news was round the town and the market-square was packed. The Town Hall, a fine relic of Kelsall's eighteenth-century days, was offered by the Town Clerk for a meeting, but it was hopelessly inadequate. The square was jammed with humanity.

The little group of Trades Council officials went on to the Mayor's balcony. There were cheers and just a little booing.

Those faint boos put Joan on her mettle. "Oh, for a loud speaker!"

"There is a megaphone we use for the police sports," timidly suggested the Town Clerk.

With the aid of it they tried to address the crowd in turns. Gerry's voice carried much the best. New power seemed to come into his overtired body. The curt, simple sentences he barked through the megaphone carried right across the square.

"You must preserve your front unbroken. You stood together in the trenches, don't let your pals down now. You came out together. You must go back together. Let all here pledge themselves not to go to work till every striker gets his job back. All or none. Hands up as your pledge."

Every hand seemed to go up at the signal. It was a great sight. Gerry had stopped a stampede back to work. Joan was thrilled. This was a new side of the careless lad; this was the Gerald Blain who at eighteen had commanded men and won his D.S.O.

"He's the man I want beside me in a tight corner," said Harry Browne to her. "That other pal of yours was a bit too anxious to get back to his fleshpots when the fun was over."

"That's horribly unfair," said Joan hotly; but Browne shrugged his shoulders. "Blain hasn't slept much this week with the pain in his old wounds, but he wouldn't leave us to face the music," he said, as he turned away.

Next day the whole country was acting on the advice that Blain had instinctively given to the Kelsall engineers. Employers tried to take advantage of the *débâcle* by demanding, as the price of getting back their jobs, that the men should accept less pay and, in some cases, leave their unions. The railwaymen were the shock troops in that battle, and though the agreement they had to sign was humiliating they went back as a body. Victimization was worst in the engineering and printing trades. Very regretfully Gerry and Joan had to leave these difficulties to the local officials, once the main question was settled.

Tony handed over Red Joan to Harry Browne. "I bought her for the strike. Let her finish the job. Sell her for what she will fetch, and use the money for anyone left out," he said.

Browne smiled his gratitude, and as they drove away in Mary Maud's Lanchester, Joan looked back at the young man standing on the steps of the Trades Hall Yesterday he had been a dictator, to-day he was a victimized workman. For a week he had shown his mettle as an organizer, had risen to a great occasion. Now, if he were lucky, he would get a job as an engineer at forty-five shillings a week, and if unlucky — Joan shuddered as she thought of the hopeless tramp for work — the Labour Exchange queue. "We must do something for Harry Browne if he can't get a job," she said to Tony, who was sitting with her in the back of the car.

"Of course we will. I'll see him all right," and Tony slipped his arm round her, but as she laid her head against his shoulder, and felt his lips brush her forehead, Joan was thinking of the hundreds of Harry Brownes the strike would leave stranded, and whom no one would see all right. And because she was silent Tony was happy in the belief that she was responding to his wooing.

· · · · ·

Gerry dropped Tony and Joan at Gordon Square. He had not spoken more than half a dozen sentences on the three-hour drive, and he refused Joan's invitation to come up and see Mary Maud. "I don't want to see anyone just now, Joan. I'll ring up some time," and with that he drove away.

Mary Maud received them with rapture. "My dears, at last you are back. Now I shall know what really has happened. Is the strike on or off, and what about the miners?"

"Steady — one at a time," laughed Tony.

At a glance she saw that he was excited and happy and that Joan was silent and rather miserable, but as they sat round the fire Joan huddled at Tony's feet, with her arm round his knees.

"They've gone quite a long way, then," thought Mary Maud, as she got out drinks, for the hospitable woman could not have a guest in her house for even five minutes without insisting on their taking refreshment. It was Tony, not Joan, who told the story of their adventures.

"Gerry was A1 at that last meeting," he concluded. "Honestly, I didn't think he had it in him. He could be a big figure in the Labour Movement if he'd chuck this pacifist stunt of his and go in for Parliament."

"You'll have to persuade him, Joan. It would be nice for the two of you to go there together," said Mary Maud.

"Yes," said Joan. That was her only remark during Tony's tale.

"Joan is dead tired, and a bit hipped at the result. Ought to get her to bed. I'll move along."

"Where to?" asked his hostess, with an embarrassed little laugh.

"Home, of course. May I use your 'phone? I'd better ring up Helen and tell her I'm coming."

Joan looked up startled. "But — after all this ... the O.M.S. ..."

Tony bent over her. "Dear heart, the strike is over now, and I've got to keep Helen sweet for lots of reasons."

Joan flushed hotly. Tony turned to Mary Maud and said lightly as he picked up the telephone, "And I simply must get a change of clothes."

"That you, Helen? Yes, Tony speaking ... yes, I'm in London ... just got back to Mary Maud's ... I'm coming over ... I'll be along in five minutes."

Joan didn't move from her huddled position by the fire as Tony bade good-bye to Mary Maud. He bent over her. "Get a good rest to-night, dear one. I can come over and see you in the morning, can't I?"

Joan looked up at him and smiled. "Of course, my dear."

After he had gone, the two women sat silent before the fire. Mary Maud was one of those rare persons able to give silent sympathy and ask no questions.

When Tony left Gordon Square he did not walk very rapidly towards his own flat. His telephoning to Helen had not been the casual business it had seemed to Mary Maud and Joan. Fifteen years of marriage to Helen Hanray had left Tony with an almost morbid fear of showing what he was really thinking about any personal matter. During the drive from Kelsall with Joan's slender body in the circle of his arm, he had been considering how best to tackle Helen. He came to the conclusion that if, as seemed likely, he had to ask her to agree to divorce him quietly, it was no use beginning with a row about the sides each had taken in the strike. He stood for a moment by the railings in Russell Square and looked across at the silhouette made by the towers of the Imperial Hotel against the sky.

It was barely a fortnight since he had first met this girl from the North, and yet he was contemplating breaking the habits of fifteen years and, for her sake, plunging into the thing he dreaded above all others — a stand-up fight with his wife. But Joan was worth it. She had dragged him out of his comfortable life, given him excitement, the feel of power, of being in touch with reality. The man who had sat at his desk polishing his witty, cynical stories, leaving any practical decisions to his wife, had been made to take part in a fierce class-struggle, drive night and day, live hard, speak at great meetings, be accepted (of all the comic things) as a Labour leader by virtue of the trade union credentials which through Joan's influence he had been given. He had loved it. Tired and grimy at Kelsall, he had sighed for his London comforts, but as he stood in the square under the bright May moon he felt he couldn't go back to the old quiet existence, to the old exclusive circles of experts and critics and Bloomsbury *littérateurs*. He would be forty this year. He and Helen would soon be the typical middle-aged couple, getting on each other's nerves, yet keeping together because no one else wanted their love. Joan, at that moment, meant more to Anthony Dacre than a woman with whom he had fallen suddenly and violently in love. She was youth, life, excitement, reality — something challenging and inspiring, which made his old, cushioned world seem not only tame but rather dingy. Yes, Helen and he would have to face things. He would see Joan to-morrow. If she were willing to take him without a formal divorce, then things might be arranged with a minimum of disturbance and fuss, but what Joan wanted she must have. No price, he felt, was too high to pay for her love and inspiration.

As he turned the key in the door he had not entered for a fortnight, Tony could not help a little sinking in his stomach — a wish that he were coming from a victorious rather than a defeated army. But Helen was a very clever woman. She welcomed him as casually as though he had merely been out to dinner. A supper-tray was laid beside her and she was making coffee. She had a message from his publishers about his new book of short stories, and that tided them over the first awkward moment.

To have ignored the strike completely would have left Tony with an uncomfortable feeling of inferiority, of the victor being generous to the defeated, so Helen laughingly told yarns about her side, ridiculous incidents — how Bowyer-Blundell had tried to drive a train with a book of instructions in one hand, and was heard to declare that the bally bits ought to be labelled; how Lord Rossalber had stormed round the O.M.S. headquarters wanting to know what on earth was the use of having a general strike if a man couldn't bring out his newspapers to tell people about it, and demanding sympathy because the scoop of the century was being cornered by Churchill. Did the fellow think he could hatch newspapers by sitting on all the available paper supplies? Tony roared with laughter at Helen's deadly mimicry, and they talked far into the night, apparently the best of friends. He was dimly aware at the back of his mind that Joan and Gerry would have been in a fury at Helen's cool assumption that the whole thing had been rather a lark, and that if Cook and Churchill could be hanged together on the same apple-tree, everything would comfortably settle down and be as things had always been.

But Tony was essentially middle-class. He had none of that rigid, working-class patriotism which was Joan's inspiration and which Blain had so wholeheartedly adopted. Helen made you look through the other end of the telescope — at little figures very far away doing rather ridiculous things. Actually, she was feeling her way very carefully. The strike had given her a bad fright about this husband whom she had come to regard almost as part of the furniture and to treat accordingly. His march out of the house had awakened her to the danger she was in, and made her respect him. This mere girl, Joan Craig, would have to reckon with Helen Hanray if she tried to annex Tony.

As he rose with, "Good Lord, two o'clock, we must get to bed," Helen said quietly, "We ought to do something for the miners' children, Tony. Farmiloe has agreed to let me have the theatre for another month, so we could arrange some matineés. You will help, won't you?"

"Rather, it's a fine idea," and Tony went to his room sleepily feeling that Helen wasn't a bad sort after all.

CHAPTER XIII

Helen felt quite satisfied with the results of her careful reconciliation. She would have liked to have continued the treatment, but for that she had no time. Farmiloe, the lessee of the Princess's Theatre, had been generous, but the production of *Resurrection* had to be put in hand at once. They were to open on the following Monday and in the days that were left Helen had not a minute to spare. She telephoned to Mary Maud to make sure that the promised financial backing would be still forthcoming, and finding her friend apparently quite amiable, Helen ventured a kindly inquiry after Miss Craig. Joan was overstrained and had a cold. She was resting quietly at Gordon Square for two or three days before going back to her work in the North, she was told. All this seemed satisfactory, and Helen plunged into her own absorbing work — Joan, her husband, and the General Strike fading like shadows into the background of her mind.

Tony was thus able to devote himself completely to Joan during her brief holiday, without having to make any explanations. As he breakfasted late, and came back to his own rooms at night, he hardly saw Helen during the whole time. The lovely weather of the summer of 1926, which was to play such an important part in defeating the miners in their seven months' fight, set in early. Joan and Tony enjoyed to the full the long, warm spring days. They drove every day out into the Surrey moorlands. They took books which they never looked at and picnic baskets which they found most useful. Mary Maud lent them her car and did not interfere. She felt vaguely uncomfortable, but did not quite know what to do. She would not warn Helen. Curiously enough, Miss Meadowes, who of the whole group had had least to do with the strike, felt most vindictive towards Mrs Dacre and the O.M.S. Hers was the bitterness of the non-combatant, familiar enough in all wars. She would have withdrawn her financial guarantee from Helen's production if it hadn't been for Tony. She wanted to keep in touch with Helen for his sake, but beyond that Mrs Dacre must look after herself.

One perfect afternoon the two lovers had camped above the Devil's Punchbowl,[89] Joan sitting on the motor cushions, her chin cupped in her hands, gazing across at the lovely distance, while Tony smoked on the heather beside her.

"Two more days of this — and then Leeds."

"My darling, it's impossible. I can't let you go." Tony pulled himself up and drew her to him.

"I must. My work is waiting, piling up fast."

"Oh, Joan, I can't live without you. What shall we do?"

"I've got to get on with my work, Tony."

The man bit savagely on his pipe. Damn this business of women's work. Why on earth did attractive girls like Joan want to work? Why couldn't they leave that to the plain women who had no other goods to take to market? It was all right getting keen on work till their mate came along, it made them more interesting, but it was time to drop all that nonsense when a lover's arms were waiting. That brought him up sharply against another thought. What was he to offer Joan? He wanted to suggest that he should take a flat for her. They could have great fun furnishing it. It would be a lovely cosy refuge from Helen's house. He could afford to give her an income, and they would be wonderfully happy together. One glance at Joan's clear, honest face made Tony realize afresh how impossible was that pet scheme of his. Joan Craig would be no man's kept toy. Joan was worth his all. Tony removed his pipe from his mouth, and took her hand in his.

"Joan," he said, very earnestly, "if Helen will divorce me quietly, will you marry me?"

"Yes, of course, my dear" she said.

At the back of his mind, even as he took her in his arms, Tony felt the faintest little flash of irritation. Joan seemed to take his offer so completely for granted, as if he were a free man. Did she think a man could walk up to his wife and remark, "Oh, I want you to divorce me," as calmly as if he were saying, "I won't be in to dinner to-night?" But as Joan melted towards him, all that was forgotten in the sweetness of her, and her white neck below her strong black mop of hair.

• • • • •

It was nearly eight when they got back. Mary Maud met them in a flurry, dressed as for an important evening function.

"Really, this is too bad, Tony. Have you forgotten it's Helen's first night and the play starts at eight-fifteen?"

"Good Lord!" said Tony. "And I promised to be at the theatre early. I must scramble into dress togs."

"Take the car, and call back for us as soon as you can," called Mary Maud, as he darted down the steps.

"I haven't an evening dress," objected Joan. "And, anyway, why do you want to go dressed up like that to the theatre? Nobody sees you in the dark."

"My dear, every one sees you. That's what most people go to first nights for — the intervals, not the play."

"My people go to see the play." Joan was stubborn.

"Now there isn't time for any arguments about the class-war, Joan," said her friend, her irritation quite forgotten, "and you have got an evening dress, because I've bought you one. If you don't want the whole world to see you in that frock, let alone Tony, then you're no woman but a shameless, unsexed hussy. Suzanne is waiting to help you, so do hurry."

There was a squeal of delight when Joan darted from the bathroom into her bedroom. "Oh, Mary Maud, it's too heavenly!"

The dress laid on the bed was of soft gold lamé, with a wide bow on the hip of gold shot with purple and red. A too critical eye might have said it was a little old for Joan, but when she was arrayed in it, with gold slippers to match, it gave her a touch of dignity which her thinness required.

"It's too lovely for me, Mary Maud."

"Not it. Hello, here's Tony. He *has* been quick. Let him see you in it, and then I'm going to wrap you in my fur cloak."

Mary Maud was well satisfied with her purchase when she saw Tony's eyes, but he said teasingly, "Some strike leader, my word."

"I know. I feel a pig, but it's all Mary Maud's fault," laughed Joan.

The production of the Russian play was certainly marvellous, though Joan found herself wondering why it was necessary to go to so much expense to be miserable, and why some one didn't advertise throughout Czarist Russia for at least one cheerful person. There must surely have been some, but apparently no Russian author had ever met one.

They went behind the stage with Tony when it was over, to congratulate Helen and the actors. Mary Maud had cause to wonder whether she had not made a mistake in giving Joan such a frock. For the first time Helen saw Joan as a rival in her own sphere. Mrs Dacre was magnificently attired in an unusual robe of red with Russian embroideries. It was not a kindly dress to a very overstrained woman of forty. Mary Maud felt that by Joan's frock, in which the girl looked not pretty-pretty, but a beautiful and distinguished woman, she had given Tony's wife a danger signal of which full advantage would be taken.

Dacre, of course, realized nothing of this. Manlike, he chose the following morning, when Helen was resting at home and thus had 'a moment to spare,' to broach the subject of the divorce. What actually passed between them Mary Maud never knew, but it was a very subdued Tony who called on her in the early afternoon.

"Helen won't hear a word about a divorce. Simply went up into the air about it," he said, thankful to find his trusted confidante alone.

"What did you say?"

"Oh, of course, I said that if she didn't I should simply go and live with Joan."

"And how did she take that?"

Tony refilled his pipe. "She said that if I did she would start proceedings, citing Joan as co-respondent," he said slowly.

"But, my goodness, that mustn't happen." Mary Maud was thoroughly alarmed. "It would end Joan's career completely."

"You all seem very concerned about Joan's career," he said bitterly. "Perhaps when she is up against this, Joan may actually put her love for me before this precious career."

Mary Maud stood up and, what was very rare for her, addressed Dacre as though he were a public meeting.

"Listen, Tony," she said earnestly, "you must understand this. Joan is a very unusual girl. She is young yet, in some ways younger than her years, but she has a great future before her. This strike has shown that to people who matter. I am not going to have her life wasted by a miserable, sordid business in the courts. It's just not going to happen."

"Then perhaps you will tell me what is going to happen? I love Joan. She tells me she loves me. I'm going to have her on any terms she will accept. If she agrees to face the music, what can you do?"

Mary Maud sat down again. She played for time. "Don't tell Joan anything of this yet, Tony. Let me see Helen first. I have a scheme. It's just possible I can induce her to change." Dacre was only too glad to be relieved of another scene that day. "Well, if you can work miracles, I'll be grateful. You know as well as I do what Helen's like when she has made up her mind, but I'll leave it to you. When's Joan coming back?"

"She is out to lunch with Gerry Blain. He came back from Kelsall last night. They said they would be back before three. When they come in, will you take Joan out as soon as she'll go and leave me to talk with Gerry?"

"Has Blain anything to do with your scheme?" Tony's voice was rather hard. He could not help being a little jealous of his friend and Joan.

"I must ask you to trust me in this, Tony. Oh, bother, here they are back again. You will trust it all to me, won't you?"

"All right," said Tony hurriedly, as Joan and Gerry came in.

Dacre was honestly shocked and grieved at Blain's appearance. His face was white and drawn with pain, and he was limping badly. "Good God, man, what have you been doing? Where on earth have you been?"

"I'm just back from Kelsall." Gerry wearily lowered himself into the nearest chair. "The employers there have been playing merry hell with the men. There are hundreds victimized."

"Oh — er — ye-es. I believe I did see something about it in the papers."

Blain coloured at the older man's detachment. "Very nice of you, I'm sure," he murmured.

The women tactfully intervened, but Gerry now rose to go. "I'm sorry, I must be getting along." Mary Maud was desperate. If Gerry slipped through her fingers now, goodness only knew when she would get him again.

"Could you drop me at Swan and Edgar's?[90] Would it be out of your way?"

"Of course not, if you are going now."

Mary Maud soon returned in her hat and coat, but when she was in his car she said very earnestly, "Gerry, I don't want to go shopping. I want to talk to you. Could I come to your rooms, or will you come into a café with me?"

"I'm not much in the mood for talking, Mary Maud, especially if it's Joan you want to talk about."

"It is, and you must, Gerry. I'm sorry, but you've got to help me."

"Righto, come to my digs. I can't even pretend to drink any more tea.."

Mary Maud had never been to Gerry's rooms, and she looked round the shabby sitting-room in Great Ormond Street with dismay. Certainly no decorators had been at work here. The furniture was fairly comfortable but obviously belonged to the landlady. Gerry's only possessions seemed to be a desk and the books overflowing the old-fashioned bookcase.

Gerry saw her glance. "It's a hole, but it's comfortable," he smiled. "I got the landlady to remove all the pictures — they were war scenes — and all her ornaments, which got in my way. Now it quite suits. Do you mind if I lie down?" He pulled a long, wide sofa-cushion out of a corner and stretched himself wearily upon it.

"Gerry, you are crocky. Aren't you doing too much? Won't you come down to my place at Ashstead and let me nurse you?"

"No, thanks. I'll be all right. All this knocking around gives me gyp, but the old body has damn well got to get used to it. Now fire away."

Mary Maud found it hard to begin. She threw off her coat, slowly removed her gloves, and then said, looking into the fire, "Joan has promised to marry Tony if he can get a divorce, but Helen won't hear of it."

"Joan told me the first, and I guessed the second would happen," said Gerry, lighting a cigarette. "What about it? Will they live together, anyway?"

"If they do, Helen says she will go for a divorce all right then and cite Joan."

"Phew!"

"Quite. That means the end of Joan's career."

"Well, you wanted her to be sacrificed, do you remember? — but this is a damned funny altar to choose for the ceremony."

"She is not going to be sacrificed on that altar. That's where you are going to help."

"Joan doesn't know about Helen? I rather gathered from what she was saying at lunch that she assumed Helen's nobility as a matter of course."

"No, she doesn't know. Tony was telling me when you and Joan came in after lunch. I made him promise not to tell her until I saw you."

"No wonder he wasn't frantically interested in my Kelsall engineers," said Gerry, feeling he had done his friend an injustice. "But where do I come in? Am I to offer myself as a consolation prize to Helen? Man, one, rather damaged, but can be used as fireside ornament?"

Mary Maud had to laugh. She leaned forward to take a cigarette from his box, and then said quietly, "Do you remember, Gerry, that when we were talking about Tony and Joan before the strike you said that if Helen was ever cruel to Joan, or difficult about her and Tony, you knew something that would make her see reason?"

"Did I say that really?"

"It was something like that, Gerry. Why is it you hate Helen so much? You have been a close friend of Tony's ever since the War, but you never go to his house or meet Helen if you can help it. You used to be quite friendly with her during the War. I remember now."

"What observation! What memory!"

"Gerry, don't be aggravating. If there is any way you can help to make her change her mind, now is the time."

"But do I want her to change it?"

"What *do* you mean?"

"Well, suppose I wanted to marry Joan myself? If she can't marry Tony, perhaps in time she might be persuaded to marry me."

"But, Gerry, when I suggested that, when I hoped you would care for her, you said you were too much of a crock to marry anyone, and, anyway, you wanted to devote yourself to work."

"I wasn't in love with Joan then. She was a fine girl, and I liked her immensely. When I saw that Tony was keen I advised him to go ahead. I thought that anything that gave Helen Dacre a shock was all to the good."

"But you can't play fast and loose with people, Gerry. If you withdrew then and let Tony have a free field, you can't come in now and take advantage of his difficulties."

"I'm not taking advantage. I haven't said a word to Joan."

"But this is unlike you, Gerry. What has happened to you? And what has made you change your mind about Joan?"

"The strike, Mary Maud. She was magnificent. You should have seen her at

Kelsall when we knew the truth about the surrender. She was a man in a million, the way she seized on just what had to be done to save the situation. And then, when I came back to London, things had altered."

"How?"

"My father is dying. I went to see him. The doctors say he cannot live another three months. His heart is in a dreadful condition."

"Oh, Gerry, I'm sorry."

"I am, too. He wasn't a bad old sort in some ways, though he gave my mother no sort of a life at all."

"But what difference does this make, Gerry? You always said you wouldn't touch his money."

"I am not going to, at least for myself. But he told me that I was his only heir, subject to Mother having what she wants. If I don't take it, it goes to the Exchequer after her death. The old man won't make any alternative provision."

"You had reckoned on that, hadn't you?"

"Yes, before the strike. I thought it a good way out. Sort of poetic justice that all those war profits should go back to the national treasury. But since the strike I realize that Father's money would simply be a windfall over which that blighter Churchill would smack his lips, and, by God" — Gerry started to a sitting position — "not one farthing above the death duties shall he touch."

"So you are going to accept it?"

"I promised the Pater I would. That made him awfully happy. Poor old chap, it's little enough one can do for him now. But I'm going to use every cent of it to fight this crowd, the crowd that made the War and that are out to beat the miners. I've been talking to Joan, and she is full of ideas. I'm going to found a Labour Training College,[91] and train a lot of these lads who have been victimized as propagandists. Then I'm going to pay them a salary and turn them loose as organizers and propagandists. It will be a new order — a sort of Socialist Order of St Francis, with all the guile of the Jesuits.[92] That will hit this Tory crowd where it hurts. In every village my lads will go, and by the time the General Election comes we will have made a difference to some of their 'safe seats.' Joan is keen as mustard. The college is her idea. I only thought of paying salaries, but training a good corps is better. And she wants women propagandists too."

"Joan could help you with that, even if she were Tony's wife."

"Of course, but I want her to help as my wife."

"Then, Gerry, you've got to fight fair, and leave the choice with Joan herself."

"That's what I'm doing."

"Not if you are free and Tony is bound. Not if you can provide money for her pet schemes, and going to Tony means giving up her work altogether."

"If she loves Tony she won't hesitate."

"Oh, what cant you men talk about love! You seem to think that anyone of you is worth giving up all that a woman has lived for. See the other side. Do you want Joan to marry you when she loves Tony because you can give her the means to do all the work of which she has dreamed?"

"That is not what's worrying you. You are afraid she will chuck her work and go away with Tony."

Mary Maud's eyes filled with tears. "Gerry, I want to save Joan for her work. It may be she will have to face the choice, but I want to save her if I can. She is so young yet."

"It would be better if you let folk stand on their own feet and face their own problems. Joan has had to face plenty, I guess."

Mary Maud sat silent, but the tears quietly rolled down her cheeks. Gerry was silent too. Then he put his hand out and clasped hers. "Cheer up, my dear, I'll tell you everything; though whether you will feel any more cheerful when you know …" He shrugged his shoulders.

Mary Maud blew her nose, wiped her eyes and rather nervously lit another cigarette.

"You've often teased me about my hating women," Gerry began quietly. "Well, this is why."

Mary Maud held her breath as he paused. She was going to hear Gerry's mysterious story at last. He went on:

"You knew Gilbert Murchison, didn't you? He was senior to me and my great pal. One of the earliest Flying Corps men to do big things."

"Yes, I remember," she said softly. "A queer man, I thought, a bundle of nerves, though he must have been very brave. He was killed at home in an accident, wasn't he?"

"That was the story. Did you know that he was Helen Dacre's lover?"

"Goodness, no!"

"He was desperately in love. Spent all his leaves with her. You remember Tony was out East practically the whole war?"

"Yes, I know."

"It was at the beginning of 1918. We were given special leave, Gil and I. We had just been through an awful time, and Murchison's nerves were in a bad state. I don't mean he was ever funky in the air. He did incredible things — he was our biggest stunt merchant, but on land he sort of went to bits. I kept with him all I could. Our colonel was one of the most understanding blokes I ever met, and he kept us together. On leave with Helen Dacre, Gil was absolutely happy. He idealized her beyond all reason. On this leave we had to go back on the Sunday night. I was rather keen on a friend of Helen's — Violet Legarde —"

"Not the dancer?"

"That's the girl. She was only a kid, of course, but great fun. We were spending the last evening together, and I was to meet old Gil on the midnight from Victoria. Something was queer about Vi that night. Talked about not missing the leave train till I asked her if she was anxious for me to go. About eleven she insisted on my 'phoning Helen's flat to be sure Gil was catching the train. They weren't there, and she broke down with some wild story about Helen making him miss his train. I told her no power on earth could make Gil do that. We got to the train about eleven-thirty, having called at Helen's flat, but it was all in darkness. I said they must have gone out to supper and a show. But as the train was moving, there was still no Gil. I shouted to Vi and made her promise to find him and get him off by the morning train."

"I suppose it was pretty serious missing the leave train. Had Helen kept him on purpose?"

"It wouldn't have been so very serious if he had caught the morning train. Chaps did miss their trains often enough and there was a row — but with a man of Gil's standing the colonel wouldn't have said much if he had produced anything that could stagger as an excuse."

"Didn't he catch the morning train?"

"He never came back."

"Gerry, what had happened?"

"He was posted as a deserter, of course. But he had simply disappeared. He reported a month later to the R.F.C. headquarters. While he was waiting to see the colonel — the orderly didn't know him, of course, though he was just an officer with a message and put him in a waiting-room — he blew his brains out."

"Gerald! Oh, my dear, what *had* happened?"

"Before he went to see the colonel he posted a letter to me, telling me all about it. He blamed only himself — he couldn't face another fight ... but I knew the truth. I'd often had to deal with him in that mood. If Helen had helped him he would have caught the leave train and got over it. She didn't. She persuaded him to desert. Took him disguised (the letter said he had disguised himself as an old man, but you can guess who had done that) to her little cottage in Norfolk. After a month — God, what a month it must have been — he decided to give himself up. His letter said he would pay the full court-martial penalty for his desertion, but evidently the waiting shook his nerve and he took the easiest way out."

"Gerry, what an awful story; but, really, was Helen to blame? She might have been trying to be kind."

"Helen knew his weakness as well as I did — and his strength. The decision must have rested with her, and she helped him to desert. She killed him, and she killed his mother too."

"Gerry, they didn't tell his mother? She didn't get to know really?"

"Of course she did. They went to her as soon as the military police were warned of his desertion. It was terrible. And, of course, there was no pension, and she hadn't a bean. Her husband had died when Gil was a baby, and all her hopes were built on him. She had nearly starved herself to educate him. I went to see her on my next leave. She was dying in poverty. Her feeling against Helen was terrible, though of course she didn't know the whole truth. My mother took her in and looked after her, but she only lived a few weeks."

There was silence in the room. Then Mary Maud said in a tense, hard voice, "I never really liked Helen, but I always admired her. I knew she was hard, but how could she do a thing like that? Does she know that you know?"

"No, she wasn't in London when I came home on leave. I had ideas that if ever I met her I'd lend her my revolver and one cartridge and tell her she could take Gil's way out as the price of my silence. But I crashed when I went back, and by the time I had struggled or to my feet again Tony was at home, and somehow I'd seen so much violence and death I couldn't face any more, so I just kept out of her way. But I couldn't stand women after that — silly, I know — and the women I met after the Armistice didn't improve matters."

Mary Maud dried her eyes. "Thank you for telling me, my dear. I know what it must have meant. You will leave it to me, then. I can use it as I like." She rose to go.

"As you like, Mary Maud. Forgive my getting up, will you?"

As she left the room Miss Meadowes looked back at the tragic, broken figure stretched before the fire, alone with its pain of body and mind, and a great lump came in her throat. Tony or Gerry? She felt that if Joan could have seen him then her choice might be difficult.

CHAPTER XIV

Mary Maud felt she must see Helen at once and confront her with Gerry's story. If she slept on it she knew her courage would ooze away. There was just the possibility that Helen would not have gone as yet to the theatre.

Hurrying to the flat, Miss Meadowes found her quarry writing letters, though dressed to go out. Helen stiffened as Mary Maud was shown in. After the conventional greetings she waited for the older woman to begin. Mary Maud was terribly nervous under that cold gaze, but pulling herself together she began in a low voice, "I've come to see you about Tony and Joan."

"Then I'm sorry, because I do not propose to discuss the matter. I have told my husband my decision and it is no concern of anyone else."

"It concerns Joan, and because of that it concerns me. I'm sorry, too, Helen, I don't want to intrude, but you simply must listen. I have certain things to tell you."

"I do not want to hear them. Frankly, Mary Maud, I'm astonished at your coming here. You have thrown this girl at Tony's head. You have made endless opportunities for them to meet. For all I know, they have been living together at your house" — Mary Maud made a horrified gesture — "I say, for all I know," went on Helen.

"Whenever I heard of Tony he was at Gordon Square, and so was that girl. After having done all the mischief you can, you actually come here to plead that I shall divorce the husband with whom I have lived happily for fifteen years in order to please a girl he has known for less than a month. I am ashamed of you. And you call yourself my friend."

"I do not think we shall call ourselves friends much longer," said Mary Maud. "Gerry Blain has told me the whole story of Gilbert Murchison and you."

Helen Dacre grasped the arms of her chair — as still as if she were frozen. There was silence. Mary Maud, fluttering, gentle soul, was afraid.

Then in a low, hard voice Helen said, "And so it has come to this. You entice away my husband with this girl, and then you come to taunt and threaten me with my tragedy of eight years ago. What have I done to you, Mary Maud, that you should persecute me like this?"

"Oh, Helen, I am not persecuting you. I didn't think of that. I just thought that neither you nor Tony were particularly happy and ... Oh, I am sorry but ... when Gerry told me that awful story I ..."

Helen was hardly listening to these protestations, but at Gerry's name she looked up. "Yes, you have heard Gerald Blain's story, now you shall hear mine. You always say I have never loved Tony. Well, it's true, but I didn't deceive him. I told him before we were married that I didn't, but he was willing to take the risk. I was a hard-up art student, and even then, young as he was, I knew he would be a success as a writer. We got along all right. When Tony was sent out East because he knew Arabic, I was very much on my own. He never got leave. Then I met Gil Murchison, through Gerry and Vi Legarde. We were soon desperately in love. There was something about Gil, not only his physical strength and beauty and courage, but a queer sensitiveness of mind. We knew we were mates. He spent all his leaves with me — he was fairly fortunate in leave — I suppose because he did such extraordinary stunts. Between each leave I went through agonies. I knew the awful risks he ran. Tony didn't exist for me. I could hardly bear to read his letters. He was in a perfectly safe billet in Cairo, and my Gil was facing a horrible death every day."

"Helen's voice choked for a moment — then she recovered her self-control, and went on:

"It was amazing how Gil escaped for so long, but the effect on his nerves was terrible. He couldn't get away from the thought of the men he had brought down. He had been at Bonn for a year before the War broke out and had lots of German friends. The climax came just before his last leave. A man was brought down, not by Gil, but near where he was. Gil helped to get him out of the wreckage. He was alive, conscious even, but horribly injured. And they recognized each other. They had been to the same lectures at Bonn. That finished Gil. He declared he wouldn't go up again. His colonel ought to have sent him to hospital, but he didn't want to lose him — and so got him leave. He came home to me unexpectedly — you can imagine my joy, Or can you? — I don't know. Anyway, after our first joy in each other, he told me that he had decided never to go back. He had made up his mind to enjoy this leave and then commit suicide."

"Helen, how awful, he couldn't have been sane!"

"Wasn't he? I'm not so sure. Feeling as he did, it was probably thoroughly sane. He would not go on murdering the friends of his student days, for the profit, as he said, of men like Gerald Blain's father."

"What *could* you do?"

"I tried all I knew at first to make him change his mind — in spite of what Gerald Blain has told you, I did do the conventional thing. Then he made me see the horror as he saw it. So I began to think too. I said, 'If you mean to go out, let us have a month together, a perfect month. If you go back now and you kill yourself the first day, we shall have had nothing. Let us have a month and leave me with your child.'"

"But, Helen, how could you, when it meant certain death if he deserted?"

"It meant certain death either way, and I wanted him — my God, how I wanted to be with him."

Helen was silent for a moment. The tears were choking Mary Maud. Helen's voice went on:

"I had this little cottage in the depths of Norfolk. My father had been living there for a time. I disguised Gil as an old man like him — Daddy was tall, fortunately. I had to trust Vi Legarde — except for that one lapse to Gerald Blain she played trumps. We got safely to that little hidden cottage, and then we had our month."

"But, Helen, wasn't it too terrible, knowing the end?"

"While there's life there's hope. I suppose I couldn't have stood it if I had thought he would really die. But I had all sorts of wild plans — pretending he had lost his memory — shell-shock — he had such a marvellous record that I didn't believe they would shoot him for desertion. I still don't think they would have. Gil was wonderful. Whatever happens to me, I had that month of him."

"Couldn't you have stayed on there, hidden?"

"I don't know. It would have been awful for Gil to have been arrested in hiding. But, anyway, we simply didn't think of it. We had fixed our month. We travelled back to town openly by train on the last day — Gil in uniform and I dressed as a nurse. No one took any notice. The Tommies[93] saluted him. It was queer. He left me at my flat, and went to the R.F.C. headquarters. I couldn't believe that I should never see him again. I felt somehow it would come out all right."

"Did he intend to commit suicide, the poor boy?"

"I don't think so. I believe he intended to give himself up, but he was kept waiting — the colonel, whom he knew very well, was busy — and he just went out. Perhaps his subconscious mind had always been determined on suicide. I don't know. Anyway, I was in agony, because, you see, I couldn't get to know anything. In desperation I sent Violet Legarde to see one of the officers she had been very friendly with. That was three days later. He told Violet what had happened."

Mary Maud was sobbing heartbrokenly.

Helen remained quite calm, but her voice, which had softened in the telling, went hard again.

"I had to go on living. I was carrying Gil's child. When I knew this for certain, my one purpose was to keep going for the child's sake. But the strain was too great. I broke down — brain fever or something. Anyway, I was delirious for days — and I lost the child. They told me it would have been a boy.''

Mary Maud knelt by Helen's side and wept into her lap. "You poor lamb, the poor boy, oh, my dear, what you must have gone through."

Helen stroked her hair, and then said very quietly, "This was the tale you were to tell my friends to force me to divorce my husband — who at least has given me a home. But there is always Gil's way out, Mary Maud. If you tell this, I shall take that way, and then your Joan can have Tony."

Mary Maud hugged Helen's waist tightly. "I'm an utter beast, a pig, and a hateful horror," she sobbed. "But, oh, I'm glad I know. I never understood you before, Helen. We all thought you so cool and hard and self-sufficient. You know it is all safe with me whatever happens."

Helen put her limp friend back into a chair and wiped her eyes. For a little while the two women talked of Gil Murchison. Mary Maud was glad of the slight acquaintance she had had with him. Then suddenly she said:

"Helen, forgive me, but I must just say this. Suppose you could get in touch with him now, and told him that Tony loved Joan as he loved you, wouldn't he say, 'Let them be happy'?"

That went straight home. Helen was silent for a time and then said, "Do you believe that Joan Craig really loves Tony like that? I have only seen her twice, but she seems to me more concerned with politics and her work than with loving anyone."

"The strike has been like the War, Helen. People's barriers are down, and feelings grow quickly. I don't believe Tony ever loved as he loves Joan. You denied him your own love, Helen; is it fair to thwart him again?"

Helen remained very quiet, her arms stretched in front of her along her knees, her hands tightly clasped. Her hair was slightly disarranged, her face had become softer.

"I have given up so much, Mary Maud, but I will not stand in the way of their love. If they really love each other they shall be happy."

"Oh, Helen, that is a great thing to say."

Helen stood up and kissed Mary Maud. "Be as good a friend to me as you are to Joan."

"I will, Helen, I really will."

Mrs Dacre went to a mirror and powdered her nose.

"Now I must be getting to the theatre," she said. "I shall be very late. Will you ask Miss Craig to come and see me to-morrow morning at eleven?"

"You want to see Joan?"

"Why not? She and I are the two people most concerned. Tony, apparently, has become merely the prize for the victor. I suppose most men are that, though they don't know it."

Mary Maud was relieved that Helen could joke, even grimly. "It would be a good thing for you both to have a talk," she said lovingly. "I won't keep you. The production was marvellous. You must be happy at the Press cuttings."

"Yes, they are pretty good about the production, but I do wish they didn't want Russian plays to be written by the editor of *Comic Cuts*."

Mary Maud walked back to Gordon Square, having seen Helen into a taxi. She cried silently all the way. Joan and Tony were going to be happy, and she would make it up to Helen. Anything that money could buy Helen should have. If only another Gil Murchison could be found somewhere for her, the dear, unselfish soul felt that the world would indeed be bright.

Friends were filling the house. Mary Maud had forgotten she had bidden them to meet Joan, but Tony and Joan were entertaining manfully.

"Mary Maud looks as though she had been to the dentist and then got a sudden reprieve," said one girl.

"That's just what has happened," laughed her hostess, seizing on so plausible an excuse for her red eyes. In the press she managed to drop a hint to Tony that Helen might not be unreasonable. He gazed at her in amazement.

"You are some miracle-worker, Mary Maud."

"No, I'm not, but try not to see Helen to-night. It would be better not."

"Anything you say goes, bless you," he murmured before claiming Joan for a dance.

CHAPTER XV

Joan was not very anxious to meet Mrs Dacre and her steps dragged as she walked across Russell Square. It was a pouring wet morning and she hated rain like a cat. Feeling thoroughly depressed, she found herself wondering what Gerald Blain was doing. He always cheered one up, but he hadn't been at Mary Maud's party the night before, although he had promised to come. Absorbed in her depression under her umbrella, Joan bumped into a man coming the other way. She started to apologize and found her arm tightly held. It was Tony.

"You look as though you were going to an execution," he said teasingly.

"Perhaps I am. Mary Maud, heaven knows why, promised I should call on your wife at eleven." Joan was both miserable and irritated.

Tony took her umbrella, shut it, and drew her under his. "I'll spare you that, anyway. Let's get out of this infernal rain. Here, taxi —"

"But Mrs Dacre will be-expecting me."

"No, she won't. I was coming to meet you. Get in. What about that pet coffee-place of yours in Henry Street?"

"You are extravagant about taxis," Joan smiled as he sat beside her. "It's only up the street and round the corner."

"No reason for getting wet. Besides, I can be alone with you in a taxi even if it is only for two minutes, and isn't that worth any fare?"

Seated in a discreet corner of one of those little cafés which mild-faced ladies make in the front rooms of Georgian houses in Bloomsbury, Tony felt a little embarrassed knowing what he had to say, but Joan had the knack of curling up and making any little outing into a picnic. She wriggled in her chair, sipping the good hot milky coffee.

"Wish I could sketch."

"Why?"

"Well, wouldn't it be jolly to keep sketches of all the jolly little sprees one has? A book with pictures of all the places where one has been perfectly happy."

"Are you perfectly happy now, Joan?" Tony leant towards her, his voice deep and his eyes hot.

"My dear, what else — good coffee — my pet *café* — a fire on a wet day, and *you*."

"Bless you for the 'you,' even at the end of the catalogue."

"A crescendo of blessings," she smiled. "And now tell me why I am here instead of talking to your wife." Joan's calm directness helped Tony round an awkward corner. He put some more sugar into his coffee and stirred it thoughtfully.

"Shall I begin at the beginning?" he said.

"No, tell me what's worrying you and we can talk all round it afterwards." Tony looked gratefully at her. He liked the way she went straight to the centre of things. "Well, then, this is the position. Helen wouldn't hear of divorcing me quietly when I asked her, but Mary Maud saw her yesterday and I had a long talk with her this morning."

"Yes." Joan selected a chocolate biscuit with much care.

"Joan, it's hard to tell you, but it's like this. Helen and I were never much more than pals to each other. The love side of marriage bored her. She was keen on her work. Perhaps I wasn't very wise … anyhow, it's over … and we settled down to a life together that was quite bearable. At least, it was till I met you." Tony added yet another lump of sugar into the coffee he was not attempting to drink, and stirred it with deliberation.

"Yes," said Joan softly.

"I didn't think that under the circumstances she would take it too badly, but — Helen is as proud as Lucifer, and also — well, I suppose she has a very strongly developed property-sense. I suppose our wanting to be together has hurt her pride and her feeling of possession in me — it couldn't have been any love for me; and so she wouldn't hear of any arrangement. Then Mary Maud saw her yesterday …"

"What happened?"

"I don't know. Neither of them would tell me. Perhaps Helen felt a bit different when she had slept on it, or Mary Maud got her to see reason. She was a brick this morning."

"Yes," said Joan.

"My dear," Tony now plunged boldly in. It was obvious that he hated discussing his wife but was determined to get through with it. "My dear, she did try to understand. She said that Mary Maud had made her realize that she could not stand in our way if we really loved each other; that because she had never been able to love me, well — we ought to have a chance. But there was this difficulty … I think you'll see it, Joan. Helen's work is mainly in the theatre, and a divorced woman in the kind of work she is doing would be in a very difficult position. I have seen such women trying to earn their living among men and I know what Helen means. They are considered any man's fair game. I don't know why it should be, but however innocent the woman may have been — well, there's a sort of atmosphere that a certain type of man will take full advantage of, and Helen has to meet a lot of that sort in her work."

"Yes," said Joan.

"Well, you see, dear — and I know you of all people will see her point of view — Helen says that she has done her duty by me, made my home and all that, and that after fifteen years she ought not to be deprived of the protection of my name. I know that sounds Victorian, but her world is very different from yours, Joan, and she meets very different people."

"Yes," said Joan. "Give me a cigarette, there's a dear." Tony produced a case and his lighter and then went on:

"Darling. Helen says why can't I take a flat for you? We could have a lovely nest together and no one need know. I would stay a night or so every week at home, just to keep up appearances, and turn up to act at Helen's shows and parties. You and I could be ever so happy together, and as Helen would be satisfied, well, it would be all right all round."

"Ye-es." said Joan, in a low, doubtful voice.

"Darling one, I haven't shocked you, have I?" Tony cursed himself for bringing her to a *café* to tell her this. He felt that if he could only take her in his arms now, things would look so different to her.

"I should be your mistress, Tony." He noted her hesitation over the word.

"Do names mean anything between you and me, my dear one? You would be my wife in everything that mattered. It's the only way that Helen will agree to … and I do owe her something … I mean, I've got to treat her decently, haven't I?"

"Of course, dear, or we couldn't be happy. But, Tony, it isn't as simple as you seem to think. It would be difficult enough to fit in ordinary marriage with my work, but there would be all sorts of complications this way."

"Joan" — Tony put his elbows on the table, rested his chin on his hand and looked straight into her eyes — "Joan, let's face this now and get it over. Does your work mean more to you than I do?"

"You know I love you, Tony," Joan said very quietly.

"Yes, you have said that, Joan, and I could have kissed your feet when you said it — but what do you mean by it? Do you love me enough to give up your work?"

"Tony, I can't do that. You have no right to ask it. If I agree to Helen's scheme … and perhaps we could manage somehow … you can't want me to give up my work as well."

"I do want it, Joan, and you must."

"But why? Isn't my work for Socialism as important as Helen's decorations?"

"It's because my life went shipwreck before that I'm not facing that again. I can't, Joan, and I won't. I've tried sharing a wife with her job and it doesn't work. I love you, Joan. I want you to be all mine. We can build a wonderful life together if you will come to me, and I can't share you."

"Will you give up *your* work, Tony?"

"Of course not. We must eat, silly" — Tony smiled — "and I only have what I earn."

"Then why not let me earn too?"

"Because I shall earn enough for us both, and because your job — oh, well, we'll talk lots about that some day. I hope your life will be full enough without work outside."

"It's not only the money, either in your job or mine, Tony. If you have your work, why can't I have mine?"

"Because a woman can't have everything, Joan. I know it seems a hard choice, but the choice is there and it's got to be faced. How shall I put it?" Tony felt that somehow the right words would touch her. "It's like this, my dear. When there wasn't any choice, when getting married was a woman's only hope of a decent status, well, she just had to put up with it, and I can understand independent women hating it — people like you, Joan. And I can understand, too, how when chances opened out, when they were allowed to work and do things, how they must have revelled in it. Marriage could take its chance and get fitted in anyhow. They did too much, they overworked at their job, or in their homes, but I can understand that phase, can't you?"

Joan nodded — pleased at his insight. "Well?" she said.

"That phase has passed, Joan, or at least it is passing. It was all right when women were more or less amateurs, when the surprise was not that they did a job well, but that they could do it at all; but now they want more — the best of them, and it is right that they should. They want the entrée into the best jobs, they want to get to the top of the tree — Parliament, the judge's bench, big business."

"Why not?" asked Joan, interested, but unable to see his drift.

"Why not — I'm all for it. But they still remain women, Joan. They can't get away from that basic fact."

"You mean children. But two or three children don't take up a woman's whole life, Tony. She can engage a competent nurse for them."

"Can she engage an equally competent substitute for her husband?"

"Tony, what *do* you mean?"

"Just that, Joan. We hear a lot about women's rights these days. Now let's talk about the man's side of the case for a bit. You unmarried women, and a lot of married ones who ought to have more sense, talk as though making a home was a side-line which any intelligent woman could do in any odd moments, provided she could earn enough to pay a housekeeper and a nurse. It doesn't work, my dear. I know. Women who talk like that have never loved, Joan. Loving your mate and bearing his children and bringing them up is a whole-time job. You can't leave it to servants."

"Kirk, *kinder*, and kitchen,"[94] mocked Joan. I didn't expect this Victorianism from you, Tony."

"If you think what I am trying to say is Victorianism, then I am not getting my meaning across to you, Joan." His voice was stern.

"Tony, I didn't mean to laugh. I want to understand, but isn't all this rather old-fashioned?"

"No, Joan, perhaps I am thinking a bit ahead — to a time when equality is unquestioned, as it is now among intelligent men and women. Given that, a woman, a worth-while woman with the brains and the power that you have, Joan, has to make a choice. She may decide on a career, she may think her work the most important thing in her life. Then, if she is to compete on equal terms with men of her calibre, she has to make it a whole-time job. She may have love affairs, as a man has — she may even marry — but in such a life, if she means to do big things, then work is in the front of the picture, as it would be in a man's life of that type — other things, love, marriage, pleasure, will fall into their place in the background."

"Yes," said Joan, her eyes were shining, "and the alternative?"

"The other choice, my dear — well, its success doesn't appear on the surface, it will not get into the newspapers, but the women I am thinking of, the woman I believe you are, Joan, may find their mate, and they may choose to be his mate. Such women, Joan, could be great lovers and great creators. The wealth of spiritual power that could raise them to a great career could give a new meaning to marriage. In the ecstasy of their passion they would create wonderful children and train them finely. To their husbands they would bring fulfilment and the peace that passeth understanding. These men could do great things for the world. They would express not merely themselves but the inspiration of their union. Does that seem a narrow life to you, Joan, a choice not worth reckoning in the scale with Parliament or leading movements?"

Joan's eyes had filled. She looked at Tony with a new admiration. She felt the quality in him that had made him, deeps that were usually hidden under his pleasant, rather hesitating manner. She wanted to rise to his level.

"I'm not sure that I am worthy to walk that road, Tony."

"Oh, my dear, it is I who am not worthy of you. There are depths in you that you yourself don't know. I feel that. You are not awakened yet, my darling. You have to make the choice without knowing the ecstasy that can be yours. You could be a great lover, Joan."

They were silent. The girl had clasped her hands on the table as though in prayer, her eyes gazed through the window, unseeing and very dark. Dacre wondered what she was thinking. Was it wise to have spoken to her like this in a *café*? If only he could have taken her in his arms. But no, perhaps it was better so. He was deeply in earnest. The choice had to be made. Joan would become completely absorbed in whatever she gave her mind to. He was determined not to be a complacent background to her political life. He loved her with his very soul and she must give him all or nothing.

She turned her eyes slowly to his. Her face was very white. "You would not want a hasty answer, Tony. I must think. I mean — Oh, my dear, you understand, don't you — I've got to look at things afresh."

"Of course, my dear. Let me take you home." He paid the bill and followed her outside. The rain had ceased and the sun was peeping through. He drew her arm through his and held her hand. She felt the nearness, the maleness of him. If only it could always be just like that. At the moment she wanted to give herself utterly to him and let the world sink out of sight. Though they walked slowly, Gordon Square was reached too soon. He looked down at her as they stood for a moment on the steps.

"I won't come in now. May I see you to-night? Will Mary Maud be in then?"

"I don't know. Shall I telephone? Will you be at home?"

"Of course. Then I'll expect you to ring me — say after seven?"

"After seven. Yes."

"Till then, good-bye, my darling one." He stood with his hat raised until she had passed within.

• • • • •

Joan climbed the stairs slowly. When she passed the sitting-room door Mary Maud called to her. Joan had hoped to escape to her own room, but she went in to see what was the matter. Miss Meadowes was not alone. She was sipping chocolate, and a friend, introduced as Miss Legarde, was drinking a cocktail. "Have some chocolate, Joan. It's so bad for my figure, but you can stand it. I don't know why I drink it," she turned to her guest pathetically, "but Suzanne makes it to perfection."

Violet Legarde laughed. "You ought to call her Satan, not Suzanne — she tempts you so often."

Joan refused the chocolate. "I'll go to my room if you don't mind." She looked very white. Her great eyes seemed too big for her small face. She pulled off her hat with an odd little gesture, and the mop of black hair seemed to overweight her slight figure. Mary Maud wondered what had happened, but she said lightly:

"Do. Have a rest before lunch. I'll call you when it's ready."

Utterly unconscious of the part this stray visitor had played in her affairs, Joan went thankfully to her bedroom. Slipping off her mackintosh and shoes, she crept, fully dressed, between the sheets, and pulled the bedclothes over her head. It was an old habit, dating from childhood in her crowded little home. Warm bedrooms were an unknown luxury then. The only chance of any privacy was to slip between the sheets in the dark, cold little room and hope people would forget her.

She tried to think, but found herself praying instead, praying to a God she had almost forgotten since her childhood. She was in a fever of indecision. Longing for Tony, yet wanting to leave this easy London life and get back to work, to her own people, to find out what was happening after the strike. She hated herself for spending this lazy week in London, and hated the thought of going north and leaving Tony. It was in this state that Mary Maud found her. She drew back the bedclothes and pressed a cool hand on the girl's hot forehead.

"Dear child, I don't want to pry if you don't want to tell me, but perhaps I can help a little. Was Helen very difficult?"

"I haven't seen her. Tony came to meet me, I have been having coffee with him."

"I see. Then has Helen been making things difficult with him?"

"Oh, no. She has been generous in her way. Says she is willing for Tony and me to live together, provided Tony will keep up appearances because of her work."

So was this the trouble! Had the little Puritan Northerner been shocked by the suggestion? Mary Maud stroked the girl's hair rhythmically and said aloud: "And did that seem quite impossible to you, my dear?"

"Tony says it is only possible if I will give up my work."

"Give up your work! Tony says that! But surely the whole point of such an arrangement is that all three of you can go on with your work?"

"It sounds like that — but would it be? The decent people trusting me and all the time I should be afraid of being found out. I hate deceiving people."

"Did you say that to Tony?"

"No, we didn't talk about my side of it. I wasn't thinking of it, anyway, when we were talking, but I realized it afterwards."

"What was Tony's point, then?"

"Tony wants all of me or nothing. He says — oh, I can't put it like he did. He made it seem wonderfully fine — and I do see what he means — the woman's choice — a career or a great love."

Mary Maud thought that this was not for him to say, but Joan was in no state for argument. The main point seemed to be that Tony was trying to get his woman all to himself. Naturally, but if Joan was not willing Mary Maud had other plans for her. To the thoroughly lazy woman her *protégée's* life-work had become a very important thing.

"Just splash cold water on your face, and change that crumpled dress. You will feel heaps better. Then come and have a quiet little lunch with me. Suzanne is tempting you with a mushroom omelette. There is nothing so good for a crisis as a really perfect omelette."

Joan had to smile. Mary Maud was always sure that food was the final argument. She dragged herself out of bed and put her head under the bath-tap. Mary Maud was much amused, and helped her rub it dry until the hair stood out all round. "You golliwog. I never knew any woman do that. I wish I could."

"Why don't you? It's a great freshener."

"My dear child — my perfect permanent. Jules, my hairdresser, would have a fit."

"You have too much money ever to do anything you want, Mary Maud."

"True, my child. And if I had no money it would be the same. Doing what one wants is a mirage, a lovely thing we all think is possible sometimes, but quite impossible just now."

The two women talked very little over lunch. Joan told Mary Maud something more of Tony's conversation with her, but she obviously didn't want to discuss it, and her friend did not press her. After Suzanne had brought the coffee they sat silent, each busy with her own thoughts.

Mary Maud's thoughts were very mixed. It was very seldom she ever troubled to think. She prided herself on her instincts. But by this time even she began to realize that instincts can lead one in all sorts of directions at once. She felt that she had tried to interfere in Joan's life and had made a thorough muddle. She had hoped that Joan would be a way of escape for Tony. At the same time she was keen on Joan's work. Now, when through Gerry and Helen's generosity a way seemed to have opened to combine these desirable ends, both Tony and Joan seemed to be raising perfectly idiotic difficulties. Why couldn't they seize happiness when it was offered to them? There weren't too many chances of it in this world. She glanced at Joan's set face, and recalled her talk of sacrifice to Gerry. Why had she always thought of sacrifice in connexion with Joan? This girl needed no urging to be a martyr. Was there anything she could say? ... But at that moment the door-bell rang, and Suzanne came in with a telegram for Joan. The girl opened it almost in a dream, read it, then sat up very straight: "Well, that settles it."

Mary Maud took it from her. "Trouble at Shireport big strike likely return here for instructions to-night if possible." It was signed "Royd."

"Must you go?"

"Of course. Is the boy waiting, Suzanne?"

"Yes, ma'm'selle."

"The railway guide, Mary Maud. Let me see. St Pancras[95] is best for Leeds. There's an express at five o'clock." Joan looked at her watch. "It's half-past three now. I can do it easily. Have you a telegraph-form?"

"You promised to meet Tony at seven, you know," said Mary Maud, handing her a pad of forms from her desk.

"I know. It can't be done. That's just a shilling, Suzanne, and threepence for the boy. Thanks ever so much."

"Won't you at least 'phone Tony to see if he is in? He could see you off at the station."

"What's the use, Mary Maud? Don't you see this settles it?"

"What does it settle? A telegram calling you away to-night, when you were going home to-morrow anyway. Tony will understand if you just explain."

"But — don't you see? — this is what would always happen. Whether I had been married to Tony, with fifteen archbishops at the ceremony, or if I was living with him as he wants, and a call like this came, I should go — whatever promises I had made. Tony sees that. I've been slacking around here since the strike and things got blurred, or I couldn't have hesitated as I did."

"But, Joan dear, you love Tony. I'm sure you do, and you are not the sort to take things lightly."

Joan stood — grasping the top of a table, her knuckles showing white as she pressed it. She wasn't looking at Mary Maud, but across the square in the direction of Tony's home.

"Love. What does that word mean, Mary Maud, the word that every flapper, every cheap journalist is always using? Do I love Tony? In my way, yes. In his way, no." Her voice choked. Mary Maud saw her lip quiver. She put her arms round the girl's shoulders.

"But you wish you did, little one, don't you?"

Joan let her head fall on Mary Maud's soft silk shoulder, and then her backbone stiffened. "This isn't any good, Mary Maud. I'll write to Tony. He will understand. Now I must get ready."

"It's been a hectic time since you woke me up that morning," said Mary Maud when, Joan's packing done, they sat drinking their tea.

"Yes, but Shireport won't be exactly dull if this strike is coming off. And, oh, Mary Maud, I'll be glad to be in the thick of it again. It's where I belong."

When she had seen her young guest into her taxi, Miss Meadowes walked slowly up the stairs to her sitting-room. She nibbled a biscuit very thoughtfully, and then suddenly sat down at her desk and wrote a long letter. The address which Suzanne read as she posted it was: "Captain Gerald Blain, D.S.O., D.F.C., 238 Great Ormond Street, W.C.1."

CHAPTER XVI

Joan wallowed in misery during her four-hour railway journey to Leeds. She had left Mary Maud's flat almost waving her telegram as a flag of independence, but alone in her compartment all she could feel was that the train was taking her farther and farther from Tony. When seven o'clock came, she thought of him sitting near the telephone waiting for her to ring. She heard the bell, saw his eager clutching of the receiver, and then his face when he would hear Mary Maud's voice instead of hers. Hiding herself behind a newspaper from the curiosity of any passer-by in the corridor, she wept till her head ached. By the time she reached Leeds she felt herself a complete martyr. She took a taxi straight to the Royds' house at Roundhay, badly wanting sympathy.

Joan was very fond of Royd's wife, whom every one, even her children, called Bunny. She was little and round and plump — very plump in these days. Her hair had been red in her youth, and even in middle age — she was nearly ten years older than her husband — she still had the soft white skin that usually goes with her colouring. She would have been pretty but for a long upper lip over rather prominent front teeth, from which came her nickname. Bunny Royd expressed quite a lot of things by the twitching of her long upper lip.

"Why, here's our fine London lady at last," was her merry greeting as she opened the door to Joan. In the dimly lit little hall she did not notice Joan's swollen eyes.

"William will pay your taxi. Will-yum," she called, but Royd was behind her. He passed out silently into the garden and Bunny drew Joan into the living-room. It was very much a living-room. Royd's big desk filled the recess by the fireplace, his books and papers flowed from bookshelves on to chairs. The girls' painting, their home lesson-books, and Bunny's sewing were scattered around over the solid table and cheap, easy chairs, but the homely litter gave an atmosphere, not of untidiness, but of just every one comfortably doing what they liked. The place seemed home to Joan's overstrained mind.

"It's nice to be here again, Bunny."

"I am glad you feel that, Joan. William has been expecting you and was rather worried you stayed so long after the strike."

"But he gave me a holiday — he said I might stay a few days."

"This is nearly a fortnight, Joan, and the men are up to the eyes in victimization cases." Royd's deep voice answered as he closed the door behind him.

"But I came as soon as you sent for me."

"The Joan I knew would not have needed sending for."

This was too much. She had come to Leeds feeling a martyr because she had torn herself away from London, and now this … She put her head on her arms and sobbed as though her heart would break. Royd was horrified at the effect of his words, but Bunny realized that there was some deeper cause for such terrible sobbing. Waving her husband away she said:

"Come upstairs with me, Joan. There's no sense in your going back to your digs to-night. You shall have Edna's room."

Bunny took the girl upstairs, lit the gas-fire, took off her dress and shoes, slipped on to her a warm dressing-gown and slippers. Joan was still sobbing and quite limp.

"Now, Joan, out with it. Have you been falling in love with some one down there? You've got to tell Bunny all about it, and get it off your chest."

Through years of friendship Joan trusted Bunny as she could never trust Mary Maud. Bunny was the only person to whom she could lower the reserve of her secret pride. With Bunny's arms tightly round her, she got her self-control back and told the whole story. When it was finished Bunny still said nothing, just stroked Joan's hair quietly, rhythmically.

"What do you think, Bunny?" Joan asked at last.

"I think Mr Dacre is a very wise man," said Bunny, "and he evidently understands you though he hasn't wasted much time. You've only known him a month."

"What does that matter?" said Joan.

"Not much, I admit, with rapid youngsters like you," Bunny smiled, "but, as I say, he understands *you*, my dear. That arrangement couldn't have worked if you tried to go on with your job."

"Other women do it."

"My dear girl, some women can have a husband, three children, half a dozen love affairs, and do a man's work in the world without turning a hair. Some women, just like quite a lot of men, can file their work and their heart-affairs and their consciences all in neat separate dockets and never take any two sections out together. But that's not you nor me, and you know it, Joan. You knew it when that telegram woke you up from your day-dreaming in Miss Meadowes' chocolate-box. Now, pull yourself together. Isn't it so? Where would Mr Dacre be if there was a big strike or an exciting by-election? Joan, if you marry — and I hope you will, for you are far too attractive to be left lying around loose to upset all sorts of men — you will either have to marry someone who will work with you, or else won't mind being parked until you have time to remember his existence."

Joan had to smile. "The neo-Georgian husband succeeds to the Victorian wife," she said.

"Why not? Quite a lot of men like it. Uses up the wife's superfluous energy and makes less demands on him."

"How?"

"Well, think of it — the number of men who come home, tired after a day's work to a strong, healthy woman, fresh as a daisy, who has done nothing all day but potter round after a servant or play golf. The Victorians kept their wives under par — corsets, no air, heavy clothes — used 'em up — but these young Amazons[96] round here want their husbands to dance all night, race round with them — I guess the husbands would be glad if they worked off their energy in any sort of cause."

Bunny was deliberately riding away on a pet hobby-horse to take Joan's mind off her troubles. But the girl was too interested in herself just then.

"That's all true, I suppose, in marriage — but ours would be different."

"Much worse, much more difficult, my kidlet. Marriage was invented to get people safely out of being in love. It's a good buffer. Its very ordinariness prevents people trying to live on their emotions. But a love affair without marriage — Joan dear, it needs a woman with a head as cool as an icepack to steer that through the rapids. I know — I've tried it."

"*You*, Bunny!"

"Yes, even ordinary little me. After a year of it I was exhausted and glad to slip into a real comfortable jog-trot marriage with my William. But the trouble with you, Joan, is that you pour yourself into whatever you are doing like water out of a jug. That's why you are a success where other women fail — but if you go pouring yourself all over the place — well, there'll just be a mess, that's all. Anyway," she went on, as Joan sat gloomily looking at the glow of the gas-fire, "there's no need to be so tragic about it just now …"

"I've made my choice and I'm not going back on it."

"Nonsense. You have made no choice, and don't flatter yourself that you can choose. Deeper things than your mind settle issues like this, Joan dear. You go and get to work at Shireport — get back into harness and away from London and from Mr Dacre. Then the deep desires of your heart will do the choosing. Now, are you coming downstairs to talk to William, or will you just slip into bed and see him to-morrow? It's past eleven."

"I feel sleepy now, bless you, Bunny. It's been a real relief to talk. I'll be bright and shining to-morrow, you'll see."

She was soon in bed, but as Bunny kissed her good-night and switched off the light Joan suddenly remembered that she had not told her one word about Gerry Blain.

CHAPTER XVII

At Shireport, where she went next day after a brief interview with Royd, Joan found the situation sufficiently complicated to leave little time for thinking of any other worries. Shireport, as well as being an outlet for a coal area, was rapidly developing as a light engineering centre. The federated employers of the older-established firms had always maintained pretty good relations with their men through the equally old-established craft unions. But a new firm had recently built a large factory in the place. It would not join the employers' association and openly declared its determination to have nothing to do with trade unions. "I pay a man what he is worth to me," Mr Ben Lewis, the young American-trained managing director, boasted on every possible occasion, and as he paid higher wages than the older firms he had attracted the best workers. But these men remained in their unions. During the General Strike they came out with the rest on that Wednesday morning when the strike was called off at noon. This gave Lewis his opportunity. At first he refused to take any man back who would not sign a form to leave his union. When the men refused as a body, he tried a fresh line of attack. He posed as the friend of the general labour unions, who did not have these irritating habits of saying which job was to be done by the members of this craft union and which by that. He decided to reorganize his factory, using much more girl-labour and unskilled men, with a few highly paid men as overseers. When the craft unions struck against this, the wages he offered to a few picked men were so alluring that they accepted. They could set the tools and so the way was clear for the semi-skilled labour.

The problem Joan had to face was that the cheaper labour used to supplant the craft union men were members of her own union. The executive officers of the Industrial Union of Labour realized that there was no ultimate advantage to their members in breaking down the craft union conditions of labour, but it was not easy to make the rank and file see this. Joan found that the members of her union were not so strong against Lewis's tempting offers as she could have wished. It seemed as though a curtain had rung down on the enthusiasm of the General Strike of less than a month ago, and that curtain was a wet blanket. "Why not?" was the sullen answer when she met the local committee of her own union. "We've been let down, why not make the best bargains we can?"

"Don't you see you will let down every one else?" she pleaded. "Once break rank and you go down as a mob."

"We came out solid and the leaders broke our ranks," was the invariable reply, repeated at every turn.

When Hadfield, the square-headed, red-faced secretary of the Trades Council suggested that she should go and talk to Lewis himself, Joan in desperation telephoned at once, and a pleasant, rather American voice suggested she should come right now. Being careful to see that her hat was at the right angle and her nose properly powdered, Joan went along to beard the lion.

When she was shown into his office she met a youngish, well-dressed man, obviously a Jew. He looked rather puzzled. "You are rather young for this work, aren't you?" he asked as he set a chair for her.

"Yes, aren't you?" was the calm reply.

He laughed, and this put them on terms.

"I like young people. I'd rather talk to you than these men who come to see me with ideas a hundred years old. How old are your ideas?"

"I got the best of them in the General Strike," replied Joan, "so they are about a month old and very prickly!"

"Well, I'm sorry for you, then. Of all the pieces of idiocy, that was one. What on earth did you think you could gain by it?"

"We might have gained a great deal," said Joan stoutly, "but we were trying to fight a twentieth-century battle with nineteenth-century machinery. There were too many unions, too many executives, and much too little thinking."

"But I agree," said Lewis — and the two plunged into an argument in which they both arrived at the conclusion that what was wanted was one big union headquarters that the employer could treat with for his whole works. Lewis felt he had got a really intelligent listener.

"I don't want to fight the men," he said, "but I want to be able to move them about. These rules as to which union man shall do which job cost us thousands of pounds a year in sheer inefficiency and waste."

"You can't use men like pawns. They demand some knowledge of what is going on, and some say in their work," retorted Joan.

"I agree — my directors don't, but I want the men to understand." And they plunged again into Lewis's conception of a new idealized rationalized industry. So intent were they, so close together their heads as Lewis put down figures on paper, that they didn't hear some one enter the room until that some one coughed and said in a loud and ominous tone, "Ben."

Lewis sat up suddenly, and Joan saw quite the most appallingly dressed woman she had ever beheld. Hard-featured and middle-aged, she had a frock of bright green with much embroidery .She wore a heavy ruby and diamond necklace, obviously — too obviously — real, a heavy fur coat thrown open to show a gold silk lining, and a large and expensive brown hat.

"Good Lord," thought Joan, "who's this?"

"Oh, my dear, is it you?" Lewis was in a nervous flurry. "Let me introduce you. My wife. Miss Craig."

"And who is this person, pray?" asked Mrs Lewis in a deep voice.

Joan repressed a terrible tendency to giggle. This couldn't be real. There weren't women like this outside comic cartoons.

"Miss Craig is a trade union official, and she has come to see me about the men who are still on strike."

"I thought you had promised me to see no more of these pernicious people," said the vision magnificently.

"Ah-ah, here's the nigger in the wood-pile," thought Joan.[97] But she was having no more of Mrs Lewis's impertinence. Turning to the man, she held out her hand and said in very business-like tones: "Thank you for granting me this interview, Mr Lewis. I will report to my committee."

Lewis looked his apologies as he took her hand, but he merely said, "I thank you, good-bye." He held the door open. Joan looked straight at his wife. "Good afternoon," she said politely, and vanished quickly, so as to spoil that lady's parting snort.

Joan, however, did not return either to her union offices or to the very uncomfortable commercial hotel where she was staying. Instead, she drifted into a café to think out a plan of action. It was Shireport's rather pretentious 'best *café*' — *papier-mâché* 'oak' panelling, cheap Jacobean chairs, rickety tables, rather dingy chintz, and highly decorated 'cream'-cakes — but the pottery was bright and pretty and the lights softly shaded. After a hard day's work in the grimy streets of Shireport, Joan felt grateful for its refuge.

As she looked round for a corner seat, a young man rose from one and came to greet her. It was Alaric Martin, the reporter from the Shireport Standard. "I was on the look-out for you and thought you might drop in here," he said. "Are you with people or can you join me?"

"I'd love to," said Joan, "especially as you've bagged my favourite seat. Also, I want some information."

"Let's exchange, then. Shall I order? Indian or China? Is this your meal, or are you just afternooning?"

"Baked beans on toast. I've a meeting at seven, and I can't face a commercial high tea at my hotel."

"Antediluvian horrors, aren't they?" grinned Martin. Joan liked this man. He was about thirty-five, and had travelled a lot as a foreign correspondent. But his health had been ruined by the War. He lived in a shanty on the coast about ten miles south of Shireport and tried to persuade himself that his lungs would soon be fit enough to let him return to Fleet Street. Meanwhile, he was all but the nominal editor of the *Shireport Standard*, and had galvanized that small, respectable local paper into such active life that the eyes of two big newspaper trusts were attracted.

"I hear you've been to see Lewis," said Martin, as Joan accepted a cigarette while waiting for the beans. "What do you think of him?"

"Oh, as one who loathes capitalists on principle, I think he is not so loathsome as he might be," parried Joan lightly.

"No, but frankly. Did you get him into any discussion of his new ideas?"

"Didn't I just, and we got so keen on the argument that we didn't hear Madame walk in."

"Phew! You've met the Dragon, then?"

"Well, the Dragon has inspected me through a jewelled lorgnette, and I believe will report unfavourably on results. I say, that pill must have been well gilded for a man like Lewis to swallow it."

"It was. Madame's father is the type of far-sighted Jew who believes in investing in brains rather than bonds. Ben Lewis was his confidential clerk, with ideas and a patent in his pocket he had bought for about twopence-halfpenny. Rose was not easily marriageable and — well, there you are."

"Don't tell me its name is Rose," pleaded Joan.

Martin laughed. "Yes, Rose is the name of our little Ben's thornbush, and she's *some* thornbush, I can tell you."

"She can't be at the bottom of this trouble, can she?"

"Not directly, of course. She hasn't the glimmering of an idea of what's in Lewis's mind in this fight with the craft unions. All she knows is that he's keeping men out of work who won't knuckle under. She approves of that all right, but she is furious with him for paying more than the district rate. Apart from that, all she cares about is getting into Society."

"Society in Shireport! I should have thought she could have bought her way into any that was going."

"Look here, fair lady. If there is anything in these rumours that you are to be asked to be Labour candidate this burg, you'd better know more about its little ways."

"Its 'Society' doesn't interest me, not politically, anyway. They won't vote Labour. But tell me — who the 'best people,' the top-notchers? There are engineering wives, of course, but I should have thought they had money enough to live in London."

"Shireport is an old town, you know, or perhaps you've never bothered to know," answered Martin, "and has a county tradition. Somehow, quite a number of the old county families retain some sort of connexion with it. Their houses are near, and as most of them invested in works at the beginning, they haven't had to sell out like the families that only had land to live on. Mrs Lewis is dying to get into that circle — would give her ears for a leg-up. But — well, you've seen her."

Joan, having finished her baked beans, lit a cigarette meditatively. "The lady seems to be the Achilles' heel of this business, as well as the nigger in the wood-pile, to mix metaphors a bit."

"Got any plans? I'm very discreet, you know." Alaric Martin respected Joan. His own taste in women was for the fluffiest of flappers, of which there were plenty to be had in Shireport, as elsewhere. But he did not think of Joan as a woman. He liked to meet her as would any man who came in from the outside world.

"I want to get these men back to work quick," answered Joan. "Of course it isn't my job. Their own unions should be looking after them, but with so many unions for such a comparatively few men I don't see them doing it, do you?"

"No, there's been no settled policy except a stone-wall obstinacy, and that's no use in this case."

"Quite, and I don't want trouble blowing up between the Industrial Union of Labour and the craft unions at Shireport of all places. I haven't any right to negotiate for the craftsmen, only to keep our men from blacklegging on their jobs, but if only one could get Lewis to take them back pending a settlement with their own unions, it would be a good way out."

"A fine stroke of business. But it cuts across Lewis's plans. He would have to begin all over again, and might not get such a good chance again. There's no public sympathy with the men just now."

"My dear man, I've been in too many strikes now to worry about public sympathy," Joan retorted. "Public sympathy is only of any use when you are strong enough to win without it. But I haven't any plans at the moment. I feel that Mrs Lewis's social ambitions are a clue, but I don't quite see to what."

"She is having a garden-party on Thursday," replied Martin. "She's had to make it an affair for charity to get any county people to go. It's for Disabled Soldiers' and Sailors' funds. I suppose any demonstration wouldn't do, would it?"

"No, not at an ex-Service men's affair, no—o." Joan wrinkled up her nose, an odd trick she had when thinking, that made her thin face in its bushy black hair look like an amusing elf's.

Martin thought: "She *is* an attractive little thing sometimes. Funny I never saw it before. Wouldn't call her pretty. Wonder what she's like off duty."

Joan rose and signalled to the waitress. She paid her own bill quite naturally and without any fuss. Then she turned to Martin. "Well, thanks very much. I have to look in at the office before the meeting. Have to think it out."

"Afraid I've not been much use with my odds and ends of gossip, but I know in my own work how all sorts of apparently irrelevant scraps can be useful. Here's another, by the way, that might link up, though I can't see how. The Anti-War Federation is having a meeting on the night of Mrs Lewis's garden-party — a sort of damn-your-charity demonstration. They've wired to that airman chap who did so well in the war and he's coming — Captain Gerald Blain."

"Gerry Blain! He never told *me* he was coming."

"Well, it was only fixed this morning. Do you know him?" Martin was amused by Joan's proprietary exclamation.

"Yes, I know him quite well — thanks for telling me. Of course, he wouldn't know I was here."

"Well, perhaps you can give me some personal notes about him. I've promised the secretary to write a puff — have to be discreet, of course."

A puff for Gerry Blain! Joan's cheeks went hot at the thought, but Martin had got out his notebook. She had to say something.

"Oh, he got very smashed up in his last flight in the War — his father is very wealthy, lives in Park Lane, but Gerry won't touch the money — at least, he wasn't going to, but now he is going to use it for Labour work. I don't know if I ought to tell you — is that what you want?"

"Admirable," said Martin. "Just the ticket, in fact. We'll have a portrait of the lofty-minded young hero — should make a good column."

"Gerry would be mad if he knew I told you, but he is so splendid people ought to know about him," said Joan.

"No journalist ever tells where he gets his things from. He would be stuck to death with the pens of his colleagues and drowned in the inkpot for letting down his profession," smiled Martin.

"Well, bye-bye. It's been jolly meeting you." Then she went straight to the post office and sent a telegram to Gerald Blain.

• • • • •

After the meeting with the members of her union, Joan walked back alone to her hotel, feeling very lonely and discouraged. As a contrast to the luxury of Miss Meadowes' house, the cheap hotel seemed drearier than ever. The little commercial room was not inviting. There was the usual faded red plush furniture, the table set as for a perpetual meal, the cruets and sauce bottle remaining as they had done since early morning. At little tables, facing the wall, the commercial men were writing out what orders they had obtained during the day, while round the very low fire the usual group were explaining at length why it was so difficult to get orders, and competing with each other in inventing tortures for Mr A. J. Cook. Least of all things did Joan want to be involved in a discussion about the coal dispute, so she went upstairs to the usual single bedroom of a provincial hotel — one ugly iron bedstead, a cheap oak suite with drawers that never open properly, lined with rather dingy news-paper, and an assortment of unwanted oddments left by previous tenants.

Joan lay down on the bed fully dressed and pulled the much-used eiderdown over herself. She realized with rather a shock as she lay there that this was the first time that day that she had thought of Tony. While her mind had been occupied with the problem of the Lewis workers she had been interested and happy. But at the end of the day she was tired and lonely. It would have been so nice to have been able to go home to Tony and talk things over — but, even as she said that to herself, she smiled, for Tony would not have the least idea of why a strike should happen on such a point. What to her was a vital principle would have seemed sheer nonsense to him — the men were getting more money for the job, what on earth was the trouble? ... Gerry, ardently soaking himself in the Labour Movement, would have understood — but then she could never be thrilled by Gerry as Tony thrilled her — Gerry could not make her feel as though an electric current were running up and down her backbone.

And then Tony and Gerry faded out of the picture and she went to sleep with the light full on. She would have lain, dressed, like that all night, if some convivial hotel guests hadn't chosen the landing outside her door to wish themselves and each other very hearty, audible good-nights, and so awakened her. Wearily tearing off her clothes, Joan got into bed. Just before she fell into the sleep of a healthy tiredness she found herself wondering if Gerry would be able to come and help.

CHAPTER XVIII

Next morning Joan was having rather a late breakfast, having given the commercial men ample time to be served and get away on their affairs, when the dining-room door opened and in walked Gerald Blain.

"Gerry, you here — so soon!" In her delight at seeing his friendly face Joan's welcome was of the warmest.

"Well, you sent for me, didn't you? When I got your wire I got out the old bus and came along."

"But you've surely not driven all through the night?"

"Well, not strictly — I got as far as Doncaster and put up there, and came along this morning. Good run — but, I say, even the remains of your eggs and bacon look positively tempting. What about a spot of the same for old uncle? Are there myrmidons[98] within?"

Blain rattled along gaily to cover the slight embarrassment they both felt. Joan kept the game going.

"If you call Maggie a myrmidon you'll think you've struck an earthquake."

"I always grovel before waitresses," Gerry assured her soothingly. "They are the most important people one can meet, the arbiters of destiny. Is my destiny bacon and eggs this morning, Maggie?" Gerry turned to the rather haughty waitress who had just come in. Maggie recognized the officer type she had served during the War and rose to the occasion.

"A bit of ham, sir. You just leave it to me."

"Not fair," laughed Joan, when a handsome dishful was set on the table. "You men get an advantage with waitresses. Now, I've never had even one smile from Maggie … I went in awe of her."

"It's my fascinating little ways, Joan — haven't you noticed them? No? Now, how can you say that when they've been working at full pressure? Not that other egg, Joan — your fair Maggie is a little wholesale, even for my appetite."

"That isn't too much of a plateful, Gerry?" Joan said reproachfully.

"True, true, fair lady, but 'tis my pleasure to pretend to a real he-man's capacity. Now, about this business of yours. This lad was awfully flattered you sent for him."

"Oh, Gerry, bless you. I'm glad you didn't mind, but I thought as it only meant a couple of days earlier than your meeting we might concoct something."

"Mind! Uncle was feeling lonely without a strike to play with. Now, pour forth thy tale."

When Joan had finished, Gerry, who had turned to the fire and was meditatively hacking at the coal with a poker, said thoughtfully: "Then there are three factors in the situation. Lewis and his strikers, Mrs Lewis and her garden-party, me and my anti-war meeting. There is also a possible fourth in a friendly reporter, this Alaric Martin, who, I gather, my dear Watson, does not love Madame Lewis."

"He dislikes her intensely. I don't know what she has done to him, but he likes Ben Lewis."

"Love me, hate my wife. Not an unusual situation," commented Gerry with a wise air.

"They seem four rather disconnected things, Gerry, but I had a feeling that we could get at Lewis through that awful female's snobbery."

"This is the moment for me to give a realistic study of a great man thinking." Gerry struck an attitude. "Look close upon it, Joan, for you may never see its like again."

Joan grinned. "Not I. Such efforts would appal me. I'll get my coat and hat and be down soon."

When Joan returned, Gerry was still poking the fire. "Got it, Sherlock?" she inquired.

"Such flippancy ill becomes a Watson," replied Gerry severely. "Anyway" — changing his tone — "we've got to blackmail that garden-party somehow. I think I'll call on the lady — disabled airman goes to plead with fair lady to soften her husband's stony heart and take back his late comrades-in-arms."

"Mrs Lewis as a fair lady — the joke of the century, Gerry. Wait till you see her. I don't see even you softening her heart. You would have far more chance with the husband."

"She probably won't see me — or will be very rude if she does. That's what I'm banking on. Then you and I will hunt up Martin and see if we can get any kind of Press stunt against her. I shall denounce her at my meeting for her hypocrisy in turning a disabled ex-Service man from her doors, who only comes to appeal in the name of humanity for his comrades, at the same time that she is running a garden-party for disabled men's funds."

Joan looked at him understandingly. "It won't exactly be pleasant for you to exploit those wounds of yours, Gerry."

"Heavens, no; I'm all for jolly old Coriolanus's way of thinking.[99] But if that woman can exploit our chaps to give her a leg up on the social ladder, I guess I can play the game to help them to get their jobs back." Joan felt her lip quiver, but Gerry rattled on. "Incidentally, I notice your complete scepticism as to my charms being able to subdue the lady instead of blackmailing her."

"Wait till you've seen the lady," said Joan. "If you charm Mrs Lewis, I'll hand you the biscuit — that is, unless you can produce some relations with titles, then you might have a chance but, unassisted — no, Gerry, not even you."

Gerry pulled a face.

Joan laughed. "Righto. Good luck, anyway. Now I must see Hadfield. He's a great lad. You'll like him, Gerry. He's got a joint committee of the different unions going and putting heart into the men. Shall we meet at the Cosy Café in the High Street? Martin is pretty sure to be there, but I'll 'phone him to make sure."

"Right you are, then. One o'clock. I should have settled with this daughter of Herodias by then."

• • • • •

Joan had plenty of time to tell the full story to Alaric Martin before Gerry appeared at the *café*. He was greatly elated, and greeted Martin like a brother when Joan introduced them.

"Gee, a great story for you, Martin, if your editor will let you use it. Setting bloodhounds on the poor battered warrior!"

"Not bloodhounds, Gerry?" said Joan, horrified.

"Well, perhaps not blood, but the two quadrupeds were indubitably hounds. Don't spoil my artistic efforts just as I'm trying to impress the Press, Joan."

"But what did happen, Blain?" laughed Martin.

"Well, as I didn't really want her to see me, I rather carefully explained my exact business to a very decent butler and sent in my card."

"And you mean Mrs Lewis wouldn't see Captain Gerald Blain, D.S.O.? I can hardly believe she wouldn't jump at the chance, whatever your errand."

"Never use that screed," said Gerry. My card is just 'Mr G. Blain.'"

"Ah, that explains it. Did she tell the butler to turn you out?"

"Did she! She arrived in person complete with two dogs — vicious little brutes — look at my trousers ——" and Gerry showed the torn hem.

"But, Gerry, you might have been badly bitten. I'll strangle that fiend," exclaimed Joan.

"We'll deal with her," said Martin in a very quiet tone. "She actually set those dogs on you?"

"She did, with a highly coloured description of me that it is a shame should be lost to posterity. That woman could give our sergeant-major a beating. She was beside herself with rage. Some temper, my hat! It evidently wasn't her morning for being a lady."

"No, first and third Thursdays, I believe," said Martin.

"How did you get out without being bitten?" Joan was not concerned about anything else just then.

"That butler was a sportsman. He held the dogs, soothed the lady, and opened the door for me without losing his dignity. His 'Good day, sir, I'm sorry, sir,' before the lady's face was one up to him. I hope she won't sack him for it."

"She won't. That butler is an expensive item in the Lewis household. I wonder what Ben will say when he reads my column. By the way, you live in Park Lane,[100] don't you?"

"Not I. Wouldn't be seen dead there. My father bought a house there, which Mother won't live in. I live in Great Ormond Street, Bloomsbury."

Martin chuckled. "For the purpose of this yarn you'll live under the parental roof, and what Rose Lewis will say when she reads that she has set the dogs on a distinguished officer who lives in Park Lane — well, I'd give a lot to be there. This will be a great advertisement for your meeting, Blain."

"Good, but it's that garden-party we've got to scotch. If only we could get some big-wig to write in and say that she couldn't dream of attending Mrs Lewis's garden-party for disabled men, in view of her treatment of one of them, that would spike it, wouldn't it?" said Gerry.

"Yes, but we want to get the men back, and merely spoiling the garden-party would make things worse," replied Joan. "The question is, could we have such a letter in prospect, and threaten her with it? Are there any of your girl friends among these county people here, Gerry?"

"Let me see," mused Gerry. "The only people I know anywhere near are the Hallam-Hastings, who used to have a place at Ayscliffe during the War. But I know they only rented it. Are they still here, do you know, Martin?"

"The Hallam-Hastings? By Jove, if you have any influence with them you've got a trump card. Sir Geoffrey Hallam-Hastings holds a majority of shares in my paper."

"Young Hallam-Hastings trained with me. I spent a leave at his home, and then I went up to see his mother after he was killed. I was with him when it happened, you see." Gerry's gay voice had gone very flat and quiet.

"Oh, Gerry, would it be fair to see her then? Perhaps it would bring it all back to her," said Joan quickly.

"Bring it back to her! I don't think that poor woman has forgotten much, and she would be glad to see me for Geoff's sake. I'll toddle out there this afternoon. It's about twenty miles, isn't it?"

"Will you telephone me at the office if she is willing to do anything?" said Martin as they stood at the counter waiting for his change. He had insisted on paying for the lunch. "It will make a lot of difference how far I can go with my old man."

"Right you are," said Gerry Blain.

Leaving Martin to go back to his office, Joan and Gerry strolled slowly back to the hotel where Gerry had left his car. A rather embarrassed silence fell between them. Joan was longing to ask: "Have you seen Tony Dacre since I left London?" but she felt too shy to mention Tony's name. She knew nothing, of course, of Mary Maud's letter to Gerry, and she did not know whether he knew anything from Tony of what had passed. They were nearly at the hotel door when Gerry said: "I may have to stay the night at Ayscliffe, Joan. Lady Hallam-Hastings will want to talk about Geoff and it will be a little difficult to break away immediately after asking a favour."

"Of course," said Joan, "and, anyway, it will be more comfortable for you. This is rather an uncomfortable hotel, but the Wellington is worse."

"Lord, that doesn't matter — but what I was thinking was — well, I would like us to have a quiet talk before I go back to London. There doesn't look like being much chance here. Are you staying here long?"

"That depends on this job. If we can pull anything off and can get the men back to work, I finish here and go back to Leeds for fresh instructions."

"Good," said Gerry, "then I'll drive you back."

"Optimist!" laughed Joan, as he got into his car. "Well, good luck with Lady Hallam-Hastings — you are well among the ladies this trip, Gerry."

But as she went up to her room she wondered what it was that Gerry wanted to talk about.

CHAPTER XIX

Having received a message from Blain, who telephoned from Ayscliffe that Lady Hallam-Hastings was willing to take steps to protest against the treatment he had received from Mrs Lewis, though she did not want to be drawn into anything connected with the strike, Alaric Martin felt it safe to spread himself. Not since the last local murder, quite three years ago, had Shireport had such a sensation.

FAMOUS AIRMAN GOES TO PLEAD FOR
HIS COMRADES

DOGS SET UPON HIM BY LADY

WILL PROMINENT RESIDENTS ATTEND GARDEN PARTY?

flared in headlines across the page.

The news, properly spiced, was served up hot in the columns. There was a photograph of Gerry in the centre which had been supplied by the Anti-War Federation for their meeting — but for such publicity as this they could never have hoped. Martin rubbed in the fortune of Blain's father, the house in Park Lane, with Gerry as Sir Galahad[101] coming to Shireport to lend his aid to his old comrades-in-arms. Fortunately several of the strikers had been Air Force fitters, Shireport being near a big air-training centre, and a group photograph of them had been secured by the indefatigable Martin.

Joan was just a little afraid that the stunt might be too successful. The object was not to ruin Mrs Lewis socially, much as Martin apparently enjoyed that aspect of it, but to get the men back to work. Gerry brought back with him next morning a very dignified letter written by Lady Hallam-Hastings, which he had her permission to use as he thought best. This was a short note saying that Lady Hallam-Hastings felt that it was now impossible for her to attend Mrs Lewis's garden-party, but that as she did not wish the funds for disabled men to suffer by her absence she enclosed a cheque, which she would be glad if the editor would forward to the right quarter.

"She was awfully decent about it," said Gerry, when he came in to see Joan next morning. "I stayed on to talk about Geoff. Now she's got our stunt connected up with him. She was quite willing for us to use this privately as a lever to get the men back, or print it to scotch the party, but, of course, she cannot do anything that appears to side with the strikers in the actual dispute because her husband is chairman of the Employers' Federation."

"But Lewis isn't on that."

"No, but they want him to be. He is a nuisance outside. And, of course, it would be better for the unions in a fight like this if he were."

"Gerry, you are a genius. It's just marvellous to work with you. You think of everything." Joan glowed at him.

Blain lit a cigarette with some care. "Yes, we pull together quite well, old thing. I like working with *you*."

His tone was quite calm and ordinary, but Joan found her cheeks growing hot. She rose from the table. "My turn to do a little lion-bearding. I'll 'phone up our Bennie. At least he won't set the dogs on me."

The voice of Mr Lewis was none too pleasant over the telephone this time, but he would be glad to see Miss Craig at once.

"So long, old girl. Best of luck," grinned Gerry. "If not heard of in three hours I'll rout out Martin and we'll search for the body."

"Whose?" said Joan cheekily, as she picked up her gloves and ran out.

"Do you call this fair fighting?" was Lewis's greeting. They did not shake hands.

"No, I don't. Nor is yours. You are refusing work to men who, with all this unemployment, have no other prospect of a job. Is that fair?"

"They can come back if they accept my conditions. I am not asking them to take less wages. They can come back to-morrow at higher wages than any other employer in this town will pay them. Isn't that fair enough?"

"You make the price of their job the betrayal of their unions, and letting down their pals, not only in this town but all over the country."

"Other men out of these unions are working here on my conditions."

"Yes, and do you really think any better of them for it in your heart of hearts?"

"They are sensible fellows and know which side their bread is buttered."

"If your ancestors had accepted that philosophy the history of your race would have been different, Mr Lewis."

That shot went home, for, like every decent Jew, Ben Lewis was secretly proud of his blood. "My wife had nothing to do with it, anyway. Why couldn't you fight me and leave her out of it?"

"Have you left the strikers' wives out of it when the men have no wages to bring home? And —" Joan couldn't help smiling — "if it comes to that, Mrs Lewis has done the fighting up to now, and with dogs, too."

"I'm sorry about that, Miss Craig. My wife is very excitable. She has well —
er — sometimes a rather violent temper, and she had already been upset yesterday
morning by some carters holding up the chairs for her garden-party, because of
sympathy with the strikers. She connected Captain Blain's visit with that, and, of
course, she was worried as to what other things would be held up."

"I don't think she need worry about extra chairs under the circumstances," said
Joan politely.

Lewis drew his chair closer to the table and looked straight at her. "Did you
send Captain Blain to call on my wife?"

"Yes."

"Did you arrange for the publicity in the *Standard?*"

"Yes."

"And what do you propose to do next?"

"Unless the strikers are at work on the morning of the garden-party, this letter
will be published in the *Standard.*" She handed him Lady Hallam-Hastings' note.

Lewis read it. "But the editor won't print it. Two can play at this game. I'll put
the wind up old Middleton all right."

"Sir Geoffrey Hallam-Hastings, I believe, owns sixty per cent of the Standard
shares. Do you own any?"

"The devil he does? Well, I hand it to you for thinking this out all ways, but
that won't get your men back to work. My wife's garden-party can just go to the
devil, that's all."

"Will your wife enjoy being cut by the County?"

"The County won't side with the strikers."

"The strikers have nothing to do with Lady Hallam-Hastings. Your wife has
insulted the chum of her dead son."

"Then if the strikers have nothing to do with it, she won't come anyway now."

"On the contrary. If I ask Captain Blain to bring her, she will come. You get
on the 'phone with your wife and tell her that."

"But after she has insulted him —"

"Easy enough to stage a reconciliation. We can say Mrs Lewis was completely
misled, the dogs were excited and out of control, and all that. We can have a
happy ending with Captain Blain all smiles and the pet of the party. You see if
your wife wouldn't like that." Joan could not quite interpret the look Lewis gave
her.

"I'll 'phone my wife," was all he said, and he left the room. When he came
back he looked relieved. His anger was replaced by the pleasant friendliness of
her first interview with him. "Thank God my wife will be livable with again. It's
been awful this morning. I don't mind telling you now. I've put it to her that all
this is my arranging. I hope you won't mind that."

"Rather not. I understand. You tell her anything that fits in."

"And you'll make it all right with the *Standard*?"

"I'll see them at once and get it all fixed up."

"Very well. Then tell the men to report for work to-morrow. It will take some time to get them fitted in, but they will be paid full wages meantime. You don't want a formal agreement, I suppose?"

"No, they are not my members, you know, and it would be awkward. I know it's all right."

Lewis held out his hand. "Good-bye, then. I hope we shall meet again soon, and not as enemies either. Will you come to the garden-party?"

"Better not."

Lewis smiled. "Perhaps you are right. I shall look forward to meeting Captain Blain."

CHAPTER XX

It was the afternoon of the garden-party. Joan sat alone in the commercial room, drinking tea for the sake of something to do, but feeling curiously alone after the last few hectic days. The men were back at work. Joan and Hadfield had hastily collected them the night previous. True, the strikers were a little astonished at the sudden change in their fortunes, for Joan obviously could explain nothing beyond the fact that negotiations had been successful in securing their reinstatement on the same terms as operated previous to the General Strike.

Joan would have liked to share the joke with these men whom she had got to know so well, but that would have made an impossible situation for Mr Lewis. Fortunately, a too intelligent Communist, who insisted on asking awkward questions, made the mistake of personally attacking Joan. This roused the ire of the men. They were to go back to their jobs — what did he want to worry for? — and the meeting concluded with a hearty vote of thanks to Joan and an adjournment to stand Hadfield a drink.

The *Standard* that morning had wriggled out of the situation perfectly, with photos of Mrs Lewis and Captain Blain. Martin and Gerry had gone off in high spirits with Lady Hallam-Hastings and her friends to the garden-party, and Joan, having written a report suitable for publication, with a private account of the proceedings to William Royd, was left with nothing to do but wait until Gerry returned to drive her back to Leeds, the anti-war meeting having been cancelled by general consent. She had written a cheerful note to Mary Maud, and toyed with the idea of writing to Tony, but what could she say? She couldn't tell him about the work he hated, the work that was keeping them apart. Joan gazed out of the window across the grimy, dismal street. These few days had been a specially exciting adventure. Most of her daily work was the hard grinding routine of organization. Even so, she felt that this was her life. There was very little pose about Joan Craig. She didn't strike a mental attitude and declare that everything should be sacrificed to her life's work. She was a very human, practical person who didn't want to do any sacrificing at all if she could help it. She wanted to marry Tony, but she disliked the deceit of the life he proposed. She hated to think of the shock it would be to those who trusted her and looked up to her for leadership, if she lived with Tony and the truth became known. It was characteristic of her age and generation that it was not the religious or moral aspect of Tony's proposal that worried her, but the desire to play straight with the men and women she worked for. Would she go to Tony if he agreed that she could go on with her work? With Tony near her, and the thrill of his presence running through her veins, Joan would have been willing then, but since she had had time to think, she more and more disliked the idea. Yet she loved Anthony Dacre. Gerry was a fine pal, a great comrade to work with, she admired and trusted him, but he had no power to thrill her, as the mere whispering of Tony's name under her breath could thrill her.

What was the way out? Joan's mind went wearily round the situation for the hundredth time. She realized Helen's generosity. It was not fair to make Tony worry Helen for a divorce. She must stop thinking about him, but it was so much easier to resolve that than to do it. In the press of work, yes, but in the quiet times, in the evening hours when there was no work to do and little to occupy her, away from her own rooms in the dreary round of provincial hotels and lodgings, it was then that she could not keep her mind from Tony Dacre.

Joan was roused from her thoughts by hearing a car draw up at the door, the sound of voices, and in came Blain and Martin.

You've missed it, Joan," said Gerry, dropping himself into the nearest chair. "It's been great — Shireport hasn't had such a sensation for years."

"Do tell me what has happened. I've been all out of the fair this afternoon."

"De poor li'l', and it was her stunt, really. Well, to begin, I'll hand it to Lady Hallam-Hastings. Quite cool, rather like a prize Persian cat. Well, of course we were beautifully late — and she tooled up to the Lewis — my dear, the dress that woman was wearing and the jools would have kept all the disabled soldiers I know in beer and baccy for centuries."

"What *did* she say?" laughed Joan.

"The Lewis? Well, Lady Hallam-Hastings presented me as though nothing had happened. 'You haven't been properly introduced to Captain Blain, have you, Mrs Lewis?'"

"And Rose?"

"Oh, the Rose was all blushes under its paint and was going to say it was sorry, but hubby was on the careful watch, and made some happy remark, took Lady Hallam-Hastings on his arm, and I followed with the Rose clinging to mine."

"You should have seen them!" Martin exploded with laughter. "Every one had turned up for miles round. Never been such publicity for such a show, and they all wanted to shake hands with Gerry. It was like being Prince of Wales."[102]

"Well, if the P.O.W. has to do that for his living every day, all I can say is that I'd join the Republican League if I were he, and agitate for the prohibition of handshaking. No, *no* more tea, Joan. I'm the colour of it. What I want is a double whisky. Why do you stay in a temperance hotel — a sensible woman like you?"

"And my flask at the office is empty," said Martin, "or I'd run round and get you one. But —"

"I know, old man. And this is the country we fought for. Ungrateful, I say."

"Did you say that in your speech?" asked Joan.

"No, thank goodness, I got out of any speech. Now, what about it, are you ready to go, Joan?"

"So soon?" Martin looked his keen disappointment. Two friends like this were rare in Shireport. "I was hoping you'd come out to my shack this evening, as your meeting was off."

"Sorry, old man, I'd love to, but I've promised to take the lady out of harm's way. Guess she's done mischief enough in this old burg."

Martin held out his hand. "Well, so long, then. It's been a great rag. Let's meet again some time," and he was gone.

"A sportsman, that lad," was Gerry's comment. "Now all aboard the lugger." With Gerry busy with the car's mechanism and his eyes fixed on the road ahead, Joan somehow found it easier to talk. "Have you seen Tony lately?" she made herself say.

"No, I called to see Helen. He was out."

"You called on Helen! I thought you never met her if you could help it?"

"Mary Maud hasn't told you the story, then?"

"What story? Is there some mystery — ought I to know?"

"I can't tell you, Joan. It's Helen's story, and I expect Mary Maud felt the same. But after she told me the whole story I realized that I had done Helen a big injustice. I had condemned her without hearing her side, and I went to tell her so."

From his tone Joan felt that it would be tactful to change the subject. "Will that end your anti-woman complex, Gerry?"

"My anti-woman complex? What on earth are you talking about, Joan?"

"Well, Mary Maud said …"

Mary Maud! *You* ought to know by now that she's not happy until she has fitted up all her friends with nice neat little complexes. I didn't like Helen, and I do like you and Vi Legarde and Mary Maud. Does that make a complex?"

"But you always are so freezing when women are about. You know you are, Gerry," retorted Joan, feeling an unreasonable hatred of Violet Legarde at that moment.

"You should have seen me with Madame Rose this afternoon," he chuckled.

Traffic in the narrow winding streets of the Yorkshire mill towns claimed all the driver's attention till they got to Leeds, and they didn't talk much. Gerry drew up at Joan's door.

"What's the etiquette in Leeds?" he inquired. "May I come in and talk, or shall we go out for a meal?"

"Oh, come in, it will be all right. It's early yet. If you can live on a boiled egg or two, we'll manage that. I can borrow them from the landlady, but it's the only thing I can cook in my room."

"Great," said Gerry, "if you're sure it's no fag for you. A *morceau*[103] of mouse-bait and a biscuit will do for me."

Climbing rather stiffly up the stairs behind her, Blain felt his heart beat more quickly at going into Joan's room, for he knew she had only one. But there was no sign in the little attic that it was ever used for sleeping.

"What a jolly comfy place," said Gerry. "It reminds me of you, Joan."

"Why?"

"No, that's fishing. But it's nice without being frilly. Can't stand the women who have to put pink silk bows even on their toothbrushes."

The divan was large and comfortable and Joan insisted on his stretching himself on it while she made supper. Gerry looked round appreciatively. The walls were papered with a plain blue paper, against which some bold black and white lino-cuts in narrow black frames gave a distinction that no colours could have done. The furniture, a heavy table, some chairs and a small plain writing-desk were obviously of cheap wood and had been painted black. There were a few pieces of thick dead-white French pottery. The curtains which Joan drew across the window exactly matched the walls. As Gerry had said, there were no frills — but it was a restful room.

Joan made some coffee, scrambled some eggs in a saucepan, and made toast on an electric gadget in less than ten minutes. Gerry liked watching her moving about. She fussed so little and she did not chatter. He wondered what was passing in her dark head, but didn't like to ask.

"There, Gerry. Sorry there's no whisky."

Blain rather painfully pulled himself off the couch. He was stiff after the tiring day, and lowered himself into a chair by the low fireside table.

"I talk about more whisky than I ever drink," he smiled. "This is comfy, Joan. Can we talk now?"

"Yes, Gerry," she replied quietly. "Just about anything you like."

He matched her directness. "Mary Maud sent me a letter when you came north, telling me something of what had passed between you and Tony Dacre. But it was her usual muddle and almost incomprehensible."

"Could I read it?"

"Sure," and Gerry drew it out of his pocket and passed it to her. It had evidently been much read. Joan glanced over the letter and handed it back.

"Mary Maud had no right to write to you, but what she says is quite correct."

"But, Joan … this letter says that Tony asked you to live with him, and stipulated that you should give up your work!"

"Yes, well …"

"But … oh, look here, I know I've no right to discuss this, but we've got to have it out. It surely wasn't for him to make conditions, under the circumstances."

"It wasn't a condition. At least, neither he nor I felt it to be that. Just simply that he felt I had to make the choice between my work and life with him. Frankly, the more I think of it, the more I see that he was right."

Gerry was silent. Joan pushed a box of cigarettes across to him. "I'll move the supper tray if you've finished. Do smoke."

"Not in your bedroom."

"It isn't that yet. I'm going to smoke. I can open this window wide afterwards."

Gerry took the cigarette gratefully, lit it, and smoked silently. After a time he said:

"Joan, I must ask you this. Have you decided not to go and live with Tony?"

"Yes."

"Even if he did get Helen to agree to a divorce? When I saw her, poor girl, she was utterly miserable. She would have agreed to anything to make Tony happy."

"I'm awfully sorry about her, Gerry. Sorry she had to know, as things have turned out. I believe it would be much easier if we were married, but Tony doesn't think so. I've got to choose between my work and him."

"And you choose your work?"

"Yes."

"Then, forgive me, Joan, but I must say it, that means that you are not really in love with him, doesn't it?"

"Why not? It's not been an easy choice to make, Gerry."

"I can see that, Joan … But if you loved him you would go to him, Joan. Oh, I know it's rotten that the woman has to make that choice, and, God knows, I can't see what he's driving at. But if he does feel that way, and if you loved him, you would go. I know jolly well if the position was reversed, I'd want you on any terms you liked to fix."

Joan looked up with a very red face. Gerry's face went hot too. He leant over and patted her hand. "Forgive me, I hadn't meant to blurt it out like that, but … well, you know I love you, dear."

"One doesn't know that till one is told."

"Well, I'm glad I've got it off my chest, but I don't want to worry you now. All the same, I just can't understand either of you."

"Gerry" — Joan's voice was deep and she spoke slowly — "don't think it's all been thought out carefully. I know it sounds as though I had weighed my love for Tony and measured it against my work. It isn't that. It's just that deep down

I know I love Tony. I can't see myself ever loving anyone as I love him. But, also, I *know* I can't leave my work. If I did we wouldn't be happy. It's part of me. Tony doesn't see it, but it's part of the me that he loves. I can't go into retirement and just love him — Milton's idea, you know — 'Him for God only, me for God in him.'[104] I think it would be fine if I could do it. I realize that Tony isn't being selfish — that he has a big idea of what the perfect love of a man and a woman should be. But I couldn't live up to that, Gerry. I might do it for a month or two, but after that — well, if a call came, say to a job like we've been doing in Shireport, I should go."

"But it's Tony Dacre, of all men, acting the sheik, that's what I can't get," said Gerry, completely mystified. "Now some men I could understand — the lads who like to think they're beefy he-men, who want their women hanging round them all the time, and not having one other blessed interest in life — but Anthony Dacre, and all he's said and written about the freedom of women. Well, I give it up."

Joan said nothing. She knew it was impossible to make Gerry understand what was in her lover's mind. Blain's sheer practical common sense made her idealize still more the mystical perfection of the union which Tony desired. Her heart grew very heavy. "Oh, Tony, Tony, I want you," she breathed within herself. Her hands were tightly clenched, but she made no other sign.

After a time Blain looked at her and smiled. "Look here, Joan," he said in a determinedly light tone, "it seems to me that the obviously sensible thing to do, if you can't marry the man you love because of your work, is to marry the man you don't love and let him help you."

Joan responded with equally forced cheeriness: "But why marry at all?"

"Well, all sorts of reasons *are* given. The best I've heard is my landlady's, and *her* husband's no catch, believe me. She always says: 'What I wants is a man. I'd rather have a good 'un than a bad 'un, but I'd rather have a bad 'un than none. A bedroom don't look furnished unless there's a couple of dirty collars and a pair of braces about.'"

"Then lend me a couple of your collars."

"Not without the man along with 'em, like a present with cigarette coupons. Wouldn't be proper." Then Gerry's laughing tone became very serious. "Is it quite impossible, Joan?"

Joan didn't answer. Gerry pulled himself on to the arm of her chair and rested his cheek on the top of her hair for a moment. Then very reverently he brushed her forehead with his lips.

"Is it hopeless, Joan? I do love you so much. I know I shouldn't ask you … I'm an awful crock and all that."

Joan pressed her hand on his. "You know it's not that, Gerry, but …"

"Couldn't you think about it, Joan? There isn't any hurry … but if at any time you wanted me …"

Joan looked up at him. His face was close to hers. Their lips met in one long kiss.

Realizing how embarrassed she must be, Gerry got up from Joan's chair and went over to the divan. They both lit cigarettes. "Touching on this marriage business," he said with an air of elaborate detachment, "or may we touch on it? When must I go, Joan? Will you say 'Time, gentleman, please,' when the landlady is likely to be sniffy downstairs?"

"I think you ought to go at eleven, Gerry, this not being London."

"So soon! Well, that's just time enough to solve the marriage problem. Most people solve it in a couple of minutes —"

"And spend their lives wishing they had found some other solution."

"Cynic. Can't be allowed at your age, Joan. But I've often wondered whether what we call love stands the test of life — I mean, is it absolutely necessary? It always seems to me, as an outsider that's seen quite a lot of other people's games, so to speak, that a successful marriage is more a question of brains, sheer brains, than love. Of course, love is desirable — I don't mean that — but given two people who like each other and want to get the best out of life, I don't see why they shouldn't make a bigger success out of being pals than two people who are hectically in love, and then find after they marry that they don't share the same interests or the same outlook on life."

"I should think love, the real thing, would be safer to bank on than comradeship, Gerry."

"Well, but would it? Take the case of Vi Legarde, for instance."

"She's married to Caldecott, the scientist, isn't she?"

"That's the chap, and a more unpromising beginning to a marriage I never saw, and I knew them both pretty well."

"What happened?"

"Well, Vi went the pace to the limit during the War. She was a dancer, you know, and very popular with the lads. She and I were great pals" — and Joan noticed that Gerry went very red, but he went on — "Caldecott was in the R.F.C. for a time, but they took him for some special work in Whitehall, something connected with the mathematical dropping of bombs on Huns,[105] and he saw a lot of her in London. He was desperately keen on her."

"Yes?" said Joan encouragingly. She wanted to hear all there was to know about Vi Legarde.

"Well, after the War, she got herself into an awful mess, and Caldecott just married her."

"She was very grateful, I suppose?"

"Yes, I suppose so, but Caldecott didn't bank on that. He just put his brains to work on making that marriage a success. He knew Vi didn't love him, but he wasn't shutting himself up in his lab and leaving her to mope herself into some other fellow's arms in the best romantic tradition. They both recognized they were facing a stiff proposition and they put brains into making it go. And a jolly fine thing they made of it. They've got what I call a *real* home."

"She's back at her work, isn't she?

"Yes, after their son was born she went back. She told me it was their safety-valve against being too wrapped up in each other — each did their own job and enjoyed life all the better for it."

Joan's answer was a deep sigh.

Gerry pulled himself off the couch. "Perhaps I'm not being exactly too tactful, my dear, but there's all sides to the question. Now it's chucking-out time, I suppose."

"Bless you for coming, Gerry, and for all you've done."

Gerry swept a deep, mock-ceremonious bow. "The pleasure, I assure you, moddom, has been entirely mine."

She helped him into his big leather motor-coat.

"When shall I see you again, Joan? Can I call on my way to London to-morrow?"

"Best not, Gerry if you don't mind. I'd rather … well, you know …"

"I understand, lady dear." He kissed her hand. "Good-bye. You'll let me know if ever you want me — for anything."

"Bless you, Gerry I will."

She heard him clumping rather slowly down the narrow stairs. She knelt by her armchair and buried her face in her arms. And somehow as she tried to think she found herself feeling no longer so alone. Gerry was a good friend to have on the earth.

CHAPTER XXI

Royd was much amused at the account of the strike which Joan gave him at his office next morning.

"It's sheer buccaneering, Joan, but, so long as it comes off and no one asks questions, I don't see any harm. But you'll land us into a terrific scrape one of these days."

Joan laughed. "It was good fun."

"Better than London?"

Joan looked up sharply at his tone. Royd looked straight into her eyes. The girl lowered hers. "Of course," she said.

"I'm glad you feel that, Joan. We don't want to lose you, least of all to one of that crowd."

"What's wrong with my friends?"

"If you mean either Blain or Dacre, nothing. I think they are as decent a couple of fellows as I've met. But there was too much softness and luxury about Miss Meadowes' house for a woman like you. We always seem to lose the best of our Movement when they are tempted by the fleshpots."

"Well, a few people go over, but …"

"I'm not thinking of those who go over to the other side. If they could do that, they weren't much good to us when they were with us, but it's our own people, those who lead the Movement. It's not that they change their beliefs, but all the edges get blunted. Poverty doesn't press on them so much. It's hidden, it becomes a matter of statistics. Just an objection to poverty isn't any good, Joan. You've got to be up against the real thing to hate it hard enough to be able to fight it."

"That's an argument for putting all your organizers on thirty shillings a week," said Joan. She would have argued as Royd was arguing if she had been talking to Tony or Mary Maud, but she could see their point of view when Royd argued the other way.

"No, it isn't. Grinding poverty doesn't make one necessarily a rebel, sometimes it makes one a toady. I want our staff to have enough to live on simply, but to keep in touch with reality all the time."

"I'm willing, you know that, but I do like an occasional binge."

"I don't want to come the heavy father," he smiled; "just keep the binges as side-lines, that's all I ask."

"What's my next job?" Joan changed the subject.

"Talking about poverty, I have to lend you one of the mining areas for a bit."

"You think the dispute's going to be a long job, then?"

"I'm afraid so now that foreign coal has started to come in. You will have seen a lot of it at Shireport?"

"Not so much yet. They're working on stocks and use a lot of electricity. The dockers and railwaymen will handle it, I suppose?"

"Yes, they'll have to. My God, I wish they could hold it up. It's awful to think of them having to take the stuff through the ports to defeat the miners after what they did for them in the General Strike."

"Why on earth couldn't they have enforced the embargo on foreign coal right from the beginning? That's what I can't see."

"Because it needed brains and planning and a central headquarters with power and a disciplined movement and all the things we never get in England, either in the Labour Movement or anywhere else. There'll be enough money lost over this business all round before we are through to have reorganized the entire coal industry of the country — but will it be done? Not likely. It means that some vested interests would have to be fought, some of the innumerable parasites would have to be cleared out." While he was talking, Royd was pacing up and down the room with his hands in his pockets. It was rather unusual for him to make 'public speeches' to her, and Joan saw that he was very deeply moved.

"It's a horrible business. What can we do as things are?"

"Help to prolong the agony by keeping the miners' wives and kiddies," said Royd bitterly.

Joan was indignant. "That's not like you, William. Should we let them starve so they will have to give in more quickly?"

Royd stopped his walk and stood looking down at her. "There's no hope of winning, or even a draw. Once the transport and railway workers agreed to handle foreign coal the miners might as well throw in their hands, take a ten per cent reduction, and work up for another fight when they can start with an agreement with the other unions to boycott foreign coal. But, of course, no one will dare to say this. We will all follow Cook round the country and urge the miners to stand firm, God help them."

"William, what has happened to you? It's wicked for anyone in your position to talk like this. It's sheer defeatism."

"Because I want the miners to organize for victory instead of being led into a starvation competition where they haven't a ghost of a chance of even keeping what they've got now? Well, have it your own way, Joan. The Executive have

agreed to let me use the staff for charity organization. There'll be precious little
other work on hand while this drags on. So go and organize soup-kitchens and
urge the miners to stand firm. I wish you joy of it."

He sat down at his desk. Joan suddenly realized how terribly the failure of the
General Strike had told on him. He had seen it as a great uprising of the workers
to help their miner comrades, and the ignominious ending had been a bitter blow.
Joan didn't quite know what to say. She knew to what extent she and all his staff
depended on this man for encouragement in their harassing work. When he was
down, it seemed as though life sagged like old elastic.

"Where am I to start?" asked Joan.

"There's a Women's Committee, started by the Labour Party.[106] You'd better
see what they think is the most urgent job for you. I'll put through a trunk call
to London and ask them."

Joan's services were welcomed by the efficient secretary of the Relief
Committee, and she was sent to take charge of their relief work in a small neglected
mining area some miles south of Shireport. Joan was accustomed to poverty, but
she thought she had never seen such sheer ugliness as in these little mining towns.
Coal dust and the mud of the mines saturated the whole place. The coal-pit was
the only thing in each village that mattered, the only part of life on which capital
and care and brains were expended. Human beings were usually fed into its mouth
at eight-hourly intervals, and just as regularly coughed up again. Now the wheels
of the winding cage were silent, but the domination of the pit remained. On the
refuse-heaps men, women, and children grubbed like maggots trying to find
precious bits of coal to sell for bread. "I could pray to those wheels that they
should turn again," one woman said to her, and Joan thought of Chesterton's
poem:

Call upon the wheels, master, call upon the wheels.[107]

The local authority was dominated by the colliery manager. He was a powerful
man, strongly built, stern of temper. He would hear nothing of feeding the
children in the schools. The pit was open, he said, work was waiting for their
fathers. If they refused work then they were not destitute and the law gave the
Guardians no power to relieve them. As the law was undoubtedly on his side, if
he chose to take this attitude, Joan realized it was no use wasting time on him.
As she got to the door she turned to him and said, "All I wish for you is that the
time shall come when you yourself shall know what it is to lack bread." The
manager remained unmoved by her dramatic attitude.

"Thank you, miss, and the same to you. Please close the door after you."

This little incident put the devil into Joan. She had a personal hate against that gruff, rude manager. She would show him!

She found an unexpected ally in the vicar's wife. When Joan called on her and met a rather gaunt, horsy-looking woman of fifty, she expected to be treated to a lecture on the sins of the miners, but Mrs Armfield bluntly said, "The miners are all right if they are treated right. It makes me sick when people who are too dainty even to put coal on their fires themselves, tell me that miners don't work hard enough. They'd sell coal in little packets in a chemist's shop before we'd go down a pit, so we might be decent enough to appreciate the men who do."

Thus encouraged, Joan told Mrs Armfield of her interview with the mine manager. "That man!" snorted the good lady. "He hasn't the manners of a hog. He was playing partner with me at a little friendly bridge, and swore at me when I played a wrong card."

"That was rather beastly," said Joan hotly.

"Yes, and when my husband demanded an apology, the man turned to me and actually said: 'I beg your pardon, ma'am, but I'd have said that just then if I'd been playing with God Almighty!'"

Joan managed to keep her face straight, and to look suitably sympathetic, but she realized that whether the motive actuating Mrs Armfield was love of the miners, or hatred of the manager, here was a stout ally for the soup-kitchen, some one who could get more out of those in authority than a stranger ever could hope for.

Joan's colleague in the relief work was James Firth, the secretary of the local Miners' Lodge. He was very different from the typical miner of the cartoons. Small, stooping, with a thin, rather scholarly face, the most striking feature about him were his soft brown eyes. During all the time she knew him Joan wondered at the shy expressiveness of those sympathetic eyes. Somehow they reminded her of Tony, though Mr Firth was his senior by twenty years. He had a nervous politeness of manner which hid real strength of purpose, the curious strength of the shy man who forces himself to face an awkward, hostile world. He knew his miners. In the twenty-five years he had been their secretary, there had been no trouble, however personal, that had not been brought straight to James Firth.

As he took her round the streets to call on the most suitable women to form her committee, Joan found in him an attitude very similar to Royd. "We can't win. We've got the best trade union material in the world, but mere willingness to starve doesn't win fights. It's brain work that is lacking, the building of a real union out of these competing little county unions, the linking up with the only unions that can really help — rail, docks, and transport. And, even then, striking isn't enough. We must get reorganization on national lines, or the whole industry will go bankrupt."

"Socialists have been preaching that for twenty years," said Joan earnestly.

"Yes, but there have been too many platitudes, too many vague phrases, too many promises. I grant you theirs is the only idea that has any hope to it, but the *idea* isn't the only thing. It's the detailed planning that is wanted. How tired I am of all the comfortable people who say: 'It will be all-right-on-the-night.'"

"The miners are all Socialists pretty well now I suppose?"

"Yes, except the boozing crowd. They are keen, but it is a race against time till the workers in other industries catch up."

As Joan talked to influential women among the miners — the wives of the county councillors, the officials of the Women's Co-operative Guild, women guardians,[108] the committee of the Labour Women's Sections, she was struck by the power these women wielded in the area. The domination of the whole district by the one union had given important positions to simple working women to an extent that she had not met with in other parts. A finely efficient type of woman was being evolved. Joan badly wanted to bring Anthony Dacre into some of these villages and say to him, "You say I can't be your wife and lover and do my job. Look at the work these women have to do. Take Mrs Cocks — she is on the County Council and the Education Committee, and does every scrap of her own mending, washing, and baking." She laughed to herself, imagining Tony's face. Would he accept that, or would he seek to prove that William and Mary Cocks had not achieved the perfect union he dreamt of? At this impious thought Joan's mind closed. Unconsciously she felt that her adoration of Anthony Dacre, and her admiration for her whole Bloomsbury circle, must be kept carefully shut away from any contact with her sense of humour.

Talking to these responsible women showed Joan one difficulty of working-class life that was a constant annoyance to sensitive people. Rules for local authorities grew up when it was never dreamed that the working class would fill such positions of authority. These rules assumed that county gentry, comfortable tradesmen, the clergy, would become the magistrates, councillors, mayors, and guardians as a matter of course, not such people as miners and even unemployed men and their wives. Joan soon began to understand the harassing difficulties of men and women in these positions without a penny of margin for lunches, fares, or postage stamps. While the unions might pay for certain of their own direct representatives, the little local Labour Parties were too hard up, and expenses had often to be found by the councillor himself, at the cost of absolute necessaries. The men and women who were guardians were in a terrible plight, for, however long they had been unemployed, they could not receive a penny of relief without forfeiting their seats. Very sensibly, collections were made for them among the miners. The London Press called it "bribing the guardians."

This Councillor Mary Cocks, a comfortable, motherly woman, and a pillar of the local Methodist church, became the secretary of Joan's committee.

"It's a shame to pile more work on to you," said Joan apologetically, as she sat by Mrs Cocks' clean fireside.

"It's always the busy folk who can squeeze a bit more in," she replied cheerfully, "and now my man's idle he can turn the mangle and wash the floors. So long as I don't ask him to do anything the neighbours can see him doing, like windows or steps, he's very handy. The miners chaff them as do women's work. I'm glad they've sent you down," she went on; "you are one of us, so to speak, if you don't mind my saying so, but Lord-a-mercy, the fine lady who came down to see me from some fund or other, not ours, she was a treat. When I tried to tell her about the needs of the folks — and, after all, there's not many in this street getting even one square meal a day — not what you'd call a square meal — she said haughtily-like: 'But your husbands have only been out a month. You can't be starving yet surely.' I told her that the men here have been on short time for eighteen months. I wonder what she thought we were doing — drawing cheques on our bank balances?" and Mrs Cocks laughed. Joan was indignant, but Mrs Cocks merely thought the good lady a joke.

"I don't know how you women manage," said Joan as she rose to go.

"Wait till you've five of your own," said Mrs Cocks, patting the girl's cheek, and then smiling at her blushes.

"Five of my own! Great heavens," thought Joan, as she walked on to her next call, "I wonder what Bloomsbury would say to that." Then savagely putting up her umbrella, for the rain was falling heavily, she said: "It would do us all good to have to face these women's problems for a bit; my hat, wouldn't there be a revolution quick!"

CHAPTER XXII

By the time she had got her Women's Relief Distribution Committee well started Joan was accepted by the rather critical and very clannish Yorkshirewomen as one of themselves. "She's got no side," said Mrs Greenhalgh, who was Mrs Cocks' next-door neighbour and the secretary of the Women's Co-operative Guild. "I can do with folks who've got no side. It's when they send slips of girls from college to teach mothers of nine how to bring up children that I draw the line, but Joan's none of that about her. I do like folk with no side." And what Mrs Cocks and Mrs Greenhalgh were agreed upon was usually the general opinion of Carey's Main, the mining town which was the centre of Joan's district.

Joan felt their acceptance when they dropped the "Miss Craig" and "Joan" became universal among men and women alike. Miners don't stand on ceremony with people who have won their approval.

One effect of this was an invitation to move from the little local public-house which called itself an hotel, and to stay with Mrs Cocks, who was the only woman in the district who could boast a spare bedroom. "My three lads were killed in the War," said Mrs Cocks, "and there's no reason why you should live in this hole," as she looked round the shabby bedroom with its soiled counterpane. Joan really didn't need much persuading, and as Mrs Cocks would not receive payment for her hospitality, except a little for the extra food required, her guest solved that problem by paying the equivalent of an hotel bill into the relief fund every week.

Joan flung herself into the work of organizing soup-kitchens, distributing clothing and parcels of food, appealing for funds, making reports to headquarters, investigating cases, all the thousand little duties of such a job, and found therein the satisfaction that comes from watching an organization grow under one's hands from nothing to a bustling hive of active men and women.

Her crowded rooms at the miners' offices reminded her so much of the General Strike days that sometimes in a lull of work she would look wistfully at the door and almost expect Tony to walk in. How it hurt to know that he would never come!

But after her first few days at Carey's Main there began to come from Tony little thoughtfulnesses that warmed her heart. He sent her the latest worth-while novel, then an interesting coloured German wood-cut for her little bedroom, a new book of poems, or a box of chocolates, amusing cuttings from odd magazines, or a quaint jar for flowers on her desk. Twice, sometimes three times in the week, parcels would come, each showing that he had spent care and time in thinking of the right little comfort to send. "Just to cheer up the troops in the front-line trenches," he wrote, when she felt bound to utter a squeak of protest. Joan salved her conscience by always sharing the eatables with her committee. Mrs Pickard, a tiny, weazen-faced woman, once said when Joan had handed round a box of Tony's sweets, "I can make a hard choc last nearly five minutes and it's heaven after bread and marge."

"It's the unending monotony of the life in these mining towns," Joan wrote to Tony, telling him of this incident. "The margin is so small now that a penny bag of sweets or a threepenny seat at the pictures is a treat of which the last drop is to be tasted — and that is not only true for children but for fathers and mothers of families. The ugliness is everywhere, the things in the shops are so cheap and nasty and ugly. There is hardly a modern book in the Free Library, anything decent has long waiting lists, there's just nothing to break the awful monotonous dullness except the home-life in the over-crowded little houses, and the socials they get up among themselves at the church or chapel. I think the ugliness is worse than the poverty."

Tony's answer was to send her still more beautiful things for her own personal use, a Batik[109] cover for her bed that Joan was half afraid to show her hostess for fear she might be offended. But that dear woman just stroked gently the beautiful dyed silk — "Oh, the lovely thing, the lovely thing, isn't it a joy to see!"

"Have it for your parlour," urged Joan. "We could hang it as a door-curtain." But Mrs Cocks wouldn't hear of such sacrilege. Almost reverently she took all her own ornaments and pictures from the little room, and against the bare, clean walls the Batik cover glowed like a jewel. Mary Maud sent little luxuries also, and soon the room was an oasis of colour amid the grime of the coalfield.

Mrs Cocks was greatly elated and allowed a few very carefully selected friends to see the presents from "Joan's rich young man," but Joan felt it was all wrong. Tony was seeking the refuge that conscience with money so often takes — "Let my loved ones at least be comfortable if there isn't enough for every one."

"It is the flight from reality," muttered Joan, but she did not send the Batik cover back to London. There was the same conflict inside Joan herself.

The Relief Committee in London, under whom she was working, urged the regular visiting of all mothers with new babies, and it was this part of the work that brought Joan into contact with a still darker side of life in the overcrowded villages. One morning she was called to a house by Mrs Clark, a dear, old-fashioned midwife, who was one of her favourite cronies. "It is as well you should see this for yourself, Joan, and tell them up in London." When she went into the little house, she found that the mother had been confined in the kitchen, her four little children being taken care of by a neighbour. There was no hot water, no milk for the mother, and but for the midwife's own shawl the baby would have had no clothes at all. Horrified, Joan dashed back to her offices for clothes and food, and wired desperately to Mary Maud, who had already been very generous, "You must send me some money for the babies."

Mrs Armfield had invited the committee to supper at the Vicarage the following night, and Joan came in waving a cheque for five hundred pounds which Miss Meadowes had sent. "Now let's discuss the best way to spend it." The obvious things were suggested, patent foods, milk, outfits for the new arrivals, but Joan was conscious of being up against some reserves, a feeling that these married women would have talked more freely if she had not been there.

At last Mrs Greenhalgh burst out impatiently. "Why don't we tell the truth? What the women in this place want is to know how to stop having any more babies while we're all so poor. Every one of the younger of us in this room is scared to death of conceiving another child when she hasn't food to give them."

"But miners like large families," said Mrs Armfield.

"They did, you mean. There was a time in this coalfield when a child was an investment — the only investment the poor could make." Mrs Greenhalgh had studied at the Labour College economics class and loved to expound a theory. "It was hard work while they were young, but every lad could get a job at fourteen, and three or four strapping men made a difference to the housekeeping money."

"What about the girls?" asked Joan.

"They were another pair of hands in the house to help with the cleaning," retorted Mrs Greenhalgh.

"But it's different now. What hope have these lads of getting work in the pits, even if the lock-out's over next month? What's the use of bringing children into the world that we can't feed and that there's no work for?"

"Because God sends them," put in meek little Mrs O'Brien, a devout Catholic.

"Then why doesn't He send food and clothes along wi' 'em?" said another woman hotly.

"Just look at my list for the relief this week," went on Mrs Greenhalgh. "There's Mrs Robson with four children under five, and three of them down with whooping-cough. Her baby is only four days old and without a rag to its back. There's Mrs Muddiford, with seven children, and her eldest is only ten. They've pawned some of the bedding, and she's expecting, and her husband is as decent a chap as ever stepped in shoe-leather. Then there's Mrs Higgins — her husband's a wrong 'un, I grant you, treats her something shameful, but it's not her fault that she's got eight and expecting another."

Mrs Armitage intervened. "It is a problem, these large families, I agree. The women are too under-nourished to bear them. But, really, it all comes back to the responsibility of the individual. There is such a thing as self-control."

Mrs Greenhalgh blazed. "Does your class practise that? Your class who can get any advice they pay for. What do you mean by self-control, anyway? If the wages coming into my house can only feed three children, does that mean that me and my man only dare be lovers three or four times in twenty years for fear of having more than we can feed? It's absurd, Mrs Armfield, and you know it. It wouldn't work with cold-blooded codfish who had to live in the conditions we live in, much less with strong men like our miners. Your class keep us women in ignorance and then you treat us as though we had committed a crime when we have another baby that you won't tell us how to prevent." To the embarrassment of everyone Lizzie Greenhalgh burst into tears and rushed from the room. Mrs Armfield followed her to comfort her.

"Eh, poor thing," said Mrs Clarke. "It's her Minnie she's thinking of. She was going to have her fourth and took pills and tried falling downstairs to get rid of it."

"But surely that was dangerous," said the horrified Joan, fascinated by this discussion.

"It was to her, poor thing. She injured herself internally and died of peritonitis,[110] and she's not the only one I could tell of, by long chalks."

The barriers were down now. The women had never talked of sex before Joan; she was an unmarried woman, and they stood a little in awe of her, anyway; but from the gusto with which they entered into the fray, Joan saw that this was a favourite subject of discussion, and that, apart from the Catholics, these intelligent women were desperately anxious for some medical advice to be available to them.

"Well, anyway," said Joan, to bring the long discussion to a close, "it's a bigger job than we can tackle, and we can't offend people like Mrs O'Brien and Mrs O'Callaghan who are among our best workers."

"The Catholic vote, as usual," Mrs Cocks smiled. "That's what our M.P. says, good Socialist though he is, when we ask him to raise the matter in Parliament." Joan squared up. "Well, it's true. If some of our best supporters think it's a matter of religion, what can we do?"

"But I'm of a different religion, why should they dictate to me? I don't want to dictate to them. They needn't go to the clinic if they don't want."

"You start reasoning with them yourself," laughed Mrs Armfield, who had returned with a pacified Lizzie and wanted to change the subject. "And, remember, you've got the vote now and you'll get what you want if you make enough fuss about it. It's our job, not the men's."

The discussion was ended by the appearance of two large meat-and-potato pies and steaming jugs of coffee. Mrs Armfield knew her guests. The vicar came in to say grace and give a welcome. He was a tall, white-haired, scholarly-looking man, who would have been more at home in Oxford than in Carey's Main. His wife got him out of the room as soon as possible, for the women's tongues froze with respectful awe in his presence.

"It's Mrs Armfield who is the real vicar," murmured Mrs Cocks to Joan, "and she'd preach better sermons than he does if they'd let her."

There was a little packet from Tony waiting for her when Joan got back to her room, a slim little volume of poetry. Turning the leaves, her eyes were caught by a verse:

> There is a pool in the convent garden. Still is
> the amber basin where no fishes leap,
> but slowly cruise between the water-lilies
> in sleepy gold, as those in silver sleep —
>   sleep on and on,
> their sleep itself a quiet breathing orison.[111]

She warmed to the simple beauty of the poem, and then her thoughts went back to Carey's Main. Carey's Main didn't read poetry. Some of the miners were well read in economics and history, but poetry would have seemed too grim a mockery in the mining towns. The young souls who might be thrilled by it had to keep this a dark secret like some fearful vice, unless they could stand endless chaff, and the souls that were unmoved by chaffing were not the type to whom Humbert Wolfe's work[112] would appeal. Carey's Main was up against life in the raw, and they lived in a world that was frightened they should know too much.

"That's it," said Joan to herself, "London, Parliament, the folks that make laws and regulations, are afraid of the miners and the steel-workers and the other manual workers. They must be kept poor, or they mightn't stick at their jobs, they must be kept ignorant of their bodies or they mightn't produce enough cheap labour, they must be kept overcrowded when slums could be swept away in five years, because, oh why — because we must have someone to look down on, just as we won't give them enough State hospitals for fear we shan't be able to give ourselves the luxury of feeling charitable."

When she had reached this very final conclusion, Joan undressed and got into bed. Had that little speech been made to Royd, he might have noticed that the feared poison was beginning to work. Already influential London was 'we' in Joan's mind. She could feel a rebel when talking to Tony or Mary Maud, but here in Carey's Main in a position of authority, able to distribute money from her rich friends, surrounded in her personal privacy by their gifts, then, though she hated with her whole soul the conditions that made Carey's Main, Joan was already unconsciously on the path of those who draw a distinction between 'we' and 'they.'

CHAPTER XXIII

Joan received very short notes from Gerald Blain during this time. "I would give my ears to be with you in a fight like this," he wrote, "but I can't leave London. Dad's affairs are in an awful mess. I have got power of attorney now and am trying to sort things out. He is suffering horribly, but he is fighting for life like a tiger. He is a stout old chap to put up the scrap he is doing. But Mother is in an awful state, so I can't leave her. Dot the old manager one on the boko for me, and I will try to deliver the K.O.B.[113] in person before long." Gerry was never much of a letter-writer, and except for occasional humorous postcards she heard nothing else of him. Mary Maud's long letters hardly mentioned him except to say at intervals, "Gerry Blain's father is still very ill. We see nothing of him these days."

The post one morning brought a letter from Helen Dacre. She was arranging a *matinée* for the Babies' Fund and she wanted an appeal made direct from the coalfields. Wouldn't Miss Craig come and speak of her own experiences? That letter was a terrible temptation to the girl. A dash to London — Mary Maud's house for a couple of days — seeing Tony, perhaps even meeting him in that little *café* where for the last time she had said she was perfectly happy. And what was the harm? She would be doing urgently necessary work, her committee would applaud her for going; besides, it would be useful to see the Central Committee in London who were mainly the women she had worked with during the General Strike. It would be good to see Beryl Gaye, Blackburn, and the rest. Joan's quick mind produced fifty perfectly excellent reasons why she should, nay, must, accept Helen Dacre's invitation.

But Joan was good stuff at heart, and not given to overmuch self-deception. "You know why you want to go, so don't cover it up," she said to herself sternly. "You want to see Tony, and all the rest is eyewash. Mrs Greenhalgh or Mrs Cocks could tell the tale just as well, and it would be more of a sensation to have a real miner's wife. You've just got to keep out of Tony Dacre's way, or heaven knows what he'll get you to promise."

Feeling a bit like a very virtuous martyr, Joan put Helen's letter before her committee, and on her suggestion Mrs Greenhalgh was appointed to go. "Me talk to those fine ladies! Lord, I couldn't," and the usually determined little woman was quite flustered.

"You go and tell 'em off as you tell us off," advised Mrs Clarke. "You let 'em know what it's like up here!" And with much encouragement from Joan, Lizzie Greenhalgh, who secretly wanted to go very much, was persuaded to agree.

Some one brought in a belated copy of the *Daily Herald*, and looking through it hungrily for news of the outside world Joan saw that Gerald Blain's father was dead.

So Gerry was free at last. Would he really be a millionaire, would he be able to finance that Labour Training College they had talked about so much? There was so little money in the Socialist Movement, so few pounds of any kind that did not belong to the trade unions, that wonders might be done by a young man who had the right spirit as well as funds. While she was checking lists and supervising the packing of parcels, Joan's mind wandered round the new possibilities that Gerry's wealth would open to pet schemes they both shared. She felt that of all the people to have great wealth Gerald Blain would be the least likely to be spoiled by it. She telegraphed her sympathy, and a few days later came a letter from him:

> I have got things sorted out more or less, and the position is much worse than I had feared. The Dad has left everything to me, but that is not going to be much. His brain must have been going for months before he actually went sick. He has been speculating wildly, got loaded up with wads of worthless shares, and thousands on which there are heavy calls. Some grafter must have been selling the old man whole litters of 'pups.' He appears to have been worth well over a million when the War ended, and now when I have sold everything off and met his debts, and invested enough to make Mother comfortable, I doubt if there will even be a few thousands left for all the schemes we planned. Well, I suppose I ought to be the last to growl after all I have said, but it makes me wild to think of those City grafters collaring money we might have used for the Movement. I suppose it serves me right for being so uppish and not going in to help Dad when he wanted me. I'll breeze round as soon as I have got Mother settled. She is going on a voyage with some friends. Just prevent the home fires burning a bit longer and the miners ought to win.

This was an unusually long letter for Gerry, and it was a blow to Joan. To do her justice, she had never thought of the Blain wealth in relation to herself. She had assumed as a matter of course that even were she to marry Gerry this money was to be used in trust for the Labour Movement and not spent on themselves. Of Gerry's adamant decision on that score she thoroughly approved. But it had been so marvellous to plan great projects like the new Labour College, without worrying where the money was to come from — and now an old man had piled silliness on to wickedness, and the war profits had vanished like fairy gold. The women who worked with her wondered at the cause of Miss Craig's irritability that morning. "Perhaps her young man is vexed that she stays here all this time without going to see him," ventured one of the helpers, but she was immediately crushed by Mrs Cocks, who would have no gossip about her guest.

Three days later Joan got back from her visiting to find Gerald Blain talking to Mrs Cocks and Mrs Greenhalgh.

"Well, here you are at last. This poor blighter was beginning to think he'd never see you any more."

"Oh, Gerry, it is good to see you." Somehow Mrs Cocks and Mrs Greenhalgh faded away into the outer office, and they were alone. Gerry was looking straight into her eyes, and then seemed to realize this would not do.

"Thank you for your telegram and letters," he said rather awkwardly.

"And for yours. Oh, Gerry, I'm awfully sorry about things."

"Well, I don't know if I am, now I've had time to think things over. I never was comfortable about that money except when I had decided not to touch it. Once I thought of using it for the Movement all sorts of doubts crept in. It didn't seem right somehow. I should be buying power. I couldn't help that, even though I never spent a farthing on myself. But don't let's bother about it now. Here's you and here's me. Is there anywhere in this hole where we can go and have a coffee and a chat, away from the eagle eyes of your estimable females?"

"No *cafés* in Carey's Main, Gerry; nothing nearer than Englefield, I'm afraid."

"That's only about ten miles, isn't it?"

"Nearer fifteen."

"Less than twenty minutes' run. Just put on a hat and tell your dear old trouts that you're having a morning off."

It was a lovely day. "Why go into a stuffy old town café?" said Joan as they drove out of the town and on to the hills behind. "Let's sit on these moors."

"They spread the car rug on the heather and looked down on the valley scarred with coal-tips and pit machinery.

"It's dragging on, I suppose," said Gerry. "I went into the House of Commons the other night to hear Baldwin weep over the sorrows of the miners. Personally I thought he might have spared them that."

"It's getting awful," said Joan. "The relief money is running out now. The guardians simply haven't got it, and they've cut the relief tickets down by half. They can't help it, of course; the money simply isn't there. Our funds are coming in well, but the need is so great and the people are short of everything. You'd think anyone could buy soap, wouldn't you now, but they can't get it on their relief tickets and the guardians can't give any more relief. The women were quite shy about it until Mrs Greenhalgh raised it on the committee. Said they hadn't had a piece of soap in their house for a week."

"Do your committee get relief as well, then?" asked Gerry.

"Yes, of course, they are all in the same boat. That's what makes this work so different. There's no nosey charity about it. All the women know each other and it's help from equals to equals. Mrs Armfield and the Wesleyan[114] minister's wife are the only middle-class women on the committee. But ours is a small district compared to some and we could use, and use well, all the money that is sent for the whole county."

"It is rotten," sympathized Gerry, "and there looks no reason why it should ever end, with all this foreign coal. My God, what a mess things are in."

"Well, that's enough of my troubles, old man," said Joan. "Now I want all yours. Gerry, you look older since we left Shireport, and it's barely two months ago."

"I feel a positive patriarch, a giddy old antique," replied Gerry. "It's been awful. Anyway, thank God we avoided any open smash and had enough for Mother. I reckon I've about five thousand left to play with."

"Does that mean you are going on the dole?" Joan laughed.

"Well, I like that, madam," said Gerry, throwing a handful of heather at her. "Here have I been keeping myself for six years and earning what these miners would think a princely screw, and she asks me if I'm going on the dole."

"Diddums get its pride hurt, then." Joan threw back the heather. "But, seriously, what are you going to do? You spoke of new plans in your letter."

"My dear, I'm all plans, always was. Well, I'm going to put the whole five thousand into a Labour weekly paper."

"As good and quick a way of losing it as any other," remarked Joan.

"Optimist."

"Well, really, Gerry, you *don't* want telling that."

"But this is going to be entirely different."

"They always are. It's only the end that is the same."

Gerry looked up at the clear blue sky. "These helpful, sympathetic women who stir us on to great deeds," he began plaintively.

Joan laughed. "Sorry. Now tell me all about it and I'll do the sympathizing angel to perfection."

"Well, once upon a time ..." began Gerry teasingly.

"There was a prince who had some money and dropped it down a hole," finished Joan. "But let's take that for granted. Now, what about it?"

"Well, seriously, Joan, I think there's a chance for a really live Labour weekly that doesn't try to sell propaganda but does get good writers and sells as a really interesting paper. No capitalist millionaire could sell capitalist propaganda. He sells jam, and you don't notice the powder till you lick the spoon. Well, my idea is this readable weekly — we'll probably call it something non-committal like the *Wednesday Weekly*, and produce something that is not highbrow but is really lively."

"But you can't do that on five thousand pounds."

"Not likely. This little fruit is out for a thicker branch than that. Theophilus Dodds is coming in as editor, and though he hasn't a bean of his own, he is beloved of all the Quakers and can get money. His uncle is rolling in dough and has promised to help. All the people one wants have promised to write, Tony and Parma de Pratz and their crowd. Horrabin has promised some cartoons, and Maxton will write for us."[115]

"And are you going to be the editor?"

"Not likely. I know my limits. That's for Theophilus. I shall be the honorary publicity wallah and make my living as usual out of the capitalist Press, which I shall continue to denounce in our own squeaker."

"It's a bit topsy-turvy that they'll let you."

"Damned good proposition for them to get our Labour writers. We give good value for their money, and the folks who want to read our stuff buy their papers and — I suppose — to some extent absorb their dope, God help 'em."

"I know, but there is a funny kind of tolerance in England, Gerry."

"But we can't say what we want to say. We have to go into their journals with, at best, non-committal stuff, and then simple innocents like Milady Joan say: 'See how tolerant is the British Press!'"

Joan laughed and pulled a face at him.

"You are going to help with this, Joan."

"Me! I've never written a line in my life. I'll pack up parcels if ever I'm in London, which isn't often."

"No, we shall do all our packing very professionally. The only amateurs that we shall encourage will be the writers, and you, my Joan, are going to do a series of 'Simple Stories from a Woman's Heart.'"

Joan lay back on the heather and howled with glee. She had not had such a laugh since the Shireport strike

"Me," she gurgled, "me, with a simple woman's heart. 'How to help your husband.' 'What to say to Rudolph when he is seen with another girl.' Marvellous, Gerry."

"'s all right. It's not 'Aunt Alice's Heart-to-heart Talks with Girls' I'm thinking of, but you *can* do the stuff I want. You sit down and write week by week the stories about Lizzie Greenhalgh's daughter and the woman who had her fifth baby with the other four in the room. No propaganda, no moral, just the plain yarn at a thousand words a time. It will be the goods, Joan, and you've got to do it."

"Do you really think I can, Gerry? It's not because — well, because we're pals that you are asking me, is it?"

"No, no sentiment, strictly business. I'm the new Napoleon of the Labour Press. I choose my minions." Gerry struck a fierce attitude and then he too rolled in the heather with laughter.

They were young and the sun was hot. Hope and interesting work lay ahead of them, and life with all the stimulation and interest it can offer to those on whom no iron collar of routine is fastened.

"It will be a great lark, and I'll try my best. I'd love to help."

"Good egg. Oh, must we get back? No, look here, you must have some eats. You can surely have one day off after two months. Let's drive to this other place you spoke of."

They drove to Englefield in high spirits and got tea and food at a picture-house *café*, while Gerry gave a racy account of the London crowd. As they were driving home in the early evening Joan said: "It was awfully decent of Helen Dacre to run that *matinée* for my babies. Of course, I couldn't keep the whole lot for here, it had to go to the Central Funds, but they let me have a third of it. I did think it was decent of her."

"She is a decent sort in her own way. She has softened a lot lately." Gerry apparently fumbled around with his gear handle, and then went on: "She is having an awfully unhappy time, Joan, and she looks rottenly ill."

"I'm sorry, Gerry. I'd do anything I could, but there is nothing I can do."

"You might make up your mind, for example. I don't think Helen would mind which way, but she feels now as though anything may happen at any time — and you must admit it's a bit devastating."

"Gerry, I'm sorry, deadly sorry. Everything is in the world's most ghastly mess and, somehow, against this fight, well, one's own personal woes seem a bit small."

"Yes, when one's got a job like yours on hand, but Helen isn't doing anything just at the moment. That *matineé* was a godsend to her, really. And, meanwhile, she hasn't much else to do but think about her troubles."

"I feel an awful beast," said Joan, "but how can she go on living with Tony and expect to be happy when she knows? It seems to me too humiliating."

Gerry pressed her hand and changed the subject. He had to return to London early next morning and did not want to talk about the Dacre affair just then.

Joan was sorry at the moment, but she didn't waste much time on Helen's troubles. Her panacea for all worries was work. She was hard on herself and life had touched her too lightly as yet for her to realize how deep the wounds of the spirit can be. Her own love for Tony caused her suffering which, at times, was very acute, but Joan could always "fill in," as she called it, and, though she would not have admitted it, she was thoroughly enjoying her position of power and responsibility at Carey's Main. It was hard luck on Tony that his call to her should have come at one of the most exciting periods of the Labour Movement's history. Away from his influence, from the pull of his personal charm, Joan felt less and less inclined to sacrifice such interesting work for his love, and motherhood seemed a much less mystical event since she had helped with dozens of new babies in the narrow streets of Carey's

Main.

Gerry's project touched her imagination. Now that her organization was on a sound basis and running almost of itself, with more willing helpers than she could possibly use, Joan began to keep her evenings free for writing. It was a thrilling secret, and with great care she produced three such stories as Gerry had suggested, stories whose characters would have been easily recognizable in Carey's Main. She sent them off with fear and trembling, and got a wire from Theophilus Dodds.

"Excellent. Do more while you feel in form."

Thus encouraged, she sent copies of them to Tony and asked his opinion. His reply came almost by return of post. "This is excellent copy," he wrote; "you have freshness and real talent that ought to be developed. Why not make this your life-work? I have not worried you during this trouble. We must all do what we can to help the miners. Ordinary standards do not apply. But when it is over, here is the answer to our difficulties. Let us settle down together and I will help you to become a writer. You can reach bigger audiences this way than ever you can by speeches. My darling, I feel so happy. I feel as though a way was opening out. It has been miserable without you, my beloved, but now we can soon be happy. Write and tell me yes."

This letter amazed Joan. If he objected to one independent career, why not to another? If the organizer, why not the writer? And then Joan saw that it would be no independence. Tony imagined himself leading and directing her, helping her with publishers, her writing being an interesting little hobby to fill in her time when he was writing too. She would have no life apart from his, and could she write at all the? Joan had sense enough to realize that the whole value of the work she had sent to Dodds and Tony lay in the freshness of its material, its contact with the raw life of the coalfield. But in Bloomsbury, or in the little cottage in the Pyrenees that Tony had once talked about, would she have anything to write about? She would have no first-hand contacts with life, nothing fresh to say that literary London had not already said in a much more experienced fashion. But how could she answer Tony? To write all this would be equivalent to telling him that she didn't love him now. Of course that wasn't true. Joan was indignant, even to herself, but somehow, nowadays, whenever she sat down to think about Tony, her mind always drifted to Gerry, to his exciting project of the new weekly, his active life, living slummily but gaily in a back street in Bloomsbury, and working always at worth-while things. She answered Tony with a vague wait-till-the-war-is-over letter, and scolded herself for being a beast.

CHAPTER XXIV

Gerry had spoken to the miners in the village hall the night before he left for London, and Joan had over-heard him promising James Firth to come back later and speak at some union meetings in the district. This had made her feel rather ashamed of her own neglect of the men's side. She had taken their solidarity in the dispute for granted, and, apart from a few meetings when she first came to Carey's Main, she had thrown all her energies into the relief work. By the strength of her personality, because of the money from outside which she represented, and because of the workers' desperate need, Joan, without realizing it, had made the relief organization overshadow everything else. The miners would, she assumed, go on being good boys and stay put, while Joan and her energetic committee of miners' wives got the thing done that really mattered.

It was this overheard conversation between Gerry and the quiet James Firth, in which, of course, her name was not mentioned, that awakened Joan to the fact that the men were resenting her well-intentioned domination. In a coalfield it is the man who counts. The women fit in — there is no other course open to them. Joan suddenly saw that all this relief organization had shifted the balance. The men could not now provide for their families; that was done through the women and children. All charitable appeals were made on their behalf, and the money went to the mother. The guardians could not, by law, relieve able-bodied men when work was, in theory, available to them. The relief had to be paid to the woman for herself and the children. The man's bread had to be taken out of their mouths, he had to share in what was sent for the mother and children if he ate at all.

"My goodness, how the men must hate it," thought Joan, all conscience-stricken, "and we've never done a thing to bring them in. We women have been so proud of doing it all ourselves here. We've been getting to feel that it's our nice little war." She put this idea to Mrs Greenhalgh, but that fierce little woman was more of a feminist even than Joan. "Do 'em good. The men are too uppish, anyway. Let 'em see what we have to put up with for a change."

"I don't know about that, Lizzie," said the wise Mrs Cocks rather slowly. "I don't know but what there's a lot in what Joan says. Of course, every one shares and shares alike, but the men are being made to feel that they are eating the children's bread instead of providing it, and it's cutting deep with many of those as don't say much. You can't alter the course of nature without upsetting a lot of other things."

"Well, the course of nature wants a bit of upsetting in the mining towns, and I've often said so, Mary."

"Are you thinking of putting on the pit clo'es and going down the shaft when the pit opens?"

"Well, there's other things besides digging coal, Mary. The women have the children."

"Yes, and the men have to provide for them, which is a harder job in Carey's Main. It's no use you going on so, Lizzie; where brawn rules, whether in war or coal-getting, the women are the underdogs when it comes to the bit, and they've got to put up with it."

"For ever?" asked Joan.

"Yes, or until they get rid of war or coal-digging, which, please God, may not be so far off, if these inventions that Captain Blain was talking about could be got started. I wish we women could get a-gate organizing that job." Mrs Cocks was a fierce politician and dreamed often of that body of sensible men and women who she felt must surely exist somewhere, if only some one could get hold of them and put them into Parliament and let them "get on with the job," in her favourite phrase. It was the theme of all her speeches to the little gatherings of women in the district.

Joan didn't discuss theories of sex equality with James Firth, but she went in a very subdued, almost apologetic mood to ask if she couldn't be allowed to help with the men's meetings. Firth was touchingly grateful: "The men are getting a bit stale. There's been no blacklegs at all to keep things lively. Of course, there couldn't be, with the men locked out and the pits just shut down. What about running a bit of a meeting in the smaller villages? We've only had them in the bigger ones."

Characteristically Joan swept aside any such small ideas that Firth might have. Her apologetic mood disappeared with his acceptance of her help. There must be the biggest demonstration Carey's Main had ever known. The men must be brought in for miles round. Of course, A. J. Cook must come and special trains and 'charas'[116] be organized. "It would be immense," she glowed.

"But isn't it a pity to bring Cook here when everything is solid, and there's so many places that are shaky and need him," said Firth mildly.

But no. Joan was sure she could get him. Captain Blain knew him well, he would motor him over. Leaving Firth rather uneasily conscious that he would count very little in this show, Joan dashed off to the post office to send a telegram to Gerry to secure Cook at all costs for the earliest available date; she sent such a wire to the miners' secretary himself as to convince that overworked but impressionable man that there must be something seriously wrong in an area which he had hitherto regarded as impregnable. He cancelled another urgent meeting in a very weak spot and wired an early date for Carey's Main. Cook's telegram went to Firth in such terms as made him rush round in agitation to Joan to find out what she had said in hers.

"Oh, just that we wanted him very much," she said casually, "but I signed it in your name, because obviously it would have more influence. See what a lot he thinks about you to come at once when you ask him."

With that the conscientious man had to be satisfied, but he had run his district quietly with a hundred-per-cent.solidarity through all the trying weeks of the lock-out, and had been proud that he had not had to ask once for outside help. What had that girl said to Cook?

"I do wish women wouldn't interfere," he said to himself as he went home. He had to say it to himself, as his wife was in Joan's innermost circle, and was never at home these days to be talked to. "But, of course, we couldn't have managed without this Relief Committee, so I'll have to put up with it," and he turned resignedly to do his account books — but, alas, there was so little to account for these days.

The women were wild with delight at the idea of the Cook demonstration and set about the organization of it at once. Joan was determined that the men should be brought in this time. They were sent out with the news to the distant villages, chalked the walls and wrote out posters. There was no need to do anything as far as the miners were concerned, but pass the word round that Cook was coming. But Joan was determined that the women should hear him too. A letter to Miss Meadowes brought a promise to defray the cost of a dozen char-à-bancs. It was Joan's demonstration. Firth privately thanked his Providence that there was no man with whom Joan was likely to settle down in his district, but he gave his blessing to anything about which he was consulted, which wasn't often. "Why do you let t'women boss t'show like this, lad?" asked the burly miners' secretary from Englefield. "I tell you, I wouldn't stand it. I'd put that Women's Committee of your'n in their places. We have none o' that nonsense in my area."

"No," said Mrs Firth, who had overheard that remark, "perhaps that's why they've appealed to us to help the babies."

"The bairns are doing all right," he retorted. "Food and no fancy trimmings is my motto. All money for food. They can do wi'out clo'es this weather if they aren't clemmin'."

Joan was completely immersed in these arrangements when a letter came from Helen Dacre saying that she was arranging for a *musicale* in some fashionable West End rooms from which she hoped to raise a lot of money for the Babies' Fund, and could Joan come herself to make the appeal? This time Joan did not even hesitate. London did not exist for her at the moment. Hilda Gallagher or Lizzie

Greenhalgh could go. But with the afternoon post came a letter from Mary Peters, the general secretary of the Relief Committee, saying that Joan must attend the *musicale*. It was to be an important affair and an experienced speaker was wanted, with actual experience of the relief work. "We also think," went on the letter, "that your committee at Carey's Main should be able to carry on the work without you. You have some very experienced helpers, and we need you for other work. Please make arrangements to hand over immediately and report here for further instructions as soon as possible."

The sun seemed to go out as Joan read this letter. Leave Carey's Main just now! It was too bad, and with Cook coming, too. But when she had cooled down a little Joan had to admit the justice of Miss Peters' letter. There was nothing now that her committee and James Firth could not manage perfectly well between them. She wrote to say she would report in three days' time. Once this decision was taken, Joan's mind veered round completely. London, perhaps work at headquarters, and live with Mary Maud. To see Tony and Gerry, to be at the centre once again and recapture the thrill of the General Strike days. The girl who had found it utterly impossible to leave Carey's Main for even a night managed to clear up all her work, hand over the responsibility for the Cook meeting, pack her belongings and say good-bye to her friends in less than two days. She was in the 5.10 train to London the next day but one after Mary Peters' letter had torn up her roots.

Half the women in the town seemed assembled at the station to see her off. Those who had little gardens brought her flowers, and piled them on the cushions until her railway carriage looked like a harvest festival. Mrs Armfield came with a box of chocolates and a book from the vicar, and enough sandwiches and cakes for the journey to feed her for a week. They sang *The Red Flag* and *The Internationale* over and over again, and the train streamed out to the passionate chorus:

> "Then, comrades, come rally,
> The last fight let us face."[117]

But as Joan leaned far out of the window, waving her handkerchief to the last possible moment, the thought crossed her mind that this was almost entirely a women's celebration. A good number of men had come along to say good-bye, but somehow they had been elbowed to the back of the crowd.

Mary Maud met her at the station. "My dear, what are you going to do with all these flowers? They are fading already. Why on earth did you let them load you up with all this vegetation?"

"Oh, Mary Maud, they are darlings and it was all they had to give." But it was a bit of a problem to know what to do with it all, and with a qualm of conscience

Joan picked up one small bunch for her bedroom and left the rest for the porters to deal with. Carey's Main was already fading a little out of the picture. It was lovely to be back again in Mary Maud's house, sitting by the fire, to eat one of Suzanne's perfectly cooked meals, and to hear all the gossip. And after supper — a long luxurious smoke, snuggling in the cushions, wrapped in the soft beauty of the charming room.

"Oh, Mary Maud," sighed Joan, "this is all wasted on you. You ought to go and live in Carey's Main where the only beautiful thing is the sunset over the smoke-blackened moor. Then you'd appreciate your mercies."

"I'm glad you like coming here so much. It's one of the excuses I make to myself for it all, that I can give an overworked warrior a rest now and again," answered Miss Meadowes comfortably.

Tony called after supper and Gerry 'phoned to ask if "a li'l' orphint boy could have a cup of coffee if he put on a clean pinny and washed his neck." It was like old times, this meeting of friends, without the grinding anxiety of the General Strike in the background. Gerry brought Theophilus Dodds, the editor of his paper, with him. Theophilus, in spite of his name, was large and hearty. He called Joan by her Christian name at once, and was evidently quite at home in the Gordon Square house. Joan had to tell her adventures, but the young men were chiefly interested in their new paper. The first number was due in a week's time. They had had all sorts of difficulties. Dodd's father had cooled somewhat and his help had been rather meagre. Gerry's five thousand pounds was swallowed up in preliminary expenses and Mary Maud had had to come to the rescue as usual.

"Oh, isn't it maddening, Gerry, all that money of your father's to have gone down the dyke just when it was wanted so badly! Just thrown away, too."

"I don't know about that," said Tony. "I've been trying to convince this dutiful son that his father wasn't such a fool as he thinks. If he hangs on to that big packet of International Wireless shares, I think he'll get back more than he has lost. The old man knew a thing or two."

Joan glowed. "Gerry, wouldn't it be marvellous if Tony is right?"

Dacre knocked the ashes from his pipe. "Are you as anxious as all that, Joan, for Gerry to be rich?" Blain looked up at his tone, but the girl was quite unconscious of any other meaning.

"Of course, aren't we all? Fancy having money for all the things one wanted to do, and being able to do them properly. It just makes all the difference. Sometimes I wonder why it is with a case like ours, with all the poverty there is, we don't sweep the country at every election and hold the power against all comers. And then when one thinks of all the wealth against us, the Press, all the ways money can talk through the cinema, books and magazines, I wonder we poll as well as we do."

"Well, I'm going back to my old views about money, Joan," said Blain. "I don't believe shovelling it out to causes does much good. Somehow folks can get the money for the things the people really want. It's not giving them our things but making them *want* them that is our problem."

"But surely advertising ..." said Dodds.

"It's useful, of course, as a good Press is useful, and heaps of other things, but money can't give you the root things."

"And what's that?" — there was a chorus.

Gerry, who was lying stretched flat on the floor in his favourite attitude, trying to get relief from the ever-present pain, hitched a cushion under his head and said: "Sufficient people with character and guts."

"Thanks," said Theophilus, "present company excepted, of course."

"I except nobody, least of all myself — but I do say this. When we've finished all our explaining and apologizing to Rothermere and Beaverbrook[118] we remain a revolutionary party — at least, that part of it that's worth anything does. Well, that means leaders, and it seems to me that old man Lenin[119] got right at the root of things when he insisted on the necessity for trained leaders."

"Professional revolutionaries — a damnable idea," said Tony sternly.

"Gerry, you don't mean that — people paid to go round upsetting things." Mary Maud's voice quivered. This nightmare of things being upset was continually being held before her by her beloved Gerry. She did wish he wouldn't. He was so nice himself, why should he have this mania for upsetting things?

"Paid agitators? No, I don't want people paid for agitating. That's the devil of things as they are now. As soon as any member of the working class shows ability as a leader, if he's too rebellious to be collared as a foreman by the boss, the men make him an official and he steps right out of their class. Take Joan there. Now think what a power she would have been if she could have been kept in that shop where she used to work. Of course she would have got the sack and had to get another, but she'd have gone on fighting. What happens? She's pretty (don't blush, Joan), she's clever, she is made an official. Then come along the Mary Mauds and the Anthony Dacres." ("and the Gerald Blains," put in Dacre). "Quite. She is now a member of the middle class. Then she'll get into Parliament and be quite a lady. Shall you be presented at Court, Joan? Women M.P.s can be if they like, I understand," he said teasingly.

Joan went bright scarlet. "Gerry, you are a beast. It's not true I'm middle class. It's not true I want to leave the workers. What about Carey's Main and all my other work?"

"Sorry, Joan, I didn't mean to be personal, but you are a bit of a red-rag personality — it tempts one to go for you — but I'm not getting at any individual. You asked me what could get things altered in this country, and I say the only thing is for the men and women who can lead the workers is to stick with them, live their life, eat their bread, and resolutely refuse to go one step beyond the standard of living of the people they are leading. I tell you, that would create the revolution quick enough. Just think how ten thousand times more effective a man like Jimmie Thomas would be if he were leading the men from the guard's van of a Great Western train."

"And I say you are talking nonsense, Gerry, like any left-wing ranter," said Tony. "You would deprive the workers of any real leadership. A man can't conduct delicate wage negotiations and remain a railway guard or a miner."

"Yes, he can, and a damned sight better. He'd know how the shoe pinched," said Gerry. But to go back to where we started. If these wireless shares do come to anything, you lot here can handle the cash and see if you can do any good with it. I believe that I can do only as much good as the life I'm leading helps to influence folks, and not one jot more, though I gave away Rockefeller's fortune, with the Rothschild siller[120] thrown in as makeweight."

"Our budding St Francis," laughed Dodds. "Never mind, old man, we'll scatter the pelf all right if it materializes."

Joan was silent. Quite irrationally she was thinking of a Batik bed-cover and some lovely silk cushions. She wondered ...

"When did you have a meal last?" said Miss Meadowes suddenly.

"God knows," said Gerry.

"There. I knew it. He always gets so St Francis-y when he's hungry." Mary Maud was quite unconscious of irony. "Goodness, it's gone midnight. You poor dears. Let's all have sandwiches. I told Suzanne to leave a pile in a damp cloth. I was sure we'd all talk our heads off. Switch on the percolator, Tony. Joan, you boil the milk."

They were all soon merrily bustling around, and Gerry was the gayest of the party that hungrily ate Suzanne's sandwiches and drank the hot milky coffee which Joan produced.

CHAPTER XXV

Joan went to the Relief Headquarters the next day with a gay heart. It was a beautifully clear morning after rain in the night. On the luxury of Mary Maud's special spring mattress she had slept for nine hours. She had awakened in the soothing beauty of the mauve and silver bedroom, and splashed in the perfectly tiled bathroom. At Carey's Main she had only been able to use a tin bath in the scullery once a week. Mary Maud had a present for her at breakfast — a sports suit she had had made to her friend's measurement by a fashionable dress-maker. There was a pleated skirt of soft wool, in just the shade of soft red that suited her, and a cunningly combined coat and jumper in red and beige, with a quaint little *beret* to match.

"Oh, Mary Maud, you shouldn't — I mean, with all the miners out and all that."

"It's an investment for them, my dear. Miss Peters wants you to go round getting money, and a well-dressed woman is the best money-extracting apparatus that was ever invented."

Certainly the outfit gave Joan a delightful feeling of confidence as she drove down to the Relief Committee in Mary Maud's car. Her shabby serge suit had been hardly treated in the strenuous days at Carey's Main, and even after Gerry's lecture of the night before Joan could not help the satisfaction that comes to any woman who knows she is perfectly and suitably dressed. She squashed firmly any little twinge of conscience that tried to make itself felt.

Mary Peters, the secretary, Joan had met during the General Strike. An impressive, even imperial figure, surrounded by scurrying helpers, she was a woman accustomed to receive obedience and looked very surprised if, by any chance, it was not accorded implicitly and instantly. She received Joan amicably enough, and the girl waited in her room while messages were received, decisions made, and orders given.

"Things are always like this on Fridays," said Miss Peters, and Joan felt that she was put on terms of equality at once. She wondered if this was the lady's habit with officials, or whether Mary Maud's backing had anything to do with it.

"You've managed to raise a good deal of money for Carey's Main, apart from our funds," was Miss Peters' first rather enlightening remark.

"I'm sorry," murmured Joan, "I know it all ought to have come through here, but Miss Meadowes liked to send it direct to me. She is very rich, and Mrs Dacre helped."

"Oh, it doesn't matter particularly," and Miss Peters' tone was that of one who had had to get used to the caprices of the charitable wealthy, "except that they will miss it now and it is fairer if every one shares alike in any funds that are going. Now we want you to do a series of meetings round London — first-hand experiences always get money, and we are desperate about this Babies' Special Fund."

"Isn't the money coming in so well?"

"Oh, very well, really, considering it's mostly in small donations from people who can't afford it, though of course there are big subscriptions as well. That's why I wanted to see you specially. We are particularly concerned about this *musicale* that Mrs Dacre is arranging. She is taking endless trouble and it really is good of her as she is so strongly opposed to us politically. It will reach a class of people we haven't been able to touch — really wealthy fashionable Society people. It is most important that it should go well."

"Wouldn't Lady Christina Hatherley," mentioning a recent Society recruit to Socialism, "be better for it than me?" asked Joan.

"No, she hasn't the contacts you have. She is helping, of course. But I want you to talk it over with Mrs Dacre beforehand, and prepare very carefully for it."

"Of course I will. I know I mustn't tread on their corns."

"Of course I can trust you to be tactful," smiled the awe-inspiring Mary, as she dismissed her to the care of the Meetings secretary.

Joan spent a pleasant morning at the office renewing old acquaintance with Beryl Gaye, and her tall, thin helper with the humorous eyes, Stella Kaye, and then went off to lunch with Tony.

Joan had just enough work during the following days to prevent her conscience troubling her. She spoke at one meeting, sometimes two, each day. There was nothing she could do at the offices, where the voluntary helpers had shared out all the work quite efficiently. Tony was a perfect companion for enjoying London. He knew the odd corners and the quaint bookshops. He had artist friends in Chelsea and lawyer friends in the Inns — men of youngish middle age like himself, who told good stories and had odd chambers up winding stairs. They gave her tea in old rooms that looked across fine lawns, though the noise of Fleet Street could be clearly heard from the distance. They joked about their wares: "I can do you a cheap line in divorces just now, Miss Craig," an Irishman with a clever, hard face remarked casually. "We're putting through a few shop-soiled cases at ninety pounds each. Pity they are no use to you." Joan went scarlet, and Tony turned the awkward corner. Tony's own friends never saw Helen. Some of them vaguely knew a wife existed, or had met her at a *première* of one of her productions, but Helen's parties in the Dacre flat had consisted exclusively of her own friends. Tony's friends would, of course, have been invited he had insisted, but Helen had never been interested enough to inquire if there was anyone he would like ask, and Tony grew more and more secretive about own interests. There was something pathetic in his anxiety to show Joan to his own cronies and his own pet bits of the city. And in the easy-going tolerance of semi-Bohemian, semi-professional London, Joan was accepted and welcomed as Tony's friend without question or remark.

Joan chattered of these expeditions to Mary Maud, and in the new and deep friendship which had grown up between the two older women Mary Maud felt that at least Helen ought to have a tactful hint as to what was happening. Mrs Dacre shrugged her shoulders: "I wish Her Highness would at least make up her mind whether or not she wants my husband. This uncertainty is a little trying." Casual words, but Miss Meadowes had seen the difference that even a few weeks had made in Helen Dacre. She was taut and strained, where always she had been cool and indifferent, perfectly groomed as ever, but the dark-rimmed eyes told the tale of sleepless nights, and the tightened lips spoke of a pride that would raise no complaint and ask no quarter. The proud woman was being made to suffer all and more of the pain her selfishness had inflicted on Tony in the days when his love placed him at her mercy.

Mary Maud felt that matters could not be allowed to drift indefinitely, for, after Helen's *musicale*, Joan would probably be off to the North again on her usual work. One evening when Joan had come in late from a meeting, and they were sitting having supper by the fire, Mary Maud decided that this cool young lady must be tackled.

"Joan," she said suddenly, after a pause, "how are things between you and Tony now? Have you made up your mind whether you are going to have him?"

"I made up my mind right at the beginning. I'm not giving up my work."

"But is he still insisting on that? I don't want to meddle, Joan, but you are going about together such a lot. Is he coming round on that?"

"I don't know. We haven't discussed it. What's the hurry, anyway?"

The callousness of emancipated youth! Here was a girl free from all the conventions that had shackled Mary Maud's childhood, and spoiled her own romance, and what was the hurry, anyway, to decide which man she wanted, or whether she wanted any? The only fixed point in Joan's conscience seemed to be her work. The gentle Miss Meadowes could not keep a touch of asperity out of her voice. "There may be no hurry for you, Joan, but have you considered the effect of all this on Helen?"

"But Helen doesn't love Tony, and she has her remedy."

"And what may that be? You certainly haven't given her any cause to divorce him, even if she wanted to."

"She needn't go on living with him if she doesn't want him. Frankly, Mary Maud, I'm sorry for Helen and all that, but the way you and Gerry talk about her, I might have taken from her some trinket she possessed and valued. She says herself that she never loved Tony. You said she treated him abominably until he got too indifferent to her to care how she treated him. The time he spends with me he wouldn't spend with her, anyway. Why does she go on living with him when he has told her he loves me? I could understand the woman who has children, or who is dependent on her husband for food and shelter, but Helen earns her own living, and can earn as much as Tony when she likes. She wants his name as a convenience. Well, she has got that, and if she thinks the humiliation of living under the same roof with a husband under those circumstances is worth that convenience, well, what has she got to grumble about?"

Mary Maud was silenced for the moment, and could only reply: "You haven't been married, Joan, or you would talk differently."

"No, I've not, and what I've seen of my friends doesn't make me so particularly anxious about it either. I agree with Bernard Shaw.[121] I'm not going to get married until I can have it on fair terms, but I believe in being fair all round, to the man as well as the woman. Helen has taken all she wanted out of her marriage and has given precious little in return. I believe in fifty-fifty, Mary Maud. I'm sorry for Helen, but she is only reaping what she has sown. I'm rather tired of women who take all and give nothing, and then expect sympathy from all their friends when their husband meets another woman with some sense of fair play, just as I am sick of middle-aged men who've taken all their wives could give them and then go hunting round for any pretty girl who'll listen while they tell her how they are misunderstood at home. Tony's swallowed his smoke without complaining and Helen will have to do the same."

Mary Maud sat by the fire a considerable time after Joan had taken herself off to bed. She had not been able to answer Joan's directness by any talk about the sacrament of the marriage tie, because Joan knew by now, having at last heard the story from Gerry, that Helen herself had not observed that in Tony's absence. Besides, abstract appeals to general principles, she had noticed, did not affect Joan and Gerry's generation one hair's-breadth. "But why?" they answered to any argument based on maxims. Things must have been so much simpler in the days when elders could simply say: "I am not arguing, I am telling you." Modern girls with their own salaries, their own careers, their well-trained minds, their decency, too, that had to be admitted, demanded reasons for any sacrifice. "Fifty-fifty," Joan had said, and Mary Maud realized that if she could have appealed to Joan on the strength of Helen's helplessness, or dependence, or children, Joan would have been recklessly generous at the expense of her own happiness. But Joan, in this talk, had at last said what she really felt, namely, that Helen was as capable as she was of earning her own living and the fact that she had married Tony fifteen years before was no absolute claim for complete possession of him now. It was a hard doctrine, and, though in theory she might have to admit the logic of it, Mary Maud was an ageing woman, too, and could see a side of the argument that had not yet occurred to twenty-six-year-old Joan in the glow of her youth.

Anthony Dacre was equally anxious to know Joan's mind. He also reckoned that time was getting short, and that the Joan who was content to be his companion while speaking at meetings and awaiting Helen's big event for the miners, would certainly be off north again as soon as that was over, and that date was only two days off.

On the day following Mary Maud's talk with Joan, there was an afternoon meeting and garden-party arranged by the Kew Committee, at which Joan made the appeal for the miners' funds, and afterwards Tony drove her through Richmond Park and on to the Surrey Highlands, where first Joan had confessed her love for him. It was a beautiful evening and they sat above the Punchbowl, looking at the soft glow of green and blue, and the mist over the moorland. Helen was having a dinner-party that night to which both Joan and Mary Maud were invited, but it was hard to leave that glory in order to drive back and dress and eat food in town.

"The South is lovely," said Joan wistfully. "We never get quite this beauty up in the North. It's wilder of course, but this heavenly soft colouring is just Surrey."

"Will you be going north after Helen's affair?" asked Tony, slowly sucking at his pipe.

"I expect so. My London meetings will be finished by then. That's the last."

"You've enjoyed this little spell we've had together?"

"Oh, Tony, it's been heavenly. I do love London, I can't help it. I adore the very smell of its taxis, and I can't say more than that, can I?" she smiled.

"And what about me, and you and me?" He knocked out the ashes from his pipe and put it in his pocket. He did not touch her. She sat huddled up with her arms round her legs and her chin on her knees, looking at the hills. She did not answer.

"Joan, dear one," he drew nearer and stroked her wrist with his finger, "I've been thinking a lot since we last talked together here, and since we talked that wet morning in the *café*, you remember?"

"Rather," said Joan.

"Well, I think I was much too — how shall I say it? well, much too wholesale then. I don't take it back — the ideal, I mean — but I'm sure we could fit things in all right if we tried, Joan."

"How?"

"Well, Helen is willing for a divorce now. That will simplify things a lot, won't it?"

"Ye-es. Do you want it, Tony, honest?"

The suddenness and straightness of the question startled the man. "Of course," he said.

"There's no 'of course' about it. Do you really want a divorce — now, honest Injun? We must talk straight, it's all so desperately important."

"All right, then, my dear, I'll be equally straight. I don't mind saying that I hate the publicity of it, and what I shall have to pretend to do in order to give Helen the evidence and keep your name out of it. If both she and I weren't so well known it wouldn't matter perhaps, but even under this new law, well, we're both celebrities, I suppose, in the newspaper sense, and they can't resist a tit-bit like that. And, oh, my dear, I've got to confess it, I feel a bit of a cave-man about you too. Somehow I loved the idea of just a cave for you and me that no one knew of and no one could come to except a few extra special friends. I hate society. I've lived in the middle of the street, so to speak, people always calling and dining, or wanting us to call or dine or week-end. I wanted a private life all hidden away, but I realize all the risks for you, my dear, and so we'll manage the horrid part somehow."

Joan squeezed his arm. "Tony, you are a decent soul," she murmured, "but, why, oh why, couldn't you fall in love with a modest violet sort of girl who could have just given you that? Why me?"

"'Cos you are you — obvious reply, but true."

"And then?"

"Dear heart, I don't see you being able to go on with this paid job you've got now, but there seems to be plenty of unpaid work that wants doing to make folks happier, and that the Labour Movement would be glad for you to do. And if you feel you must earn your own money, you really have a talent for writing. Why not develop that?"

"There's Shireport and Parliament — well, possibly, anyhow."

Tony's arm went round her and she relaxed against him. "Joan, dear, couldn't that come later? You are very young for that yet. It's a big job to tackle, and, oh my dearest, if we were married you wouldn't like not to have children, would you?"

His tone was very soft and earnest and shy. Joan's eyes filled with tears. She had the impulse to take him in her arms, to soothe his head against her breast, to make up to him for all those frustrated years — and yet ... even as she pressed against his shoulder, she knew that she felt differently from the time when they had sat together on just this spot after the General Strike. Then Tony had swept into her life like a knight of romance, the first of his kind she had met. Only because his demands had been so imperious, so exacting, had she been able to resist at all, but now somehow she knew things were not the same. Shireport had made a difference, Carey's Main and the position of authority she had held there, Gerry too. But here her mind sheered off, she didn't want to think of Gerald Blain just then. Joan hardly knew what to say. She wanted to plead for time again, yet that seemed unreasonable when Tony was going so far to meet her and giving up so much.

It was Dacre who unknowingly got her out of the awkward corner.

"Good Lord!" he said, catching sight of his wrist-watch. "It's half-past seven and Helen's guests come at eight. I'm awfully sorry, we simply must dash."

Joan's relief made her enthusiastic. "My lad, how ghastly, let's race for it. Can you make it in half an hour?"

They raced for the car, threw themselves in, and Tony drove madly towards town.

"Whew, that was a near thing," he said, as he shaved by a horse's head and swerved to avoid a rapidly oncoming car. "Did I startle you?"

"Rather not. I'm time-keeper. Quick as you can."

"You *are* a sportsman," but Joan was relieved at the need for haste which prevented him talking. She wanted to have time to think before she and Tony were alone again.

He dropped her at Gordon Square and raced off. Mary Maud was dressed, and for the first time almost angry. "Really, Joan, this is too bad. Was that Tony who drove away? It's a quarter-past eight, and he will have to dress. If you haven't any consideration for Helen, I think you might avoid humiliating her openly."

Joan was utterly contrite. "I won't be five minutes." She kicked off shoes and tore off stockings, pulled on the fine gold ones, swilled her head and shoulders in the bathroom, and dashed back all glowing to pull over her head the lovely gold evening frock that Mary Maud had bought her for the first night of *Resurrection*, and which she had never worn since.

Joan was ready in well under twenty minutes, and Mary Maud sighed to think of the long and careful creaming that her own toilet had necessitated. She couldn't be angry with the girl for long. "I wish I had your energy. Here, wrap this shawl round you and come along. There are sure to be others later than us, thank goodness."

There weren't. Every one was waiting, and they had a disconcertingly public entry. If Helen was annoyed, she certainly showed no sign. Carefully dressed, under the shaded lights, she looked very distinguished in a curious robe of silver and red which made her part of her own decorations. It was a typical Helen Dacre party. The guests were chosen because they were either interesting, or the wife or husband of an interesting partner. The number was small enough to feel a party and not a mere feeding squash. And the meal was perfect. Joan enjoyed herself immensely, and was herself so novel as to have quite a success. Captain Bowyer-Blundell took her in to dinner and her other neighbour was Commander Knowsley. It was not to be expected that such a combination could keep the talk away from the General Strike, but Joan had no wish to disturb a pleasant party by a hot political argument, and carefully steered the discussion into a flippant repartee about plus-four volunteers and pretty providers of hot cocoa. In Mary Maud's mind, however, the discussion she had had with these two men on the morning of the General Strike still rankled. She wanted those points settled.

"What about those fifteen-pound-a-week miners now, Captain Bowyer-Blundell?" she remarked from her place directly across the narrow table. "You ask Miss Craig about them. She ought to know."

"Who are they?" asked Joan, all innocence.

Bowyer-Blundell fixed his eye-glass. "Portia[122] shall decide," he said solemnly. "Miss Craig, I told these people that I myself have seen authentic pay checks from the colliery in which I am a shareholder, where a miner got fifteen pounds for a week's work, and they refuse to believe me."

"Joan won't believe you. There's not a miner she's heard of getting a quarter of that," put in Tony.

"Which are your collieries?" Joan asked.

"The Pinxton Pits."

"Oh, then, fifteen pounds wouldn't be an unusual pay check. I should think you could have been shown some at twenty or twenty-five that were quite authentic."

"There now. Perhaps you'll believe her," said Bowyer-Blundell, proudly looking round at his friends. "Now am I a liar trying to slander the poor miners? Here it is, straight from the horse's … er, I mean, the fountain head."

"Have you ever heard of the butty system, Captain Bowyer-Blundell?" Joan asked sweetly.

The captain dropped his eyeglass. "Now don't tell me there's a catch in it after all," he pleaded. "What's the butty system?"

"It's a system by which one man contracts to work a place, or a stall as they are sometimes called. He may have four or five men working with him, but he is responsible. The output is checked to him and he draws the wages for the lot. So, as he always gets the biggest share, and would probably have five men working with him, the actual wage of these men on the check you saw wouldn't be much above two pounds a week, when deductions have been reckoned."

The company, which had grown silent to listen to this exchange, roared with laughter. Any friend of Bowyer-Blundell's had heard about this fifteen-pound-a-week miner until they were tired, and the simplicity of the explanation tickled every one. The soldier took it handsomely. "I grovel, I bow to the judgment of Portia, but honestly I gave the case in all good faith."

"Of course I know that," said Joan sympathetically, and drew him back under cover of a private conversation from the laughter of the crowd. Bowyer-Blundell was grateful, and the table generally appreciated the tact which did not follow up an obvious advantage.

When the men drifted back into the red and silver room for coffee, Joan found herself the centre of a little court, all anxious to talk about the miners and to air their views on the General Strike. Quite modestly, but firmly, Joan kept her end up without getting excited, and the men liked the novelty of being able to discuss such issues on level terms with so young and attractive a girl. It was but natural that she was a little elated when Mary Maud took her home. Tony had pressed her hand: "You were in great form to-night." Helen had said, "I am so glad it is you who are coming to my *musicale*. You put it so clearly, I know you will convince these very difficult people." Bowyer-Blundell had been frankly disappointed that she was in Miss Meadowes' charge and that he could not take her home. "Do let us meet again some time," he pleaded. "It's been most interesting to meet you."

Mary Maud hugged her when they got home. "I wish I knew all you do about things, my dear. I knew there was an answer to Bowyer-Blundell, though he obviously wasn't lying, you could see he believed it. But, oh, I'm glad you were there to put them right. What I have suffered from them since the strike. It was really splendid."

As Joan stretched herself luxuriously in bed that night the world, especially the London world, seemed very good. These people were so clever, yet they were so nice to meet. It was jolly to be in arguments that really mattered and where people didn't lose their tempers. It had been stimulating to hear the good stories, the talk about books and ideas. It would be marvellous to write books like Tony, to write things that made people really respect one as his clever guests obviously respected him. And Tony was such a darling. Of course, to marry him did mean giving up all the things she had planned to do with her life. It meant amateurism, it meant fitting in work somehow amid the conflicting calls of husband, home, and perhaps children. Was she fitted for that life? Joan knew right deep down in her heart that she wasn't — that she wanted to do her job and do it thoroughly, and that Tony wouldn't fit in. He would say so now perhaps — no, to be fair, he hadn't even said now that he would. *Her* work must be fitted into his life, he wanted her as a wife and a lover and a mother. Did she want that? Joan tossed herself round impatiently. Why were things so difficult for women who wanted to do things with their life? Why had such a choice to be made? Surely if Tony were different she could fit everything in somehow. But then — Tony was Tony, and there you were.

CHAPTER XXVI

Joan had promised Gerald Blain to help with the final stages of the new paper, and she went down to the offices after breakfast on the morning following Helen's party. Joan was secretly very proud of being asked to help. She got a real thrill out of the shabby little offices at the top of a narrow crooked staircase. Every Socialist paper the world over has been brought to birth in little attic rooms, with trestle tables littered with newspapers, paste pots, magazines and Press cuttings, with cartoons and photographs pinned on the bare and grimy walls. But to Joan it was all excitingly new. It was the thrill of a lifetime to cross Fleet Street, actually to see the name on the street corner, and to look up at the advertisements for every paper one had ever heard of. Then to go up a narrow alley straight into the heart of the world, and up a staircase where every little door bore the name of a Press agency or a magazine, to the very top where one was welcomed as a colleague and treated as part of the scheme of things — this was life.

Joan was busy reading galley-proofs when Gerry limped in. "Hello, didn't expect you so early after your gallivanting last night, and the great success and all that you were."

"How do you know?"

"Lawrence Redfern was there. Didn't you meet him?"

"Oh, yes, I *was* introduced to him, I remember — the dramatic critic of the *Fleet Review*, isn't he?"

"And of our beloved *Weekly*. He's our latest capture; didn't you know? He's going to do a special feature: 'What would Marx[123] think of this.'"

"Humorous, I suppose?"

"Very — and it's no use Madame being superior because some one's been telling tales about her. They were very nice tales."

"Such as?"

"I thought she couldn't resist that. I was assured that Madame was the belle of the evening, that she wore a wondrous frock of gold, and slippers to boot — no, that isn't a pun — and that altogether she was a great success."

There was something in Gerry's light tone that made Joan look sharply at him. If this Lawrence Redfern had wanted to gossip about last night's affair, he might at least have had the decency to talk about the Bowyer-Blundell incident and not her dress.

"It was a lovely party," she said composedly, "and charming people. We talked a lot about the miners."

"Yes — I heard Bowyer-Blundell was thinking of taking out a card in the I.L.P."[124]

Joan met his eyes steadily. "Get it off your chest, Gerry. Don't you think I ought to go to Helen's parties or wear a gold frock that Mary Maud gave me?"

Gerry sat himself on the edge of her table, and ruffled some papers idly, smoothing them out again.

"Of course you must do as you like. Why not?"

"I wasn't asking your permission, Gerry. I'm not likely to. I asked you what *you* were thinking."

"Is that important?"

"To me, yes — don't fence, there isn't any need."

"I'm sorry. Well, all right, if you want to know, I hate the thought of your getting mixed up in Helen's crowd. I know them pretty well, and they're damned dangerous for a girl like you."

"I like that. I'm not a baby. And they were some of the nicest people I've ever met. They were awfully decent about the miners, and were as pleased as anything when I showed up that nonsense of Bowyer-Blundell's fifteen-pounds-a-week miner. Redfern didn't tell you about that, I suppose?"

"Yes, he did. I know they have nice manners. They don't care enough about the miners — at least, when they are not dangerous — not to be perfectly charming to anyone who cares enough to defend them. But you think of what that crowd did during the General Strike. Ask Mary Maud. We saw them with bared teeth all right when their class-privileges were in danger. It's not people like that uncouth fool of a mine manager in Carey's Main who are dangerous to the workers. They carry their own antidote. Decent people like that vicar's wife will help the workers to do 'em in. But it's these kindly wealthy people who play the devil with people like you, Joan. They are so reasonable and they can be so kind. It seems a shame to fight them, and after a while you'd find yourself not wanting to put things so strongly — it might hurt your new friends' feelings."

"It wouldn't make any difference to *me*."

"Oh, yes, it would. I've seen it happen to people much less susceptible than you, and I've not lived very long with my eyes open, either. And they can be so useful. You let them know you are writing, Joan, and they can give you such help — a boost here, an odd 'par' there — a word to an editor friend, and it's done."

"You mean they'd try to buy me over?"

"Not consciously, but you'd become one of their circle. It's not what their class consciously does to the workers' leaders that matters, Joan. It's easy to fight against that, but it's the mass of ideas which they take for granted, and which they assume, as a matter of course, that all decent people will take for granted, the atmosphere they create that is so difficult to fight against. Of *course* workers are always ill-advised when they strike; of *course* industry can't pay any better wages in the face of foreign competition; of *course* Socialism is a very fine ideal, but you can't alter human nature — and so on. You can't convert people like these though you produced every statistic there was in the universe. All their class-privileges are bound up with not being converted, not seeing the ugly truth. If you beat them on one point they shift to another. You've only two things to do, keep out and fight them, or go in and accept all they have to give — and it's a lot if you are worth while. But you can't go in with them and fight them at the same time, Joan, so don't you make the mistake of thinking you can." Gerry was unusually in earnest

"You talk as if it were these people I cared about. They are Helen's friends, not Tony's, and, anyway, if Tony left Helen for me, they'd fight me anyway, so there's no danger of their friendship."

"Don't you believe that. Their solidarity is a class thing. It doesn't enter into internal personal affairs. That kind of woman will never take a woman's side in a love affair — there's no sympathy among them for the woman who loses her man. The pack is on her, and the men follow. Helen knows that and she is afraid."

"Gerry, you are very profound this morning. Why all this philosophy?" Joan's cool tone was a little malicious because she was feeling uncomfortable.

Blain pulled himself off her table. "I am sorry," he said politely. "Of course, I have no right to criticize your friends."

Joan leaned over and gripped his wrist. "Come off it, Gerry, and I'll come off it too."

Blain grinned. "That's better. I can't stand it when you are being the perfect lady, Joan."

"But honestly, Gerry, what about yourself? You are every bit as much of that class as any of Helen's friends. I could quote you, yourself, against every one of your generalizations."

Gerry shrugged a shoulder. "My father started life as a manual worker, and but for his luck I should have been a factory worker too. And Mother never let him or me forget it — but, anyway, I don't mean to imply that Helen's lot are the usual silly-ass type of 'best people' who can only maintain their superiority by not letting other people come near enough to them to see how silly they really are. They are a damned sight too intelligent and interested in life for that. They'll pet you, Joan, and make a fuss of you, because you are unusual and yet can fit in with their conventions, and they will feel they are no end advanced and democratic. But between them and the working class the gulf is fixed, and when a crisis like the General Strike comes they make no bones about which side they are on, even when the best of them admit that the workers have a case."

"Well," said Joan slowly, "there's Tony and Mary Maud and Lady Christina — one can think of a good many more than the five just men to save Gomorrah."[125]

"Oh, I know there are exceptions," said Gerry rather impatiently, "but take the exceptions, the best of them like Tony and Mary Maud. Sympathetic with the workers, yes, but it's all a show to them, an interesting exhibition of unusual types. They are bored with their own crowd, so they stand outside the struggle, like keen spectators at a boxing match, and cheer the workers on to victory. But they are never *in* the fight. And if you go with that crowd, Joan, you will be out of the fight too. You'll be comfortable and sympathetic and interested, but it won't be long before the fight will be in the ring and you'll be in the stalls." He looked up at the clock. "Good Lord, time's getting on and me holding forth like a stump spouter. Guess I'll get on with the doin's. By the way, Mother is coming home next week. You must meet her, you'd love her."

"I guess I should. She made *you,* anyway," said Joan impulsively. They both went rather red. Gerry picked up his papers. "Forward the Light Brigade," he laughed, and limped to his own room. Half-way through the morning he put his head round the door: "You'll be staying to lunch, won't you? There's a crowd coming to talk over last-minute ideas. Harry Browne is here from Kelsall — he's doing the dispatch side.

"Rather. I'd love to," said Joan.

It was a gay lunch — Parma de Pratz, who was responsible for a witty column that Joan had been proof-reading, a delicious guy of the typical Woman's Page; Redfern, who had worked off some of his repressed anti-capitalist complexes in his review of the week; a couple of young Labour M.P.s; the cartoonist; a tall, grave young man, with an outsize in collars, who seemed to be regarded as an encyclopaedia on how to run a Socialist state; and a little grey man in a grey suit, who had been a diplomat for thirty years, and seemed to be determined never to be polite to anyone any more.

In this editorial group of the new *Wednesday Weekly,* Harry Browne and Joan were the only genuine proletarians. Browne was very quiet and obviously on his guard against every one but Gerry. It gradually dawned on Joan that Browne's relation to that group was nearly as suspicious as Gerry's attitude to Helen Dacre's amiable friends. Browne was equally afraid that contact with Redfern and Parma and the rest might dilute his rebel fervour.

"What a complicated business English social life is," thought Joan. There must be a line between capitalist and worker somewhere, but whenever you think you've got it, it's always somewhere else. There's an obvious gulf between Harry Browne and the Duke of Northumberland, or Mr Gordon Selfridge,[126] or his own immediate boss, but where does the line shade off?" It was a difficult conundrum, but, meanwhile, the talk was good.

Parma had been to a Society wedding that morning — a peer and stage affair — and had tried to get an interview with the bride's mother. "She looked at me as though I was an insect," said Parma, "and asked: 'Are you from a real paper, or from the penny Press? I cannot talk to the penny Press.' Fancy Rothermere's little efforts being ticked off as the 'penny Press.'"

"Not in this year of grace, Parma. I can't believe there's anyone anywhere who isn't dying to get into the papers," said Redfern. "It would be the only excuse I could think of for putting up another statue in London, if such a one could be found."

"My dears, I assure you …"

"You know, Blain," said Rupert Rivers, the ex-diplomat, in his slow way, "I am convinced there are whole pockets of English life that are as unknown as Darkest African tribes to the public, simply because they never get into the papers and never come into contact with people who write. My sister told me once of meeting a woman-teacher from a boarding-school, who had never spoken to a man except on business since her father had died fifteen years before. Horrible."

"Saved her a lot of trouble," said Parma flippantly. "I'll do you a series, Gerry, on 'Unknown Britons.'"

"Do. It would be great." Gerry looked at her so gratefully that Joan felt a sharp twinge of jealousy. Joan, like most other young women who work with men in men's jobs, was not accustomed to having other women around much. She would have protested hotly if she had been told that she liked being the only woman to be doing any particular job. But somehow it was nicer when they were much older like Helen Dacre or Mary Maud. Parma de Pratz was too much her own age, and Parma's finished metropolitan air made Joan feel gauche and provincial. Not even Mary Maud's sports suit could make her feel equal to this cool young Press 'sob-sister.' Mary Maud had ascribed Gerry's improved manners with women to Joan's influence, and clearing up the Helen Dacre story, but Joan could not help wondering if this fascinating Parma hadn't something to do with it. Gerry joking with her was Gerry in a new light, older, more a man of the world. Joan asked herself a little viciously whether he regarded Parma as being in the workers' struggle or merely in the stalls. "Joan Craig, you are being a cat and you know you are. Now stop it," and she turned to Browne to talk shop about Kelsall. "One can always 'fill in,'" she thought, returning to her favourite maxim.

Joan had to beg for the miners' children at a Wesleyan sisterhood in the north of London that afternoon, and on the top of the bus in the pleasant summer weather she tried to sort out her ideas. Why had she been so suddenly and so violently jealous of Parma de Pratz at lunch, she who had thought herself above that type of meanness? And what was she to say to Tony? It was Helen's *musicale* tomorrow — and either then, or the day after, she must make up her mind what she was going to do; besides — and her mind drowsily drifted along — if she didn't decide soon Parma might … at this Joan pulled herself up sharply.

What was she thinking of? Of course she loved Tony — but did she want to marry Tony? Tony, London, Bloomsbury — her mind was away on a new track. She saw herself as Tony's wife — a lovely flat, his friends, all the pleasant people she had met, holidays abroad, and writing. It would be lovely to write — jolly way of earning money and being able to say what you wanted — but, of course, you couldn't do that, not Labour things, well, perhaps one could sometimes say what one wanted, very tactfully, and there would be no more tiring journeys, no more beastly cheap hotels, and — her mind again pulled up with a jerk — nothing worth doing at all. Did she really want a soft-cushions-and-hot-baths life? It would be nice for a time — but Shireport, the thrill of leadership, of getting jobs done, of being in the battle with the workers, of doing things that mattered …

With Gerry one would be on the stretch all the time, working at top speed. Gerry never spared himself. Pain and utter fatigue might pull him down, but somehow he went on. There would be no possibility of Gerry's wife watching things as an interested spectator in the stalls. She would be expected to do her job and anyone else's that needed doing. Suppose she married Gerry and had a baby — well, that would have to be fitted in, as Mrs Cocks and the women of Carey's Main fitted theirs in. The universe wouldn't be expected to stand still, as at some miracle, to allow Gerry Blain's baby to be born. Its mother would probably be correcting proofs or planning speeches to the minute of its arrival, while Tony would have been clearing the world around her for the miracle from the moment he knew it was on the way.

Joan found herself laughing at her own comparison of the two men. "They are dears," she said softly.

"Your stop, miss," called out the conductor, and Joan hastily got down from the bus, her dreamy attempts at thinking things out not having taken her much farther.

CHAPTER XXVII

Joan was really more nervous than she cared to admit to Mary Maud as they sat having a quiet lunch at Gordon Square before Helen's great effort. For this *musicale* Mrs Dacre had secured, among other celebrities, a Polish 'cellist who had recently achieved fame, and who was himself the son of a Silesian miner.[127] The expensive tickets had sold well. According to the beautifully produced programme which Joan had received that morning there was to be tea at four-thirty, then music, an interval for her speech and a collection, then some more music. It seemed odd to see her own name in such company. "Miss Joan Craig, who has just returned from relief work in the Northern coalfields."

"I do feel awfully nervous about it, Mary Maud. It's so absolutely off my beat, this sort of thing. There are far more experienced women than I am, who have done far more work. I can't think why Helen Dacre insisted on having me."

"Helen always has an eye for dramatic effect," Mary Maud said shrewdly. "An older, sober-sided woman would seem too familiar — it would be too much like any other charitable affair. Your youth, and the fact that you can speak well, and that you are straight from the trenches, so to speak, will have the maximum effect. But do be careful, Joan. I mean, you simply must not upset their susceptibilities by telling them their class is responsible, or anything of that kind."

"Well, I believe they are."

"Believe anything you like, but your job is to get money this afternoon."

"Don't worry. I won't give them a 'Variations on a Class War' theme, much as I'd like to. I've prepared this wretched speech so carefully that it will be too dismally diplomatic for anything. I shall coo like a dove, drat 'em."

"Joan, Joan," laughed Mary Maud, "as an angel of charity, really ..."

"I know, but charity-begging isn't my line, Mary Maud. However, I'll be good."

The beautiful old rooms were well filled when Miss Meadowes and her charge arrived. Blain and Dodds and their crowd had undertaken the stewarding and were busy handing round cakes and tea. Tony was helping his wife to receive people. "I hope you won't feel nervous. Everything is splendid," whispered Helen as Joan greeted her. Crowds and success always made her appear years younger, and she looked very distinguished this afternoon in a close-fitting dress of soft brown chiffon velvet and a turban of dull gold.

Captain Bowyer-Blundell was hovering round and promptly took charge of Joan. "Let me introduce you to people," he said, "they'd love to meet you." Joan would have liked to have sat quietly in a corner and looked at the frocks. The affair seemed like a fashion parade. It was utterly different from her world and she was too alive not to be interested in new people and fresh types. But Bowyer-Blundell insisted on introducing her to fashionable ladies who seemed to have some vague idea that she ought to be able to stop the whole trouble.

"Couldn't something be done about this man Cook?" they murmured. "Wasn't he too dreadful? Didn't she think it was all his fault, really? And these Russians — wasn't it true that Cook had promised them there should be a revolution; weren't millions of money being sent from Russia to help him to do it? Of course, the children ... but wasn't it true that the miners were getting much more in relief and strike pay than when they were at work?" Cook, Cook, Cook — it was useless to explain to these ladies that Cook had to obey the resolutions of his own committee; useless to point out that most of the men were not on strike, but were locked out; useless to talk about the wages the miners had been trying to live on — these women wanted a bogy, and Cook had replaced the Kaiser.

Joan wondered why most of them had come at all. She felt that the bait of the 'cellist and a famous actress must have been well emphasized by Helen and helpers like Lady Christina. And why should they be asked to give to the miners? thought Joan, as she sat on the dais beside the chairwoman, and the music began. Their class was at war with the miners — why should they be expected to feed their enemies? — yet some of the most fashionable women there had really worked hard to get funds. Individuals were all right, she said to herself, lots of them, but it was this rigid system that kept people from knowing each other. Was there another country in the world where the class barriers were so high as in England, and where it was so loudly proclaimed that none existed at all?

The Polish 'cellist was playing, and Joan's thoughts were caught up in the music. It seemed to her that he was expressing all the longing in the souls of people like Harry Browne and James Firth, and her committee at Carey's Main — the revolt against ugliness and repression, their passionate cry that man was not a mere thing to grub in darkness beneath the ground all his days. Then, in a wild sweeping movement of the music, the doors of that room seemed to fly open and the miners came in, grimy from the coalfield, black with the coal-dust, and the fashionable throng seemed to break and flee. Triumph — Joan's heart rose with the 'cellist's bow. Victory in the fight against all the odds, and then low, sweet sounds that told of the hope of a better world.

Joan had been so completely absorbed in the music and her own thoughts that it was an effort to come back to earth with the applause, and to hear the chairwoman's few words of introduction and the call on her to speak.

If the compilers of that programme had wanted pleasant soothing syrup, tales of the coalfield with just the right amount of pathos to get money and not enough tragedy to make the fashionable audience uncomfortable, it was not wise to allow a Polish 'cellist to play the music of revolt before an impressionable girl like Joan had to speak. Whatever the 'cellist had meant to the audience, to Joan it had been a call to sacrifice, a rededication of her life to her cause. She saw the well-dressed audience as a garden of temptation and she wanted to proclaim her mission and throw her challenge before them. But she was too experienced a speaker to be entirely swept away. Forcing herself to be calm, she started on the speech she had so carefully prepared, the recital of actual experiences at Carey's Main. But these stories took a deeper tone from the passion in Joan's own heart. Sincerity grips even a hostile audience, and this one, at worst indifferent, was held by the feeling in the speaker's voice.

"Good, so far," whispered Helen anxiously to her husband, "but I hope she doesn't lose hold on herself and get into a ranting propaganda speech. It would be fatal."

"She's all right. I think she is getting 'em," answered Tony.

But Joan's stories were having more effect on herself than on her audience. She went on to speak of what the country owed the miners, what they had done in war-time, the lives they led underground, and to contrast this with the easy life led by those who owned instead of produced. The deep bitterness she was feeling could not be kept out of her speech. Flinging away discretion with a gesture, Joan concluded with the fiery words that Dacre had last heard in the crowded drill-hall at Shireport:

> "Whenever a mine's blown skyward
> We are buried alive for you,
> There's never a wreck drifts shoreward
> But we are its ghastly crew.
> Go search for our dead in the forges red
> And the factories where we spin,
> If blood be the price of all your wealth,
> Good God, we have paid it in."

Said with all the force of the passionate contempt she was feeling for her audience just at that moment, it was magnificent, though not tactful.

"Damn," said Helen Dacre. "I felt she would spoil it."

"I'm not sure she has done," replied Tony. "It was a great speech and this audience is impressed."

If only it could have been left there! But the conscientious chairwoman, with a programme confronting her, dutifully intimated that if anyone would like to ask any questions there would be time before the collection was taken.

A stout woman dressed in some kind of uniform rose. The chairwoman called on her as Lady Fortescue, and Joan remembered her name as a noted worker among city girls.

They had just listened, she said, to the kind of speech that was at the root of the whole trouble. If there was no money in the industry, it couldn't be given to the miners; but people like Mr Cook and Miss Craig went round the country telling them that they were the sole producers of wealth. The men were led to disaster, and people like Miss Craig had then to go and beg for help for the families which the foolish vanity of the leaders had ruined. "I shall help the miners' children," she concluded, "in spite of Miss Craig's speech, but I shall not give one penny to this fund. I will not let the authors of disaster be the distributors of my charity."

Joan wanted to leap to her feet to reply to this speech, but the chairwoman placed a restraining hand on her arm and called on a grey-haired woman, prettily dressed in a loose gown of blue and grey, and wearing much hand-made jewellery. She was so sorry Miss Craig had spoken so bitterly. All that was wanted was peace. If only people had kind thoughts everything would be well. She was sure every one had kind thoughts for the miners just now. The good Premier had spoken so beautifully of peace in our time, and every one was being so nice about helping, and she was sure that if only dear Miss Craig, who was so sincere, would go and ask the miners to have kind thoughts for their employers, everything would be so nice and settled and we should all be so happy.

"You had better take the platform and get on to the music, Helen," advised her husband. "Nothing else will keep Joan from tearing this woman to bits."

Helen took the hint, but before she could reach the platform a younger woman had risen, a fashionable Society girl. With a little giggle she said she wasn't used to speaking, *she* wasn't a paid agitator, but she did just want to say that really it was all nonsense, this talk of people starving. No one starved in Britain. They could all go on the dole. Every one knew that was why no one could get decent servants nowadays, the workers just lived on the dole, and their children were fed at school. But they weren't properly grateful. No one was grateful, nowadays, and really, with taxes so high, it was the rich that were to be pitied, and why didn't Miss Craig and Mr Cook go to Russia if they didn't like England? With another little giggle the girl sat down to laughter and applause that showed she was voicing the exact feelings of the greater part of that audience.

No chairwoman could hold Joan back then. She stood in front of the dais with her hands clenched, her face dead white. She was too moved for passion, her voice sounded cold and hard.

"I came to speak to you to-day against my will," she said. "I have always earned my own living and I have come to beg from women like you — you who are kept in luxury by the efforts of other people. I humbled myself to beg for your charity for the miners, the men without whom the workers of this country could not have won your war, the war that kept your dividends safe and your homes unscathed. These men risk their lives every day for the comfort of selfish, idle people like you, and I have to come and beg for charity for them. What I am saying now will close your purses, but I believe that if the men I know in the coalfields had heard what has been said here to-day, they would be grateful to me for sparing them the final humiliation of your grudging almsgiving."

With that Joan turned and left the platform, walking rapidly to the ante-room amid the hisses of some of her audience and the outraged glances of others. Helen Dacre was in a state of nervous collapse. Half the audience rose to its feet in insulted dignity. Tony leapt to the platform. He was popular. He was a celebrity. He had a good voice. Joan heard him appealing for order as the door swung behind her. She felt a hand grip her arm. It was Gerry. His face was set and white.

"Come along," he said. "let's get out of here. There is a stairway at the back."

Joan was in no mood to argue. She was just beginning to realize what she had done. Gerry took her down to the street to his own little car. "Get in. We'll drive to my digs, if you don't mind."

"Oh, Gerry, I'd love it. I don't want to see anyone at this moment. I couldn't face a *café*, or Mary Maud at home."

"So I thought." His face was so grim that Joan wondered what he was thinking. They swung through the crowded streets without speaking till he stopped the car at Great Ormond Street. He hurried her up the stairs and put her into his big upholstered wicker chair.

"Some brandy?" he asked her.

"No, thanks. Could we make some tea?"

"Rather." He went out and came back with the kettle, which he put on the gas-ring in the fireplace, and then, still without speaking, put out some tea-things and a biscuit tin. Joan sat with her hands gripped in front of her, staring at the hearth. The kettle boiled. Gerry made the tea. "Drink this," he said.

Joan roused herself. "Gerry, what have I done? I've ruined all Helen's work. I've spoilt the collection. They won't give a penny to the funds now, and Mary Peters will be furious. Every one will be furious."

"Let 'em. I don't think — I never did — that we should get much from that type of audience beyond the price of their tickets. Why should they give when the men are out? Nothing you said would make any difference to the decent people like Lady Fortescue. But, Joan," and Blain's voice sounded quiet and very determined, "You had got to make that speech some time or go under."

Joan looked up in surprise.

"I don't mean those words or that place, you know that. But you had either got to raise your flag of independence some time soon or be swallowed into their life. You realise that now, don't you?"

Joan drained her cup, grateful for the hot tea, and put it on the floor beside her.

"Gerry, you were right," she said. "It's difficult when you get to the fine shades between class and class, but the big broad issue is there. It's the issue that this century will be occupied in fighting out. We don't want to face it, but it's there."

"It's there all right," answered Gerry quietly.

There was silence for a time, and then Joan said in a low tone:

"I'm sorry about dishing Helen's show, but this afternoon showed me where I had been drifting. I've got to stick with my crowd, Gerry, and work with them. I've got to be in this fight. You were right. One can't live in luxury and pretend one is working with them just the same. I'm in the ring from now on. No more trips to the stalls," and she smiled at him.

"Is there any reason why we shouldn't be in the ring together, Joan?"

She did not answer for a moment — and then said slowly: "Not if the work comes first, Gerry."

"It will — with both of us." He did not touch her. He stood with his shoulders against the mantelshelf, looking down at her.

"But Tony?" she asked. "I feel a beast about him."

Blain kicked a hassock meditatively. "I know, and I've felt I ought to clear out, but that would have been no good, Joan. I didn't realize it at first, but you two just wouldn't have hit it. I've seen that ever since we talked at Leeds — that is, not unless you gave up your career. And I want you to go all out on your job like me, Joan, and we'll fit in together because we're both keen." Then Blain smiled for the first time since they had left the hall.

"We shall be living such a life that perhaps he will be thankful that he has had a lucky escape."

"I like that!" and it was the old Joan rising to his teasing bait.

"Well, the general verdict on *me* after this afternoon will be: 'Poor lad, but he married her with his eyes open!'"

Joan jumped to her feet indignantly. "Of course ... if ..."

And then she saw Blain's eyes.

Explanatory Notes

Chapter I

1. (p.4) From 'Jerusalem' by William Blake, Preface to *Milton* (1809-10), ll. 35-36. The anthem has been adopted by and is sung in the labour movement and by the Women's Institute.

2. (p.4) Cistercian or trappist monasteries (founded in the twelfth century) were renowned for their silence and austerity.

3. (p.4) A conservative-leaning daily newspaper. During the General Strike the government took control of *The Morning Post* building and worked with their compositing staff to produce *The British Gazette* on 3 May.

4. (p.4) On 31 July 1925 ('Red Friday') the Conservative Government gave way to miners' demands and introduced a wage subsidy for a period of nine months.

5. (p.4) Twelve leaders of the Communist Party of Great Britain were imprisoned in 1925 for publishing seditious libels and breaching the Incitement to Mutiny Act of 1797.

6. (p.6) The governing body of the Trades Union Congress.

7. (p.6) See note 4.

8. (p.6) The Royal Commission on the Coal Industry (usually known as the Samuel Report) was set up in 1925 to look at the options for rationalising the industry, the issue of nationalisation, and miners' wage levels. The Chair of the Commission was Sir Herbert Samuel (1870-1963), a liberal politician who has just finished a spell as Governor of Palestine. The Report, published in March 1926, rejected wholesale nationalization of the mines and recommended that the government subsidy should end, but it also recommended various modernisation reforms and the continuation of minimum wage agreements. The Samuel Report can be regarded as precipitating both the beginning and the end of the General Strike. Although the rejection of the report by both the mine employers and the miners started the General Strike, negotiations based on a revised version of the Samuel Report's recommendations (known as the Samuel Memorandum) formed the basis of the capitulation over the strike by the leadership of the General Council of the Trade Unions Congress.

9. (p.6) Unknown: perhaps 'Westminster Parliamentary Bulletin', or 'Workers' Post Bag'.

10. (p.7) Stanley Baldwin (1867-1947), three times Conservative Prime Minister: during 1923, between 1924 and 1929, during the General Strike, and from 1935 to 1937.

11. (p.7) Winston Churchill (1874-1965), British statesman, Chancellor of the Exchequer 1924-29. During the General Strike he edited the government newspaper the *British Gazette*.

12. (p.7) Winston Churchill was a war correspondent during the Boer War of 1899-1902. He was captured but escaped.

Chapter II

13. (p.9) A fashionable address in Bloomsbury, and the home of Leonard and Virginia Woolf.

14. (p.9) A group of writers, artists and intellectuals which included Roger Frye, Duncan Grant, Lytton Strachey, Maynard Keynes, Leonora Carrington and Virginia Woolf.

15. (p.9) Anton Chekhov (1860-1904), Russian dramatist and short story writer, Feodor Dostoevsky (1821-1881), Russian novelist, Percy Bysshe Shelley (1792-1882), Romantic poet. Wilkinson is ridiculing the pretentiousness of fashionable metropolitan intellectuals.

16. (p.11) A government subsidy of ten million pounds was given to the coal industry in 1921 and a further subsidy of twenty-three million pounds in 1925. See also note 4.

17. (p.11) A Russian Communist or a British Marxist who advocated revolution and support for the Soviet Union.

18. (p.12) A famous Greek warrior renowned for his strength. The reference to the earthquake is obscure, as in Greek mythology Ajax was shipwrecked and drowned as punishment for his anger at being refused the armour of Achilles at the siege of Troy.

19. (p.12) A novel by Leon Tolstoy published in 1899. Helen Dacre has supposedly adapted it for the stage.

20. (p.13) On 29 April 1926 over 800 delegates representing 141 trade unions affiliated to the TUC met at the Memorial Hall, Farringdon Street, London. The General Council of the TUC was given the authority to call and direct, if required, a General Strike.

Chapter III

21. (p.15) Ben Tillett (1860-1943), English trade union leader.

22. (p.15) The Methodist hall in which the Memorial Hall conference was held.

23. (p.16) A popular chain of tea-shops.

24. (p.16) Acronyms of trade unions: A.S.L.E.F.: Associated Society of Locomotive Engineers and Firemen; A.U.B.T.W.: Amalgamated Union of

Building Trade Workers; A.S.E.: Amalgamated Society of Engineers.

25. (p.17) James Henry Thomas (1874-1949), General Secretary of the National Union of Railwaymen and a Labour Party politician. Thomas was a leading member of the TUC negotiating delegation during the strike.

26. (p.17) A daily paper that supported the Labour Party, edited by Henry Hamilton Fyfe.

27. (p.18) The elected Executive Committee of a trade union.

28. (p.19) Fashionable silk cloth.

Chapter IV

29. (p.21) Popular and political songs. 'Swanee River' was composed by Stephen Foster in 1851 and adopted by the state of Florida in 1935. 'Annie Laurie' is a Scottish folk song with lyrics by William Douglas (1685). 'The Red Flag' is the anthem of the Labour Party, with lyrics by James Connell (1889).

30. (p.22) A painting of naïf or ethnic origin or influence, very much in vogue among modernist artists and intellectuals at this time.

31. (p.22) The Dacre household or establishment. Something unconventional is suggested.

32. (p.24) The patriotic fervour which drove men to enlist in the 1914-1918 war.

Chapter V

33. (p.27) The successor to the Social Democratic Federation.

34. (p.27) The refrain from the traditional community song, usually accompanied by dancing, 'Knees Up Mother Brown'.

35. (p.28) James Ramsay MacDonald (1866-1937), first Labour Prime Minister, leader of a minority Labour government in 1924 and the National Government in 1931.

36. (p.28) Herbert Smith (1862-1938), President of the Miners Federation of Great Britain 1921-1938.

37. (p.28) Jimmie Thomas (see note 25).

38. (p.29) A constituency Labour Party in a fashionable area of north-west London.

39. (p.29) The Organisation for the Maintenance of Supplies (O.M.S.) was established in the summer of 1925 to co-ordinate the work of volunteer strike-breakers.

40. (p.31) Military medals: D.S.O.: Distinguished Service Order; D.F.C.: Distinguished Flying Cross.

41. (p.32) The end of the First World War on 11 November 1918.
42. (p.32) A hotel named after the Savoy and the Ritz, two of London's top hotels.

Chapter VI

43. (p.36) The votes cast were 3,653,527 in favour of the strike and 49,911 against The unions exercised block votes on behalf of their members.
44. (p.36) Ernest Bevin (1881-1951), General Secretary of the Transport and General Workers' Union 1921-1940, Minister of Labour 1940-1945.
45. (p.36) A Conservative daily paper owned by Lord Rothermere.
46. (p.37) A Justice of the Peace.
47. (p.38) An area in the West End of London famed for its restaurants and night life.
48. (p.40) Saladin (1138-1193), a Kurdish warrior and leader of the Islamic forces responsible for recapturing Jerusalem from the crusaders.
49. (p.40) Chaired by Sir John Sankey, the Royal Commission on the Coal Industry (1919) recommended the nationalisation of the mines.
50. (p.42) St. Francis of Assisi (1181-1286), founder of the Franciscan order and patron saint of animals.

Chapter VII

51. (p.45) A term referring (usually in a derisory sense) to indigenous South African peoples.
52. (p.45) A delicacy derived from goose's liver.
53. (p.46) A portable flask in which to transport hot liquids.
54. (p.48) This refers to the fact that the mines had been run by the government in the First World War. Despite promises to the contrary, and despite the recommendations of the Sankey Commission in 1919 that the mines remain nationalised, the Liberal government returned the mines to the coal-owners in April 1921. The miners went on strike to protest against planned wage reductions but were forced back to work.
55. (p.48) The decision by the government to return to the Gold Standard in 1925 required cuts in public spending.
56. (p.48) Jimmy Thomas. See note 25.
57. (p.52) Idiot.

Chapter VIII

58. (p.54) A.J. Cook (1884-1931), secretary of the Miner's Federation of Great Britain 1924-1931.

59. (p.54) Lord Birkenhead (1874-1930), barrister, Secretary to India (1924-1928 and an influential member of Baldwin's cabinet.

60. (p.54) A member of a small, exclusive religious sect founded in 1825 by John Nelson Derby with strict rules about contact with outsiders.

61. (p.54) Sir Arthur Steel-Maitland (1876-1935), Minister of Labour 1924-1929.

62. (p.54) A reference which seems to conflate two different books: William Booth of the Salvation Army's *In Darkest England* (1890) and Charles Booth's *Life and Labour of the People of London*, published between 1891 and 1903.

63. (p.55) A reference to the fact that Lord Birkenhead was a vigorous supporter of Edward Carson during the Irish crisis of 1914 (see note 64).

64. (p.55) Sir Edward Carson (1854-1935), a barrister and advocate who led the paramilitary Ulster Volunteer Force in opposing Home Rule for Ireland in 1914. He became the leader of the Irish Unionists in parliament. During the General Strike he was the Lord of Appeal.

65. (p.55) Lord Birkenhead's name was Frederick Edwin Smith. The suggestion is that he is looking after his own interests.

66. (p.56) Neville Chamberlain (1869-1940), Minister of Health 1924-1929, Prime Minister 1937-1940.

67. (p.58) Pericles (500BC-429BC), the architect of Athenian democracy, who divorced his wife and scandalised Athenian democracy by living with a foreigner, Aspasia of Miletus. She was described by Socrates as the most intelligent and witty woman of her day. In defiance of convention Pericles treated her almost as his equal.

68. (p.58) Mount Olympus in Greece was traditionally thought to be the home of the Greek gods.

69. (p.60) The 'wireless' was a name given to the early radio. Many households did not have radios in 1926 though they were to be found in most homes by the 1930s.

70. (p.60) Sir William Joynson Hicks (1865-1932), Home Secretary 1924-1929, colloquially known as 'Jix'.

71. (p.62) During the night of 2-3 May 1926 a row erupted between the workforce and the owner of *The Daily Mail* concerning its editorial for 3 May, 'For King and Country', which attacked the trade unions. When the editor Thomas Marlowe refused to withdraw his editorial the workers downed tools. The government used the incident as an excuse to break off negotiations and demand the rescinding of the General Strike decree. *The*

Daily Mail had also published the notorious Zinoviev letter in 1924, which had discredited the first Labour government.

72. (p.62) Harold Sydney Harmsworth (1868-1949), proprietor of the *Daily Mail* and a supporter of the Conservative Party.

73. (p.63) Hardliners, or those who refuse to compromise.

74. (p.63) Jimmie Thomas was in fact a moderate trade union leader.

Chapter IX

75. (p.65) The Lanchester was a luxurious British limousine.

76. (p.65) A reference to the fashionable Hotel Russell but also to the fact that the Miners Federation of Great Britain had its headquarters at 55 Russell Square.

Chapter X

77. (p.72) The TUC official paper produced during the strike, edited by Henry Hamilton Fyfe from the offices of the *Daily Herald*. Its premises were raided for evidence of subversion but publication was permitted.

78. (p.75) 'My darling', an Irish term of endearment.

79. (p.75) The lines are taken from 'The Internationale'.

80. (p.78) Nancy, Lady Astor (1879-1964), Conservative politician and first woman to sit in parliament.

Chapter XI

81. (p.80) The offices of both the TUC and the Labour Party were located in Eccleston Square in central London.

82. (p.80) The warrior queen of the Iceni tribe in Britain who led a rebellion against the occupying Romans in AD 61-63.

83. (p.80) A military acronym for General Headquarters.

84. (p.81) In Greek mythology, one of three snake-haired women whose look turned the beholder to stone.

85. (p.82) Latin for 'father'; in this context, upper-class slang.

86. (p.82) Sir Herbert Samuel returned from holiday in Italy on 6 May to begin secret discussions with the Negotiating Committee of the TUC.

87. (p.82) The statue of Horatio Nelson (1758-1805) in Trafalgar Square, London, erected in the mid nineteenth-century to celebrate his victory at the Battle of Trafalgar in 1805.

88. (p.83) The Archbishop of Canterbury (Randall Davidson) clashed with

Churchill. The Archbishop's proposals for a settlement of the strike (made public in *The British Worker* on 7 May) were rejected by the employers. The BBC refused to broadcast his proposal for a compromise settlement.

Chapter XIII

89. (p.93) A beauty spot near Hindhead in Surrey.
90. (p.97) A department store in Regent Street, central London.
91. (p.99) Blain probably refers to National Council of Labour Colleges, the Marxist rival to both the Workers' Educational Association and to Ruskin College Oxford. Wilkinson wrote regularly for the NCLC journal, *Plebs*.
92. (p.99) The Society of Jesus, an order of Roman Catholic Priests known for their zeal and their teaching.

Chapter XIV

93. (p.105) A colloquialism for English soldiers.
94. (p.112) Usually *'Kirk, Kinder and Kuche'*, a German alliterative phrase which stands for a patriarchal view of women's lives, supposedly devoted to 'church, children and kitchen'.

Chapter XV

95. (p.115) A major railway terminus for trains between London and the north of England.

Chapter XVI

96. (p.119) Derived from the legendary, physically imposing female warriors from Scythia, the word 'Amazon' was used to denigrate powerful women.
97. (p.122) A colloquial term used to denote something dark and hidden which emerged unexpectedly. The derogatory implications of the term were not as widely understood at this time as they were in the United States.

Chapter XVIII

98. (p.127) Originally a member of Achilles' feared personal guard in the Trojan wars, the word 'myrmidon' came to refer to a minion or hired ruffian.
99. (p.128) Gaius Marcius (fifth century BC), a Roman general who captured the town of Corioli from the Volscians, but who, after he was banished

from Rome, aided the Volscians in many victories against the Romans. He is the hero of Shakespeare's *Coriolanus*.

Chapter XIX

100. (p.130) Park Lane was and is one of London's most exclusive residential areas.
101. (p.132) One of the knights of King Arthur's Round Table, he successfully completed the quest for the Holy Grail.

Chapter XX

102. (p.137) Edward, Prince of Wales (1894-1972), the future Edward VIII and the eldest son of George V, King of Britain 1910-36. He donated £10 to the Somerset Miners' Distress fund.
103. (p.139) French for a piece or morsel.
104. (p.141) From Milton, *Paradise Lost*, 4: 299 (slightly misquoted).
105. (p.142) A colloquialism for Germans.

Chapter XXI

106. (p.146) The Women's Committee for the Relief of Miners' Wives and Children.
107. (p.146) The lines are from 'Song of the Wheels' by G. K. Chesterton (1874-1936).
108. (p.148) The Women's Co-operative Guild was a women's organisation formed in 1883 to further co-operative principles. It campaigned for women's suffrage, equal rights between women and men and maternity benefits. Local Poor Law 'Guardians' were responsible for administering relief to families in distress. Women had served as Poor Law Guardians since the nineteenth century.

Chapter XXII

109. (p.151) Fabric made from a technique originating in Java.
110. (p.153) An abdominal infection.
111. (p.154) Not traced.
112. (p.154) Humbert Wolfe (1885-1940), a popular poet.

Chapter XXIII

113. (p.155) 'Boko' is a slang word for nose. 'K.O.B.' is a slang acronym for 'knock-out blow'.
114. (p.158) Wesleyanism or Methodism was the religious denomination founded by John Wesley (1703-91). It traditionally had a strong following in mining regions.
115. (p.159) J. F. Horrabin (1884-1962), the political cartoonist and Wilkinson's collaborator on *A Workers' History of the General Strike* (1927). James Maxton (1858-1946), Labour MP and Chairman of the Independent Labour Party and the League Against Imperialism.

Chapter XXIV

116. (p.163) Charabancs or motor coaches.
117. (p.165) The lines are from 'The Internationale'.
118. (p.167) Max Aitkin (1879-1965), proprietor of *The Daily Express* and *The Evening Standard*.
119. (p.167) Vladimir Lenin (1870-1924), leader of the 1917 Russian Revolution, Marxist theoretician, and first premier of the Union of Soviet Socialist Republics.
120. (p.168) John D. Rockefeller (1839-1937), the founder of the Standard Oil Company and one of the richest men in the world. The Rothschilds were a fabulously wealthy family; 'siller' is here a corruption of 'silver'.

Chapter XXV

121. (p.172) George Bernard Shaw (1856-1950), playwright and Fabian socialist.
122. (p.176) The heroine of Shakespeare's *Twelfth Night* who disguises herself as an advocate.

Chapter XXVI

123. (p.178) Karl Marx (1818-1883), political theorist and founder of international Communism.
124. (p.179) The Independent Labour Party was founded by Keir Hardie in 1893 and was one of the radical organisations which helped found the Labour Party. The ILP remained to the left of the Labour Party in the 1920s and 1930s.

125. (p.181) The biblical town destroyed with Sodom because of the sinful behaviour of its inhabitants.
126. (p.182) The Duke of Northumberland was a hereditary peer and one of the richest landowners in Britain. Gordon Selfridge (1858-1947) was the American-born founder of Selfridge's department store in Oxford Street.

Chapter XXVI

127. (p.187) An inhabitant of southern Poland. Silesia is a region which overlaps Poland, the Czech republic and Germany.